THE KING'S GAMBIT

The Vault Guardian, Book One

THOM L. MATTHEWS

Illustrated by
ELENA GARRIDO

CONTENTS

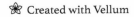 Created with Vellum

INTRODUCTION

This novel is the first part of what will *probably* be a 5 part series. There is information about my writing process in the Afterword, as well on my blog.

I tried to put a lot of thought into the backstory, characters, locations, and religions that are found throughout this book. For your convenience, I included a glossary and pronunciation guide at the end of the book. I did my best to make the glossary spoiler-free so you can refer to it anytime you wish. I have found glossaries to be very helpful in books that have many names, so I hope you find it beneficial as well.

The pronunciation guide was made to follow the way I imagine the names are spoken, with the capitalized letters being the accent of the word. I made the guide to follow phonetical pronunciation, and did not use any conventional method for it. This way, hopefully, anyone can understand it.

Lastly, many of the early reviewers requested that I add maps to the novel. These are also placed at the back of the book. Please keep in mind that this map is not all-inclusive. I tried to focus on the main areas in which the story takes place; however, there are some places that do not appear on the maps. This is because they are too far away and would require vast amounts of land to be covered in between that are not yet relevant to the story. Future novels will have more maps added on as needed for the story.

For Irmajeanne, watching me with the Ascendants.

"Far more real than the ticking of time is the way we open up the minutes and invest them with meaning. Death is not the ultimate tragedy in life. The ultimate tragedy is to die without discovering the possibilities of full growth."
—Norman Cousins

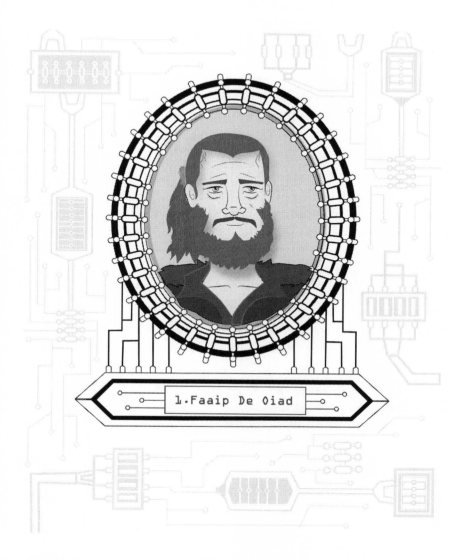

1.Faaip De Oiad

"**H**ave you wondered if even the smallest decision could impact the fate of the world?" the man asked Sam, the young woman sitting opposite him. He voice was so familiar but Sam couldn't bring herself to look him in the eyes. "I didn't either," the man continued, "until a loud and incessant siren echoed throughout the undercroft, and a stranger invaded my home, the Grand Vault. I suppose that is the best place for me to start."

None of this made any sense to Sam. The last thing she remembered was the closing gate, an explosion, and then the ominous sound of nothingness. She needed answers, so she would remain silent, and let the man finish his tale.

"When the sirens went off," the man continued, seemingly ignoring Sam's discomfort, "my initial concern went directly to the sealed compression units in each of the corridors. If they were breached, then my work would be for nothing. I could not remember the last time I had checked the units, for the need had never before arisen. This was the first time I had ever heard the alarm. 'Was the power finally failing?' I asked myself, knowing it would only be a matter of time. Everything must stop working eventually—that was something I had always known.

"Each of the corridors were maintained at standardized settings, each set to the same precise conditions for the treasures they contained. How was I supposed to run the diagnostic scan? For some reason, the procedure eluded me. The temperature inside each chamber needed to be exact. Anything less than perfect would have been unacceptable and disastrous. I supposed the best way to start my analysis would be by checking the temperature in each chamber. That would not be too difficult. I thought that it would at least give me something to do.

"The first corridor extended about twenty-five meters and had refrigerated chambers with glass doors on both sides. There were roughly fifty units within the chambers on either side of the corridors: each containing the essence of the future. The contents of each unit were completely unique from those adjacent and were all subjected to the same conditions. The cooling units and standardized pressure behind the glass refrigerators maintained the integrity of each chamber. This was the same for each of the dozens of corridors within the place I once called home. There was no greater treasure in the world than what these sealed units contained, and it was my job to watch over them.

"After about an hour had passed, I finished the inspection of each of the units in every corridor and ultimately found nothing. Thankfully, none of the chambers in any of the corridors were breached. I asked myself, 'If the chambers were still safe, then what was causing that dreadful sound?' Before I could determine the cause, I noticed another sound, though it was significantly fainter than the alarm. It was outside. I had never been outside, for I was born within the mountain. I always imagined I would die there, too."

Sam felt a chill run down her spine as she thought of the man's death. She couldn't quite remember why, but something about it greatly unsettled her.

"It must have been years since I had last checked, but it seemed that the outside cameras were in working order," the man said. "They were my eyes from the inside, and they showed me people outside the front gate. I instantly regretted the decision to look, for the sight was a most gruesome one. A chilling reminder of why I needed to stay indoors.

"It was dark, and the moon was absent. White clumps of snow covered the stony ledge lingering beside the mountain. The snow was tainted by the blood of men everywhere I looked. A man with his back to my eyes was standing with two hands tightly clenched around a glowing sword. The blade emitted a green light that grew with intensity as the man blocked the incoming fire from the horde in front of him. From my calculations, there must have been well over five hundred men fighting against the one with his back to me. The host carried automatic rifles alongside primitive bows and arrows. A fair-skinned man with green eyes held what, at first glance, appeared to be a silver revolver. Upon a second glance, I realized it was actually a solar pistol. Closer examination revealed more solar weapons among the attackers, though none were as powerful, nor as impressive as the pistol. I did not understand how that could have been possible: the only way he could have acquired these weapons was from another Vault, and they should have all been sealed just like the one I was guarding. Unless he was an Enochian, he should not have been able to unlock any of the Vaults."

The man paused a moment and sighed, as if he were disappointed in himself. "But you know all about that, Sam. That is why all this happened."

Sam opened her mouth to reply, but no words came out. Instead, she nodded to acknowledge the man's comment but still refused eye contact. She wasn't ready yet.

The man continued his story. "The green-eyed man with the solar-powered pistol continued to fire at the swordsman, and each shot dissipated less than a meter from the intended target. The blade glowed a brighter green with each failed attempt. All the while, bullets and arrows soared through the air and each burned into ash the instant they met the swordsman's blade. Occasionally, a man from the crowd would close in on the swordsman only to have himself disemboweled, beheaded, or both.

"The fight continued like this for quite some time, exactly how long I cannot say. A part of my inner being found the scene to be an absolute atrocity. And yet, I found myself unable to look away, for I was utterly fascinated. I wondered who these men were and why they were fighting outside my home. The mountain would not fall nor receive any damage from their presence, so why did the swordsman appear to be defending it?

"The siren, I eventually discovered, was merely a precaution to warn me of any possible invaders. Though why such a measure was needed I did not know, for only the Old Ones could enter. And I still wondered how these men came to possess solar weapons. I continued to watch in awe and wonder, for despite my immense knowledge I did not know what in the wide cosmos the green blade could possibly be.

"Eventually, the man with green eyes realized his assaults were only working to make his enemy more powerful. He stopped firing and commanded the other solar-armed men to cease while he let the rest continue their futile attacks. He merely watched and waited. It was a smart plan, I must admit, for it worked. The glow from the swordsman's blade grew fainter with each use. Before the glimmer faded into the blackness of night, the man made a wide horizontal stroke through the air and let out a loud bellow from his gut. An enormous arc of green and white light sliced through the air behind his blade and sailed towards the mass of attackers. Each man it touched fell to the snowy ground with burns across their bodies. They screamed as they smelled their flesh boil and watched their comrades die. Suddenly, the swordsman's blade shattered, and the hilt flew like a rocket from his grip. It was a vain effort, it appeared, for there were still fifty or so men standing. The man with green eyes raised his pistol again, a smile etched across his stubbly face.

'You're surrounded,' the man with green eyes said impatiently and with a quiver in his voice. 'Give up before I do something I will regret.'

"The swordsman shook his head. 'You should not have followed me. The Vault is not meant for you.'

"Another man stepped forward, pressing his black hat close to his head as a gust of wind blew past him. Most of his face was hidden below the hat, though I saw that he had a thin black mustache. 'You don't know me,' he said to the swordsman. 'Nearly everyone from my home village died a few years ago. It finally succumbed to the violence, famine, and illness that have overtaken our world. Both my wife and daughter are gone, and I only barely made it out alive with my nephew. Many more will continue to die without your aid. Please, sir. Help us.'"

Sam continued to stare at her hand, and she clenched it to a fist. Her grip was so hard that she felt her nails digging into her skin. She could feel the warm blood oozing from within her palm. She didn't care. The mention of the man in the black hat made her furious.

The man paused, perhaps to look at Sam as she balled her hand into a fist. When she still didn't look up at him, he decided to continue. "Another growl of wind roared by, picking up the snow and dusting the men. The swordsman sighed heavily. 'I am sorry to hear about your tragedies. Sadly, I cannot change my mind. I've been entrusted to the Vault for a reason, and it is not meant for you. So long as I shall live, this world shall never again be the playground of tyrants. It's not what she would have wanted.' A strange statement, for he was not an Enochian either, and I had never heard of any others being assigned to guard my home. That was a duty all my own either until they returned or until my death. I was not sure if either would ever happen.

"The man with the black hat hung his head low in bitter disappointment. He wrinkled his face and looked to the green-eyed man, appearing to be just as angry.

'She? So you know of the Eternal Mother as well? What makes you think she chose you instead of me?' the man with the green eyes asked.

"The swordsman remained silent and seemed to take a moment to collect his thoughts. He coughed violently and, as he did, the horde approached him slowly, perhaps unsure if he had any other tricks up his sleeve. 'Do not come closer,' he finally said as his cough subsided. 'You and your men are not prepared for Svaldway's cold winter nor are they true fighters. A decade was not enough to truly prepare you against me with the Voidsweeper.'

'Your weapon is broken!' boasted the man with green eyes, walking closer and pointing his pistol at the swordsman's chest. 'No more tricks, brother! It's over, now let me in so I can *save* our planet.'

'The loss of the blade is inconsequential. I will enter the Vault. You will not.'

'Do you think you're somehow worthier? Because of your blood? I am the Sun's Chosen! She bestowed her holy weapons to me—not you! I am the one who should enter the Vault. Think of the good I could do with it!'

"I did not understand of what they were speaking. Entering the mountain had nothing to do with worth or human blood—only the blood of an Enochian. I was even more intrigued now, wondering what would happen next. Surely no one could enter, I told myself, for acquiring blood of the Enochians would be impossible.

"The swordsman backed up slowly. 'Those are not holy weapons —such things could never exist. Enochian technology is the very reason that I will never let you into the Vault.' I gasped when the swordsman mentioned the Enochians. I did not think it possible for anyone else alive to remember them. The Enochians had been gone for centuries.

'Enochians are about as real as the Vänalleatian Ascendants,' the man with green eyes said. Only the Sun is true. She blessed me with these weapons with the purpose of reuniting the world, and entering the Grand Vault is the last step I must take to achieve that goal!'

"The swordsman groaned. 'Do not test me. I did not bring you here for a reason. Go back home to our family. They may even take you back.'

"The man fired his pistol at the swordsman only to find himself shooting the mountainside as the swordsman dove to the ground. The swordsman crawled toward the entrance and placed his hand against the Vault's doors. At this point I panicked. I feared for what would happen next, hoping beyond hope that it would not. Another part of my being, this part stranger and less familiar, found myself wanting it to come true. Despite my duty to the treasures within the Vault, I also wanted the swordsman to enter. I wanted company—a friend.

"The man with the green eyes reloaded his solar pistol with another fusion cell and readied his aim at the swordsman. His companions dared not make a move without command. A grave miscalculation, for the swordsman had ample time to smash the glass vial against the glowing blue gate to my home. Another siren blared through the halls asynchronously with the alarm which I had nearly forgotten. As the doors were opening I found myself faced with a choice, the first I had ever needed to make. Was I to let him in and risk everything for which I dedicated my life? Or was I to override his access and let him die?

"The doors closed, and my decision was made. It was the first of many that would alter the course of the planet's future. I did not think about that at the time: I only wanted a friend. This supposition both excited and frightened me. I had the profound desire to make contact with a person after an eternity of isolation. Yet people are notorious for their selfishness and destruction. That is why my undercroft was constructed—human greed and their devastating tendencies.

"I rapidly shifted focus to the inside of the Vault and overrode the sirens blaring through the halls. My eyes found the swordsman as he passed Sector 1. I finally had my first clear glimpse of the man, and I was surprised because he did not look like an Enochian; the sun must have damaged his DNA enough to throw off my scanners, but not enough to deny his entry to the Vault.

"He was of a taller stature, nearly two meters in height by my estimates. He had very broad shoulders and was well built, broad and muscular. He was very pale and a cough that continued as incessantly as the alarm. He was dressed in heavy furs from the waist down and carried a fur coat over his shoulder, evidently too warm with it inside. He wore what appeared to be a long-sleeved sweater, riddled with holes revealing an undershirt underneath. The sweater was covered in dirt and patches of blood, both old and new. The man wore thick leather boots that were sopping wet; he seemed to pay no mind to this any more than he did the blotches of blood covering his body.

"The man had dark, brown eyes that looked intently at everything before him. There seemed to be a kind spirit behind these eyes—one that also carried a heavy burden and sorrow. He had a large and prominent nose that widened every few seconds as he inhaled deeply with great satisfaction. His hair was long and dark, pulled back and tied behind his head, roughly level with the middle of his ears. The tie that he used to put his hair together seemed to be from some kind of thin and tattered rope. His hair extended down between his shoulder blades. The man had a dark beard to match the dark hair on his head, and it was nowhere near as long or as neat. The beard protruded quite a few centimeters from his chin and cheeks. It was messy and unkempt, though it seemed practical to keep his face warm enough to protect him from the cold weather and harsh winds that he must have been exposed to outside.

"His mustache was much shorter than his beard, and it revealed full lips that were severely cracked. The dried lips were extended and spread apart, revealing a full smile on the man's face. The sight of the chambers behind the entrance to Sector 5 seemed to bring immense joy to the man. He took off his wet boots as well as the stockings on his feet and placed them on the floor next to the entrance of Sector 5. He opened the door and entered.

"At long last I was no longer alone. I had to keep myself from rejoicing just yet. This man could be here to steal from me. I initially doubted that it was a simple coincidence for him to be in Sector 5, given what the units in its chambers contained. Yet the man's demeanor seemed so peaceful and pleasant. The look of awe upon his face as he explored the corridors implied that his intentions in coming to my home were not malicious. His head turned left and right, looking at each of the chambers down the corridor as he examined the units within. He never spent too much time to look at any particular one. He did not seem to be looking for anything. Instead, it appeared that he was simply exploring and embracing the moment.

"I decided to keep watching the man. For so long, I had been alone watching over the chambers and the treasure contained within them. But the treasure was not for me to use. Instead, they were placed here to help the people of the future. I was stationed here to watch over the treasure and to make sure it remained safe and regulate that all the standardized settings. I supposed I had just assumed that I was supposed to protect it from invaders as well. I then wondered if I needed to protect them from this man if he was indeed an Enochian. The Vaults were, after all, made for them.

"I continued to watch the man and noticed that he had begun to mutter to himself as he paced down the corridor. 'Well, Jean, I finally made it. I only wish you were here to see it. I wonder what he would think of this place, if I brought him along. I suppose he's safer where he is. They can watch over him better than I ever could. I just wish you didn't have to go....'

"The man seemed ecstatic as he continued to investigate the corridors within Sector 5. As he sauntered down the hall, he continued to mutter in a low and relaxed tone. I felt as though I was beginning to know him. I became desperate to learn more about this man. In the short time I spent watching him, I became certain I could trust him. The risk of exposing myself—of making myself vulnerable —was worth it. I could finally talk to someone and end the life of isolation I had suffered for far too long. Not only that, but I was enthusiastic about the chance to help this man. I could learn more about him and about his backstory. Maybe I could find a way to reunite him with his son and discover what happened to the other Enochians."

The man paused once more and took a deep breath. "Pardon me, Sam," he said. "I still forget to take breaths between my words." He forced a laugh, and Sam could tell he was trying to ease the tension.

The man took another deep breath before resuming. "The man made his way to the Sector 5 exit. He returned to his belongings and sat down on the floor next to them, leaning against the wall adjacent to the Sector's entrance. He donned his boots, apparently drier than when he had left them due to the strong air circulation within the undercroft. He returned to his feet and gazed around him. It was at this point I noticed how heavy his eyes were. He seemed exhausted, unsure of where to go next. This was my chance to establish a relationship with the man.

'Greetings, stranger!' I said.

"The man shook with a great fright. He was apparently startled from hearing my voice, and he looked all around him to determine where my voice originated.

'Please, do not be frightened. I am speaking to you from the overhead intercoms. There is ample space in Sector 23 that can serve as temporary living quarters. Why not go there and rest?'

"He circled around again, unsure of where to look. The man then responded with a slight tremble in his voice, 'Where are you? How can you see me?'

'I have been observing you through the cameras scattered throughout the facility since your arrival, uncertain as to whether I should make contact. Your presence here caught me off guard, but I welcome your company. Please, go to Sector 23 and rest. Perhaps we can get to know one another after that. Until then, allow me to introduce myself: my name is Mimir.'

"The man hesitated, then slowly nodded his head. He made his way forward, to Sector 23, and the world was ready to change."

Sam smirked and sat up straight in her chair. She was ready to hear the full story of her savior, Benedict Limmetrad. She finally shifted her gaze from her right hand to the man telling her the story. She looked him in the eyes; they were bright green.

2. Sanctuary No More

"Again!" Rakshi shouted, swinging her iron sword across Ben's chest, missing his sun-cloak by barely an inch. He recovered his own dull blade from the withered grass and hoisted himself off his knees. He readied his stance, gripping his sword with both hands. He stood sideways with his weapon positioned at a downward angle toward the Sentinel Commander and made himself as small a target as he could.

It wasn't an easy thing to do, for Ben was not a small man. He towered over everyone else in the village at six feet and five inches. He looked down at Rakshi, a much smaller target, but no less worthy an opponent. Her might behind a blade was rivaled only by her ferocity behind a bow. And *that* was matched only by Rose's proficiency.

He dodged another swing from Rakshi's short sword and slid to her flank with great speed. He made his counter, slashing forward at her non-sword arm.

She pirouetted, then parried without hesitation.

"Good planning," Rakshi said, sweat dripping from her chestnut-shaded forehead. Though her dark eyes looked at Ben sternly, he guessed that there was a slight flicker of approval in them.

"But it's too predictable," she continued as she made her follow-up attack. She wasted no time and spoke as she fought. It was a way to teach the mind and body all at once, she would tell Ben. "If your opponent only has one weapon in one hand, then they're going to know to protect the open side. More often than not, you'll find an enemy with something occupying each hand. A shield, another weapon, or both hands on the same one. Always assume they know their weak spot."

Ben nodded and parried each attack, working hard to concentrate on both the conversation and the blunt blade waving dangerously close to his face. Rakshi pushed him back, closer to the fence near the twins, swinging through the air with a whir of screeching metal.

"You may find you need to kill your opponent. But only if you see no other way."

Ben took a slight pause, and his teacher knocked the sword from his hand and swept her leg beneath him. He fell to his back and nearly lost the wind from his lungs. Kristos laughed until his twin brother pushed him off the fence. Then Zechariah had a laugh himself. Ben would've hoped the twins' little ruse would've been enough to distract Rakshi in time for him to recover his weapon. He had no such luck.

Rakshi stood over him and pointed the sword at his neck.

She was in her element, and it was quite a sight to see her thrive and to listen to her teach. She meant every swing she took, calculated the precision of her actions, and had a fiery passion in her eyes. She had been training since before Ben was born and became Sentinel Commander over men and women older and more experienced than herself. She was even younger than the twins, the otherwise youngest members of the Freztad Sentinels.

"If I were a wastelander, you'd be dead," she said, still pointing her blade at Ben's throat before helping him to his feet. "Since you were defenseless. and in a position to be restrained, I'd much rather spare you."

Ben finally spoke up with a slight hesitation in his voice, as was common. "You're saying it's okay to kill someone?"

"Only if you can't help it. If you're going to die, or someone else is because you didn't stop your opponent, then you need to make that choice."

"I thought our job was to stop killers."

"*My* job, Benedict. You still have a lot of training to do before I can name you a Freztad Sentinel. You're still just a farm boy." Rakshi spoke in a flat and harsh tone, but Ben noticed a quick grin flare as she teased him.

"You know I hate being called that."

"A farm boy? Then don't work on Kabedge's farm. There are plenty of other workers."

"That's not what I meant," Ben said, gritting his teeth.

Rakshi shook her head with disapproval. "There are far worse things to be called than your own name. Get used to it. Embrace it. Make it your own, Limmetrad."

Ben rolled his eyes. "At least Rose shares that one, too. I'd like to share as few things in common with my father as possible. I want to be better than him."

"Better how?" his teacher inquired. She was never satisfied with a superficial answer. Just like the strokes of a sword and angle of an arrow soaring through the sky, Rakshi believed in making deliberate actions. And to Rakshi, actions included words.

'The entire Sentinel Guard must be decisive and exact. You must never act with only half a heart', Ben recalled her once saying to him.

Ben flexed his arm across his chest and stretched, sore from the training. He would be rather be sore on the outside than within. *Pain fades easier when it's physical*, he considered as he resisted the aches he felt at the thoughts of his father.

"I want to protect people," Ben replied. "Do something useful for the village. Even if the village doesn't want my help I want to be here to make a difference. That's more than I can say for Alphonse."

Rakshi untied her hair and let the black tangles free themselves and flow to the small of her back. She laid down her weapon and approached Ben, looking up at him. "You don't know why he left. No one does. You can't judge the actions of another without so much as a hint at their experiences. That's why you must be decisive when you take a life, for it is no easy thing. You must be absolutely sure of their intent or of the consequences of their actions. One misinterpretation and you disturb a balance not only externally, but within yourself. And even if you're sure you've made the right decision, you must be able to live with that decision for the rest of your life. Only then can you be trusted to guard people's lives."

A lump grew in Ben's throat. He swallowed hard, but it did not go away; rather, it only bothered him even more. It was the first time he faced the true meaning of the idea. Were these people whom he really wanted to protect? Was he only here to train with Rakshi to spite his faceless father for abandoning him? Surely even that would make Ben better.

There are lives worth protecting, he thought. The lives of those who made Ben feel like he really belonged. His only anchors to the dwindling village he called home. The only reasons he didn't make the same choice as his father to leave and explore the world, no matter how much his heart begged him to do it.

"Decisive action. Got it. Speaking of which," Ben faced toward the farm across the road and tilted his head toward it, "Kabedge needs me to finish up with the harvest. If gathering the last scraps of food before summer hits isn't being trusted with people's lives, then I don't know what is."

Rakshi nodded and extended her forearm. Ben clasped his arm around hers and shook it firmly. He turned toward the village street. Suddenly he felt an aching smack to the back of his head and the sound of a loud *thud*.

"Rakshi what the—!"

His teacher smacked him upside the head again and shook her head before landing her eyes on the bastard sword resting in the dirt. "Forget something?"

Idiot, Ben cursed at himself. "Right. Sorry about that."

"Who wouldn't be sorry after a smack like that!" Kristos yelled from the side. "Damn, Benny, that must've hurt. Another decade like that and you'll be as strong as me and Zech!"

"Fat," Zechariah coughed.

"What's that?" demanded Kristos, raising a fist against his brother.

"You mixed up being fat with being strong."

"Bugger off, I'm not fat. No one's fat. That's just a myth Kabedge put out there to stop people from stealing his food after hours!"

Rakshi rolled her eyes at the twins. *There's that grin again*, Ben thought to himself as he watched his teacher hide another smirk. Though the three were some of Ben's only friends, he couldn't help but feel left out. They had years of friendship and stories to build the foundation of their friendship. Years *without* Ben. It made Ben hate his aunt even more for rarely letting him visit the other settlements without supervision.

"If you don't take care of your weapon, it won't take care of you," Rakshi said, trying to ignore the twins' antics.

"It's just a training sword."

"Aye, and if you can't treat that well then what makes you think you'd do any better with the real deal? Take it back to the armory, and make sure it's wiped down and clean. I want to be able to see my face in it by the time I'm done with those two fools."

"Hey!" the twins protested in unison.

"Rakshi, come on. I have to get to the farm. I don't have time. I don't want the old man overexerting himself having to pick up my work *and* have to worry about Vic at the same time."

"Fine. Go on," his teacher said while raising her hands in defeat. "You can clean it after you're done at Kabedge's. I don't want to have to pick up your work either, so I expect it to be done by morning."

Ben nodded. He picked up the sword and placed it into its scabbard. He rushed across the village, past the Tree of Mathias, to drop off the sword. He was sure that leaving it on his bed would remind him to clean it before tonight.

It was still dawn, and the sun chased the moon out of its place, ready to shine and burn above the land. The light grew behind Valhaven, the Limmetrad ancestral home, and illuminated it from the blackness of night. The building was taller than any other in Freztad, and it was long and wide, enough to hold the entire village during a meeting or storm. Its roof was thatched with bales of hay and wooden beams, just like every other structure standing in the village. The walls were made of stone, coarse and gray like the clouds before a spring rain with mortar of lime to keep it together. Other houses were made from oaken lumber and hides of boiled leather to insulate the walls; some were even made of scrap metal from the old days. Valhaven was the only stone home in the entire village, the oldest and sturdiest of them all. But even after almost sixteen years it was hardly a home to Ben.

He hastily entered the front door of the house, hoping not to disturb his aunt. He left the door open so as to not risk making a sound upon closing and darted to his room. Considering the size of the grand hall in which he lived, Ben's room would perhaps be more accurately described as a large closet. Across the room and to the right lay Ben's tattered feather and wool bed. It rested upon the floor on a wooden frame that he had built for it when he was barely ten. Though it wasn't much, it allowed Ben to occasionally drift off to sleep after staring at the stars through his window. At the foot of his bed were two baskets, a rucksack, a quiver holding arrows and a knife, and a bow. Ben smiled at his possessions.

Though they were few, they were things he had earned and could call his own.

The only possession Ben couldn't quite call his own lay in a metal box at the bottom of his dirty clothes basket. For no reason in particular, Ben decided to look at the box once more. Perhaps another glance would give him another clue. He walked a few steps from his door to the basket on the floor. He rested the iron training sword against the wall before bending down and pulling out all his dirty clothes to reveal the small metal box at the bottom. He slowly reached his hands toward the bottom of the basket and grasped at the resting silver object. He turned from the basket to his bed. He sat down and stared at the only other thing given to him by his father besides a name.

He removed the metal lid from its base and revealed its contents. Inside the small box was a silver bracelet, comprised of many interconnected links. At the center of the bracelet was a rather large and clunky circular object with a glass face. It was a watch. On the back of the watch was an odd geometric design with concentric squares and a circle at its midpoint.

The watch had a circle of numbers with three needles protruding from the center as well as a smaller circle with twelve dots and a single needle. The long thick needle pointed at the number '7' and the short thick one pointed at the number '8'. The long thin needle pointed to the number '1'. On the smaller circle, there was only one needle and it pointed to a '5'.

He had no idea what the watch was used for or what the needles pointing to the numbers meant, nor had he ever thought to ask anyone. The watch was the only connection between Ben and his father. It was a way for Ben to pretend that he was alone with a father who acknowledged him, loved him. Talking to someone else about it could ruin that connection of pure fantasy.

Ben had taken the watch apart many times in the past and had determined that the needles were supposed to move on their own. How they did so, Ben couldn't figure. It appeared that some pieces were missing, for he found a small key inside where it seemed something else ought to have been. After each time he had taken the watch apart, he put the needles back to their original positions. For years, Ben had been wondering why his father had left him this seemingly useless trinket. It had always bothered him, reminding him of his mysterious father who had abandoned him. And yet he couldn't bear to get rid of it. As much as Ben tried to pretend that he wanted to forget his father, he would never be able to do such a thing. He couldn't forget someone he never knew.

Ben bit his lip and decided to put the watch away. He placed it into its box and laid it on the floor as he prepared for the rest of his day. He put on his sun-goggles and donned his wide-brimmed hat and set out for another day of work in the unforgiving sun.

Ben walked next door to Kabedge's with his usual medium length and loose-fitting robe that extended from his shoulders to just above his knees. He entered the produce shop and walked to the far end of the shop where he saw Kabedge. The old man was probably in his mid-seventies and had a long gray soul patch and hair to match it hidden underneath his faded green turban.

"Morning, Kabedge. I'll have the usual."

"For you, kid? Sure, why not. Let me tell you, it's gonna be a hot one out there today. Not sure what's worse, the storms or the accursed heat."

"Yeah, tell me something I don't know. Got any more stories for me while I eat?"

Kabedge shook his head and wagged his finger. "No stories until my crops are done, y'hear? Can't have you out there late with blood bugs. Gonna be swarming after this storm. Think it'll be a big one."

"You going senile on me now, Kab? You *love* those stories!"

"Another time, kid. I gotta think of one you don't know yet." The olive-skinned man turned around and finished Ben's meal, humming to himself.

Minutes later, Kabedge handed Ben a small clay bowl of steam and greens. "Here you go, kid. Kabedge's famous cabbage casserole, if you can even call it that. You know, I hear casseroles were a lot different back in the Old Days. Did y'know they had books back then that were dedicated to nothing except for recipes? Pages and pages of different ways to cook a meal. Wish I could get my hands on one of them recipes. Then maybe I could make some *real* food. Say do you even know what a book is?"

Ben took a spoonful of the soup, nearly burning himself as he choked back a laugh. "See, I knew you had a story in you! And of course I know what a book is! You tell me about them all the time. Lydia's room is full of them! That's how I know they're a waste of time."

"Oi!" Kabedge barked. "Don't you go bad mouthing the chief! She's your aunt for crying out loud. Be grateful!"

"*Was*," Ben corrected Kabedge.

The old man raised an eyebrow. "She's still alive, and she hasn't relinquished her duty. I believe that makes her the chief unless Freztad made a new law without me."

"Rose is the real chief. She has been for years. She'll be old enough for the title in the fall and I'll bet you the farm that Lydia will ask her to take up the mantle."

Kabedge raised his hands in surrender. It was clear he didn't want to argue with Ben on the subject. He turned to cleaning the dishes and setting up shop for the day.

"Say, were books actually that important back in the Old Days?"

Kabedge gasped and clutched his left side as if he had been grievously insulted. "Important? Of course they were important! Books are what taught people proper back then! They were loads smarter because of them!"

"Then what happened? Why aren't things like the Old Days if they were so smart?" Ben asked with a shrewd smile.

Kabedge shook his head and suppressed a smile. "Because there is such a thing as being *too* smart, kid!"

Ben chuckled. "What else you got for me? Got any more stories about people moving around in horseless carriages or men jumping to the moon?"

The cook dismissed the comment and went back to wiping down his counter and washing his dishes. Then he suddenly threw the wet rag at Ben with a boisterous chuckle. "Get on outta here, kid, and do your job before it's too late! I'm sure I'll have a story by then."

Ben squealed as the grimy cloth nearly landed in his bowl. He looked up at Kabedge, red in the face by the sound he made. Then, the two shared another laugh.

"Yeah, yeah, I'm going. Say hi to your husband for me, will you? I haven't seen Vic in a while. I'll see you in the afternoon before the sun gets too bad. Take it easy, old man." He offered Kabedge another shrewd smile and threw the rag back at the cook right before darting out of the shop.

The farm was the most grandiose thing Freztad had to offer. To outsiders it wasn't much to look at, especially compared to Mathias's Tree, but it was far better than any farms the other settlements had. What Kabedge's farm lacked in quality, it more than made up for in diversity. In the few acres of farmland outside the residential area of Freztad, Ben tended to its various crops. While many of the villagers worked on the farm as well, Ben spent more time on it than anyone else. He knew everything there was to know about the farm. Kabedge and Vic had once run the farm together for decades, before Ben's father and aunt were born. They were getting older now and Kabedge's husband was ill as of late. Ben had taken up most of their responsibilities in the past few years, never minding the hard work. Management was still left up to Kabedge and Vic—Ben tried to avoid the other workers as often as possible. It was better that way.

Besides, working on the farm meant Ben got free food from Kabedge during mealtimes, and that was too great an opportunity to pass up.

The farm had a decent irrigation system fed by the sacred Gjoll River. The river was Freztad's salvation, the only reason any villager drew breath. It was as wide as a tall fir and flowed hard and fast from the highlands of Sydgilbyn to the great lakes of Vänalleato. It roared behind the Eastern and Southern walls of Freztad; its water pouring through the pipes into the village's farmlands. Many found the blessing of the Gjoll to be accompanied by a curse. At the edges of the river were pockets of water where blood bugs grew and thrived, having once carried a deadly disease that had plagued the village.

The fear of blood bugs never stuck with Ben. He had been bitten more times than he could count and never once had so much as a cough. It was for this reason that Ben had been chosen to work on the farm. Ever since the outbreak, people had been fearful of approaching the Gjoll for any reason other than to praise whatever spirit may sleep at the bottom. They had grown careless with repairing and replacing the piping, and the irrigation system became rusted and clogged, spoiling the crops. When he was eight years old, Ben had offered to work the repairs, never afraid of the consequences. Reluctant though they were, Kabedge and Vic accepted Ben's help, and the crops continued to prosper. As he grew older, he slowly picked up more jobs around the village that dealt with the Gjoll, such as setting out fishing nets and carrying the deceased's ashes to the river. On occasion he would even enjoy a relaxing sail on the river.

Ben walked out from behind Kabedge's store and looked over the fields. He had finished getting all the edible corn and cabbages yesterday, so he figured it would be best to work on the tomatoes and beans today. If he finished harvesting those today, he would be able to take the next few days off until the wheat and hay were ready. With that notion in mind, he thought about how he might be able to spend time with Rose and hunt like they used to.

Ben smiled under his scarf and got to work.

I t was sundown when Ben finished his work. He returned from his day's work to Kabedge's store for him to inventory. While Kabedge sorted through the crops, Ben made himself a quick meal. He thought about how he could spend the next few days relaxing, something he rarely did anymore. Ben only worried that Rose would be busy taking over for her mother. He hoped he would be able to convince her to take at least one day off.

Finishing the last few bites of his dinner and gulping down the last of his water, Ben cleaned up and said goodbye to Kabedge before returning to Valhaven. Once inside he noticed Rose's door was open. It was triple the size of Ben's living quarters. *A proper room.* Rose's bed was raised from the ground on a wooden frame with bannisters reaching toward the ceiling. A canopy of green silk cloth surrounded the bed at the bannisters and hung down to near a foot from the floor. Across the bed was a paint and oiled portrait depicting two women surrounded by a forest. Ben never knew who could have been so skilled as to capture the likeness of toddler Rose and young Lydia. The real testament to the artist's talent was not the detail, but showing his aunt smiling. It was probably the last time she ever did.

Luxurious though it was, Ben was not jealous of Rose's living space. He did not mind his small room and he enjoyed gradually filling it with his own possessions. He was jealous, however, of what Rose's room meant. It was a constant reminder that Rose had a parent who loved her. All Ben had was a watch and a name.

"What're you doing?" a soft voice asked from behind Ben's shoulder.

He turned around to his best friend and couldn't help but grin. Rose stood at the threshold of her doorway with her wavy chestnut hair tied behind her ears and reaching below her shoulder blades. At only a head shorter than Ben, Rose was rather tall for a woman though this was not her defining feature. The cousins looked quite similar, their Limmetrad traits prevalent. They both had bronzed skin with dark hair and sharp, square jaws and smooth chins. Their noses differed somewhat, with Ben's being larger and more prominent than his cousin's. Her key feature that set her apart from all others were her eyes. The windows through which she looked were leafy green, bold and bright. No one else in Freztad nor, to his knowledge, any of the other settlements had eyes like hers.

"Everything alright?" Ben asked, noticing the grimace on his cousin's face.

"Of course not. Mom's having an episode right now."

She's your mom, *remember? I don't have one.* "Again? What is it this time?" It was hard for Ben to sympathize with his aunt. Her melancholy had been dragging her down for years now, and Ben found it hard to believe she could get any worse. First, she stopped leaving the village. Then the house. And then her room with nothing but books and drink to keep her time. Yet she always seemed to find the energy to criticize Ben, even though he did more for the village in a day than she did in a year.

"Oh, I don't know. She got upset when I told her that I wanted to discuss summer rations with the other leaders so early. I want to do it before next month." Her voice shook ever so slightly as she spoke as though she felt a pinch of guilt.

"Next month? You mean before the solstice? We never ration that early." The harvest wasn't exactly bountiful this year, and he hadn't accounted for rations when he decided which crops would go to the animals. There wasn't nearly enough time to plant anything that could grow in just under two months.

"This spring has been a particularly bad one," she said. "With the storms we've had lately I doubt the full summer heat will wait more than a fortnight after the solstice to arrive. We need to start preparing as soon as possible."

Ben pinched the bridge of his nose and sighed heavily. "I finished the bulk of the harvest today and let me tell you, there isn't much left. I can look at things again in a few days, but I was thinking of taking tomorrow off and seeing if you wanted to go hunting..."

Rose's leaf-green eyes drifted to the floor. "Ben, you know I'd love to go." There was a tone of sadness to her voice. "We haven't been able to go in so long, but I just told you how much I need to do. With the condition that Mom is in and the village...It's just not practical."

Ben let out a long, drawn out sigh. "The village can go a few hours without you in the morning. Besides, you'd be doing them a favor by going out to hunt. We haven't had good meat in quite a while, and you're the best one with a bow in Freztad. You'd be doing them a disservice by not going."

"Even so, I can't leave Mom here. What if something happens and I wasn't here to help her?"

"Rose, you have your own life, you know. You can't live her life for her. I know you love her. She's a strong woman," Ben admitted with difficulty. "If she weren't, Freztad wouldn't still be here. It might even be good for her to have some extra time to herself." Ben tried to sound as reassuring as he could. He wasn't just saying all this to convince Rose to hunt with him. He knew that it wasn't healthy for Rose to bear her mother's burdens all the time. She needed time for herself, too.

Rose groaned and rolled her eyes. "Fine, you've convinced me. I guess a few hours in the morning couldn't hurt. I hate when you make sense."

Ben gave her a shrewd smile and chuckled. "Hey, I don't claim to make sense. I just say whatever I think is right. The two aren't always the same, you know. Anyway, let's try to leave at first light, shall we?"

"Yeah, we can do that. We only do a few hours, okay? I want to be back well before noon. I'll go clean up my bow, replace the string, and make sure I have enough arrows," Rose exclaimed. It was obvious that she needed time away from the village and a break from the overwhelming responsibility that weighed on her.

Ben raised a wide smile and returned to his room. He saw his cousin smile and nod as she closed her door. "Oh, and don't you go changing your mind on me last minute!" he shouted.

Ben closed his own door and collapsed on his bed, asleep before his head touched the pillow. It was the best sleep he had had in months.

Dawn couldn't come soon enough. Ben paced around his room for at least an hour before daybreak, getting ready for the hunt. He counted the arrows in his quiver and made sure his hunting knife was adequately sharpened. Ben dressed himself for the forest and laid down on his bed, planning a route for the hunt.

The forest next to the village went on for miles and contained diverse wildlife. It wasn't uncommon for deer to appear outside the village to drink water from the river, so Ben knew there were still some in the forest. He had also heard howling emanating the thick woods recently and worried that a pack of wolves had settled nearby. If there were indeed wolves then not only would spotting deer be difficult, but stomping around the forest carelessly could mean death.

Ben heard a soft knock at his door and got up from his mattress. "Morning! Ready?"

Rose nodded, with her long dark hair tied back and bow wrapped around her torso and across her left shoulder. "Yeah. I talked to Mom about it, and I think she'll be okay if we're only gone for a few hours."

The two left the house and walked straight down the village main road. Sleeping homes and silent shops lined the path, watching the cousins as they walked in the early morning. Kabedge's shop was the first building they passed on the left, adjacent to his and Vic's house. Freztad only had a few shops scattered throughout the village, many of which sold goods traded from neighboring settlements. The majority of buildings in the village were houses for the eight hundred or so remaining villagers. A handful of the houses were empty.

According to Kabedge, the population had been dwindling for the past fifteen years, which Ben knew was due to his father's leaving, and then even more so from the plague ten years ago. Yet anyone who thought his father's abandonment was a bad omen couldn't have been more wrong. Lydia had proven to be an extremely effective leader before the blood poisoning and melancholia had gotten the best of her. Before

Rose was born, Lydia formed the Penteric Alliance with the other neighboring settlements and set up trade agreements. She obtained the resources necessary to make Kabedge's farm flourish in comparison to all the other settlements. She bought plows, horses, and cattle for the farm, all of which could be bred and raised for further prosperity.

Surrounding the village was a large stone wall standing just shy of twenty-five feet tall. The wall enclosed all the buildings and the farm, though Freztad's territory extended far beyond the village to parts of the forest on its outskirts. Between the walls and the forest was arid land with scattered patches of wilted grass. A few abandoned Sentinel towers stood outside the village along with an old dried up well. Two towers stood tall at the village entrance, each within the wall on either side of the gate. Another like them stood behind Valhaven to overlook the river. These days, only the two western towers at the village front were ever actually manned while the remaining Sentinels patrolled the roads between settlements. There just didn't seem to be any point for them to man the towers outside of Freztad, too.

Reaching the end of the village, Ben and Rose approached the gate and lifted the drawbar. Rose called up tower, "Hey—Rakshi! Do you think you could open the gate for us? Ben and I are going out to hunt."

Rakshi peered over the ledge at the two and nodded with a smile. "Be safe out there, you two. I heard howling in the woods last time I was on duty." She waved to Neith at the other tower, and the two pulled the levers at their stations. Ropes ascended and descended along the wheels of metal pulleys like the gears in Ben's watch as the gate creaked open upon its track.

Ben and Rose made their way outside and waved to Rakshi, thanking her as she closed the gate behind them. The deep green and brown forest loomed over the small village at only a few dozen yards beyond the village walls. Rose shifted her gaze from the withering woods to her cousin. "Which way, O' Master Tracker.?"

Ben chuckled. "I think if we go to the left, closer to the river, we're more likely to find some deer tracks. I sometimes see them out there when I'm fixing the pipes."

Rose frowned. "Let's not get too close to the river. The blood bugs might still be active, and I reckon they've still got the blood poison."

"It'll be fine, trust me."

"I spoke to Kabedge the other day inquiring about Vic. Haven't you noticed he hasn't been around lately?"

Ben's belly churned, and he grew pale. "I figured he just couldn't get around as easily anymore. He is getting pretty old."

"I thought so, too," Rose said. "Then I spoke with the Elder. They've been experts on the poisoning ever since the plague. He said all of Vic's symptoms fit."

No, it can't be, Ben told himself. He couldn't lose Vic. Worse, how would Kabedge deal with it?

"I've been by the river plenty of times," he said. "If anyone were to have been bit, it would've been me. I feel fine."

Rose shook her head, not buying the protest. "That doesn't count. We all know you can't get sick for some reason. Some people aren't as lucky."

Rose's voice felt like a bitter sting. "You survived, too," he said.

"That's different, Ben. Mom kept me inside. I didn't leave the house for over a year, so I was never exposed."

"And Lydia didn't give a damn about me. She let me come and go as I pleased."

"We've been over this! She did what she could to keep you inside. Like always, you just didn't listen to her."

"Well, I never got sick and still haven't. The blood bugs don't carry the sickness anymore. Vic will be fine." Ben wasn't sure if he was trying to convince Rose or himself.

"Don't take this so lightly. It affects people differently depending on how old they are. It crippled Mom. It killed all the other children. We're the last ones, Ben. You need to consider for a moment that *maybe* another plague has started."

Ben shifted his eyes to the Gjoll. The river had always been a like a silent friend. He could go to it when he wanted to be alone, knowing no one would bother him. Rose knew that about him, so why would she all but forbid him from going there?

He groaned and accepted defeat. "Fine. I'll just get a good look of some tracks from a distance. I should be able to pick them back up once we're in the forest."

The pair arrived at the edge of the forest and took a left, toward the river. Closer than Rose liked, though not close enough in Ben's opinion. Sure enough, Ben spotted tracks. He then found a clearing in the woods and beckoned for Rose to follow him. As he had predicted, Ben found the tracks with relative ease. The deer the tracks belonged to didn't appear to be going fast; it was about medium-sized, too. It probably left no more than an hour ago. Not bad for their first catch.

They kept silent as they traversed the forest. The wind carried a scent of fresh rain and dank crevasses past their nostrils while the wilderness remained hauntingly silent. An occasional crow cawed to remind the pair that they were not alone. They continued to walk deeper in the woods, slowly heading southwest, their bodies arched close to the ground to avoid being spotted.

"I think we're getting close," Ben whispered.

"How can you tell?"

"The tracks are quite fresh. They're wet, and the mud is packed down. Probably from that stream we passed."

"I can't believe you can figure all of this out from just a little bit of mud."

"Well, I got it from the mud *and* the broken branches over there that are still wobbling," Ben said with his shrewd smile, still leaning down next to the tracks.

"Don't give me that look, Ben. We need to keep going or else your precious mud will dry up."

Shortly thereafter they spotted their prey, a young buck with a decent set of antlers. None of this deer would go to waste. Its antlers would sell nicely, and the meat will make a decent meal. He slowly removed his bow from around his shoulder. He nocked an arrow and took aim. With a slow breath he released the arrow.

The arrow squealed through the air and landed in the buck's rear left thigh. It let out a loud wail and darted away from its predators. Ben and Rose quickly hopped over the fallen tree and gave chase.

The buck eventually stopped about a quarter mile later, exhausted and groaning in pain. The cousins found a pair of thick trees to hide behind. It was Rose's turn to take the shot. She nocked her arrow, then seemed to notice Ben look of disappointment.

"Ben, what has gotten into you? You love hunting. We're supposed to be having fun."

"I do love it. I am having fun. But I hate when I get a lousy shot like that. I might as well have missed it completely. It's been so long since I've hunted and even longer since I've missed that badly. Most of my shots would at least slow them down enough for me to get it over with quickly." In truth, Ben hated causing anything undue pain. He told himself he should've waited for a better angle. They should've been closer.

"I'll get it over with quickly, don't you worry." Lifting her bow to take aim, Rose readied to unleash the final shot. As she pulled back the arrow and readied to release, something fierce let out a horrific howl. At the sudden sound, she accidentally let her arrow loose and completely missed the equally shocked deer. Ben and Rose looked at each other, both with their eyes widened.

A white wolf, nearly the size of a small horse, lunged at the deer from behind the cover of some nearby trees. The deer quickly ran away from the wolf, having been given a head start by the wolf's warning howl. With the injured leg, the buck's speed was no match for the wolf's. There was no way it would be able to outrun the giant beast.

Ben looked over at Rose saying, "We should get out of here! That thing is huge!"

"No, we can still get the deer if we keep our distance from the wolf. Once it starts feeding, it'll be still, and I can make the shot!"

Ben felt his spirits lift, if only a little. He was already upset about ruining his shot, and even more upset when the wolf came along to steal their kill. Rose's confidence and self-assurance were enough to cheer him up. Now they could still go home with something to show for it. Even though the wolf's size and speed terrified Ben, he knew even that was powerless when facing his cousin.

The cousins followed the blood tracks of the deer, knowing that it had to be close by. When they finally arrived at the end of the tracks, Ben and Rose saw the deer's body ahead of them with the beast atop it. Rose drew her next arrow and took aim.

Rose could have made a lethal shot, but she froze. The wolf made no advances in their direction, but it was clear that it had spotted the two of them. Ben was convinced that the wolf was gazing directly into his eyes. After staring at the two for what felt like an eternity, the wolf howled and sprinted away from them, leaving the deer's corpse behind.

Rose released the tension on her bow and let it down. "What was that all about? Why was it staring at us like that? There's no way it could have been afraid of us."

"I'm not sure. Maybe it's seen humans with bows and arrows before and knows a losing battle when it sees one. Did you see its eyes? It looked like it was *thinking* when it saw us. As if it were making conscious decisions about what to do. Wolves don't do that, do they?"

"I certainly couldn't tell you. Let's get that deer and go home before it decides to change its mind. I've had enough of an adventure for one day," Rose said with an exhausted sigh. The two picked up the deer—Rose helped place it on Ben's shoulders after taking his bow from him. "Are you sure you're going to be okay carrying that all by yourself? I can take it from you if you get too tired."

"I should be fine. This is nothing compared to the work on the farm. I totally forgot how easy this was," he said, grunting as he adjusted the deer on his shoulders.

Rose made a face at her cousin and chuckled. "Well, let me know if you change your mind, muscle man."

Their trek back wasn't perfectly precise because they came to the edge of the forest near the village's Northern Wall, rather than facing the gate to the West. Ben put down the deer and stretched his back and neck. Noticing that it was much brighter than when they had left,

Ben decided to put on his sun-goggles and lifted his hat back onto his head from the attached string around his neck. Rose did the same before the two exited the safety of the shade.

"I can't wait to get home and have some lunch at Kabedge's!"

"Just make sure you skin the deer and drop it off at Zevi's, so he can prepare it. I have to get back to Mom to make sure she's okay, and then get ready for whatever business there is to attend."

A faint, high-pitched noise carried through the wind to the cousins.

"Rose, do you hear that? Listen!"

They were silent, trying to get a closer to listen to the screeches piercing the air. Rose broke the silence. "Oh no—the village! Ben, those were screams! I think we're under attack!"

Ben's eyes widened under his sun-goggles as a pit grew in his stomach. "Rose, give me back my bow and quiver. We need to go. Now!"

Rose, hands shaking, removed Ben's bow and quiver and handed them over to him. Without having to say anything else, the two cousins left the deer behind and ran toward the village, each with a nocked arrow in their bow.

3.Secrets Left Behind

S printing as fast as they could, Ben and Rose approached Freztad's Northern Wall. As they had feared, the sounds they heard from the forest were indeed screams. Amidst the screams from the villagers, Ben could hear voices barking orders—voices he didn't recognize. Rose ran along the village wall toward the entrance. Ben caught up with her and grabbed her by the shoulder.

"Rose! What are you doing? You can't just run in there! We don't know what's going on. It's not safe!"

With a cry of desperation, Rose turned to face him. "We need to work our way to the village front and see what's going on! Our people could be in trouble!"

"Look, it sounds like there's a whole mess of them in there, so we need to stop and think about this *before* we put ourselves in danger. Sorry to say, but I don't think these guys came here for a nice early morning chat," Ben said facetiously. "We're being attacked, and we may be our people's only hope. Getting killed because we weren't cautious isn't going to do anyone any favors."

The situation terrified Ben, and he was doing all he could to remain calm. He knew he had to for Rose's sake. She really cared about the villagers. He had to be strong for her—and for himself.

"This...this just doesn't make sense," Rose said with a tremble in her voice.

Ben was just as shocked as his cousin. To the best of his knowledge, their village didn't have any enemies, and he had never heard of any wastelanders being great enough in number or organization to attack the capital of the Alliance. Yet all signs seemed to indicate that the unthinkable was happening.

"We'll worry about how they got in later. Right now we need to get inside the walls so we can help. Like you said, we need a plan first —and I think I have one. First, we need to see the front gate, then I'll tell you what I think."

The two worked their way around the wall toward the village's front. Ben stopped and signaled for Rose to wait behind him. He didn't know if there was anyone behind the corner and didn't want to be caught off guard. He loosened the tension on his bow and pulled out the knife from his quiver, ready to take out anyone that may be around the corner. *Cover me,* he mouthed to Rose as he prepared to turn the corner.

Ben's heart was pumping faster than he could think, racing from the fear of what find might happen next. If there was someone around the corner, he would have to hurt them—possibly even kill them. He didn't like the thought, but he knew what the alternative meant. He shuddered and finally peered behind the corner and sighed with relief.

No one was at the village's front. Unfortunately, the relief was short-lived; he suddenly discovered how the invaders breached the village walls. Ben cursed at himself, since it confirmed his and Rose's suspicions. The village gate was destroyed. It was lying on the ground, splintered and ruined beyond repair. It seemed that some heavy object was repeatedly bashed into the wooden gate until it could no longer hold itself up. Next to the gate was what appeared to be a massive wooden log surrounded by an even bigger contraption made up of wooden beams that was standing on wheels. The end of the wooden log facing the fallen gate was enclosed by a conic metal point. The log, which Ben now realized was a battering ram, must have been used by the invaders for a long enough time to break down the gate. *How did no one stop them?* Ben thought to himself.

"Rose—it's clear, there's no one here. But look," Ben pointed at the battering ram and destroyed gate, "that's how they got in. These guys must be serious trouble..." he said gritting his teeth together as he continued to examine the scene. There were arrows scattered all around the battering ram. Some pierced through wooden shields that were left behind the few trails of blood that led into the village.

"I...I can't believe this is happening. This is all my fault! I knew I shouldn't have left! The village is my responsibility!" Her voice was shaking worse than before.

"Rose! Stop it!" Ben said forcibly. "You can't blame yourself for any of this. We have no idea what is going on or who's responsible. I doubt the two of us being here could have prevented anything. There are nearly forty Sentinels within the village. Maybe we can help if we keep the element of surprise."

"You're...you're right, Ben. I'm sorry. I'm just really worried about Mom—and about the people! So can you tell me about your plan now?

"You don't need to apologize, Rose, we're going to get through this." He put a hand on her shoulder and looked her in the eyes. Ben was amazed at how well Rose was handling this. She was shaken up, sure, but she was able to maintain her composure and focus on what was important. *You're a true leader, Rose. You really care about our people.* "Oh, and as a matter-of-fact, I *do* have a plan," Ben added. "You know the Northern Sentinel Tower? The one outside the village walls?"

"Yeah, it's never occupied. What good does that do us?"

Ben grinned. "Well, did you know that it has a secret passage below it? It leads to the inside of the village, and I happen to know exactly where."

Rose stared at Ben with disbelief. "Ben, my mother is the village chief. I have been in every building—every square inch—of our village. There is no secret passage. I would know about it!"

"Well, if you knew about it, then it wouldn't be secret. Come on, we don't have time to argue about it. Follow me, and you can see for yourself."

They ran back toward the forest. Rose followed, a look of disbelief on her face. Rather than going straight for the forest, Ben turned and ran toward the abandoned Sentinel Tower. Underneath was the old dried up well. He climbed to the top of the tower without a word to Rose—time was too precious to waste.

"Ben! What are you doing? This is no time for games, we need to hurry and come up with a real plan!"

Ben ignored Rose. He reached the top of the tower and found what he was looking for. After all these years, the rope ladder was still up here, untouched. He grinned as he saw his plan coming closer to fruition and grabbed the rope ladder. He threw the rope ladder down the tower and quickly descended to the ground. He then tied the ends of the rope ladder to the wooden planks that closed the well and planted it securely into the ground. He picked up the rest of the rope ladder and dropped it into the well.

"Okay, Rose. Down we go. This well has a tunnel that will lead inside the village. It's our way in without being seen."

"Ben...how do you know about this?" Rose asked with a stunned look on her face. "Is that rope going to hold us? How far is the drop down?"

"I'll answer everything once we're in the tunnel. We have to hurry! The rope is sturdy enough, but it's not a big deal if it breaks. The drop isn't more than twelve feet. Remember when I broke my arm when we were little?"

Rose nodded to which Ben replied, "Well, that was without a rope in the first place. It'll be okay, so let's start moving. Would you mind holding the ends of the rope for me?"

Rose grabbed the end of the rope ladder that extended out of the well and attached to the wooden barricade. Without another word, Ben descended the ladder. Once he got to the bottom, he checked to make sure the tunnel hadn't collapsed. "Okay! It's safe to come down now," he called up to Rose. "Just to warn you, when you put your weight on the ladder, the wooden cover will get pulled up, closing the well. You'll feel a jolt as you move down about a foot. Don't panic and just hold on."

"*Uh*...okay, whatever you say," Rose said with a nervous tremble. She turned around and put her feet on the rope ladder while still holding the well's edge, avoiding putting all her weight on the ladder. She then slid her hands across the outer edge toward her center and held onto the rope and edge at the same time. She finally put all her weight on the rope and screamed as she suddenly dropped into the tunnel.

"Ben, I can't see anything! Please tell me you have a torch or something!"

"Oh right, I forgot about the whole 'no light' thing. Give me a moment, I'll fix that!" He took off his rucksack and felt around for his flint and steel. When he pulled them out, he then felt for his scarf. Once he got everything he needed from his bag, he felt around for the torch he had used last time. *It should be around here somewhere*, he thought to himself. Once he finally found it, he wrapped the scarf tightly around it. He removed a small container of animal fat from his rucksack, placed the torch on the ground, and lathered the fat across the scarf at the torch's head. He struck the flint and tinder together until the torch finally roared aflame.

"Okay, Rose. Good to go. Ready?"

Rose nodded with a puzzled expression as she studied the tunnels around her. "You owe me an explanation!"

Ben groaned. "When we were younger, your mom and I...well we didn't get along very well, as I'm sure you've noticed over the years. So a lot of times when she and I would get into arguments, I'd run off and explore the village. I never went to you because I assumed you'd just take her side."

Ben noticed Rose looking curiously at him, and he assumed that she evidently hadn't realized that he would run away when they were younger. He wondered if she was disappointed in him for keeping secrets from her, especially about this tunnel. He liked having his own safe space to be away from everyone. Like sailing on the Gjoll, it was a place that he felt he could actually call his own.

Ben continued. "One of our arguments got really heated. I tried asking her about my parents. She had nothing but bad things to say about my father—and nothing about my mother. She told me that he left her to lead the village to chase some crazy fantasy. When he hadn't come back after a few years, she assumed he was dead. She kept making it seem like it was somehow *my* fault that my father left her. Then she told me that he finally came back with a child and expected her to raise it. She said that, you know. When Lydia told me the story she referred to me as 'it' and 'the child.' She never acknowledged me as human, much less as her own blood. She even doubted that I was Alphonse's son."

Ben remained silent for a few moments. He wasn't sure if he should keep talking to Rose about this. It wasn't right to talk about her mother this way after all Lydia had been through and done for the village and even himself. He also felt guilty complaining about his aunt who, for all he knew, could be dead right now. The thought made him shudder.

Rose looked at Ben and stopped walking. She then told him, "Ben—it's okay. You can keep going on with the story. I don't mind what you say about my mom, I just want to know what happened and how you found this place. I also don't want to take too much time because we need to get to the village."

Nodding, Ben resumed walking, taking a right at a fork in the tunnel. "After we had that argument, I had had enough. I decided to leave the village. Mind you, I was only eleven at the time, so I thought I was invincible and could survive out on my own. I packed my rucksack with my knife, flint and tinder, alcohol for cuts, bandages, and a canteen of water. I left the village through the front gate, lying to the Sentinel and saying Lydia had sent me. Not giving it a second thought, the Sentinel opened the gate for me. Once I was outside of the village walls, I realized that I didn't have any idea what to do. It was immediately clear to me that my childish sense of invincibility was just a fantasy; I wouldn't be able to survive on my own. So I decided to stay close to the village. I thought the abandoned Sentinel Tower would be perfect for me. It would give me shelter, and I could sneak into the village when I would run out of food.

"When I got to the abandoned tower, I noticed the well underneath it. At the time, I had no idea what it was. I just saw that it was boarded shut with wooden planks. It seemed as though it was closed for a reason and that no one was supposed to access it—so I naturally broke it open to see what was inside. Unfortunately for me, I didn't have any tools to pry it open or remove the nails, so I thought jumping on it would be the best way to open it up—and it worked a little *too* well. The planks all snapped at once and I fell straight down, landing on my arm. I was sprawled out at the bottom of the well, writhing in agony and screaming for help. When I realized that no one could hear me, I thought I was going to die. I examined my surroundings and noticed the tunnel before me. Once I walked through it, I noticed that the light from the well didn't travel very far. I brainstormed for some solutions and quickly discovered that I had all the necessary tools. Using one of the wooden planks, some extra bandages, and my flint and tinder, I was able to assemble a torch and explore the tunnels."

Ben and Rose finally approached the end of the tunnel. There was another ladder that extended toward the ceiling to a small wooden surface, though this time the ladder was made of wood instead of rope. Ben set the torch against the corner of the tunnel and looked at Rose. "And this is what I found. I think you'll be surprised when you see what's up top."

Rose continued to stare at Ben with disbelief. She stammered for a moment, trying to find her words. "Ben...I can't believe this. How has a tunnel leading to our village from the outside existed all this time without me knowing about it?" Before Ben could respond, her expression switched from disbelief to anger. "How could you have kept this from me for so long? This tunnel is a liability! What if outsiders—like the people attacking us right now—found out about it and snuck in? This tunnel has been a danger to our people this whole time, and you never did anything about it?" Rose yelled at Ben.

Ben sighed and closed his eyes as he put his thumb and first finger around the bridge of his nose and pinched, something he did out of habit whenever he was frustrated. "Well, they'd have a real tough time getting through that hatch up there without this," Ben said as he removed a small key from his rucksack. "You see, I didn't have this the first time around, but I was able to carry the ladder to the well and escape to the village. As soon as my arm was healed, I returned with a new rope ladder and this key, which I knew had to be for the lock behind the hatch."

Rose, puzzled by all of Ben's secrets, reverted to staring at him with disbelief. With a calmer tone than last time, she continued. "I have a million more questions about this, but I think it's time you finally show me where this ladder leads. We need to hurry!"

Nodding, Ben climbed the ladder with the small key clenched between his front teeth. When he reached the top, he fidgeted with the wooden panel at the tunnel ceiling. He finally pulled down on it, letting the panel swing open on the hinge that connected it to the ceiling. Above the wooden panel was a metal surface with a handle and small keyhole. Ben removed the key from his teeth, inserted it into the keyhole, and slowly turned it. There was a soft click, and Ben removed the key. He pulled on the metal handle until it swung open just like the wooden panel.

Beyond the metal surface was a leather rug. Ben pushed the leather rug aside and climbed through the trap door. He then looked down at Rose and said, "Leave the torch there. It'll burn out on its own, and you need the light to see the ladder properly. Hurry up here. It's safe—for now."

Rose quickly climbed the wooden ladder. Once she reached the top, Ben gave her a hand through the trap door. She examined her surroundings with her brows raised and eyes widened. "Ben...this is your room! How..."

"I'll answer questions later—provided we survive this ordeal," Ben said as he pulled down a few of the blinds to his window, peering outside.

"What do you see out there? Are there a lot of them? Is everyone okay?" said Rose, volleying one question after another.

"From here, I can make out about twelve invaders. Each of them is armed with either swords, machetes, or axes. Some of them have shields. I only see two with bows, and they're both low on arrows. I don't see any of our people. I'm not sure if that's good or bad news. At least I don't see any bodies from here," said Ben as he continued to peer through his window.

"Okay...have you come up with a plan yet?" Rose asked as she approached Ben's bedroom door to listen for intruders.

Ben released the blinds and locked the trap door, covering it up with the leather rug. He then looked over at Rose, then focused on something behind her. The bastard sword he was supposed to have cleaned yesterday still lay against the foot of his bed. *Good thing I never cleaned that sword.* It wasn't sharp nor was it meant for actual combat, but it would have to do. *The attackers don't know it's not steel.*

He smiled shrewdly. "Yeah, I have a plan. I'll need you to climb to the tower behind our house. Then I want you to overlook the village and get an idea of where the invaders are. Once you do that, I want you to find me. I'll be sneaking around the village to find out where our people are. I'll take out any of the invaders along the way. I'll be as stealthy as possible, but if anyone notices me I want you to take them out. Try to keep them alive, though." *Only kill if there's no other way,* Rakshi's voice seemed to echo in his mind. "We're going to need to know why they came here once we're done. After you've immobilized any of the invaders, I'll do my best to knock them out as quickly as possible, so they don't alert the others. Does that work?"

Rose swallowed, letting down a nervous gulp. She closed her eyes and took in a deep breath. "Yes—I think I can do that. Please be safe out there. Try to find Mom, too. I'm worried about her—and everyone else."

"You can do this, Rose. I know you can. You're the best archer I've ever met. I wouldn't want anyone else watching my back out there." He knew Rose, like himself, didn't want to kill. Rakshi taught that lesson to Ben, but he imagined it was just part of Rose's nature to preserve life. He hoped they could accomplish this without any death on their hands.

The cousins walked out the back door of Valhaven towards the rear tower. Rose ascended the tower as Ben kept watch over her, bow and arrow drawn in case anyone was to sneak around the rear of the house. As soon as she reached the top, Rose gazed down at Ben and signaled that she was ready. She drew her first arrow, nocked it in her bowstring, and surveyed the village. Ben could see that she was getting the lay of the land, determining the hostiles' location. When she was finished, she looked over the edge of the tower at Ben and held up a thumb from her chest and then quickly extended her hand and held up her middle three fingers.

That means there's sixteen of them. I missed four. He thought it may have been a good idea to climb the tower with Rose to look for himself but decided against it. *Too much movement.* It would draw unwanted attention.

Ben worked his way toward the rear right of the house and peered around the corner. The coast was clear, and he darted to the side of the next building over, Zevi's Butchery. With his back against the wall, he was facing the Sentinel Tower and saw Rose signal that his left was clear. He turned the corner and made his way behind the butchery in a crouched position to avoid making too much noise. He had his bow and an arrow in his left hand with his knife in his right, blade facing the ground. The training sword's scabbard beat against his thigh if he moved too fast. *Better to keep it slow anyway.*

He heard voices a few yards ahead of him but couldn't see where they were coming from. He wondered if they were inside one of the buildings. If they were, that would be a problem; Rose couldn't cover him there. He would have to find a way to lure them out. But first, he would need to confirm if they were indeed inside.

Ben slowly approached the Sentinel's Keep. He heard voices coming from the nearest barracks. He could distinguish some of what they were saying now.

"Look, lady—I don't need to tell you want we want! It's business, and that's all you need to know. Now, are there any other villagers that ain't accounted for or not?" a gruff voice said with an impatient tone. When there was no immediate response, Ben heard a *smack* followed by a quiet whimper.

"C'mon! We just need answers. We don't wanna hurt or kill anyone else. Things're bad enough as is. But if you won't talk, we'll have to start hurting people. We've got plenty in here with us..." the gruff voice said.

"I already told you. There isn't anyone else. Everyone, aside from the ones you *killed* are inside here with us. Will you please stop tormenting my people?"

A pit grew in Ben's stomach. *People were killed?* Maybe if they hadn't left, the village would've had enough people to protect it. There was at least some good news, Ben supposed. He immediately recognized the woman's voice as his aunt's. Rose won't be happy to hear that people were killed, but at least her mom was safe.

How can I think like that? Why should I care about Lydia more than anyone else?

He had never dealt with death like this before—the purposeful killing of other people. The village was rarely attacked and, when it had been, nobody in Freztad had died. He had heard of the deaths that happened outside their borders. But until now it had never been his concern. It was never real. He was left doubting if he could save anyone. Was he strong enough to make a difference?

Ben thought of Kabedge's antics and good food. Vic's history and language lessons with Rose. He thought of Rakshi and the other

Sentinels—whose bravery probably acted as the first line of defense against these invaders. He thought of his aunt who, despite her chronic melancholia, could revert to her strong self for the sake of the villagers. Lastly, he thought of Rose, the strongest person he had ever known. He may not have been strong enough for himself, but he owed it to his people to be strong enough for them.

Creeping forward, Ben approached the building toward the front of the village. He thought it strange that he hadn't seen any of the invaders whom he and Rose had spotted earlier. There were at least sixteen of them, excluding any who may be inside the building with Lydia and the gruff-voiced man. He had to come up with a plan fast, before anyone else got hurt.

Ben crept along the building toward the village's center road. As quickly as he poked his head around the corner, he moved back behind cover. He saw six of them patrolling the village. Three walking toward the village front, three walking down toward him. He had an idea.

Backtracking toward the opposite end of the building, Ben sheathed his knife and readied his bow. The three approached the alley and came into view. He let his arrow loose.

The intruder bellowed in agony. Ben's arrow struck the man's upper thigh and went clean through. This time, Ben meant to hit the leg. The other two invaders were just as shocked as their screaming companion. One of them stayed with him while the other cautiously walked down the alley. He was armed with a wooden shield and broad-axe. Ben knew close quarters against this man would be the death of him. He also knew the screaming would attract other invaders. His best bet now was to run to one of the other buildings, lure them there, and have Rose take them all out behind him.

Narrowly escaping his pursuers, Ben ran toward the middle of the village back into Rose's line of sight. He passed the next building and turned the corner only to see a heavyset man with an enormous, two-handed claymore. The behemoth of a man was prepared and already had his sword raised as he quickly chopped down. Ben quickly leapt to the side, scarcely missing the sword's deadly thrust. What could he do? The sword's long reach meant that Ben needed to keep his distance, and he was still too close to draw, nock, aim, and loose even a single arrow. The only thing he could do was run.

Ben knew that he could outrun the giant, so he sprinted toward the village's southern wall. He ran as fast as he could, hoping to get away as soon as possible. His heart was pounding, and his hands were shaking with fear. He turned around whilst running and saw the large man was still following him. And he wasn't alone. One of the archers from before was taking aim. The shielded man with the broad-axe was hurtling forward, too.

With the archer aiming at him, Ben knew he couldn't run straight for the wall. He'd be too easy of a target. He quickly changed direction and went left, back toward Rose. He should have been in her line of sight by then, but Rose had yet to release a shot.

The archer's first arrow narrowly missed Ben's right shoulder, landing a few yards ahead of him. He made another right, toward another house. He got behind cover and drew an arrow. He peered around the corner and aimed for the archer. *If I can get him in the hand, he'll be too injured to do anything.* The two men chasing Ben weren't far behind, but they were both much slower. He had time to aim for a single shot before he'd need to run again. He steadied his bow and held his breath, hoping to lessen the shaking of his hands. He exhaled—and released.

The arrow missed Ben's intended target, but just barely. It stuck out of the archer's left shoulder rather than his hand. *That should at least slow him down. There's only one other archer to deal with.*

Ben continued to the village's road. He was out in the open now, but he had nowhere else to run. He ducked behind one of the house's front decks and stole a quick glimpse of his surroundings. He'd likely lost Giganto and the Axe-Man by now. He noticed that the bulk of invaders were outside of the barracks. He counted seven of them keeping guard. *The man inside must be their leader, and they're protecting him.*

"Gotcha, you maddening runt!" a gruff voice snarled from behind Ben. It was the man he had heard interrogating Lydia. He was tall and brawny, though not nearly as large as Giganto. He wielded a rounded shield in his left hand and a broken steel sword in his right. He slammed his shield into Ben, knocking him over.

Ben drew his bastard sword and swung against the man's legs. The beefy man chuckled and jumped away from the attack. Ben stood himself up and gripped his sword with both hands. He searched his enemy for a weak spot as he had during training. It was a vain effort, for the brawny attacker never held a position long enough for Ben's eyes to absorb the scene. The man lunged forward with the broken sword. Ben parried and countered. Both hands gripped hard around his iron sword's hilt and swung down against Beefy's shield.

There was a crack as iron hit the steel rim of the wooden shield.

The beefy swordsman smiled as he heard the sound of broken metal. The steel blade sliced through the air between them and landed with full force against Ben's dull blade. It snapped half a foot above the hilt.

"Needs to invest in some better metal, runt. I got me self a legendary blade here. She ain't never let me down once even with only half a blade." He bashed his shield against Ben and knocked him to the dirt. He pulled his right arm back, ready to stab down at Ben. Ben crawled backwards from his enemy and hit his head on the side of the house. He was trapped. He had no way out.

Beefy grinned and readied himself to thrust his sword through Ben's heart. Ben closed his eyes and waited.

The stab through the heart never came. Instead, Ben heard a *whoosh,* followed by a deep grunt. He opened his eyes to see an arrow through Beefy's right upper torso. The man was bewildered, and Ben took advantage of the situation. He picked up his bow and smacked it against the back of the man's head as hard as he could.

Beefy was out cold.

Looking for where the arrow came from, Ben saw Rose on top of Kabedge's shop, hiding behind the chimney. He smiled and gave her a thumbs up. Now that he knew she was still watching him, Ben had more confidence. He returned to his hiding place behind the deck to once again scan the village. There was no sign of Axe-Man and Giganto. All he could see were the guards outside of the barracks. He needed to get them away from there.

Ben turned around and got Rose's attention. She seemed to be eying the same group as him. He pointed at them and made a shooting gesture. She nodded, evidently understanding what Ben meant.

He drew and nocked another arrow. He pulled it back and heard a crack come from his bow. *I must've hit the guy too hard. I won't get many more shots out of this thing.* He aimed at one of the guards closer to him, hoping Rose wasn't aiming at the same one. He let his arrow loose and hit his mark. The man was hit in the chest, but it didn't appear lethal. The other guards were caught by surprise and were suddenly standing more alert. They raised their shields and surveyed the area. But it was too late, Rose hit another one of them, knocking him down to the ground. Four more to go.

One of the guards barked orders at the other two and walked towards Ben. He figured Rose would still be able to hit them since she was higher up. Their shields were large enough that Ben knew he'd be wasting arrows and his bow's durability on them.

Ben ran left, around the building he was hiding. The guards would be walking toward his old location. Now he could catch the other two by surprise. He drew another arrow and aimed again. Another crack. Ben released the arrow and hit one through the arm holding the shield. He screamed in pain. Ben heard grunts from behind him. *Sounds like Rose got the other two.*

Ben readied to take aim at the last guard. He pulled the arrow back, but the bow couldn't handle the stress. It snapped in half and the top of the bow flew back into Ben's forehead. He let out a loud yelp.

Recovering from the blow to the head, he looked up and noticed a guard was calling for others as he ran toward Ben. All he had now was a knife, and that wouldn't do him any good in open combat.

Returning to Rose was probably the smartest decision. Ben turned around and worked his way toward his cousin. He could get back into her line of site and hopefully take the shield and sword from Beefy.

As luck would have it, Beefy was still out cold. Ben picked up the sword and shield. The sword was awkward to hold—it was not properly weighted without the entire blade. The hilt was a magnificent piece of metalwork, and he couldn't believe that he hadn't noticed it while fighting Beefy. It appeared to be crafted from a flawless black metal with a silver snake coiling around the shaft to the cross guard. The cross guard was in the shape of marvelously detailed golden wings, each feather meticulously carved and etched. At its center, the snake's head rested with a red-jeweled crown upon its head, its eyes made of emeralds. Though the hilt was just long enough for Ben to grip with both hands—just like his training sword—but there was no need with such a short blade. The sword seemed to have once been much longer but was now broken with only two and a half feet of black and uneven steel remaining. Nonetheless, a steel weapon was rare and impressive. Whoever these invaders were, they were well resourced.

Or maybe it is legendary, Ben thought with a smirk.

Beefy was lying on his side, breathing heavily and unevenly. Even though he had attacked the village and tried to kill him, Ben pitied him. He didn't want him to die. He was worried that the arrow may have pierced a lung. These feelings confused Ben. Why was he upset about the enemy being harmed? He may have killed some of Ben's people—he *almost* killed Ben. Staring at Beefy now, Ben couldn't help but feel sorry for him. Everyone has their reasons for making the choices they do. Everyone has to do what they can to survive in this world. Everyone has the right to live, don't they?

The sound of running footsteps closed in on Ben's location. He lifted the round shield and readied the unbalanced short-sword. Rose was still behind him, volleying arrow after arrow. Ben knew she had his back, so he charged to the village road.

Axe-Man and Giganto, along with four other men were drawing closer to him. Ben couldn't believe his eyes. Giganto had three arrows sticking out of his chest and he was still making his way toward Ben with rage in his eyes and a thirst for blood.

The giant of a man raised his claymore and swung fiercely down at Ben. Like before, Ben leapt backwards. Shield raised, Ben took advantage of the time it took for Giganto to lift his sword up from the ground and prepare for another swing. He flanked to his right and thrust his sword into Giganto's side.

It was no good. Giganto was wearing thick leather armor. Ben's sword did nothing. Ben leapt backwards again to stay out of the claymore's radius. Now Axe-Man was approaching. He crept closer to Ben, with his wooden rectangular shield raised to protect him from Rose's arrows. Evidently, the four men following behind had been taken out, compelling Axe-Man to tread lightly.

The broad-axe swung swiftly and violently through the air, trying to reach Ben's body. Ben continued to back away, parrying the axe as best he could until the half-blade was finally knocked out of his hands. Ben held up his shield with both hands and ran full-speed at Axe-Man.

Axe-Man was caught by surprise at Ben's lunge, and he lost his footing. Rose took quick notice and took her shot at him. Axe-Man was down. The only one left for now was Giganto.

Ben tallied up the invaders. He had taken out five of the invaders. He had seen Rose take out eight. With Giganto still working his way toward Ben, that meant there were *at least* two others somewhere.

Two assailants walked out of the barracks, and two others from the front of the village made their way toward Ben and Rose. The two coming from the front were agile women with bows and arrows. One of the attackers coming from the hostage house was also a woman, but she was built much sturdier with a broad frame. She carried two battle axes. The fourth was a man wielding a halberd, probably only a few years older than Ben, and built like most of the other attackers.

There didn't seem to be any way out of this. Ben felt like he had two options now: go back to the tunnel from his room and run like a coward or face these invaders and die trying to save his people. He turned to look at Rose. She only had two arrows left in her quiver and another ready to go. It didn't seem as though she had ever given a single thought to running away.

An arrow flew toward one of the agile archers, but she quickly dodged it and shot back at Rose. The archer next to her did the same. Rose took cover behind the chimney, cursing to herself.

The enormous sword was raised up again, nearly beheading Ben as he neglected to pay attention to Giganto in favor of watching his cousin. He decided his best chance now was to find one of the bows from one of the downed archers and lock himself in his house and shoot from there.

Rose seemed to take notice of Ben's situation, and she quickly shifted her focus. She aimed her second to last arrow at Giganto one more time and fired at his back. Giganto grunted but shrugged off the pain. Ben looked up at Rose to see what she would do next. He saw her aim at Giganto again. *What is she doing? She knows his armor is too thick. Don't waste your last arrow, Rose!*

Then Ben realized she was no longer aiming to weaken the man. In fact, Ben noticed that her shot was aimed high. She was aiming for his head.

She was shooting to kill.

Rose readied to let her last arrow go free, but just like in the forest, a loud noise erupted and startled her—she missed the shot. But it didn't matter; Giganto was lying face first in the dirt mere inches away from Ben, his back burned and smoking.

The sound was like nothing Ben had ever heard before. The best he could compare it to was the sound of thunder during a bad storm. But unlike thunder, these sounds came from much closer to the ground.

Two large metal objects came into the village, rolling over the fallen gate. The objects looked like horse carriages that moved without horses. On top of these self-moving carts were people shouting and holding some sort of device that was causing the sounds of thunder.

The two agile archers ran for cover but quickly dropped to the ground motionless. The young man and axe-wielding woman tried to run into the house they had originally exited, but they fell, too. All their backs were smoking. Then the thunder stopped. The carriages stopped moving. The people on top jumped off and surveyed the area. A door in one of the carriages opened, and a mustached man walked out of it. He pulled down his sun-goggles and looked over at Ben and then up at Rose. Then he smiled. "You know—a 'thank you' would be nice!"

4. The King of the North

The newcomers were more than happy to help the villagers clean up the mess which the invaders had caused. Some of the more well-armed militants combed the settlement in search of any surviving attackers. Most were unconscious from either the cousins' counterstrike or the onslaught brought upon them by the newcomers. The prisoners were subsequently restrained and moved into a cell within the Sentinel's Keep.

Never before had Ben been so fascinated by outsiders. He had been to the other settlements before for trading purposes, but he never had any real interactions with the people. Moreover, none of them had anything as intricate as what these newcomers possessed. The weapons that the newcomers used to defeat the invaders were apparently called 'guns'. From what Ben could gather about them, they seemed to have the same purpose as a bow and arrow. He was astonished by how small some of them could be and by how they used such little effort to achieve such profound results. *Such a simple and innovative way to harm other people*, Ben reflected.

More fascinating, and practical in Ben's opinion, were the 'sun-carriages' that carried the newcomers into the village. When he asked one of the newcomers how they worked, they simply told him that "by the graces of the Almighty Sun, these machines find strength." Ben had absolutely no idea what that meant and wanted a better answer, but it was all anyone seemed to know about them.

When the battle was over, the man with the mustache exited one of the sun-carriages and introduced himself, "Hey there! The name's Randolph—but you can call me Randy if it pleases you! I don't care one way or the other." He extended a hand toward the two cousins, making Ben feel awkward. He wasn't sure who he was trying to shake hands with.

Randolph was a man of slightly above average stature, a few inches shorter than Ben. His hallmark characteristic was his thick salt and pepper mustache that extended down both sides of his mouth to his chin. Being out in the sun, it was difficult for Ben to make out the rest of Randy's features since, like nearly everyone else, he wore sun-goggles and some sort of head covering. Randolph wore a black flat brimmed hat with a straight sided crown and rounded corners.

Unlike Ben, Rose didn't hesitate to reciprocate the greeting. "It's a pleasure to meet you, Randy. My name is Rose. I suppose I'm sort of the leader here. I cannot thank you enough for everything you did for us. Seriously, if you hadn't—"

"*Ahhh*, girl, don't mention it! We were on our way here anyway to meet you all. Freztad! Wow! I've heard a lot about this place—a lot!"

Randy said enthusiastically with his hands on his hips. He eyed the village, seemingly basking in some vicarious experience.

Rose gave Randy a look of bewilderment. Ben knew what she was thinking. *Who are these people?* But Rose shifted her attention elsewhere. "Well, Randy, I hate to cut this introduction short, but I need to see my mother and the other villagers to make sure they're going to be all right." She spoke quickly and shuffled away from Randolph before he could interrupt her again.

Randy offered a toothy smile as he watched Rose run off. He then shifted his attention to Ben. "Who might you be? I saw you giving one hell of a fight out there before we rolled on in!"

"Oh, sorry. I forgot to introduce myself. I'm Ben—Rose's cousin," Ben said nervously.

"Ah! So, you're Ben! Wow, you sure are bigger than I expected. I've heard about you! Ya see, the King knew your old man way back when," Randy said with great delight.

A violent chill ran down Ben's back. *A king? One who knew my father?* He was lost for words, troubled with the newcomer's statement. Ben knew of no kings, though he was vaguely familiar with the settlements in the Northern Realm. Perhaps one of their leaders calls himself 'king'.

When Ben didn't respond right away, Randy clapped a hand on Ben's shoulder and smiled, his black mustache rising to his cheekbones. "Ah, speaking of His Majesty, he sent me on some important business, which is why we came here in the first place. Y'see, our King has roots in this very village. A man by the name of Xander, though I doubt there are many here who would remember him. When this fine village here just didn't do it for him anymore, he decided it was time to leave. He traveled all over the wastelands until he arrived North and united the warring tribes under a single ruler. He saw great injustices being wrought upon the commoners and sought to put an end to them. King Xander has been a fine and fair ruler ever since." Randy chuckled, hands still on his hips and head moving around as he studied the village. He seemed infatuated with it.

Ben felt a beast within his belly, growling and afraid. *He means to take over our village as well.* "If he already has a kingdom to the North, then what could he possibly want down here?" Ben bit his lower lip, forcing himself to remain calm. This man was a stranger like the invaders. He could slaughter them all at any minute. But he didn't. Instead, he stood before Ben full of laughter and without a care in the world. And that worried Ben even more.

"Straight to the point! I like you, Ben!" said Randy, still smiling. "Our humble kingdom of Ænæria has been going through a bit of a famine as of late, and we've been searching the wastelands tirelessly for food. Our king mentioned in the past that his home village produced bountiful crops year after year but never wanted to return. I think it would've been too hard on him." At this, Randy offered a sympathetic frown. "I eventually convinced His Majesty to allow me to bring a small party to Freztad and see if we could strike a deal."

Ben felt his chest sink into his gut. Were his fears confirmed? *Does Xander aim to take over Freztad?* They'd reap the farm and destroy the Alliance without a care of anyone harmed in the process. The possibility sickened him. He wanted to believe this kingdom of Ænæria didn't exist.

Ben finally spoke. "You're telling me this king of yours was able to rally together multiple settlements, form alliances with them, and put himself in charge? Is that what you're trying to do with us? I don't think that will go over so well with Rose and her mother. I mean... well, what do we get out of this?"

Randy's eyes widened, and his jaw dropped with shame. "Oh, no, no, kid, you've got me all wrong! My friends and I aren't here to take over your land and make you pay fealty to us. King Xander has grown rather tired of tending to new lands. We just want to make some sort of pact, like you have with those other settlements. It'd be good for all our people, and I think the King could really benefit from getting back to his roots y'know? It's been over fifteen long years since he and his first followers left this fine village of yours."

Ben felt his heart beating faster—so much so that he thought Randy could hear the thumping stampede through his chest. Both Xander and Ben's father had left just over fifteen years ago. An exodus of scores of people left after his father, and Randy was implying the same had happened with his King. Could Xander and Alphonse be the same person? *He was the rightful chief after all. Maybe they didn't leave after him, but* with *him.* Ben continued to push his luck. He wanted more answers from Randy. Though the man was friendly, he never seemed to fully answer Ben's questions. He always left him with more questions than answers. "You still haven't answered what our village would gain from this alliance. Not to say I'm not grateful for the help that you all did for us in dealing with those attackers, but I'm still not quite sure what you're getting at here. After having just been attacked by outsiders, it's hard to suddenly put all my trust into more of them."

It was hard to tell with Randy's sun-goggles, but Ben got the impression that Randy's eyes were staring intently into his own. He wasn't quite scowling at Ben, but he sure wasn't giving him the warm and welcoming expression from before.

"Man-oh-man, it is *hot* out here! Why don't we go on inside with that cousin of yours and finish this discussion there? And while we're at it, do you think you could let me know where the water is around here? My compadres and I need to hydrate after that fierce battle we just won!"

Trying to hide a look of frustration, Ben walked in the direction of the freshwater well in between two of the houses on his left, beckoning Randolph and his crew to follow.

He thought to himself, *the fierce battle that* they *just won? Rose and I did all the work!*

The thought also reminded him of how thirsty and devoid of energy he was. He approached the well and drew a bucket of water from it. He cupped his hands inside and drank it all, savoring the cool and fresh taste of the rich spring water below. Ben took another handful and splashed his face with it to cool off and calm himself down after everything that had just happened. *Relax. These are good people. They saved Freztad. Let loose a little and hear Randy out.* He let the newcomers have as much water as they wanted.

Walking away from the well, Ben approached Randy and said, "I'll be in the barracks where Rose went. You know which one right?"

Randy looked at him and nodded, smiling.

The barracks were close to the front gate that once stood tall and proud. Ben saw some of the villagers walking out of it and getting ready to clean up and make repairs. Most of the villagers were past their prime and simply wanted peaceful living. They never deserved anything like this. Most of them would contribute as best as they could to fix up the settlement, but then they would want to go back to their quiet and peaceful lives. Ben saw seven of them near the gate, removing all the debris and discussing which parts of the gate they could salvage to build a new one.

The front door creaked ajar revealing two more villagers. Ben instantly recognized Kabedge walking slightly behind a sickly man. It must've been months since Ben last saw Kabedge's husband because his appearance had drastically changed. His once graying hair was gone; his eyes heavy with the mark of sleepless nights under them. Vic's emaciation was more than apparent given his loose-fitting clothes and bony expression. Ben wanted more than anything to check in on Kabedge to make sure he was doing well after the attack but decided against it. He knew that the incident had to have been exceptionally difficult for Vic to deal with in his health. Kabedge would need all his focus to be on his husband at this time. Instead, Ben simply offered a reassuring smile as the two staggered toward their home.

Ben saw two more villagers carrying a third toward the Sentinel's Keep. As Ben looked closer he saw that it was a woman with a bloody bandage just below her right collarbone. It was Rakshi. *No. It can't be.* He rushed to the Sentinels and asked what had happened but was stopped by Kristos.

"She needs to get to the Keep as soon as possible," Kristos said. "Can't have you slowing that down, Ben."

Ben tried to push his way past Kristos, but the Sentinel grabbed him by the collar. "I need to see her!" Ben yelled in protest.

"She was shot," Kristos explained. "The healers need to repair the wound and stabilize her condition."

"Why can't I go in to see her?" Ben asked.

"I'm sorry, Ben. The Keep is being used to tend to all the injuries. It's essential bodies only."

Ben fought the urge to attack his friend and enter the Keep regardless. He felt his insides churn as he thought about what might happen to Rakshi.

"Look, man," Kristos said. "There's nothing you can do. We'll let you know when her procedure is over."

Ben felt the same guilt Rose expressed earlier. If only he had been here instead of hunting. Maybe he could have done something. He turned from her body and ran.

He walked somberly to the barracks to meet with Rose. He would need to tell her about Rakshi. Loss was never something he liked to think about. He had grown up feeling emptier than he ought to have. While he didn't have any parents, Ben was able to cope as best as he could with the thought of being without a father. He attributed his resilience in that aspect of his life to Rose, who also never knew her father, a man named Julius who had left Freztad after Alphonse on the exodus nearly two decades ago.

Perhaps he left with Xander. Lydia will know.

The wooden steps in front of the barracks creaked with each one of his steps as he climbed the front porch to find his cousin inside. He could see that the attackers had certainly left their mark. Ahead of him was a toppled wooden dinner table with many broken chairs around it. To his right, Ben spotted slashes across the wood alongside torn and tattered curtains that were blowing into the building from the wind.

To Ben's left were the remaining villagers, too traumatized to leave just yet. Among the crowd of people were Lydia and Rose. His cousin was leaning down next to her sitting mother when she noticed his presence. She looked up at him with a hopeless expression. She turned to whisper something to Lydia and stood up to face Ben and gestured for him to follow her across the room.

Rose spoke in a hushed voice, "Glad you finally showed up. What took you so long? Mom's really shaken, up and I need someone to take her home while I deal with our guests. Oh, and get this: the attackers ransacked the village looking for someone in charge. When they finally found her, they assumed there had to be others. They didn't think that someone like her...someone with..." Rose's voice gave way, and she looked down at the floor, away from Ben.

Someone confined to a wheelchair. Someone so defeated, Ben thought to himself, knowing exactly what Rose was trying to imply. Rose never spoke of her mother's melancholia, and she certainly never resented Lydia for the position it put her in. *I need to ask about Xander and Ænæria.* But now wasn't the time. Seeing Rose so distraught, he simply couldn't bear to accuse her of keeping such a secret from him. Lydia on the other hand....

"It's okay, I understand," he replied. "I heard them talking to her earlier. It sounded like their leader was interrogating her. Is she going to be okay? It sounded like they hit her."

Rose's bright green eyes looked up at Ben. There were no tears, but her eyes were still stricken with unease. "Aside from some cuts and bruises from fighting back at the start of the ambush, she's physically okay. Mentally...I just don't know, Ben. She's a strong person in her own respect. She's been through a lot, and this certainly didn't do her any favors. I just hope this is something she can get though."

"Their leader—he was asking your mom questions about where any other villagers might be. As if they knew we weren't here," Ben said as he looked around the room one more time, further examining the damages and avoiding Lydia's gaze. "Does she blame me for all of this?"

"Oh, Ben...no, not at all. She really isn't like that, you know? Why don't you try talking to her? I know you aren't on good terms with her, but it would really mean a lot to her—and to me—if you tried to comfort her right now," Rose said softly.

"What's the point? You said she's fine and that she doesn't blame me. There's nothing for me to say to her."

Rose frowned at Ben, clearly disappointed that even in the aftermath of tragedy, Ben wouldn't talk to Lydia more than needed. Ben was anxious enough after everything that had happened, and he couldn't bear to deal with his aunt if she would just blame him. He could ask about the King and his father later. For now he had more important things to address.

"Rakshi was shot," Ben managed to say.

Rose lowered her gaze. "Zechariah told me. He was with her when it happened. He said it wasn't too deep and that he immediately took care of her. I think she'll be fine."

"Do...do you really think so?" Ben asked.

"From what I've been told, it doesn't seem like the attackers were trying to kill anyone. A lot of the Sentinels were injured in the fight. Esther's leg is broken, Joaquin was shot in the arm, and I think Quyen almost lost an arm. But none of them were killed."

"So everyone is fine?" Ben gave a sigh of relief.

"Fine is a relative term," Rose said, turning her head to Lydia, who was still sitting across the room without her wheelchair. "But everyone's alive if that's what you mean."

"Well ain't that a relief!" Randy's voice boomed.

Ben felt his body jolt, startled by Randy's sudden presence. The man walked in without a sound.

Randy took off his black, flat brimmed hat and revealed a balding scalp and bushy dark and gray hair receding to the back of his head. "D'you two have a minute?" He gave the cousins a wide and friendly smile. Ben and Rose exchanged glances, but before they could respond, Randy started speaking. "Excellent! Now that I've got some time with the two of you, I wanted to let you know why my friends and I came here in the first place. Believe it or not, it wasn't to come and save the day! Though we were all more than happy to oblige in that respect. As I told Ben here," he said looking at Rose, "I've come as a humble representative for King Xander of Ænæria with the goal of forming an alliance with your settlement. It appears you good people could do with some better protection and upgraded equipment. His Majesty has quite the surplus of tools and weapons—he even has a few sun-carriages that I'm sure he could spare. With the right equipment, you could replace that gate out there in no time! You'd certainly be able to make a significant improvement from that last one. But I digress.

"As I told Ben, we're quite interested in Freztad on account of your grand farm. Food is something severely lacking in Ænæria. In exchange for the equipment and extra protection, we'd like to establish a trade route for your crops as well as have your permission to allow some of our people to move to this village. I see that you have quite a few vacant homes that could house some of our many skilled tradesmen."

Give and take. That's not so bad. In fact, the idea was leagues better than he had anticipated. More protection sounded perfect to Ben. The village had barely enough Sentinels to maintain the patrol both outside the village and within its walls. With a recent attack, the need for protection was even more pressing. The prospect of having new villagers intrigued Ben, too. He wondered about whether they had different lifestyles which they could bring with them to liven up the village. More people meant Freztad might be able to live on for more than just another generation. *Maybe I could make some friends, too.*

"Rose," Ben said. "What are your thoughts? Do you know anything about this 'Ænæria' place?"

"Not much," Rose admitted. "We first heard about them at the Summit last winter. The Grand Elder said he had been seeing more travelers around Vänalleato and a new kind of currency circulating within the village about six years ago, I think. A few months before the Summit, Vänalleato received word from a man calling himself Legate Gatron, a solider under the rule of King Xander of Ænæria."

"I know Gatron!" Randy cheered. "Good man, though he can be rather unreliable at times. Sorry to interrupt, please continue!"

"Anyway," Rose said. "Gatron claimed he wanted to warn Vänalleato of Ænærian activity being close by but that their actions weren't to be seen as threats. They wanted no dispute with Vänalleato but rather to become peaceful allies. The Grand Elder replied saying Vänalleato was already part of the Penteric Alliance and would need to discuss it with the other settlements first. The Grand Elder heard didn't hear back from him but noticed an increase in bandit activity just outside their borders, though they couldn't confirm they were related."

"Then why haven't I heard of Ænæria before?" Ben asked, shocked his cousin had kept such a secret from him.

"It's because we couldn't come to an agreement," Rose said. "Jarl Geon was furious. He claimed Ænæria's sudden approach was a threat to our agreement, and the bandits were a way to intimidate us. Geon wanted to prepare Sydgilbyn for war and suggested we do the same. The Grand Elder scoffed at his proposal, claiming it was foolish and unnecessary. He wanted to send another message to Gatron with our 'reasoned and level-headed response to the situation' and then decide our course of action based on Gatron's reply. Geon cursed the Grand Elder, calling him weak. He looked to me and asked if we'd stand with him, as the officiator of the Summit. I of course told him Freztad would stand with the decision of the Alliance, but I would make no attempt to recklessly sacrifice my people's lives. Thane Morgiana agreed with Geon, and Sheika Thalia with the Grand Elder. Without an agreement, I proposed we simply wait to see if Gatron attempted contact again."

"That was almost five months ago," Ben said. The more Rose revealed about Ænæria the more he grew upset with her for keeping such a big secret for so long. "Why haven't you told me about this? What did this Gatron guy say?"

"Vänalleato hasn't heard from him yet. Ben, it's not like I tried keeping this a secret from you! It's nothing personal. I just didn't have enough information to tell you yet..."

"*Personal?* We tell each other everything!"

This struck a nerve with Rose. Her expression shifted from shame to anger as her arched brows furrowed and nostrils flared. "Everything? Well, how about that tunnel, Benedict? Did that just happen to slip your mind too?"

"That's different!" Ben snapped. "This affects the whole village!"

"As does the tunnel!"

Randy put himself between the arguing cousins, putting a hand on each of their shoulders. His cheerful smile made Ben want to punch his happy teeth right then and there.

"Now let's not fight, *huh*? There was so much of that today as it is, and I'd hate to see anything come between you." He looked to Rose and raised his eyebrows in sincerity. "I apologize for my friend Gatron's poor correspondence. He's been dealing with an insurgency recently, and this bandit problem of yours is likely related. He forwarded your message to the King in order to avoid making an inappropriate response. It may have been lost in transit or slipped his mind. He's quite the busy man, y'see. However, the King has since dispatched me to find this wonderful village. So, Rose, to avoid any further miscommunications, would you like to come with me to meet King Xander the Chosen?"

Ben's lungs froze, refusing to let air in or out. His heart rattled against his ribs, begging for relief. Did he hear right? *Rose can't go to Ænæria.* The village needed her, now more than ever. If Rose left and Rakshi was injured, then who would guide the village back to peace, protect it from another attack?

Ben almost spoke, but Rose beat him to it. "Normally, I would say my place is with my people. But this attack...it changes everything. I will go with you, Randy."

"Excellent!" Randy's eyes widened, and he smiled widely. "The King will be ecstatic to finally meet you!"

Ben couldn't believe what he was hearing. "Rose, are you crazy? We need you now more than ever!"

"Calm down, Ben," she said, though she didn't seem too calm herself. "I think this is the best thing I can do for Freztad. What if these attackers are the same ones Vänalleato has been dealing with? There's likely many more out there, and Rakshi isn't in any condition to train people to fight back. The other Sentinels are either injured or not disciplined enough to take her place. Sydgilbyn is the only settlement with trained fighters to spare, and they won't send anyone without blaming Ænæria." She turned to face Randy, her back now to Ben. "But your King can help us, yes? Provide us with those weapons you used and soldiers to protect us?"

A toothy grin crept up Randy's cheeks. "I can do you one better. I can leave you some sun-carriages and guns here. I'll even have my nephew Longinus teach your people how to shoot."

I can't believe this. "Rose, there has to be some other way. You can't leave. Especially not all by yourself. At least take me with you!"

"I won't be by myself. Randy and the Ænærians seem more than capable of defending themselves, and they would have nothing to gain by harming me, either. They didn't need to save us. We were *losing* that battle, Ben. If they wanted us killed or taken as hostages, then they would've done it by now."

"It's true; we would've," Randy grinned.

"And I'd offer for you to go, Ben, but the village already trusts me with these responsibilities. I know how to handle diplomatic situations. I need someone whom I can trust to keep an eye on things while I'm away. You *always* stay here when I go off on meetings."

Ben shook his head. "They won't listen to me. They don't trust me." He thought about the looks he had received as a child when parents had lost their children to the blood poisoning. *Contempt and hatred.* He knew the look well, for he saw it in Lydia's eyes every day. *I'm a stale reminder of death and the dishonorable chief.* "Let me go with you. At least I can be there to protect you."

Rose smiled her sweet grin, her straight and white teeth the only shining light in the darkness of the day. She always found a way to calm and reassure him. "I know you've learned a lot from Rakshi and the other Sentinels. But I think you'd be of more use here. Freztad will listen to a Limmetrad. They always have ever since Mathias founded the Tree by the Gjoll. To lead is in your blood, Ben. It's about time you realize that. I'll even bring a handful of Sentinels with me if that makes you feel better."

It didn't make him feel any better. If Ænæria was substantially north of Vänalleato, then Rose could be gone for weeks. The village wouldn't be able to handle that. With so many injured Sentinels, there would barely be enough left to guard the village after Rose left. Freztad would be left horribly vulnerable. *Trade will suffer, too,* Ben realized. Routes would be less protected, and the village itself would be weaker and more open to attack. A deal with Ænæria could save Freztad. But the interim could very well destroy it before Rose ever has a chance to return.

Ben was no leader, but his heart told him to listen to his cousin. He turned to Randy, who seemed quite content watching the cousins banter on and on, as though he had no place better to be. "How far is Ænæria?"

Randy stroked his mustache and looked toward the ceiling, deep in thought. "*Hmm*. I'd say it's only a two-day drive. Our sun-carriages are a great deal faster than horses, and we can keep them riding through the night if they get a good charge. The King will only need a day with her, so I'd say you can expect us back by week's end." He looked to Rose and smiled. "How's that sound, Chief?"

Ben now realized how pale his cousin looked. She must have been exhausted from the tumultuous day, and the proposal of leaving her people in shambles to meet a mysterious king in a faraway land must have terrified her. Ben feared she would overextend herself just as her mother had.

"It works for me," Rose answered. "Let's go to Valhaven and discuss the details there." She turned to face Ben. "Why don't you tell any able-bodied Sentinels about the lesson with Randy's nephew. They'll need to have proper training before the Ænærians leave."

Ben sighed. "I still don't think this is a good idea. Can't you—"

Rose stomped her foot on the floor. Villagers still making their way in and out of the house looked over to them in fright and curiosity. "Dammit, Ben! I'm the Chief of this village. Just listen to me for once, will you? Gather the Sentinels and tell them about Longinus."

Ben stood frozen. He had never seen his cousin lose her temper like this before. *Especially with me.*

"Now!" she yelled. Her face was red, and tears welled up in her eyes. What they were for, Ben could not be sure. He left the building without a word, slamming the door behind him. The wooden panel cracked and creaked from its hinges and fell to the floor. Ben simply kept walking. He didn't look back.

Randy's nephew never minced words and had no patience for incompetence or shenanigans. Aside from the red and black scar across his left eye, Longinus's face was pale and cold as though it had seen decades of misery and hardship, yet Ben couldn't imagine he was more than a few years older than himself, perhaps eighteen or so. The Ænærian's hair was a golden silver tied in a knot above his head. His voice was coarse as if his throat were full of gravel. He stood just under a foot shorter than Ben, and his shoulders were narrow. He also found it odd that the man was so clean shaven when all the other Ænærians sported some manner of facial hair. It came as no surprise that the twins poked fun at Longinus for these things, but Ben felt sympathy for him. He saw something of himself in this Ænærian and admired the way he held himself despite the criticism he surely endured from others besides the twins.

Longinus's lesson was simple yet interesting. The guns were quite easy to use and were essentially the same as a bow and arrow. Instead of nocking arrows, Ben had to load bullets. Instead of reloading after each shot, he only had to do it after every twelve with a contraption that held the next batch of bullets. After the initial learning curve, Ben found that he could adapt to the new weapon quite quickly.

Ben and the Sentinels began by learning how to use what the Ænærians called 'pistols.' After they demonstrated competence with those, they moved on to larger guns called 'rifles' that held somewhere around thirty bullets. These were much more difficult to get used to because they kept firing while holding back the trigger. The rifle's recoil barraged his right shoulder, leaving a large and painful bruise. He received some relief because after every five or so shots there was a misfire, and he had to manually remove the dud bullet. After a few hours of practice, the group decided to retire so as to save the rest of the ammunition.

To avoid Rose after their tiff, Ben worked on the temporary gate for the rest of the afternoon. He would have much rather spent the rest of the day by himself, but he felt the need to make himself useful. It first occurred to him that he could fetch the deer from that morning's hunt, but he knew that the meat was spoiled by now. Instead, he spent the rest of his day working on the gate, avoiding Rose, and wondering about the other settlements. For once in his life, he seemed to have an inkling of his father's sense of adventure. There was a whole world out there. Now that he was told he couldn't leave the village, he wanted nothing more than to do just that.

Ben and the other villagers stopped working on the gate at sundown. On his way to Valhaven, he decided that he would stop by Kabedge's house to see how he and Vic were doing. As he approached the house, he saw Kabedge at the front door talking to Rose. They stopped talking when they noticed Ben and turned to him. Rose's eyes were bloodshot and Kabedge seemed distraught.

"What is it?" Ben asked with a tremor in his voice. He worried that something may have happened to Vic—that today had been too much stress on the old man's heart.

Kabedge looked to Rose and nodded gravely. Rose sighed and looked at Ben. "It's Rakshi. She's dead."

5.Promise to the Departed

I t was a moonless night, and the flare of the burning pyre by the Tree was the only light to guide the lost soul on its way to the Great Dream.

Or so the Elder claimed.

The Elder's face was painted white, and sigils of black were etched on his forehead, cheeks, and chin. He held a long wooden staff, probably made from an old oak tree that knew the sun of the

Old Days. The preacher spoke the Great Dream, where all souls traveled after death. He claimed death was the true awakening of the soul to a world which the living could only ever glimpse in their dreams.

It was a sweet story, but Ben found no comfort in it. To Ben, Rakshi was gone forever. There was no Great Dream. No afterlife. Only silence and nothingness.

The Elder lit the final pyre, to signify the ascendance of Rakshi's soul while he hummed a tune, and the villagers bowed their heads in silence. The Ænærians simply looked away and pretended not to hear a thing.

They scorn those who worship the Ascendants. Few Freztadians followed the Vänalleatian ways, free to worship as they pleased. But they never acted as disrespectfully as the Ænærians.

A lump grew in Ben's throat at the words of the Elder as he spoke the final goodbyes to Sentinel Commander Rakshi, "...who will now join the Ascendants and watch over us for the rest of our days. Her tears will join the rain of the others who have fallen. Tears not for their losses, but for the losses of the living. We, the poor wretched souls who must continue this sad and violent life without knowledge of when we will rejoin them in eternal peace."

To this much, Ben listened. He could no longer think of the Rakshi he knew. *She was surely decisive, but did she weigh the consequences?* Ben's turmoil within fought an unfair battle as it drummed against his belly and reminded him of his loss. She fought. She chose. She died.

It made his chest feel hollow thinking about it, but he simply couldn't help being mad at his teacher. Rakshi shouldn't have died. No one should die, not even whichever thug loosed the arrow to pierce Rakshi's lung just deep enough to cause her to bleed out without the healers noticing. Rakshi's blood was on his hands, and he didn't think he could ever forgive himself for it. Ben decided to make a pact with himself, a promise that reflected Rakshi's last lesson to him. He would never end someone's life. He would find a way, no matter the situation or the consequences, to avoid it. It was the only way he could forgive himself for not being there sooner; for not saving Rakshi's life.

A hooded newcomer in a black hood stepped toward the Tree, facing the Vänalleatian Elder. "A few words, if I may?" It was a scraggly haired Ænærian. Ben didn't know his name.

The Elder mumbled something to himself about it being "highly irregular," but Ben didn't quite pay attention, lost in his thoughts until the newcomer disturbed the atmosphere.

"I am told your village recognizes no gods as your own." The Ænærian addressed the crowd with a confident and almost arrogant tone that spoke down to the heads below his own. "And yet you let this *old man* speak to you about an afterlife that cannot be promised by any but the Great Mother herself. I say to you all: pray not to the deceased, for they cannot hear you. Your friend cannot hear you. Only the Great Mother hears. She listens and contemplates only the needs of the followers of her Chosen." His eyes shot a glance at Randy and then to the crowd. "The Great Mother sent us here to rescue you. Don't allow that to be in vain." He walked back to the other Ænærians in silence.

It was short lived.

"*How dare you?*" Kristos barked as he walked toward the newcomer. His fist was raised and his feet heavy in the mud. Zechariah grabbed him by the cloak to hold his brother back from doing anything rash.

The Ænærian turned and raised an eyebrow at the angry twin. "Excuse me?"

"You heard me!" Kristos yelled. "Who do you think you are? This is a *sacred* service for beloved members of our village, and you think it's acceptable to spew your nonsense at us? You're our guests here! Have some damned respect!"

"Kris..." said a voice to Ben's right. He looked to see who it came from, but now everyone was muttering and throwing curses at the Ænærians. Slowly, stomping their feet into dirt, a score of angry villagers gathered and approached the Ænærians, whom were now peacefully making their way to their quarters.

"How can we trust these outsiders after what just happened?" one of the villagers demanded.

"Who even let them come to the funeral?" another said.

"Everyone, please," the voice muttered once more. This time it sounded like there was a choking of tears behind it. It was Rakshi's mother.

Ben thought he was the only person to notice the cry for peace as the villagers continued to rile themselves up and curse at their foreign guests.

But a calm and gentle voice finally intervened and gathered the people's attention.

"That's enough, Freztad!"

The scores of yelling voices grew quiet, and the mob froze in their tracks. They turned to face Ben, but they did not look at him. Instead, they looked to his left.

Rose walked forward and approached the Elder of Vänalleato, putting a gentle hand on the old man's deerskin cloak and furs. "We are a people of acceptance and peace. All beliefs are welcomed in our village. Some of you may worship Mathias's Tree, others the Gjoll itself. Some of you come from elsewhere in the Penteric Alliance and worship the gods of the earth, sky, or flame. I've even met traders who preach the word of the gods of the Old Days. These beliefs are all welcomed in Freztad, for we are the foundation of the Alliance. Rakshi died protecting us, and she believed in the Ascendants. She also believed in Freztad, or else she wouldn't have been Sentinel Commander. What would she think if she saw the people whom she died for fighting with guests over their beliefs. They are free to speak their mind. We owe them much more than that. We owe it to Rakshi, too."

Silence overtook the villagers, for not even a blood bug or hunter buzzed nor trilled. Only the gentle flow of the river, brushing against the muddy bank, in concert with the howling wind against the crackling fire of Rakshi's pyre dared to disturb the peace. Ben didn't understand why the Ænærians would say such things. The man had met the other Sentinels when he taught them how to use the guns. He

knew their love for Rakshi. Ben hadn't interacted with many of the
Ænærians, but Randy and Longinus seemed to be men with little
tolerance for nonsense or antics of any kind. So why would they let
one of their own act in such a disrespectful manner?

In the end, the villagers heeded Rose's words. They bowed their
heads to the leafless branches of the Tree and returned to their
homes. Only Rakshi's parents and her would-be-husband remained
by the Tree and pyre, their eyes red and cheeks moist. Rose was
walking with the Ænærians, no doubt apologizing for Freztad's ill
hospitality.

But who could blame them? Ben wondered. *That guy is an idiot for
saying anything.* Rose would likely look past that and not see it as an
excuse for treating guests in such a manner. But with her off by the
Ænærian quarters and the rest of the villagers marching toward their
homes, Ben was left alone with the broken family and the Elder—
who made no attempt to comfort the family. He simply knelt by a
basin, muttering to himself and washing the paints from his face.

Ben looked at the mourning family and noticed that one of the
Ænærians stayed behind and was talking to them. He turned around
and approached Ben.

"I wanted to offer my condolences," he said softly. His voice still
threw Ben off, almost as if it had been overused for years. "Both for
the death of your friend and for Elmer's behavior. He'll be punished."

"He was being a jerk, but Rose was right," Ben said. "We accept all
kinds of people in Freztad. Even if their beliefs are a little harsh."

"You are too forgiving, Limmetrad. Ænæria could use more like
you. I am disappointed to hear you will not be joining us when we
leave in the morning."

"Why is that?" Ben asked. He desperately wanted to leave with
Rose, but he knew she was right. His place was in Freztad. Even if he
wasn't wanted there.

"I saw you fighting before we finished off the attackers. You're
quite skilled. Where did you learn to fight?"

"I trained with Rakshi," Ben said, nodding his head toward the funeral pyre. "She was the Sentinel Commander. The best fighter in all of Freztad. Maybe even in the Alliance."

Longinus frowned. "Then it is certainly a shame that you have lost her. I am impressed that you had a woman rise to such a rank. It is uncommon in Ænæria."

"Like I said, Freztad is pretty accepting." *Except when it comes to the child of a traitor.*

Longinus nodded and cracked a smile. "And how about the skill of the other Sentinels joining me? Zechariah and...?"

"Neith and Yeong are the others," Ben responded, trying to remember who would be accompanying Rose, though he wasn't aware that Zechariah was leaving as well. "They're all skilled. Zechariah is the oldest of the three and has the most experience. The others are relatively new. You can't really go wrong with any of the Sentinels."

"You seem proud of your comrades," Longinus noted.

"Oh, I'm not a Sentinel. Not yet, anyway."

Longinus offered a confused look but remained silent. He and Ben turned and saw Rakshi's family approaching them.

"I shall take my leave," Longinus said. "I hope to see you again, Limmetrad. *Sol Invictus.*"

Ben nodded and waved the Ænærian goodbye. He turned and looked at the mourning family.

Zevi caught Ben's wandering gaze and locked eyes with him. Ben expected to see fury and flame behind the butcher's gaze, but only found the chestnut eyes to be empty and without purpose. Then, as Ben questioned whether to leave the family be or to head home, Rakshi's mother turned from the Tree and nearly jumped at Ben's presence.

Is she mad I'm here? Does she blame me?

The middle-aged woman wore a black headdress and dark purple sash across her dark gown. Her eyes widened, and she tapped on her husband's shoulder. The bald copper skinned man with the long and bushy black beard and sunken eyes followed his wife's gaze. The three were now all looking at Ben in silence, with three very different expressions on their faces—each just as hard to read as the other.

"That's him, Rohan, is it not?" Rakshi's mother asked.

Rohan shrugged his shoulders and looked to Zevi with an inquisitive look. Zevi nodded. "It is, Mother Zoya. Are you sure you want to do this?"

Ben felt the hair rise on the back of his neck, and his stomach murmur with discontent. What were they about to do?

Rohan turned his back to Ben and reached from a wooden crate that had been filled with Rakshi's belongings. It was customary for a Vänalleatian funeral to burn the body with their most prized possessions so that they may remember themselves once they enter the Great Dream. Rakshi's father turned around with something long covered in a thick beige cloth. He walked toward Ben and lifted it toward Ben's chest. "This is for you," he said with a slight tremble in his voice.

Ben raised an eyebrow and swallowed hard. This was not what he expected. He did not understand what was happening but knew it would have been rude to refuse. He slowly nodded his head and accepted the gift. Whatever was wrapped in the cloth was rather light, but he couldn't guess what it could be, given its size.

He unwrapped the gift to reveal a beautifully carved recurve bow with blue and green beads tied around its top and bottom shafts with thin braids of a tanned thread. The top and bottom limbs of the orange-tinted bow curved away from the bowstring; the handle stood perfectly straight, positioned slightly inward. It was Raskshi's bow. The weapon she had made for herself at her Hunting Trial when she turned thirteen. Ben smiled at the thought, for he remembered his own Trial, though the bow he'd made was now broken well beyond repair. He examined the bow with admiration, *bodark wood, I think. Rare and durable, no wonder it lasted all these years.*

"That may very well have been her most prized possession," Zoya said, smiling as she watched Ben stare at the bow with admiration. "We simply could not have had it burned with her. She would have wanted it to go to someone who had great need for it."

Ben raised his glance from the bow and narrowed his brow. "Why me then?" he turned to Zevi. "Why not you?"

Zevi shook his head and coughed, choking back another assault of tears. "A Sentinel's bow should only serve a Sentinel. It would be wasted on me. You were her favorite guard."

Ben shook his head. "I'm not a Sentinel. That's up to whomever becomes the next Commander." Ben bit his lip on his words. He realized that with Rose leaving first thing in the morning, he would have to oversee naming the next Commander. But how would he be expected to do that with multiple Sentinels leaving with her and with such a conflict of interest?

He didn't want to think about a *replacement* for Rakshi. No one could ever be that.

"Perhaps not," Rohan said, "but she'd want it to go to you all the same. Ascendants know what she saw in you, the parentless deviant that you are, but my daughter felt a bond with you. Perhaps she saw it her place to set you straight. Take it and do her proud by becoming a Sentinel and proving me wrong."

Ben readied a protest, but the three passed him by as soon as Rakshi's father had finished speaking. He was used to cruel words by the villagers but hearing it from Rakshi's own blood was like salt in an open wound. He had been called much worse than 'deviant' in the past by those who likened him to his father or blamed him for the plague that killed the children and left Lydia bound by chair and melancholy. He gripped his fingers tight around Rakshi's bow and closed his eyes. *I'll do you proud, Rakshi. I'll become a guardian for our people, and I'll do it the way you would've wanted: without killing.* He opened his eyes to see that he was finally alone by the Tree; the Elder was gone, and the Ænærians at their camp. Ben looked at the dwindling fires and said goodbye to his friend.

Gusts of cool wind blew over Freztad in a synchronous harmony with the buzzing of the hunter flies stalking their prey. The refreshing air on the gorgeous night was perhaps the most pleasant occurrence in quite some time. A seed landed on Ben's head, waking him from his slumber beneath Mathias's Tree. *Strange,* he thought, holding the seed against the moonlight. He had been sleeping beneath the dead wood of the Tree and wondered how a seed from the other side came to land on his head. He pocketed the seed and looked up at the Tree. It stood tall and proud, with its empty branches facing East, its leaves to the West. No one knew why the Tree by the Gjoll only flowered on one side, but it had done so for the past couple centuries. It was the first Limmetrad, Mathias the Exile, who had found the Tree, and built his sanctuary by the Gjoll. Many believed the Tree refused half its nutrients so that the soil could grow strong and fertile. Ben figured it had just been burned by the fires of the Old Days but was too stubborn to die as it lived as an anomaly among its brothers. And that's why he liked it. It was stubborn and different. Just like Ben.

Before he had drifted off, he had lain in the grass with eyes fixed upon the cloudless sky, under the light of the moon and stars. It was the brightest night sky he had ever witnessed. The moon was full and just above the forest, appearing larger than ever. Each of the stars were in attendance that night without cloud or mist to censor them. Ben could not believe that some people never took a simple moment just to look up.

Examining each star, Ben attempted to spot patterns among them. He thought of different shapes, trying to make stories out of them. *Wolf and tree. Mother and child. Mountain and Beast.* Anything to make sense of those strange yet beautiful bright dots in the sky and out of his reach. The celestial canvas gave Ben's mind some ease. Sleep could not find him that night. He needed to know that Rose was safe, and yet it had been nine days since her departure, four more than had been promised. While his body may have been exhausted, his mind had never felt more alert. It had to have been midnight by the time his aunt had gone to bed and he had snuck out of the house to enjoy the fresh air.

His whole life was measured by the change around him: the formation of the Alliance, the shrinking village, his cousin's blossoming leadership. But just like the stars above, Ben felt like he was unchanged and stuck in the same place for his entire life, which was insignificant compared to the longevity of the heavenly lights. Yet it wasn't just their longevity that made Ben feel insignificant. It was their association with his mother, and how he wondered if she was looked at the same stars sixteen years ago, or if she was as unaware of them as she was of him.

"Happy birthday to me, I guess," Ben whispered to himself in the bright moonlight, now fully awake.

Aside from the Hunting Ceremony on his twelfth birthday, Freztad never celebrated any of Ben's birthdays like they did Rose's. Lydia made a big deal of her daughter's birthday before she formed the habit of retreating into her home in solitude. By the time Rose became the stand-in for her mother, the entire village knew when to celebrate their beloved chief's birthday. Rose never made the festivities about herself, but about the village. Ben knew that was in line with her personality, but he secretly thought it was because she felt bad about Ben's birthday never being celebrated.

Like Rose, he didn't like the idea of celebrating himself and being the center of attention. But while Rose embraced it and tried to make the day about community, Ben had a more cynical disposition. He saw no reason to celebrate the day when some nameless woman brought him into the world.

Sitting up from the dewy grass, Ben cursed at himself as he buried his head in his palms. He wasn't supposed to be thinking about Rose. He came out here to *relax*, not worry.

She's going to be fine, he told himself. Yet as much as he tried to convince himself otherwise, he couldn't get his mind off his cousin. He told himself he was being ridiculous. Rose had been out of Freztad plenty of times before, and she always came back. *Not for over a week,* he argued with himself. Randy said they would be back by dawn on the fifth day.

That dawn had long since passed; Rose and the Sentinels were still gone.

Ben stood up and stretched, stiff from falling asleep on the uneven field. He figured it would be best if he just went to his room and fell to sleep. Waking up under the night sky put Ben in quite a stupor. He couldn't imagine that he had been asleep for long. He simply wanted the night to be over. He had lain awake for hours only to be teased by a short reprieve.

Ben made his way to the back of his house. He never thought Valhaven looked like much, but he stopped for a moment to appreciate how the building glowed when it basked in the moonlight. Approaching his room's rear window, Ben fidgeted with the hinge until it gave, allowing him entry into his room. The blinds behind the window rattled from the wind. He slid through the window as fast as he could and closed it just as quickly, worried the sound might wake his aunt.

A great *SLAM* sounded from across the hallway. *Too late,* Ben realized with a cringe. A knock came at his door, loud and threatening.

"Benedict! Is that you? What in the bloody wastes are you doing?" his aunt's harsh voice growled from outside his room.

Ben sighed and opened his door. Lydia sat in her moving chair, her unusable legs hidden by a red and purple quilt Rose had made for her on her forty-third birthday. His aunt looked up with dark and beady eyes, her face sallow and angry. Her hair was dark and thinning and fell only past her ears, covering old scars and bruises.

"I couldn't sleep. I went for a walk outside," Ben said. He saw no reason to lie to his aunt, for she'd spite him no matter the words that came from his mouth. Ben often wondered if she regretted teaching him to speak as much as she regretted accepting him from Alphonse.

Lydia grunted and rolled her eyes. "Make less noise next time. I feared you were an intruder."

"Sorry to disappoint." He smiled shrewdly at his aunt as his hand found the seed in his pocket. His fingers rolled around its hard shell and pinched at it delicately. Linden seeds were the most valuable in the Alliance, for they were rare and represented the center of the five villages. Ben only now realized how lucky he was to have found one when he woke. *From the dead wood, no less.*

"What're you doing?" Lydia asked as she eyed Ben's hands in his pocket. "You're fidgeting just like your father." She shook her head. "I'll never understand how you inherited his mannerisms."

It's not like he was around to teach me. Suddenly Ben remembered he had been meaning to ask his aunt about Alphonse since the attack but had been preoccupied ever since. When Rose had left that next morning, Lydia locked herself away for two days before Ben saw her again. In that time, he had been bombarded by the villagers with demands and inquiries. Every day from noon to dusk, he sat at the Valhaven's table, listening to people complain about their damaged homes from the attack; the bullets from the Ænærians that destroyed Madam Nala's clay pots and dishes; Old Man Gareth's winery was raided, and he swore it was well after the attack and before the Ænærians left; the bank's vaults were ruined and chaotic while Alyn the banker recuperated in the Keep. The village was a mess.

Then, there were those who demanded the naming of a new Sentinel Commander. Ben pushed that one off as much as he could. He needed all the Sentinels present for an election, and he had already sent Sentinel Torin with a courier to Sydgilbyn to hire mercenaries to guard Freztad in its current vulnerable state. Moreover, Neith, Yeong, and Zechariah had gone with Rose for far longer than anticipated. He tried explaining to the villagers many times that his hands were tied, but they never understood. Most of them just gave Ben a hard time because he wasn't Rose—he wasn't their real leader.

"Since we're speaking about Alphonse," Ben said to Lydia, "I wanted to ask you something."

"We're not speaking of him. I don't need any more reminders of people who leave me behind." Lydia grunted and turned her chair around, wheeling toward her room.

A fist formed around the seed in Ben's pocket. "This is important! It's about Rose!"

Lydia braked the wheels and stopped. She did not turn around. "I'm listening," she said after a moment of uncomfortable silence.

"The Ænærian King she's going to meet. They say his name is Xander, but..." he felt a cramping in his gut as he spoke, "I think he might be Alphonse."

For a moment, Lydia said nothing. The shadow of the hall enveloped her, and all Ben could see was the silver reflection of the moon on her chair's iron wheels. She must've been deep in thought, for she made no hurry to move or respond. She dared not even make a sound, and Ben waited anxiously. Then she sighed and continued to roll forward. "Your father is no king. He went off chasing some fantasy from the Old Days."

"Well, where do you think the Ænærians got those sun-chariots and guns from? That stuff has gotta be from the Old Days. I've never seen anything like them. It's as if they were pulled straight from Kabedge's stories."

"Then maybe you should ask him about it, though I doubt he knows the identity of this Xander character. But your father is no king. He couldn't even lead this village, so what makes you think he could rule an entire country? No, I suspect my brother died chasing his fool's dream that drove so many people from our village." Lydia opened her door from down the hall, ready to hide behind it and pretend Ben didn't exist.

He didn't let her off that easy. "It's my birthday, you know. You gave me answers about my mom for my twelfth birthday when I proved I was a man. Why not give me more now that I'm acting chief?"

Lydia scoffed. "*The eleventh day of the fifth month.* Alphonse beat the date into my head before he left for good. I don't know why he'd insist on telling me without a word about your mother. I recall telling Julius that I doubted you were even my own blood. I couldn't imagine someone so strange and reclusive as Alphonse being with a woman. I had thought you were some orphaned boy he'd found and couldn't bear to ignore. Alas, I've been proven wrong over the years. You're too much like your father. And just like him, you'll never be a leader.

Enjoy playing chief while you can. Playtime will be over once Rose returns."

Ben stood at his doorway steaming. His aunt's words pierced his heart in a way they never had before. How could his aunt be so belligerent and condescending? Somehow, she always found a way to beat him down lower than he'd already fallen. And what of the mention of Julius? Lydia rarely spoke of her ex-husband. Ben figured it was Julius's abandonment with Alphonse that made Lydia so bitter; the paralysis was merely the final push toward her melancholia. *And that bit about me not being Alphonse's? She hasn't brought that up in years.*

As if reading his thoughts, Lydia sighed. "You get one question before I go to sleep. Get on with it."

Ben thought intently on what to ask. He knew he could ask Kabedge about Xander in the morning, so he'd drop that for now. Instead, he formulated a different question, one he needed to word carefully to elicit the response he desired. "You always told me Alphonse made his final departure mysteriously and without a trace. So if he was no leader, then why did everyone in the village follow him, including Rose's father?"

"That's not a fair question," Lydia snapped, making for her room once more. This time Ben ran up to her and blocked the doorway. "Move, boy!"

"Only when you answer my question!"

Lydia grinded her teeth together and grimaced. "Fine. You'll want to sit for this. It's a long answer." She rolled her way toward Valhaven's hall and situated herself in the middle. Ben sat opposite her.

"Julius was the closest thing my brother had to a friend," Lydia started, "other than Takashi, who didn't call himself 'Kabedge' yet. The boys were nearly inseparable, and Takashi once told them he'd trade secrets about the Old Days with them for any relics from the outside. It was a reckless offer, because the boys took it quite seriously. Leaving Freztad in those days for anywhere but Vänalleato was strictly forbidden, but the two would sneak out of the village anyway, always coming back with an artifact for Takashi."

At this, Ben resisted the urge to interrupt. He'd never known that

Kabedge was a mentor to his father in the same way he had been one to Ben. Why was he just hearing this for the first time, and not from Kabedge himself? What other secrets did the old man have?

"As the boys got older, Alphonse spent increasingly less time in the village and Julius more time with me. Then, about a year after our mother died and months before our father's passing, when I was Rose's age and your father was in his early twenties, Alphonse disappeared for nearly four months. Despite our father's ill health and the responsibilities of chief being placed upon Alphonse's shoulders, my brother would disappear from the village for days at a time, sometimes even weeks. I would try to stop him, but he always found a way of disappearing without a trace only to return suddenly with some grandiose tale about the Old Days and relics he'd found in the wasteland. Julius and Takashi continued to humor him, but I did not. I found his behavior to be irresponsible and unfair, for he left all of his duties to me.

After his long departure, just months before our father died, Alphonse returned with his most ludicrous story yet. He told me one of the relics spoke to him. I told him the sun must've fried his head while he was out there. But he seemed as sharp as ever, adamant about what he heard. He told me the relic's voice told him about a place with a way to fix the world and put it back to the way it once was. It was too much for me. His tinkering with relics was one thing, his absconding another. But thinking he could put the world back to the way it once was seemed absolutely ridiculous. I asked him why he'd want the world to go back the way it was if he didn't even know what it was like. He claimed that the Old Days were better. People were better and healthier, but something happened to change it all. He went so far as to say that that's why the sun burns so hot and the blood bugs thrive.

"When our father died, Alphonse became Chief of Freztad. I'd hoped the position would change him; force him to stay home for the good of the village. Sadly, my wish was granted. Being chief did indeed change your father, but not in the way I had hoped. He became anxious and uneasy, unable to sit still. After two years, the mantle of chief weighed too heavy on his shoulders, and he disappeared without a single word to me or even Julius, his friend. Five years later, he returned with you, only to turn back and abandon our village once more...." A tear brushed across her cheek that seemed to shine in the candlelight. She sniffed, wiped her face with the back of her hand, and blew out the candle in front of her. She backed away from the table and set course for her room.

"Wait," Ben said with a hint of frustration. "I don't understand. Why did everyone leave with him?"

Lydia continued to roll toward her room. She did not look back to Ben as she responded. "I never said they left with your father. I said they left *because* of him. They left with Julius." The door slammed behind her.

Ben was once more alone in the place he was supposed to call home.

6.A Wild World

The rising sun on the horizon's golden tapestry had not yet bid farewell to the moon sinking over the Gjoll when Ben decided to leave his bed and find Kabedge. It wouldn't be long before the villagers filed outside Valhaven with the day's grievances. The air was cool and refreshing, and no clouds tainted the sky —a welcome change while it lasted, for he knew it would not stay this way. The storms ravaging the land were the sign of summer's coming.

In a way, Ben felt lucky that he did not live close to the sea as Kabedge often told him that the coastal lands were often decimated beyond repair when the sky's anger unfolded. Kabedge's talk of the sea had always left a longing in Ben's heart. He couldn't imagine a body of water more impressive than the Gjoll, and the thought that the world was covered by more sea than land fascinated him. It often made him wonder if his father left him to find the sea, for Ben didn't know what could be more enticing. *If he even is my father.*

A raven stood perched above Kabedge's doorway, gnawing on a worm it had won from the most recent storm. It eyed Ben cautiously as he walked towards the shop, ignoring the hunter flies buzzing by its beak. It was early, but Ben knew the old man liked to smoke a pipe on his back porch before tackling the day's tasks. The porch was a simple wooden deck with a small rounded table and two rocking chairs. Upon the table was a game from the Old Days that Kabedge and Vic had once played together in the evenings before the blood bugs woke up to feast. Many of the figures on the game board were made of clay, but a handful were of rusted metal and shaped like horses and castles. The thought now came to him that these were perhaps some of the trinkets Alphonse and Julius retrieved for the old man. Ben chuckled and shook his head. It was funny to him that Kabedge was the same obsessive old man even before he was old.

To Ben's surprise, neither chair was occupied, and they moved only from the light breeze. No pipe was found nor a tray for its ash. Ben walked up the porch to the back door with a look of concern and confusion upon his face. He readied his fist to knock on the door when it suddenly flew open against his face, smacking him in the nose.

"Oi! Watch yourself, Ben!" Kabedge hollered with great surprise. "What're you doing coming around back so early in the morning before I even got a smoke in?"

Ben rubbed his nose to make sure it was not broken only to find that it was bleeding. When he stopped seeing spots, he looked at the old man and noticed a great change about him. His pipe was in his left hand, flint and steel in his right: both were shaking and beads of sweat dribbled across his forehead. "What's wrong, Kab?" he said with a nasally tone as he squeezed his bloody nose. "You don't look so great, and you slammed that door open quite hard."

Kabedge pulled a handkerchief from his apron and handed it to Ben, only after appearing to consider whether or not to first dab the sweat off his forehead. He sat down in the rocking chair closest to Ben and lit his pipe. He blew a ring of smoke with a heavy exhale. "It's Vic. He's getting old, kid. Mind and body ain't what they used to be. I gotta clean him, dress him, feed him, move him to and from the bed. It ain't good. Elder thinks it's the bug plague come back, but I tells him that's nonsense. Ain't had a case of it for ten years!" He took another hard drag from the pipe and blew it out forcefully through his nose.

Ben sat in the chair next to his old mentor and placed his free hand on his shoulder. Kabedge brushed it off, "*Agh*, look at me—it ain't my place to be nagging a kid like you about problems like these. What'd you come here for? Planting some more crops before the heat and storms roll through?"

Ben shook his head and sighed heavily. "No, I don't plan on doing another round of crops before the solstice."

"Rose seems to think we'll be needing more crops this summer. Seems to think it'll be a bad one. She's got good judgement, that one."

"Rose is why I'm here. The other villagers will have to work the fields before the end of next month without me."

Another ring of smoke glided from the old man's lips. He seemed to stare at the ring, deep in thought as he watched it dissipate into the air. "She ain't back yet, is she?"

"No. I mean to go looking for her. And I need your help. What do you know about Ænæria?"

Kabedge took the pipe from his mouth and stared at Ben with a look of intrigue. "I know very little. And how's an old man like me to help you do that? They've always kept to themselves. My sister, if she's still alive, lives leagues north of Vänalleato where I imagine Ænæria is. But last time I spoke with her, Ænæria didn't exist.

"According to Randy, Ænæria was only formed fifteen years ago."

"Ah. That would do it. Haven't spoken with Risa since then. It's hard to communicate so far away. Is that all ya needed from me, kid?"

Ben shook his head and placed the handkerchief on his lap, the bleeding having finally stopped. He looked at the game board ahead of him and picked up one of the pieces in the back row with what looked like a crown. "This one's the king, right?"

Kabedge smirked and shook his head. "Nope. That's the queen. King's the one next to her. With the cross on his head."

"Why doesn't the king have a crown? What does the cross mean?"

"The cross was a symbol of a God from the Old Days. The king was thought by many to be the closest to Him. The man who did His bidding, as it were." He scratched his head for a moment. "At least I think that's right. Why the sudden interest?"

Ben returned the clay queen piece in her spot and picked up the clay king. It wasn't much to look at compared to the metal pieces, but Ben could tell that Kabedge had put a lot of work into making it. "Because the Ænærians referred to their king as the 'The Sun's Chosen.' I'm trying to get a better understanding of their king. He's apparently from Freztad, but no one seems to have heard of anyone named Xander. I was hoping you would."

Kabedge's expression shifted to a horror that Ben had never seen on the old man's face before. The color from his olive skin vanished, and the old man now appeared pale and sickly. He put down his pipe and muttered something to himself and shook his head slowly. He stood up from his chair and walked to the edge of the porch and leaned over the railing. "This ain't good."

"Then you have heard of him?" Ben asked, still clutching the king piece in the palm of his right hand.

"I have. And it's no wonder no one in the village remembers the name. Xander died over forty years ago. Vic and I are the only two old enough to remember him."

Ben raised an eyebrow. "I don't understand. Randy told me he left twenty years ago and founded Ænæria shortly after."

Kabedge grunted and spit to his side. "You trust this Randy? The same man who you're convinced stole Rose away?"

Ben grimaced. He hadn't thought of that. Randy could have made the whole thing up. And why not? He had no reason to be truthful with Ben. All he needed was to kidnap Rose. *Rose.* "But Rose heard of Xander. Independent of Randy."

"Kid, all I know is there's a man out there calling himself Xander, and someone stole Rose away in his name. As far as I'm concerned, that only means one thing: his name isn't Xander. The *real* Xander died of fever in his bed. Just like his parents did weeks before him. It was a nasty pox we had, and the only one of their family to survive was a little boy who Vic and I raised along with all the other orphans over the years."

"What happened to the brother? Who was he? Are you saying he's King Xander?"

"If this man is truly from Freztad, then yes. I'm positive Julius is calling himself Xander."

The piece from Ben's hand slipped and hit the wooden floor below him, shattering into pieces. Neither Ben nor Kabedge acknowledged it and instead waited in silence until it was finally disturbed by the raven Ben had seen on his way over. This time it was chasing another black bird just like it, their wings and *caws* the only sound to be heard in all of Freztad.

Suddenly everything seemed to make sense to Ben. Lydia had hinted at Xander's identity the night before. *Everyone left with Julius fifteen years ago. Rose is his daughter. He came back for her.* "Why would Julius come back for his daughter after so long?"

"How much do you know about Julius, Ben?"

"Not much. The most I know I only learned this morning from Lydia." He went on to tell Kabedge about his confrontation with his aunt, and the gut-wrenching revelation that his father wasn't the true cause for people leaving the village.

"There's more to it than Julius leaving Freztad to find his friend. But to understand that, you need to know more about the man."

He retrieved his pipe and took another heavy drag of it before beginning his tale.

"Julius was Lydia's husband until fifteen years ago, but they were together for as long as I remember. Though he was my son, he never truly saw me as a father. It was tough for him, growing up with the loss of his entire family and the sudden transition to a new one. But he grew into a very stout and stoic individual, the only one in the village able to win the heart of someone as strong willed as Lyd. When Alphonse left about twenty years ago, Julius helped Lyd keep control over the village. Helped her make deals with the neighbors and form the Penteric Alliance. He was always charismatic, that son of mine.

"After about a year of working together, Julius and Lyd finally married. Happiest couple in Freztad. Made the village thrive, they did. Between Lyd's strong temperament and Jul's charm, they brought the village to the greatest it's ever been. Traded for plows, cattle, horses, pipping, tools, you name it. With the trade routes and alliances established, the two made Freztad the central trading hub of the land. Village was bustlin' with people from all over.

"Now y'see, Lyd here was content with all that. She was just happy to have the village and her people safe and well taken care of. But Julius couldn't get enough of it. He was thrilled to see all kinds of people from all over. Interested in their cultures and whatnot. He wanted Lyd to expand the village, wanted to share the wealth with everyone else. He saw everyone here prospering and didn't think it fair not to share it with the rest of the land. But Lyd wanted no part of it. Not that she didn't care about everyone else, but she thought she had done more than she needed. Alphonse was supposed to be chief —not her. She never wanted that responsibility.

"Now the two didn't argue much about it, but it did cause a rift in their relationship. Their differences became more profound. Julius spread his ideas to other people in the village. Got lots of them to listen to him, too. Lyd didn't pay it no mind, though. By that time, she was pregnant with Rose, and that was enough for her to focus on. Well, that is until you showed up.

"As Julius kept spreading his ideals 'around the village and Lyd was taking it easy for her unborn child's sake, your father returned all of a sudden. Your father and aunt argued for hours, and Alphonse left the next day. A few days after that, Julius and his followers left the village to follow him."

"Lydia already told me that part," Ben said with a groan. "Why did everyone follow Julius? Wasn't he just going after my dad because they were friends?"

Kabedge shook his head and sighed. "If only it were that simple. Julius didn't leave to chase after his friend with hopes of finally bringing him home. He and his loyalists followed Alphonse because they hoped he'd lead them to the Vault."

A crow from across the field cawed loudly, the only sound Ben could hear amidst the waking sun.

"What is 'the Vault?'" Ben asked, thinking he had missed some detail.

"I don't know much, kid. I've only heard legends, and few at that. But I'll venture to guess it's why Julius finally came after his daughter: he's found the Vault, and now he's come for the key."

Ben looked at Kabedge narrow eyed and perplexed. "How is Rose the key?"

"Your father only gave me sparing details the day he returned with you. He claimed the Vault was the origin of the voice he heard from the metal box he found in the wastes years before. It had given him coordinates to a mountain in the frozen North, with an ancient monolith from the Old Days. He said it stored the knowledge of the past and the key to salvation for the future. And he carried with his heart the key: blood. I'd always assumed he meant his own blood, the blood of Mathias and his descendants. It's long been thought that blood holds the power of what it is to be human. It only makes sense that blood from the line of heroes would be enough to open the mythic structure. I reckon Julius sought after Rose because of her blood. He wants whatever's in the Vault for himself. He wasn't the same boy Vic and I raised when he left." The old man shuddered and looked to the dawn horizon as he tried to blink away the tears welling in his eyes.

Ben didn't put a hand on Kabedge's shoulder this time. Instead, he took a moment to digest the information. It was all so much at

once. Rose wasn't just taken by a foreign king for political gain. Somehow, that was easier for him to accept than knowing her absent father
stole her for a mysterious power left by the Old Days. It was simpler
when Ben had thought that his wayward father, not Julius, was King
Xander. He had an entire lifetime to learn about Alphonse, whereas
he knew nothing of his cousin's kidnapper. He had convinced himself
he could find Alphonse, and that somehow it would be easier to
persuade his own father into bringing Rose home. Julius was a wild-
card. Even if he could afford the time to study him with Kabedge's
aid, Ben knew it wouldn't be enough. Because when it came down to
it, Ben knew why it would've been easier to deal with Alphonse. Lydia
had reminded him of it constantly: Ben and Alphonse were nearly
the same person.

The whole venture now seemed hopeless. He thought he could
sneak out of Freztad, delegate his duties to someone else, someone
more capable, and search for Rose. He would have traveled north,
tracking the sun-carriages and stopping by Vänalleato to inquire
about the Ænærians. He would have asked if anyone knew about his
father's movements fifteen years ago. Then, he would have continued
his search for Rose until the end of his days. Because he knew that's
how Alphonse would have done it. But with Julius as his enemy, Ben
felt ill-prepared. Julius didn't know him, and he surely wouldn't have
a problem stopping Ben from getting in his way.

Kabedge straightened and stretched, then firmly gripped Ben's
shoulder. "Hey! It's your birthday ain't it, kid? Sixteen years old today,
eh? Come on inside, I've got a gift for you."

Inside the shop were a few villagers already waiting to order their
breakfasts. "Hold on, hold on! I'll be just a minute! Quit badgering
me, I'm an old man!" he yelled playfully to his guests. He led Ben
through the kitchen to a back room which was stuffed with pots and
pans, cutlery, spices, herbs, and other miscellaneous ingredients that
old Kabedge probably forgot even existed. Behind a wooden table
across the room was a faded parchment map that had seen its fair
share of use and was about the only decoration Ben could see in the
room. Toward the end of the room was a small fireplace fixed with a

metal pole to hang the kettle. The old man poured a cup for himself and Ben before sitting down.

"Not exactly, pretty is it?" he asked, looking at the faded map on the wall. "But it's all I've got for you, I'm afraid. In fact, it was always meant for you. Your father gave it to me to hold onto until you were old enough. I'd say sixteen is a good time, especially under the circumstances."

Ben sipped his tea as he looked at the map. It was bitter yet had a hint of mint hiding within. The map was sketched in fine detail on aged parchment. About three feet by two, it depicted large land-masses with islands scattered all over. Some regions of the map had X's etched over them, and others had circles. There were no words on the map, but there were numbers everywhere. The numbers followed a series of lines that formed a sort of grid.

"You don't have to get me anything. It's just a random day of the year. For all I know, Lydia got the day wrong. She didn't even believe Alphonse was my father."

Kabedge chuckled. "*Heh*, she probably believed it for a while. Julius, too. Must be why he didn't have his people take you with Rose. Can't see why else he'd make such a foolish mistake. You're just as much a Limmetrad as Rose. Grow yourself a beard and you'd look just like your father, too!"

Ben paused a moment, confused. "Wait. Why didn't the Ænærians take Lydia then?"

Kabedge turned his gaze to the map. He pointed to a spot on the leftmost landmass, slightly west of its center. His finger was placed next to a shaded mark, the only mark of its kind. "This here, kid, is Freztad." He lifted his finger and made a circle in the air over the upper portion of the land mass. "All this is north—Ænæria. You really think it'd be practical to bring someone in Lyd's condition around here? No way."

"Kabedge...why are you giving me this map?"

"Because somewhere up here is the Vault. That's where Julius is headed. That's where Rose will be. Your father found it with nothing more than coordinates and this here map. You can do it too."

"But Kab, I don't have the..." *Coordinates,* he almost said. He knew exactly where Kabedge was going with this. The revelation was surreal. Ben always thought Alphonse had left him with only the watch but learned years later that it contained a key. The key to the same tunnel Alphonse used to disappear from Freztad right under Lydia's nose. Now, he learned his father had also left him a map. He finally knew what the numbers meant. *7 ,8, 1, 5 is actually 78, 15.* He examined the map carefully and traced his fingers over its intersecting lines. Far north he found the number 80. Following it down slowly, Ben looked at the numbers to the side until he reached the midpoint between 10 and 20. His finger rested on an isolated landmass that almost looked like a diving bird. "Right here! This is where the Vault is!"

Kabedge smiled, his face looking brighter than Ben had seen in quite some time. Then a tear dripped down his cheek, and he turned away to wipe it off.

"What's the matter, Kab?"

He shook his head and waved a hand at band. "Oh, it's nothing, kid. Just happy to see you all excited is all."

Ben knew what was really bothering him. He placed a hand on his old friend's shoulder. "I'll be back, Kabedge. I'm not going to abandon the village like Alphonse did. I'll return with Rose and the others. I promise."

"I know you'll be back, kid. You're tough. Tougher than you know." He said this with great conviction in his voice. "But I wonder if it'll really be you who returns, or someone else." Reaching to the uppermost corners of the faded parchment, Kabedge removed the map from the wall and rolled it up as if it were a scroll. He placed it firmly against Ben's chest. "Take it with you. It won't be enough on its own to get you to the Vault, for it's far too old. You'll need a mapmaker, you will. Vänalleato. There's a good one there. Goes by the name of Siegfried, I reckon."

Ben clutched the map firmly in his hands. *I'll find you, Rose. I'll bring you home.* Before Ben could even question what Kabedge meant about returning as someone else, the old cook smacked him on the back. "Get on outta here, kid! You're racin' against time now! Take some food and leave as soon as you can! But don't let anyone see you. I think you're right to mistrust those Ænærians and who knows if they left spies about. Best you leave at dark. Can you do that?"

Ben smiled shrewdly. *I know just the way out.* And just like that, Ben returned to his room and packed. He spent the rest of the day gathering supplies and planning a route to Vänalleato. It was three days by horse if one took the roads, six by foot via straight path. Neither were ideal for his situation, especially if there were Ænærian scouts expecting him. Horse would require him to leave by the front gate; that would be too conspicuous. Furthermore, enough horses were missing since the attack, and Ben wouldn't want to contribute to the losses. Walking was out of the question; it would be far too long and dangerous. Besides, the Ænærians' head start was already more than he could catch up with. His only other option would be to take a boat along the Gjoll. No one would dare follow him by the blood bug infested water, and he would leave no tracks. It was nearly perfect: winds were strong this time of year, and the river flowed north all the way to Vänalleato. The only issue was the sailboat itself, for it was poorly maintained and its wood probably rotten and sails ridden with holes. That was of little consequence, he reflected, because he would take any risk to bring Rose home.

He decided to travel by the cover of night when the sun disappeared and Freztad slept. He would have to bring enough supplies with him to make the necessary repairs on the boat. For the rest of the day's light, Ben slept to retain the strength to travel. When he finally woke, he saw that the moon was high and village still. With only his rucksack of essentials, his quiver and Rakshi's bow, and the clues left by his father, Ben descended into the dark network of tunnels below and did not look back.

The sound of the flowing water mixed with the sounds of chirping crickets and humming blood bugs was peaceful and soothing to Ben's mind. He unfolded the boat's sail and found it had few enough holes that he could manage for a few miles before mending it. The boat was left on the river's shore and suffered little rot. The wooden edges were growing green with mold, and one of the paddles had been chewed to the center by whichever bugs or rodents lived nearby. He slumped his shoulders and sighed as he tossed the rotten paddle into the river; it would do him no good in that condition. One would be enough along with the rudder, which seemed to be spared much of the same decay. Ben pushed the small vessel into the flowing river and jumped inside. It wobbled and nearly turned over with the sudden jolt but was sturdy enough to stay afloat. He pulled the sails and readied himself for the voyage north.

He occupied his time on the water with wandering and racing thoughts of his journey ahead. He knew not what kind of land Ænæria would prove to be, nor did he know what challenges he may face. The first hours of the night were filled with scenarios and possibilities. Randy seemed a reasonable man, Longinus an honorable one. Perhaps he could cater to their natures and come to an agreement. *Doubtful,* he told himself. Even if they would listen to him, there would be nothing they could do. Ben pictured the balding man with the large mustache and the pale blonde nephew standing in a corner looking the other way as he pleaded on his knees before a shadow with a crown. *I'm at the King's mercy.*

When his thoughts eventually drifted from the worries ahead, Ben found himself dwelling on the roads already taken. Following the Gjoll, most of his thoughts centered around death—specifically Rakshi's. It wasn't fair. She was young and should have had a whole life ahead of her with a new husband and maybe even children. Her parents shouldn't have had to outlive her. That wasn't right. His thoughts wandered to Rose once more, and about how Lydia would fare if she never returned. Rose was so concerned about leaving her mother behind and yet she left anyway; her concern for the village had become her priority, and Ben was entrusted to care for his sickly aunt. In this he failed, for nothing but worries of his cousin's safety filled his mind. He couldn't imagine Julius would harm his own daughter. *But would 'Xander?' How heavy does the crown weigh, and what would the King do to keep it?* He simply didn't know. The uncertainty of the future and of his own decisions weighed heavy on his heart and made his first night feel long and cumbersome.

When the sun's light broke the cool air, Ben dragged the boat ashore, for he could no longer keep his eyes open. Knowing wolves were around, he wouldn't dare sleep on the ground. He climbed a tree and hung a hammock from its limbs. He slept through as much of the day as his anxiety would allow. Eventually, the racing thoughts and unease of not moving got the best of him and he climbed down to continue his path forward.

It was late day when he continued north. This time he thought of old stories he grew up with and spoke them aloud to himself. His favorite was about Mathias, the first Limmetrad. According to legend, the man was the greatgrandchild of his namesake from the Old Days, and he was of the first generation to have never known the Old Days. While the world continued to crumble, and people mourned the past, Mathias thought forward. He left his dead land from the East and explored the entire world before finally settling in Freztad. On his journey, he met his best friend and lover, with whom he had two children.

Ben remembered when he was a young boy listening to Kabedge and Vic tell the stories to him. They would tell him a new part to Mathias's adventure every week as a reward for keeping up with his studies. For as long as he could remember, Ben had wanted to be like Mathias and travel the world and make an impact. It was a nice story to distract himself from the cruel reality: he was nobody, and he would never accomplish anything. Oftentimes, Ben wondered if that's why he had actually decided to leave. The villagers clearly mistrusted him. Lydia resented him. *I'm too much like Alphonse for them.* Rakshi was dead, Rose was gone. Only the twins, Kabedge, and Vic remained. The twins were a small comfort to him, but no true reason to stay. Kabedge had enough on his plate dealing with his sick husband and own old age. *I'll only return with Rose. Otherwise there's nothing for me here.* The village would be better off without Ben, and he would be better off on his own while he discovered who he truly was without the dark cloud as Alphonse's son hanging over his head.

When the sky glowed purple with the receding sun and Ben found himself midway through Mathias's tales, a most unexpected event unfolded. Across a small creek branching from the Gjoll and between the thick trees on its edge, Ben once again saw the enormous wolf from Freztad—and it wasn't alone. The wolf was staring down a gray horse with a black and silver mane. The draft horse was a large gelding with steel shoes that it blazoned with ferocity as it bucked and reared at the approaching white wolf. *Sleipnir?* Ben thought to himself with great surprise. There was no mistaking the great horse for his cousin's own mount. He hadn't realized that Sleipnir had been among the many animals that had run off during the attack of Freztad, though he wasn't exactly surprised. Sleipnir had always been a difficult animal, even being made a gelding did little to dampen his temper. Rose was the only one in the village to have ever tamed the horse, and it made sense that no one would have been able to bring him back once she left.

The wolf made no sound and kept its distance from the horse, but Sleipnir continued to snort and neigh as he backed up against the trees behind him. Any second now and the wolf would have its next meal—unless Ben did something about it. Without much thought, he turned the boat to shore and found his feet on the ground. He nocked an arrow in Rakshi's bow and aimed at the ravenous wolf. He let the arrow loose but missed, his shot landing just before the wolf's front paw. It turned and snarled at him just before charging forward and leaping across the creek toward Ben. He fumbled for the pistol Longinus had given him and tried to recall how to use it.

It didn't matter, the wolf was too quick, and it dodged Ben's first shot as if anticipating it. He kept firing until the wolf pounced on his chest, knocking him over. As he fell to the ground, he lost his grip on the gun and dropped it somewhere to his side. The wolf was on top of him, its drool dripping down onto his face as it bared its yellow fangs. He tried to punch the wolf in its side, flailing about and helplessly trying to escape its clutches. Its cold gray eyes stared into Ben's with a strange beauty and an apparent intelligence behind them. It suddenly closed its maw and lost interest in its prey, leaping off his chest. It sniffed at the forest floor for a moment before spotting Rakshi's bow where Ben had dropped it. It picked it up between its teeth and looked back at Ben before it darted deep into the wooded darkness.

He cursed aloud after the wolf, blood boiling with fury for it stealing his precious bow. There was no way he would be able to follow the beast. It was too fast, and the night was growing dark. Rakshi's bow was gone just as quickly as it had come. Another thing Ben was powerless to save.

A whinny sounded from behind as Sleipnir trotted across the creek, his hooves splashing in the water. The horse glanced at Ben for a moment before swiftly shifting his gaze toward the rucksack in the boat. He dipped his nose in it and scrounged about, smelling the food Ben had inside.

"Sleip, hold on, big guy," Ben said as he saw the horse struggle with the closed sack. With a closer look, Ben could see the pale horse must've been famished from so long on his own. The year was growing hot, and the grasses were wilting. He opened his pack and removed a carrot. The horse snatched it from his hand the second it left the bag. Sleipnir chewed quickly with many pieces falling to the ground. While the horse scavenged the food he had dropped, Ben had an idea. He swung his rucksack across his shoulders and holstered his pistol. With a running start, he hopped onto Sleipnir's back. The horse neighed and bucked, but Ben held tightly onto the gelding's mane. The struggle lasted minutes, but those minutes felt like hours to Ben. Every buck was felt throughout his entire body, and he could already feel the bruises he'd have come morning. But he held tight, knowing the horse would give in. "It's for Rose," he kept telling the horse. "She's in danger, and I need your help finding her!" Eventually the horse was either too worn or finally understood what Ben was saying, and he accepted his new passenger. He kicked the horse in the side and nudged it to run forward. *Horseback is better than that rotting hunk of rubbish.* The boat would get him to Vänalleato, but not all the way into Ænæria. Besides, he could use the horse's company.

The ride for the rest of the night was painful and tiring, for it had been quite some time since Ben had last ridden bareback. They moved slowly through the thick woods before finally finding the road. Once Ben found the star leading north, he and his cousin's horse rode for hours toward Vänalleato. Sleipnir ran fast but grew too tired to continue once the moon sank into the horizon. They stopped by a stream to make camp, and Ben fed Sleipnir much of his remaining vegetables. The horse devoured them in minutes while Ben made a fire and warmed his own meal, thinking of the next day. By his estimates, he'd be able to make it to Vänalleato in fewer than two days now that he had a horse to ride. In the morning, Ben and Sleipnir continued to ride along the road, and soon the Vänalleato mountains were visible in the distance. They stopped as little as they could afford, most often to relieve themselves or whenever a patch of green grass appeared, though that was rare.

By midafternoon they took a break to find some water and stopped by a clearing in the forest. Ben tied Sleipnir to a tree as he looked for the stream he thought he'd heard. Just as he decided to turn back for fear of wandering too far, Ben suddenly spotted a hidden opening within the forest's depths. The scene was illuminated by the harsh day's sun without any trees to impede its reach. The field opened between the thick forest, riddled with flowers of all sorts of colors and scents. But the beauty ended there.

Horrified, Ben realized why the gap of trees before him existed. This was no natural field. The trees that had once stood there were in fact torn down for the nefarious sight in front of him. Wood was crudely chopped and shaped to form tall pillars intersected perpendicularly with long planks. The rotting corpses of the wastelanders who had attacked Freztad hung from the crosses scattered across the field. Flies buzzed around the bodies, and two ravens were perched atop the crosses furthest from Ben. Beneath the birds were the barely recognizable faces of Axe-Man and Beefy.

Ben examined the rest of the field. Twelve crosses stood, each suspending an invader at various states of decay. In the center was a thirteenth post standing four feet tall. Nailed to it was a rectangular wooden plaque that read:

sol invictus

His stomach churned, and he vomited where he stood until he was heaving, choking on the emptiness of his innards. The words before him almost made him feel even worse. His eyes were strained at the sign as he attempted to make sense of it. Who did this—who could have such blatant disregard for life to not only murder but to desecrate their remains? Ben spat at the ground, both from the taste of his sick and at the names of the culprits: *Randolph. Longinus. Julius.* The Ænærians had taken the wastelanders prisoner. It only made sense that they were the ones behind this atrocity. He had no way of knowing if Julius had been present at the crucifixions, but he somehow knew that the King would have condoned it. His only other question was the meaning of the words 'sol invictus.' It seemed to be another language, yet somehow familiar. They were the last things Longinus had said to Ben on the night of Rakshi's funeral.

Regardless, Ben now knew what kind of people he was dealing with. These people were sadistic butchers. He had seen them kill some of the attackers in Freztad, but he brushed that off as a necessity; they did it to save him and Rose. But when they took the prisoners with them, they simply disposed of them in the middle of the forest. These people took the time to cut down the trees, construct crosses, and hang them all. From the looks of it, they were left alive while crucified because he saw no mortal wounds on them. The only marks on their bodies were from the fight in Freztad, the ravens, and the nails piercing their wrists and ankles. The Ænærians were worse than the invaders responsible for Rakshi's death. *And they have Rose with them.*

"Oi! Who're you?" a voice called from the field of bodies. Ben shook with a fright. He looked around to see if one of the hanged men were alive and speaking to him.

"Well I'll be. Ol' Randolph said you'd come following, but Longs said you didn't have it in you," the voice said.

Ben turned around slowly, inching his right hand toward his concealed handgun.

In front of him was a scraggly looking man with a crazed smile aiming a small pistol at Ben's face. The stranger had long and unkempt hair that flew with the wind under his straw-colored hat. His eyes were red from the harsh sunlight. His nose appeared to be broken as it was crooked and facing the same way as his blowing hair. Upon a closer look Ben realized it was the Ænærian who had spoken out at Rakshi's funeral.

"But boy, am I glad he was wrong. I get to go back home now! Maybe I can see that pretty girl with the royal eyes...," Scraggles continued, muttering to himself.

Ben's attention shifted from the gun pointed at his forehead to what the crazed man said. *A girl with special eyes? He must be talking about Rose!*

"Where is she?" Ben yelled "If you people did anything to hurt her I, swear I'll—,"

The assailant pulled back the hammer on his pistol and said, "*Uh uh*, now don't you get a temper with me! Once I bring your cold body back to Gatron, I'll be in the King's good graces again!"

Scraggles laughed hysterically, his hand unsteady. Ben took the opportunity to whip out his own. Now, the two were pointing at each other's heads.

"*Nu uh*, I wouldn't be doing that if I was you!" Scraggles yelled. "Why don't you put that there gun down, so we can make this here situation easy."

"I'll put it down when I get answers!" Ben retorted. He noticed the man was trembling, clearly afraid. "Now tell me where she is!"

"Where who is? The girl with His Majesty's emerald eyes? Oh ho, I wouldn't know nothing about that. Legate gave me this here bruising jus' for looking at her," Scraggles said pointing at his broken nose. "Then they left me here as punishment for my 'outburst' at your little pagan ritual. If Fenwin were in charge, I wouldn't have been punished, but rewarded! Instead, I was told to wait here and see you if showed up, so I could bring your dead self with me!"

The man made his way closer to Ben. Panicking, Ben closed his eyes and pulled the trigger. He thought about his promise to Rakshi and wondered if he was breaking it if it meant he would be saving his own life. *Click.* The gun didn't fire. Ben once more felt like he was going to be sick when he realized what went wrong. He forgot to pull back the slide to load the bullet into its chamber.

Scraggles's eyes widened, and his trembling ceased. His crazed smile shrank away and, as it did, he took aim and fired his weapon.

Ben eyes squeezed tight. He heard the loud *BANG*. But he felt nothing and instead heard the stranger screaming and begging for mercy.

"*Ahh*! No—get off! *Arrgghh*! Help me! Please, help me! Get the *ack acgle* thing offa me!" he screamed, choking on his own blood.

Opening his eyes, Ben saw a most gruesome sight before him. On top of Scraggles was the large white wolf. Its enormous jaws were clenched around the man's throat. Blood splashed the wolf's cloud white coat. The wolf released its grip around the man's throat once he stopped screaming. His lifeless body lay limp as blood continued to flow from his neck. The wolf then turned its attention toward Ben. He was paralyzed with fear and couldn't bring himself to move the pistol's slide and hope to defend himself.

As it turned out, it wasn't needed. The wolf turned to its side and lifted something Ben never thought he'd see again: Rakshi's bow. It slowly walked toward Ben and dropped the bow by his feet. His eyes widened with disbelief as they moved back and forth between the bow and the dead scraggly man. He looked at the man with conflict and confusion. The man's death was not something he wanted to celebrate. Yet because of it, Ben was still alive. *What would Rakshi have thought of it? What about Rose?* The wolf's behavior was also something that puzzled him. It sat now, jaw open and tongue out as though it were smiling.

A thought popped in Ben's mind. He recalled each time he'd seen the wolf and the circumstances around those instances. First, when it attacked the deer, speeding up a potentially long hunt and allowing Ben and Rose to return to Freztad just in time to fend off the attackers. Then, once more when it had Sleipnir trapped, so Ben could break the horse and hurry his journey. Each time, the wolf stared at him as if in thought, but never once harmed him. Instead, it seemed as though it were communicating. "You want me to pick this up, don't you?"

The wolf barked as if in affirmation. Ben reached for his friend's bow and was surprised to find that it had no teeth marks; it was in the exact condition in which he had seen it last. As he examined the bow, the wolf came closer to him, slowly and hesitantly. Ben reached out and ungloved his hand before resting it on the large beast's head. It closed its eyes and groaned with approval as Ben pet it slowly and gently. He smiled and thanked any gods that may have been watching him for not having his hand bitten off. "Hey wolf, I'm on my way to save my cousin and could use some help. You wanna come with?"

The wolf howled with approval and wagged its tail back and forth.

"Great! Let's get going!" He turned toward where he had left Sleipnir, who he knew would have a fit when he saw the wolf again. Before he took a step forward, he looked once more at the bodies hanging from the carved wood and knew he couldn't leave them there. He sighed and placed his belongings on the ground. "There's just something I need to attend to first."

7.The Town of Elders

The settlement of Vänalleato bore absolutely no resemblance to Freztad. An outlander visiting the town for the first time would have no idea that they had been allies for nearly a century. Though Ben had traveled here before, he was still taken aback by the vast differences. The buildings and houses were made of red bricks from the clay by the riverbed. Vänalleato rested atop a rocky bluff that gradually climbed to a precipitous edge arching over a large lake fed by the Gjoll. The rough and uneven terrain required strategic land development. While scattered and unorganized in appearance, the small town was structurally sound.

Despite being considerably smaller in size, Vänalleato's population was nearly triple that of Freztad's. He recalled the last time he had visited the town as a kid, seeing children bustle across the town while their parents and older siblings tended to their shops. The town's Elders often communed at the central villa, discussing town matters and entertaining themselves with stories passed down by their ancestors. The livelihood of Vänalleato was both intriguing and unsettling to Ben. Ever since his first visit with Rose many years ago, he could never determine what had made it seem so different. He couldn't help feeling that Vänalleato was just *better*.

Even though the wolf had killed a man just yesterday, Ben felt oddly safe with its presence. It walked with a silent grace despite its massive size, and its cloud white coat shined from the sun's touch. He wondered if the wolf was somehow domesticated like horses and cattle. He supposed it was possible since Kabedge had told him stories about people in the Old Days keeping wolves in their houses not for hunting or protection, but as companions. The thought of having a new friend comforted him. Ben's only concern had been for his arrival in Vänalleato. He wondered if he would be able to convince his lupine companion to remain in the outskirts without causing any trouble. It was bad enough that it followed Sleipnir so closely, who was terrified and unsteady. At the onset of the trip, Ben worried that the horse would resort to bucking him off and high-tailing it back to Freztad. The steed continued to shift its gaze from the road to wolf, watching for any signs of danger. After an hour of riding and throwing insults at the horse for being such a coward, Ben finally won Sleipnir's full cooperation.

With the town finally in sight, Ben decided to try commanding the wolf to stay behind. "Look. *Uh*. Wolf. You need to wait here. So, *uh*...stay there, boy...or girl? Come to think of it, I don't even know *what* you are." Sure enough, the great beast ceased following the Freztadian pair and, with a whimper, returned to the forest. Ben and

Sleipnir trotted toward the cliff-sitting town, climbing the steady hill toward the town's gate. As they approached the entrance, Ben could hear the hunter flies buzzing all around him. Generations ago, it was Vänalleato that had first given Freztad the idea to raise the vibrant insects. They had raised hunter flies for so long that their lake was nearly devoid of any blood bug eggs. Any occasional outbreaks were dealt with by the buzzing hunter flies within nearly a week's time. As he thought about it, Ben wondered how there could have been an outbreak that killed so many people ten years ago. What change could there have been?

When he had arrived at the gate, Ben called out for a guard's attention. "Hello? I'm a Freztadian traveler on urgent business. Is there any way someone can let me in?"

A dark-skinned boy with fair hair, likely three or four years younger than Ben, peered down from the balcony at the gate's central tower. He gave a frustrated look, as if he had something better to do than his job, and said, "What kind of business d'you want with us? We ain't got time for visitors, and there ain't no trade caravan expected for another week!" He then disappeared from Ben's view.

Aggravated by the boy's rudeness, Ben yelled up to the boy once more. "I don't think you heard me right—I'm from Freztad. We've had an emergency, and I need to be let in!"

The fair-haired boy let out a loud and exaggerated sigh from wherever he was hiding. He once more came into Ben's view and said, "No, I don't think *you* heard me right. I said very clearly, 'we ain't got time for visitors' and we wasn't expecting no one. Now bugger off!" He turned from the balcony and once again retreated from sight.

Ben's heart thumped like a drum, pumping fury through his veins. Before he could get too carried away, he needed to think of a way to get the brat to listen. He yelled up toward the balcony and said, "Listen, kid! You're going to let me in, and you're going to do it *now*. My name is Ben Limmetrad, my cousin is the chief of Freztad, and if she finds out you won't cooperate, then she'll make sure the next caravan arrives 'missing' its shipment and a nice description of the fool responsible. I'm sure your town will *love* you once they find out it's your fault that they'll all starve!" He was bluffing, of course, but he could tell that any threats of public humiliation wouldn't sit well with an arrogant kid like this one.

There was a brief moment of silence before Ben heard a response, though it wasn't from the impudent boy. A deep, gruff voice from beyond the gate bellowed, "FELIX! What in the name of the Ascendants are you doing? Let the man in!"

While Ben couldn't see it, he heard what sounded like a startled jump followed by a crash up beyond the balcony. The boy didn't reappear, but a metallic grating sound came from beyond the wall, and the great wooden gate ascended. Behind it stood a large, middle aged man with a bushy reddish beard and long, tied back blonde hair.

"Sorry about my son up there," the man said. "Boy has always been poor with discipline ever since the day he showed up here one day as a kid. I've been trying to get him to show some responsibility around the town lately, but Ascendants forbid he ever put any effort into anything."

"Wulkan! You told me not to let anyone in since Master Sieg—"

"That's enough of you, boy, now get back to your post, and do your job," the man said. "Sorry again about him. As you heard, my name's Wulkan! I'm the blacksmith here," he said, reaching out his arm to clasp forearms.

"I'm Ben Limmetrad. I've come from Freztad."

"Limmetrad, *eh*? I didn't know Chief Lydia had a son. Haven't been down to Freztad since the plague, but you look far older than that."

"I'm not her son. She's my aunt," Ben answered bitterly. "And she's not chief anymore. Her daughter Rose is."

"Oh my. Shows how much I know about politics." He gave off a hefty laugh. "What brings you to humble Vänalleato, Master Limmetrad?"

"He says he's here on 'urgent business,' but he didn't bother to say what it was!" Felix shouted down to his father, once again neglecting his job.

"FELIX," Wulkan's gruff voice thundered, "I swear by the Ascendants, I won't let you enter the swim if you keep this up!"

"But, Wulkan! Arynn will be there! I wanted to impress her with my flawless form," he said flexing his muscles and pantomiming a breaststroke, "If she isn't betrothed yet, I—"

"If you keep talking, you won't be doing *anything* to impress her," Wulkan hollered.

Defeated, Felix finally shut his mouth and turned from the tower's inner balcony. Wulkan looked up to the cloudy sky and let out a deep sigh. "Anyway, you were telling me why you traveled all this way?"

Ben explained his situation to the blacksmith. He told Wulkan about how his village was attacked and how one of their people had been abducted. He withheld the fact that his village's leader was the one who had been taken. He then continued to explain that he had a lead on the kidnappers and needed someone to help interpret his map.

Nodding sympathetically, Wulkan stroked his beard in thought. "Well, our cartographer is out of town right now, but that's his shop over there." He pointed to a shack around the corner. "Think he was hired a few days back on a charting job. His daughter, Arynn, is still in the town, but I'm not sure where she is. You might want to look around. Can't miss her. She's about your age and has bright red hair."

Ben thanked the blacksmith and asked where he could hitch Sleipnir to allow him to rest. Wulkan directed Ben to a stable farther up the bluff where he could board Sleipnir for free if he purchased a night at the adjacent inn. He decided it would be a good idea to stay in the town for the night. He wasn't sure how long it would take to get his map deciphered, and he was quite tired from the poor sleep he had had on his trip so far.

Wulkan said his farewell and made his way to the forge. Finally making his way to the stable on the hilltop, Ben looked around the town in the hopes of spotting a red-haired woman. He didn't think she'd be too hard to pick out. Most of the townspeople were rather fair of skin and hair, though none had red hair.

Ben could tell that he had made the right decision about spending the night when he realized how drained Sleipnir was. The horse didn't so much as buck at the stable keeper once and only snorted at him every *other* second. He lapped up the water in his stall and devoured his feed shortly before lying down to rest. Ben was jealous of the horse, tired from his journey and recent lack of sleep. *Not yet*, he told himself. After taking care of boarding Sleipnir, Ben went next door to the inn. It was a small, cobbled building with glass windows and a single story. Since Vänalleato rarely had visitors, the inn was more like the innkeeper's home with four extra rooms that she and her husband rented out a few times per year. Payment wasn't much, only about twenty-five seeds. Oddly, the innkeeper said that she also accepted 'sols,' but Ben hadn't a clue what that meant.

The sky was leaden and overcast as Ben explored the small town searching for the girl named Arynn. He strolled down the street, trying to remember where Wulkan said her father's cartography shop was located. As he made his way down the hill, three young children dashed across his path, shouting and snickering. Two little girls lagged behind the third child, a boy gasping for air with a terrified look on his face. Ben smiled at the playful children kicking up dirt and wailing in the distance. Watching the kids play reminded him of his childhood with Rose before she took over for her mother. Before all the other children had died.

Gusts of wind roared throughout the town, and most of the its people made their way inside, anticipating a coming storm. Ben grew concerned about everyone going indoors because he still hadn't caught a glimpse of Arynn. He couldn't afford to stay in Vänalleato for another day, but he also knew he couldn't leave without someone to interpret his map. He simply had to hope that Arynn would be in her father's shop. Ben made his way in the direction Wulkan had pointed toward earlier. He wasn't sure how he'd know which building belonged to the cartographer until he saw a hut at the end of the trail with a wooden board above the door displaying a compass overtop a sailboat.

He entered a room filled with strange instruments neatly

arranged on shelves lining the walls. In places without shelves, there were framed maps, each one as unique as the next but all in the same script. Some of the framed images confused Ben because they didn't look anything like maps. There were no bodies of water or landmarks but instead series of dots and lines with names scattered all around. He saw words like *Sirius* and *Polaris*, but just like the 'sols' the innkeeper mentioned, Ben had no idea what they meant. Looking up, Ben saw dangling ornaments, all of which were spherical in shape but varied in size.

Much to his dismay, there didn't appear to be anyone else in the building. A loud and mighty thunder clap shook the instruments on the shelves and the ornaments above him. Rain poured and pattered against the roof and echoed throughout the shop. Not ready to give up and run through the storm to his room, Ben decided to wait a bit longer. He went to the nearest shelf and picked up one of the instruments. It had a semi-circular frame attached to an arm with other small parts and two eyepieces, one of which looked like a telescope. Fidgeting with the instrument's pieces, and looking through the eyepieces, Ben contemplated the tool's purpose.

"What are you doing? Put that down!" a voice yelled over the rain from the door. Startled, Ben jumped and fumbled the instrument, nearly dropping it. He put it back on the shelf and looked over to the door way. There she stood, a hardy looking young woman in a drenched gray tunic with sopping curly and braided red hair. Arynn looked so angry that Ben could have sworn the water was steaming.

"I asked you what you're doing here!" she yelled again, arms crossed.

Flustered, Ben struggled to get out any words. His cheeks burned bright red, embarrassed being caught in the empty shop and playing with the tools. Especially in front of the owner's daughter, who looked like she was ready to kill him.

"Oh. *Um* hi, I'm Ben. You must be Arynn! I was wondering if—"

"I didn't ask for your name, now get out of my father's shop!" she yelled.

"What is it with people in this town interrupting me all the time! I just need help reading a map! This *is* the cartographer's shop, right?"

Arynn maintained her spiteful glare at Ben. "He isn't here. So leave," she said, uncrossing her arms and gesturing toward the door.

Ben picked up a hint of unease in her voice when she told him that her father wasn't there. Unwilling to have made this trip all for nothing, he refused to budge. "Your dad is out on a job, right? I've got time. I'll wait here, thanks."

Her brows furrowed, and she said, "This isn't a debate. With my father out of town, I'm in charge of the store—"

"Oh, then *you* can help me! So I've got this map, but I'm not too sure about its accuracy."

Arynn groaned and wrung out her hair by Ben's feet. "Fine! Do you have it with you?"

Ben handed the map to Arynn. She took a few moments to analyze it and then asked, "This map is severely dated. You have a bunch of circles and X's. What do they mean? Which is your destination? Some of them might be submerged by now."

Checking his father's watch—which he now wore on his wrist—to make sure he had the numbers correct, Ben traced his finger over the lines on the map to the correct location: 78 vertical, 15 horizontal. "This is the spot. What makes you think it's submerged?"

"You really don't know much, do you? Lots of coasts from the Old Days are underwater now. Islands, too. Judging by the scale of this map, this place looks like an island—a big one, though. But there are plenty of other things to factor into it such as elevation and time of the year. If it's really high up, you'll probably be fine."

"What caused places to go under water?" Ben asked, confused.

"In case you can't tell, I'm your age and wasn't around hundreds of years ago," she said facetiously.

Unsatisfied, Ben changed the subject back to the matter at hand. "So, you can read the map, right?"

"I can. I know where we are and the best route to get to where you want to go."

Ben realized where she was going with this. "But you're not going to tell me without something in return. Does it have to do with your father?"

Arynn's gaze shifted from Ben, and she suddenly became very interested in the floor. "Yeah. He left well over a week ago. The job he was on should've only taken four days at most...."

"Was he traveling alone? Is it possible that weather would've been a problem? Is there anything that makes you so suspicious that something is wrong? Maybe the job just took longer than anticipated."

"Stop, stop! One question at a time, sheesh!"

The color faded from Ben's face, and his stomach swirled with unease as he looked away from her. Before he could respond, Arynn spoke up again. "We've heard strange, loud noises coming from the forests lately. I warned him not to go; I told him it might be dangerous."

"Why haven't you or anyone else gone to look for him?" Ben asked.

Arynn rolled her eyes. "Because of those noises. The town's Elders don't think it's safe out there, and they've made it very clear that they don't want anyone to leave. They can't force us to stay, but most of the townspeople are too scared to go anywhere. They think my father got what he deserved for ignoring the Elders' counsel."

Another clap of thunder struck, and the rain continued to pour heavily. "Did some of the noises sound like that?" Ben asked.

Arynn paused and thought about the sound. "Yes, a little bit—but it wasn't thunder! This is the first storm we've had in weeks. But the sounds boomed like that, and there were a lot of them."

"I believe you. I think I know what the sounds were. Freztad—my home—was attacked recently. The attackers were defeated by these other guys using these sun-powered carriages and tools similar to a bow—guns," Ben explained.

"Are you saying the people making those sounds are good?" Arynn asked with a glimmer of hope in her eyes.

Ben wasn't keen on disappointing her but didn't want to lie either. "No, I really doubt it. They acted nice to us and all, but they had a hidden agenda. Their leader took my cousin." Ben went on to explain everything to Arynn. Everything from mustached Randy, the talk with his aunt, and Kabedge revealing the identity of King Xander as his own uncle, Julius. The forest crucifixions, which still made him uneasy as he thought to himself taking down each of the hanging bodies and burying them before completing his trip to Vänalleato. He even shared details he didn't think were all that important or relevant. The only things he left out were anything about the wolf and the story of the Vault. He really enjoyed talking with Arynn, finding it comforting to talk about everything he had been through with a complete stranger. It felt even better to get it all out with someone his age who was going through something similar.

"If I go out there to look for your dad and bring him back, will you two help me navigate my way north?" Ben asked. He was nearly positive the slaver activity was related to reason the Elders placed Vänalleato on lockdown was related to the Ænærians. Investigating the sounds Arynn spoke of could prove invaluable, though he didn't say any of this aloud. He didn't want Arynn to think he wanted her dad to be in danger. He didn't want that, but he *did* want to learn more about Julius and the Ænærians.

"Yes, fine—but I'm coming with you!"

Ben frowned. "If I'm right about these guys out there, then it could be really dangerous. I don't think it'd be safe for you."

Arynn shook her head. "What's that supposed to mean? It's not safe for me because I'm a girl?" She scoffed angrily. "You're just like the Elders!"

Ben took a step back and threw his hands up in defense. "What? No! That's not what I mean! I just wouldn't want you to get hurt out there. These guys are no joke, and I've heard you've had raiders and bandits around here a lot lately. Besides, I thought you were asking for my help since you couldn't leave the town."

She sighed, slumping her shoulders and playing with her hair. "Well, there's a curfew, too. For women, anyway. When the Elders announced the lockdown, the Grand Elder himself set extra restrictions for women. He said we can't be out of the town past sunset without male supervision under any circumstances. That law *does* get enforced."

"Oh," Ben said gently. He knew Vänalleato was different from Freztad but hadn't realized its laws were so strange. "Why do the men and women get treated so differently here?"

She sighed, and her eyes dropped to the floor. "The Elders do treat us differently in many ways, but this rule actually has nothing to do with that. It's because my friend Sera went missing two years ago. The Elders thought she ran away, but I would have known if she had. Then, when more people started disappearing, the Elders thought it had to do with the bandit and slaver activity. They're worried women are more vulnerable out there alone and more likely to be taken. I just," her voice cracked, and Ben could see tears welling up in her eyes. "I don't want that to happen to my dad, too."

Ben looked at Arynn sympathetically and made up his mind. He would let her come with him, because he understood exactly how she felt. "I guess I'll need your navigational skills after all."

Arynn nodded her head and smiled.

The storm continued for the next few hours, and the rain was too heavy for Ben to go searching for Arynn's father. The visibility was poor and the mud too dangerous for Sleipnir. Instead, Ben spent his time getting to know Arynn. As her hair dried and she gave him fewer glares, Ben noticed how attractive she was. Her long red hair was complemented by her bright blue eyes. Her eyes glimmered while her cheeks dimpled with every smile or laugh in their conversation. When she talked about the tools and instruments in the shop, Ben saw her passion for navigation and exploration. He was quite jealous about how much Arynn knew about the past and the world beyond their borders. He never knew how big the world was or what happened in the Old Days—aside from what Kabedge exaggerated, of course.

By the time they finally got to the subject of the Old Days, the thunder had stopped, and the rain settled. Despite how much he enjoyed his time with Arynn, Ben decided it would be better to leave and search for her father.

"We'll take two of the town's horses," Arynn suggested. "They don't get out enough these days, anyway."

The pair mounted up and proceeded downhill toward the town gate. Felix didn't dare offer any sass about opening the gate. Ben figured that it was because he was riding with Felix's crush and that forming proper sentences in front of her would probably prove too difficult. With Ben's horse following Arynn's as they left Vänalleato, Ben turned around to look up at Felix and, upon doing so, stuck his tongue out at him. Felix looked like he wanted to retort but was too afraid to do so in front of Arynn.

It was nearly nightfall by the time Ben and Arynn found a fresh trace of her father. They found a campsite with recent holes in the ground, presumably from tent spikes. There were enough holes to account for four tents. "Was your dad traveling with this many people?" he asked Arynn. She shook her head nervously.

"No, he went along with his two clients; a man and woman— they're nomads, they said. They should've only brought one or two tents. There's no way they'd need four," Arynn said.

Ben continued to search for more clues. He didn't see any signs of a struggle, but all of the footprints were distorted by the storm, and he couldn't determine how many people had been there. He did, however, pick out prints that were by no means human. The hoof prints led him a few yards from the campsite to his next clue. He discovered tracks that seemed to belong to a regular carriage rather than the kind Randy's people used. The tracks seemed to go as far as he could see thanks to the mud from the recent storm. He and Arynn mounted their horses and followed the fresh trail that led toward a mountain range in the distance.

Part of Ben was glad to discover he wasn't dealing with Ænærians, but another part of him was disappointed. On the one hand, he and Arynn probably had a better chance of dealing with these people. There didn't seem to be too many of them and, so far, there was no indication of hostility. On the other hand, Ben wanted a sign that he was truly on the right track. He really hoped that he and Julius were heading toward the same place and that Rose was with him. So far, he had no sign of this. For all he knew, he was no closer to finding his cousin than when he had started his journey.

The sun was finally down when the pair saw a roaring campfire glowing from a cave at the base of the nearest mountain. Outside of the cave stood a regular wooden carriage without a horse tied to it. The mud was too messy for Ben to see where the hooves led, but it seemed as though most of the footprints made their way toward the small mouth at the foot of the crag. Slurred words and garbled laughter echoed through the cave from its occupants. *Looks like we found them. I sure hope they're friendly.* Ben wished he had asked Wulkan to fix his sword's broken blade because he wasn't sure how much use it would be in a fight. The bow wasn't a great weapon in close quarters. He could resort to using the gun that the Ænærians had given him, but he didn't imagine it would be exactly pleasant on his ears when fired in an enclosed space. He also wished the wolf had followed them here, too. Sure, it probably would have horrified Arynn, but it would've likely been a huge help right about now.

The two dismounted their horses and hitched them to a small tree. They slowly approached the cave entrance and listened to its occupants in an effort to get an idea of what they were up against.

"Sho, I heard dat they're on some kinda...uh...ex-expedition right now! Makes you *really* wonder—hic!—what they're after, you know?" one of the cave's occupants said. An older male by the sound of it.

"I could care less 'bout those damn Ænærians! Did you hear what they did to Frohnz's gang? Tore 'em to shreds with their crazy sun magic in one of them settlements on the river. Shoot, if they didn't pay so well for fresh meat, I wouldn't put up with them..." another male cave-dweller said.

Ben's heart skipped a beat at the mention of a river settlement and sun magic. *Could he be talking about Freztad?* he wondered.

"I co-concur—hic!—with you on that one. Shay, Dyl, you got any more mead? I'm fr-fresh out," the first man said, giggling and hiccupping at the same time.

"Silas, I think you've had enough. Drink some water and sober up. You have to keep watch at *some point* tonight, y'know?" This time the voice belonged to a woman.

"Aww, Arma, c'mon! Lighten up—come tomorrow we'll be rich with this here sh-shipment! Let's ce-celebrate now before we get back home!" the drunk man said.

"Arma's right, Silas," the first man, Dyl, said. "You're on second watch, and I don't intend on staying up for you, nor do I want your drunken-self watching my back. Like I said, those Ænærians turned their back on Frohnz's group in the blink of an eye after hiring them. For all we know, they already know where we are, and they're coming to collect and have no intention of paying out corpses."

The Ænærians hired the group to attack us? I shouldn't be surprised.

"*Agh,* y'all are no fun!" Silas said. "Fine! I'll—*hic*—get some water. Hey, what're you lookin' at baldy? You want some wa-water? Here you go!" He laughed hysterically after the sound of pouring liquid.

"Silas! Stop tormenting the prisoners and wasting water, you idiot!" the woman, Arma, said.

"Ben," Arynn whispered. "My dad is bald! These people are slavers—that's what they meant by having a shipment of fresh meat! Let's go in there, kill them, and get him back!"

"*Shh!* We don't want them to hear us, Arynn. And no killing! Got it?" Arynn rolled her eyes but nodded. "Just give me another minute to come up with a plan," whispered Ben. "I want to make sure there isn't a fourth one with them. If they're slavers, then I doubt they had a tent set up for your dad and the others."

Arynn looked at Ben furiously, as if she couldn't believe what she was hearing. Despite this, she listened and stayed quiet while Ben thought and listened.

"Did you hear that?" Dyl said.

"It's probably just Ming on her way back," Arma said. "She better have food with her."

That was what Ben was waiting to hear. There *was* a fourth with them. A woman. *She must have the horse,* he thought to himself. He now had the last part of his plan. He handed Rakshi's bow and his quiver to Arynn, who seemed confident in how to use it. Ben quietly explained his plan to her. After he made her repeat the plan to him, the two quietly walked their horses farther from the cave before returning on foot. All they needed to do now was wait.

Nearly a quarter of an hour later, the splashing sound of a horse's hooves in the mud approached the lit cave. A woman with pitch black hair tied in a short braid and a green bandana arrived on the back of a brown mare with three rabbits and a gopher hanging from its side. Ming brought the horse to the carriage outside the cave and dismounted. She tied the horse to the back of the carriage and threw some straw on the ground for it to sleep on. As she walked passed the wooden cart toward the cave, Ben crawled out from underneath and snuck up behind Ming. He covered her mouth with one hand and pressed his gun's muzzle against her temple.

"Don't say anything, and don't struggle," Ben said, trying not to sound nervous. "You're surrounded. If you fight back, you'll be shot." Ben made a clicking sound, signaling Arynn. An arrow flew from seemingly nowhere and landed right in front of Ming's feet.

"Now, listen to me: I'm going to let go of you, and I want you to drop all your weapons. I'll start by taking these," Ben said as he moved his hand from Ming's mouth and removed the arrows from her quiver and dropped them to the ground. Ming remained silent as she slowly pulled out her knife and dropped it.

"Good. Thank you. Now to business. Your people have some friends of ours. We're proposing a trade. We'll let you go free, unharmed, if you give them back to us. I think you'll find that to be more than generous," Ben said, trying to sound as confident as possible. It took everything he had to stop his hand from trembling and showing Ming how absolutely terrified he was.

"They won't make the trade," Ming said. "We aren't friends— we're partners. We see everyone as sols, including each other. The three that we picked up are worth much more than one." There was that word again: 'sols.' He still didn't know what it meant. To add to Ben's discomfort and confusion, Ming's calm tone of voice completely unnerved him. He wasn't expecting this. He didn't think anyone could be so cold as to cast away their companions. Then he remembered how Scraggles was completely abandoned by his people for simply *looking* at Rose the wrong way. He shuddered to think about how they treated their enemies when the image of hanging bodies in the forest clearing came back to haunt him.

"Maybe they won't. But when their lives are on the line too, I'm sure they'll change their mind," Ben said. "Let's get to trading, shall we?" He directed Ming toward the cave's entrance, gun aimed at the back of her head. He was happy she couldn't tell that his finger was nowhere near the trigger.

The thin tunneled entrance led to a large cavern riddled with stalagmites and small rodent bones on the cave's floor. A stream seemed to flow through the cavern because Ben could hear the muffled sound of flowing water. He also felt the occasional drip from the stalactites hanging above, seemingly threatening to impale him.

The three slavers Ben had overheard from outside were lounging around a small fire. One of the men had long, frizzy facial hair extending from his high cheekbones down to his chest. His hair was long, dark, and braided, and touched the ground from where he was sitting. The other man, whom Ben figured was Silas, had bloodshot and sunken eyes with stains of mead splattered all over his tunic. He too wore a long braid and a beard, but his facial hair grew more or less in patches and didn't extend far past his chin. The woman, Arma, had a complexion far darker than the others. She had no hair aside from a long braid that matched her comrades—and her braid was far longer.

At far end of the cavern was a large, iron cage containing three people crammed together. Two of them, a man and woman a few years older than Ben, were huddled next to each other. The third was a sallow looking man with a fully bald head and a dark red face. The young couple didn't seem to notice Ben entering the cave as they were too focused on each other and were seemingly on the brink of tears. Arynn's father, however, noticed Ben the moment he entered the cavern. Unfortunately for Ben, so did Silas.

"Oi—Ming's back! So did you—*hic*—bring some meat? My belly's got a hankering for so-somethin' to soak up all this mead!" Silas struggled to say before he noticed the tall stranger lurking behind his acquaintance. "*Eh*? What's this? HEY! WHAT'S GOING ON HERE?"

Arma and Dyl, originally paying no mind to Silas's nonsense, were alerted by his yelling. They turned their heads toward Ben's direction and quickly jumped to their feet at the sight of their partner with a gun to her head. Dyl was armed with a hatchet in each hand, and Arma held a crossbow, aimed toward Ben and Ming. Silas was still on the ground, crying about the mead he had spilled when he jumped at the sight of Ben.

"Who're you and what d'you think you're doing with our friend there?" Dyl snarled.

"Friend?" Ben asked. "See, Ming here told me she was your partner—not your friend. Glad to see she was mistaken. I'd like to make a trade with all of you. I'll give you back your friend, unharmed, in exchange for those people you have caged up over there."

"Three for one?" Arma said, inching closer to Ben. "That's no trade. Hell, I doubt that gun you got there is even loaded. They rarely are these days."

A deafening explosion rang through the cavern causing the prisoners and slavers to each cover their ears. Several stalactites fell and crumbled on the ground next to the wall that was shot. Ben suffered through the pain, knowing he couldn't drop his guard. He really didn't want to fire his pistol in the cave because he knew how terrible the echo would be. But he didn't have the patience to argue in circles with these people. He had to prove that his gun was indeed loaded and that he was willing to fire it.

"Well, there you have it—it's loaded," Ben said when the ringing stopped. "Where were we? Ah, yes, I believe I was asking for all three of those people."

"How about we make another sort of deal. We'll give you one of 'em in exchange for Ming. That's the best offer you're gonna get, kid. In case you haven't noticed, you're a bit outnumbered here," Dyl threatened.

"Am I outnumbered? Ming here can tell you that I'm not alone, can't you?" Ben said, pressing the pistol a bit harder against her head.

"He's bluffing. I don't know what he's talking about. Just kill him already! The three of you can take him! He's scared, I felt him trembling the second he laid his hands on me!" Ming yelled.

Ben wanted to shut her up somehow, but he didn't want to look like he had lost his composure. He couldn't show any signs of weakness against these people. Instead, he feigned a smile. "She's got a bit of a mouth on her, doesn't she? Believe what you want, but I'm not alone, and a fight against me won't go down as easily as you think. Back to business now. All three of them and my people and I don't hurt you."

Unfortunately for Ben, he wasn't convincing nor threatening enough. Dyl pulled back his left hand and prepared to throw his hatchet. Realizing what Dyl was doing a split-second before he did it, Ben leapt out of the way and dove to the ground just as the axe spiraled through the empty space that Ben's body had just occupied. Off balance from Ben abruptly letting go of her, Ming wobbled and happened to be in the wrong place at the wrong time. The blade of her partner's hatchet landed just above her left breast. She screamed in agony as she fell to the ground, blood spilling out of her side.

Dyl readied himself to throw his second hatchet, but this time Ben was more than ready. As soon as he landed, Ben took aim at Dyl's right kneecap. When Dyl was ready to throw the hatchet, Ben pulled the trigger once more. Dyl dropped his weapon and joined Ming's screaming. His legs buckled as his right knee was reduced to nothing but a mess of torn tissue and pouring blood.

Ben's gaze now shifted toward Arma, who was ready to shoot her crossbow.

"I heard shots and screams and came as fast as I could! Are you— drop it!" Arynn exhaled, rushing into the cave. When she saw the crossbow aimed at Ben, Arynn pulled back Rakshi's bow and aimed it towards Arma's head. This gave Ben time point his pistol at Arma as well. Acknowledging defeat, Arma dropped the weapon and put her hands in the air.

As Ben rose to his feet, he resumed pointing his pistol toward Arma. "Thanks, Arynn. Go free your dad and the others. I'll keep a watch on her...and the guy crying on the floor over there." Arynn nodded and rushed over to the iron cage, opening the lock with the key that lay on the ground a few feet away from it.

As Arynn freed her father and the couple, Ben focused his attention on the four slavers. He made eye contact with Arma and said, "Get your drunken friend—I mean partner—up from the floor and bring him closer so I can have an eye on all four of you." Arma complied and smacked Silas across each cheek to get him off the ground and closer to Ben. Looking down in front of him and then up again toward Arma, he said, "Do you have any bandages or anything to stop the bleeding?"

Arma nodded slowly, staring at the blood flowing out of Ming's still body.

"Get them quickly! If you can promise me that Mead Stain over there stays still, I'll help you get this hatchet out of her while you put them on and apply pressure."

Arma darted toward a large rucksack against the cavern wall and returned with an armful of bandages. She told Silas not to move and to stop crying over his stupid drink.

"Okay, I'm going to pull this thing out, but as soon as I do, you need to put a thick dressing over it and push as hard as you can. Keep it even, and don't stop until we can wrap another bandage around her body. Got it?" Ben said to Arma.

Again, Arma nodded. She looked confused but didn't say anything. Ben knew it must have seemed odd to Arma that Ben came in threatening to kill Ming one minute but was working to save her life the next. He never planned on hurting her in the first place, and he felt he was to blame for her situation. Ben didn't want to let someone die if he could help it—especially if he was partially responsible.

"Ben, we're all set. Let's get out of here," Arynn said as she walked back toward Ben, followed by her father and the young couple. "Ben? What are you—watch out!" Arynn yelled.

It was too late. Just as Ben removed the hatchet from Ming's side, Silas hurdled over her body and tackled him. Ben jabbed and kicked at the enraged slaver to no avail. He could hear screams from the background, but Ben wasn't sure who they were from. Silas's fists repeatedly collided with Ben's face, sparking spots of black and white until he could no longer feel the pain. He heard a loud bang that reverberated throughout the cavern. It was followed by a thick crumbling noise and a pulsating sensation from the ground. In the midst of the chaotic noises, he thought he heard someone calling his name. He tried to look for who it was and answer them, but he instead found himself surrounded in a dark, thick fog. He could barely think, much less figure out what was happening. When the voice stopped calling his name, Ben felt his body being dragged across the stony floor, tearing his shirt and shredding his back. As he was being dragged, he occasionally opened his eyes and could have sworn he saw the night sky collapse on top of him.

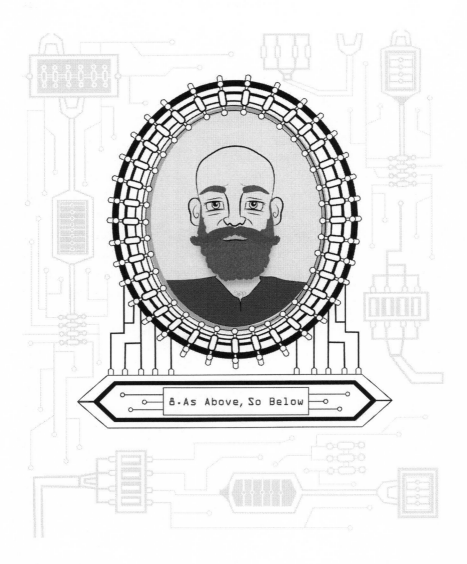

8. As Above, So Below

B en woke up in a stupor, unable to recognize his surroundings. He looked around in a daze and was bewildered by his surroundings. It took a few seconds to come out of his trance and reorient himself. The blue sheet over top of him and the window overlooking the shining clear lake reminded him of his room in Vänalleato. *How did I get here?* The last thing Ben remembered was being dragged by his legs out of the collapsing cave at night. He looked outside again to see neither darkness nor a rising sun, but the maroon and violet of the dusk sky. Worry set in, and Ben panicked that he had been unconscious for far too long. He quickly sat up and tried to stand, only to have his vision go black and fall right into bed. His stomach gurgled, and he realized he must have not eaten in over a day. Not only that, but his head was throbbing and felt like someone was pounding it with a mallet like a piece of meat.

Sitting up, slowly this time, Ben felt his head and realized there were bandages over it. He patted other parts of his head and his face to see if he could find where the injuries were. The back of his head hurt somewhat, and he vaguely remembered bumping it a few times while being dragged. What really hurt were his cheekbones and nose. There were no bandages over these, but they were tender to the touch. He felt a sharp shock of pain when he felt his nose and let out a yelp of pain. Hands shaking from the flare up of pain, he slowly and much more gently felt the outline of his nose again. It seemed prop-erly aligned, but it was obviously swollen. He figured his nose must be broken, but someone put it back in place for him. He then remem-bered the drunken slaver who pounced on atop him from nowhere and wailed on him just as he removed the axe from Ming's body. *What in the world happened back there?*

Ben heard a soft knock at the door. "Come in," he said weakly to whomever was at the door.

Behind the door was Arynn and the old innkeeper carrying a metal tray with two teapots and cups. The innkeeper placed the tray on the end table and smiled at Ben saying, "Here you are, dear. Make sure you drink up. This one will help with the pain," she pointed at the pot closest to him and then to the one further away saying, "and this one is for your poor nose and cheeks. Careful though, they're hot." She smiled again and turned to look up at Arynn. "Will you be needing anything else? I can fetch one of the Elders if you need."

Arynn shook her head and smiled at the innkeeper saying, "I will let you know if we need anything. Thank you, Genevieve."

The old woman nodded and offered a small bow to which Arynn reciprocated. The innkeeper left the room and kept the door slightly ajar. Arynn pulled a chair closer to the bed and sat down. She poured a cup from the farthest tea pot. "You'll need to sit up if you want to drink any, you know. Wouldn't want you to spill and have to treat burns, too."

Ben could not help but feel a tad uncomfortable, lying there next to Arynn. As she helped Ben drink the tea, he thought about how he never really got past the whole 'feeling awkward around girls because they're different' phase. *Rose is a girl, sure, but she's different. Well, different in a different way than most girls are. She's a different kind of different,* he thought. Ben was not sure how to rationalize it any better than that, even to himself. He never thought it was much of a problem, considering the only times he had interacted with others his age were at occasional Penteric Alliance's celebrations. In fact, it was at one of those when he first noticed girls his own age and became self-conscious. He could never explain what he felt properly, and he was too embarrassed to talk about it with anyone other than Rose. But even Rose couldn't understand the feelings Ben told her about. Here he was, barely sixteen years old, on a journey across the world to find his missing cousin, and despite having faced armed attackers and savage slavers, he was *still* afraid of talking to girls.

"Will you sit up properly and hold the tea yourself? I *do* have other things to do today," Arynn said with a halfhearted frown that seemed to imply she did not really want to do those other things.

"I...*um*...okay, sure. Sorry," Ben stammered.

The tea was surprisingly sweet and probably would have smelled quite fragrant if his nose weren't so swollen. Next to him, Arynn poured a cup of the other tea and drank it herself. He wasn't sure why she was drinking the pain tonic until he noticed the heavy bruising on her right shoulder and various cuts and welts on her hands. Her hands shook a tad as she brought the tea to her lips.

After taking a few more sips, Ben put the cup back down on the end table and asked Arynn about what had happened in the cave. As Ben suspected, he had gone in and out of consciousness thanks to the beating Silas had given him. To his surprise, it was Arma who threw the assailant off of him, not Arynn. Arma and Silas struggled with one another as the latter reached for Ben's gun. According to Arynn, Silas's finger must've slipped, and he fired the pistol straight into the ceiling. The young couple made a run for the exit as Arynn's father subdued Silas and knocked the gun from his hand. The bullet's impact was enough to breach through the stony roof revealing the stream held above. The water came rushing through the hole and broke it open wider and wider until the cavern began to implode. At that point, Arynn gave up on trying to wake Ben and dragged him by his feet out of the cavern as fast as she could, only barely making it out in time after her father and Arma. Silas and Dyl weren't so lucky.

"What happened to Arma?" Ben asked.

"She's being held in the rear tower while the Elders and Grand Elder figure out what to do with her. Even though she kidnapped my father, he's advocating for her release. He says she redeemed herself by trying to save you when that guy attacked you. If you ask me, I think he's being *way* too forgiving," Arynn said. "Not that I'm not glad she saved you, of course," she quickly added.

"What do the Elders need to discuss? They're not going to release her, are they? She's a slaver working with the Ænærians!"

"She needs to rot in a cell. I bet it was people like her to took Sera away. The rest of them got what they deserved and so should she," Arynn said, gritting her teeth.

Ben sipped his tea. He didn't know how to respond. Of course she was upset about her friend. It's the same way Ben felt about Rose and Rakshi—and the Ænærians who took them from him.

"In the meantime, they need to contemplate the will of the Ascendants to figure out what to do with her."

Ben rolled his eyes as he took another sip of tea. Arynn jabbed Ben in the shoulder. Not hard enough to really hurt him, but with enough force that he nearly spilled the hot tea all over him. "Hey! What was that for?" he yelled.

"You rolled your eyes. Why?"

Good going, Ben. Now you've offended her. His blatant disregard for belief in the supernatural was well tolerated in Freztad, where many shared his disbelief. Those who did have something to worship ignored Ben's godlessness because he was the only person who would ever bring the deceased's ashes to the Gjoll. Spending his whole life in Freztad made him forget that others were not so tolerant. "I'm sorry. We don't base decisions off a belief system or anything. I guess I found it a little silly that you would leave someone's life in the hands of some old geezers who talk to spirits."

Arynn's jaw dropped, and Ben could tell she was resisting the urge to slap him. She put down her cup forcefully, spilling some of the tea on the tray and table. "Just because you had your ass handed to you last night doesn't mean I'll hesitate to hurt you even more. Your disbelief doesn't give you the right to mock the Ascendants!"

Once again, Ben realized he had screwed up, and he felt he was closer to smacking himself than Arynn was. "I'm *uh*...I'm sorry I offended you. Again. I was just trying to lighten the mood," he said with a forced chuckle.

Arynn groaned and slumped her shoulders. "Do you even know *anything* about the Ascendants?"

"They're supposed to be like spirits or something, right?"

Arynn stared at Ben, obviously stunned. "That's an understatement. They're the collective souls of all our ancestors. Their wills grant us strength and life. It's thanks to them that we have clean water and are kept safe from wastelanders and slavers. It's only when we do things that they disapprove of that bad things happen, like my father leaving despite the warnings, or the last blood bug outbreak that took my mom."

Ben didn't know what to make of this. The idea of a culture based on such personal beliefs was so foreign to him. He offered a look of sympathy to Arynn and, hesitantly, placed his hand on her knee. "I'm sorry to hear that. What happened to her?"

Arynn suddenly became very interested with the inside of her teacup, avoiding eye contact. "Ten years ago, during the plague. Not many in Vänalleato still think about it because we weren't hit nearly as bad as Freztad. But my family was. My mom was bitten by a blood bug and came down with a nasty fever. One day she fell asleep and wouldn't wake up." She stopped talking and twirled her hair around her finger while still staring at the inside of her cup.

"Hey, it's okay. You don't need to keep going. I appreciate you sharing that with me, though. I understand now why you got so upset with me bad mouthing the Ascendants. Your mother is a part of that now, right?"

Arynn looked up at him from her teacup and gave a half smile. "Yeah, she is. I like to think she still looks down on me with the other spirits."

Even though Ben didn't share her beliefs, he appreciated how they were able to comfort her. They were able to give her meaning to tragedy. *If that works for her, then who am I to question it?* It was at that moment that Ben realized how connected he felt to Arynn. She had lost her mother, her best friend, and nearly her father, too. Ben didn't have either parents, he lost people to the plague, his friend was killed, and his cousin had been kidnapped. Maybe it was that unspoken connection that made Ben feel so close and comfortable around Arynn.

Ben noticed that his hand was still on Arynn's knee, and he quickly jerked it back to his teacup. He took a sip from it to hide his embarrassment. They sat for a moment of silence that seemed to Ben as though it dragged on forever. He suddenly couldn't form any thoughts about anything to say.

Then, out of nowhere, Arynn chuckled. "You're not entirely wrong, you know."

His brow burrowed with a look of confusion. "About what?"

"The Elders," Arynn responded, with another chuckle. "They're just a bunch of old geezers."

Ben responded with a nervous laugh. "*Heh.* I can't tell if you're messing with me now."

Arynn rolled her eyes. "No, you goof, I'm serious. I mean, I believe the Grand Elder has a strong connection to the Ascendants, but some of the laws he and the Elders enforce can be really strict. I can't see why our ancestors would care so much about such things."

Ben was starting to get the sense there was some kind of

animosity in Arynn, hidden by her respect for her beliefs. "Laws like what?"

"Oh, I don't know," she said as she waved her hand flippantly through her hair. "Things like only letting men be in charge. Women not being allowed to leave the town without a male chaperone after curfew. Who we're allowed to live with or marry..."

Suddenly Ben remembered one of Felix's comments about Arynn. "You have to be betrothed, right? Like an arranged marriage?"

Arynn twirled her hair once more. "Yeah. Something like that." She looked extraordinarily uncomfortable and got up from her chair, taking Ben's cup from him. She poured another and handed it back to him. Her disposition changed, and her tone became less solemn. "Drink another cup or two. It'll help with the swelling. I'll be back to check on you in the morning. My father wants to meet you and formally thank you for saving him yesterday. He's also working on some new maps for you based on the one you showed me."

"Why is he drawing new ones?" he asked as he blew on his steaming tea.

"They're to a better scale to help make it easier for you to read. The one you showed me was also pretty dated, so he's fixing that, too."

Ben suddenly felt unnerved. He felt his wrist and didn't feel his father's watch. *Did it fall off in the cave? What if there's more to it that I need to get to the Vault?* "Where is my watch?" he asked in a panic.

"That weird shiny thing you had on your wrist? One of the Elders took it off when he healed you. He thought any Old Days' artifacts would skew your chakra and interrupt your healing."

Ben was relieved to hear that his dad's watch wasn't left in the cave, but he still wanted to know where it was. "I don't know what a chakra is, but that doesn't matter. I *need* that watch! Do you know where it is?"

"Will you calm down for one second? I'll try to get it back for you, but you shouldn't be walking around at all. Just keep drinking your tea and *relax*. I'll let you know what I find out in the morning."

Arynn waved goodbye to Ben and walked out of the room before he could argue further. He finished his tea and began to feel very tired. He was angry with himself for being in bed for an entire day. He didn't want to go back to sleep. He wanted to get up and do something useful. But it was no use; no matter how hard he fought it, the slumber overpowered him. Ben's eyes forced themselves shut, and he slept a dreamless sleep.

~

"Are you sure this is right? It'll take weeks to get there! Is that *all* water?" It was so much information for Ben to take in at once. Arynn's father, Master Siegfried, drew out four charts subdividing the relevant parts of the map that Ben had given him. They had all the important landmarks and the most direct route to the Vault. The first two looked like they were mostly forests and marshes with a few breaks occupied by large settlements or small cities of which Ben had never heard. The third map appeared to be scanty woods and grasslands with the occasional small town. The fourth map had nearly as much ocean as land. The final map was almost entirely ocean with a few archipelagos leading up to a final massive island. *How am I supposed to travel over all that water?*

"Yes, indeed it is. I do presume you could fetch a boat and sail there. Though that may take quite a while..." Arynn's father said. His attention shifted suddenly to the watch, back where it belonged on Ben's wrist. "My, my, what an odd trinket. May I look at that for a moment?"

Ben looked at Arynn for clarification, but she merely shrugged. He didn't like that the man seemed so easily distracted, but he supposed he could trust the cartographer after all the man had done for him. He handed the watch to Arynn's father, who held it close to his eyes and gasped when he saw the symbol on its back.

"As above, so below," he whispered.

"What does that mean?" Ben asked, confused.

Siegfried handed the watch to Ben and quickly turned to the

shop's front door as though he were worried someone were looking in. "You'll want to keep this close to you, Ben. Don't lose it."

Ben and Arynn exchanged puzzled glances.

"Anyway!" The cartographer exclaimed, as though he'd already forgotten about the watch. "Before you worry about getting to Svaldway—I believe that's the name of the island you're heading toward—I'd suggest you make your way to Jordysc. You'll find it right at the bottom of the third map, which I've marked for you. I don't know much about the other settlements. I haven't been to most of them myself; got them from other maps I've collected."

Ben looked at the mark Master Siegfried made to represent Jordysc. There didn't seem to be much there: no bodies of water, forests, or anything that would've allowed a settlement to thrive. "What's so special about this place, Master?"

Arynn snickered at Ben for addressing her father this way. Master Siegfried gave her a disapproving look before answering Ben. "It has been many years since I last travelled there, but I know they're good people. They shall be sympathetic to your cause." Once again, the man stole a glance at the watch around Ben's wrist.

The answer didn't exactly satisfy Ben, but he appreciated the help nonetheless. "This is a tremendous help, Master Siegfried. So, all I need to do is follow the paths you've made here, and I'll be good to go? I wouldn't need any of those fancy tools by any chance, would I?" He said looking curiously at the instruments that lined the walls of the cartographer's shop.

"Of course, *you* won't need them—you wouldn't know how to use any of them! That's why Arynn is going with you!" said Siegfried.

"*WHAT?*" Ben and Arynn shouted in unison.

The bald map maker let out a loud, hearty laugh. "No offense to you, Ben, but I believe it is safe to assume that you do not know how to read star charts, use a sextant, or determine distance from the scale of a map?"

Ben opened his mouth to argue, but ultimately decided against it. It was true, he didn't know the first thing about navigation. He only made his way to Vänalleato because of the Gjoll and the road that led him straight here. He stood there, next to Arynn and her father in a defeated silence.

"Why do you want me to go with him?" Arynn asked her father. "The Elders say it isn't safe to leave—you and I already ignored them once and look what happened! We're lucky to be alive!"

"It is no more dangerous outside our walls than it was before," Siegfried answered calmly. "I knew the risks when I left, as did you. What the Elders say is of no consequence."

"But Father—the Grand Elder speaks the will of the Ascendants!"

"Perhaps. But what would your mother want?"

"W-what does that have to do with anything?"

"Is she not with the Ascendants?" her father asked with a slight grin.

"Of course she is! What kind of question is that?"

"I reiterate my initial question: What would your mother want? Would she not want you to follow your heart and achieve your dreams?"

Ben wasn't sure where this conversation was going, but he continued to listen and remained silent. Arynn stood speechless and deep in thought as she looked at the floor with a conflicted expression on her face.

Her father broke the silence. "Arynn, you've wanted to explore the world for years. You've begged me to take you on expeditions and I've taken you on as many jobs as I could to show you what I know. But sweet daughter, I have nothing left to teach you. Go on with this young man and help him save his cousin. Go and see the world not as something to be recorded and charted, but as a place to experience and appreciate. This is what I want for you, my child. This is what your mother would have wanted for you."

Arynn smiled and thanked her father, only to elbow Ben in the ribs the second he noticed her wipe a tear from her eye. "Ow!" he cried. "What was that for?"

"Get along you two. I imagine you'll be stuck together for quite some time now," Master Siegfried said chuckling.

Arynn groaned, as if the idea of traveling with Ben ruined the prospect of getting to explore the world. Ben, on the other hand, had a different concern. "I admit I was in way over my head to think I could find Rose on my own, but I'm not sure I like the idea of you risking your life to help me."

"Then don't think of it as me helping. Think of it as me just tagging along to get out and see the world and make new maps so I can be a master just like my father."

Ben knew he wouldn't be able to argue with Arynn or her father once their minds were set. Instead, he realized he would need to tell them the truth about his mission. "If you want to come then that's great. But there's something I need to tell you about all this first. Something *big* that I've neglected to mention...."

He went on to explain to them about the true reason Rose was taken. He told them about Julius searching for the powerful and mysterious Vault hidden far to the North. He explained to them that the King had plans to rule an empire and use the Vault's secrets to do it; how he was seemingly willing to do anything it took. Ben then told them that Julius was Rose's father, and that he believed Rose's blood held some kind of mystical power that would unlock the Vault's doors to reveal the power inside.

"The Ænærians have been encroaching on Vänalleatian territory for some time now. You've already heard the sun-carriages and guns. You've already run into slavers that are working for them. Some of your people already accept sols instead of seeds as payment—that must mean you've had some sort of contact with them whether you've realized it or not. They're becoming ambitious, as if they're ready to take over every settlement they can find as soon as they open the Vault. The people we're dealing with here are bad news. You deserve to know all this before you get involved."

As Ben expected, Arynn didn't seem to care; she wanted revenge on the Ænærians just as much as he did. Maybe even more. What *did* surprise Ben, was Siegfried's response to his story.

"I know a bit about these Ænærians," Siegfried said. "The people who captured me spoke of them in fear. They said these people were blessed with magic from the sun itself. From what I heard from them, the slavers seemed to think the Ænærians worship the sun as some sort of god and that their faith was rewarded with power. I don't believe any of the Ænærians have made their way into Vänalleato just yet, but we do have a fair amount of trading with the North. I imagine that's why we have sols."

"What exactly are sols?" Ben asked.

"They're round and flat pieces of metal. Some are copper or silver, and I've even seen a gold one once. They're much more durable and rare than seeds are, so it's no wonder they've spread so quickly. But unlike seeds, which every now and then will actually grow into something, I don't think sols have real value aside from looking pretty."

Ben had been trying to imagine exactly what sols were for quite some time, but learning about them only made him more confused. Like Master Siegfried said, seeds are valuable because they can potentially grow into something, which was no easy feat. He thought to himself about how Freztad was the only settlement he knew of that could actually plant and grow seeds with any kind of reliability. All their allies lacked good soil and enough seeds to successfully grow plants. To represent themselves as the leaders of their alliance, Freztad decided to use its surplus of seeds as its currency. Seeds would be accepted among allied settlements in exchange for goods and services. Most people tended to do a mix of things with the seeds to prevent inflation. They would plant them, feed them to animals, or save and trade them. Seeds were highly valuable because they had actual worth. *What use is there for metal pieces? You can't grow stones with them and, even if you could, you couldn't eat them.*

"They may not have intrinsic value, but that doesn't mean they're useless," Arynn suggested. Ben and Siegfried offered her a curious look and waited for her to say more. "If we're heading north and going into their territory, it might be better for us to use sols rather than seeds. That way, we blend in and won't draw attention to ourselves. If we already have some in Vänalleato, then I think it would be best for us to exchange as much as we can before we leave. There's no one else in the Alliance where we're heading anyway, so seeds are useless to us."

Master Siegfried stroked his beard and smiled at his daughter. "Right you are, my dear. Why don't you two go around town and see how much you can exchange. And—" he walked to his counter and pulled open a drawer. He pulled out a pouch and threw it to Arynn "—please take these with you. Consider it a down payment on any of the maps you make while you're out there."

Arynn opened the pouch, revealing scores of seeds. She thanked her father and promised to return with better and more detailed maps than he'd ever seen. "I look forward to your return. I won't lie, and say I won't be worried about you Arynn, but I have a special feeling about this young man here," he said as he shifted his gaze toward Ben. "I don't think it's a coincidence that you came here in need, and just in time to save the others and me from the slavers. No, I think the Ascendants have smiled upon us by intertwining your fate with ours, Ben. I would go with you, but I feel my presence is needed here. I would like to convince the Grand Elder to go easier on Arma. If they do, then she may be able to help us figure out what happened to Sera and the others who have disappeared."

Arynn smiled, her eyes shining with a brilliance Ben hadn't seen in them before. She really missed her friend.

"Anyway," Siegfried continued. "Please watch over my daughter while you're out there."

"Oh please, *I'm* the one who's going to be watching over *him* the whole time," Arynn said smugly to her father.

Arynn and her father bowed to each other to say goodbye before she and Ben left the shop to exchange the seeds. As the two of them explored Vänalleato's shops and exchanged the seeds, Ben mulled over what Siegfried had said about him. He wasn't sure why Arynn's father thought he was special. Ben couldn't think of anything all that special about himself, but it was a refreshing comment nonetheless. He wasn't sure if he believed in the Ascendants, either. If they were indeed real and had some sort of hand in his fate, he sure hoped Master Siegfried was right about them being on his side. He would need all the help he could get.

Ben and Arynn were able to clean the town out of all its sols.

They had eighty-seven copper, twenty-three silver, and two gold sols. Neither of them knew exactly how much that was worth in Ænæria, but they figured it was certainly better than nothing.

When they finished exchanging currency, Ben fetched the rest of his belongings from the inn. When he left, he found Arynn waiting at the front of a carriage hitched to Sleipnir out front.

"Is this the same carriage the slavers used?" Ben asked.

"Sure is. Now, are you ready to go or not? I've got your bow and quiver up here in case you were looking for it, by the way."

"Sheesh, even with everything going on I can't believe I forgot you still had Rakshi's bow. Do you have any weapons? Do you have my pistol?" Ben asked, as he climbed next to Arynn in the carriage.

"I have my own bow and a spear in the back with your bow and my father's tools." She handed the reins over to Ben. "And...well...no, I don't have your gun. It was lost during the cave-in."

"*Eh*, that's all right. I don't really like guns anyway. They're loud, and their only purpose seems to be to hurt people," Ben said. "Wait a minute...how on earth did you get Sleipnir to let you anywhere near him?"

Arynn let out a highly-amused laugh. "Your horse just likes me more than you, that's all. No need to be jealous."

As Arynn continued to laugh at Ben's frustration, he led the horse drawn carriage down the hill to the town's gate. Luckily for Ben, Felix wasn't on guard duty to make fun of his frustration with Arynn. Arynn gave Ben an overview of the directions while they left the town. After a quarter of an hour had passed, they reached the edge of the forest and got onto the main road that they would need to follow for the next few hours before their first stop.

Ben made sure Sleipnir stayed on the path, but didn't need to steer him much once there were no more trails forking from the road. The horse seemed to prefer drawing a carriage than having a person on his back because he snorted much less frequently. While they followed the road, Arynn told Ben about the locations on the first map they were using.

"So right here is where we are," she pointed on the map, "and I think this is where we'll end up by nightfall. I don't know of any settlements near there so we're going to have to set up camp. You do know how to set up a tent and fire, right? Because I'm *not* doing everything for you this whole trip."

"Obviously I know how to set up a camp. I originally planned on doing this without you, if you remember."

"Good, so you're not completely use—what in the Elders' names is that?" Arynn yelled, pointing to her left.

Ben looked behind him and laughed hysterically when he saw what Arynn was pointing at. "Oh, did I forget to mention I have a wolf friend?"

9.The Deserters

"WHAT IS THAT SUPPOSED TO MEAN?" Arynn shrieked as the wolf came closer to the carriage. In hindsight, Ben thought that it probably would've been better to have told Arynn about the wolf *before* they left. He didn't let that bother him, though, as he was perfectly entertained by Arynn's reaction. Once Arynn stopped screaming in terror and threatening to shoot the wolf, Ben decided it was time to fill her in on his history with it. He told her about the time he and Rose saw it in the forest, how it saved his life a few days back, and how it had been following him since.

"Do you expect me to believe that something like this just happened to slip your mind?" Arynn asked.

"Must've lost some chunks of memory from that head injury in the cave the other night," he teased.

Arynn let out a dissatisfied grunt and crossed her arms. Ben reckoned she didn't want him to see her so unnerved, but he could tell she was terrified. He pulled the reins on Sleipnir and hopped off the carriage.

"What are you doing?" Arynn asked, trying to hide the tremble in her voice.

Ben walked around the side of the carriage and met the wolf, whose head stood up to his chest. Ben put a hand on the wolf's head and gently pat it. "See? It's friendly. Wouldn't harm a thing...well, it did rip a guy's throat out once, but that's different." The color in Arynn's face vanished in response to his comment. He chuckled again. "Come on down, and let it get to know you. It's not going to hurt you, I promise."

"*Uh*...yeah, fine. If *you* can do it then I'm sure I-I'll be fine, too." She slowly approached the wolf. As she got off the carriage, Sleipnir let out a loud snort as if to tell Arynn she was crazy for doing this. She reached out her hand for the wolf to sniff. The wolf let out a soft bark, to which Arynn jumped. It then wagged its tail and panted happily.

"Told you not to worry," Ben said.

"Well, now that we got this out of the way we should get back on the road. Time is short, and we have another twenty-three or so miles left before we can make camp," Arynn said, softly petting the wolf.

"Will we make it before sundown?" Ben asked.

"If we leave now without any more distractions, then yes, I'd say so."

Ben got on the carriage and yawned as he stretched his arms in the air. "Well, let's get going then, shall we?" As soon as Arynn climbed up next to him, Ben shook the reins for Sleipnir to start moving.

After she reevaluated the maps and adjusted their course, Arynn looked back to see the wolf still following them. "So, what's her name?"

"Whose name?" Ben asked.

Arynn squinted, annoyed at Ben. "The *wolf's*, idiot!"

"Oh—that thing. No, incidentally it hasn't actually told me its name yet. The conversations have been pretty one-sided so far," Ben said facetiously.

Arynn punched him in the shoulder. "How about Sierra?" she suggested.

"Why that name? How do you know it's a girl?" Ben asked.

"Well, besides the *obvious* reason, I think most female wolves have narrower muzzles, foreheads, and shoulders," she said smugly.

"I didn't realize you were a lupine expert. You were just screaming '*Ah* what is that thing?' not two minutes ago!" Ben laughed as he did his best 'terrified girl' impression.

"Oh, shut up!" she yelled, punching his shoulder again.

"Stop, what was that?" Ben questioned seriously.

"I'll stop when you stop giving me attitude," Arynn retorted.

"Not that—listen. Does...does that sound like—"

"Crying," she answered.

The horse drawn carriage came to a stop at the side of the road. Ben and Arynn waited quietly and listened. The crying was faint and distant. Sierra's ears perked up suddenly, and she darted off in the direction of a grassy meadow upon a hill. Ben didn't hesitate to follow, and he jumped off the carriage and followed.

"Ben, what are you doing? Oh, I swear by the Elders, that boy is going to get me killed...."

Ben ran at full speed, worried he would lose track of Sierra. The wolf made no attempt to slow down as she made her way up the steep hill. As Ben climbed closer to the crest, the crying became much clearer. *Almost there. I wonder what has the wolf in such a hurry? Does she know what's crying?* He made it to the top of the hill and found that it overlooked a large valley in the distance. Resting behind a large lake were scattered mountains that brushed up against the horizon. Sulking behind a dead tree sat a small child. Ben approached the crying child and knelt down in front of him.

"Hey, little guy—what's wrong?"

The boy sniffled and wiped the tears from his eyes. He looked up at Ben, frightened. "Who a-ar-are y-you?" The boy then shifted his gaze behind Ben to the enormous wolf. He let out a loud shriek.

"Hey, hey, hey, hey—*shhhhh*, little guy. Don't be scared. That's," he tried to remember what Arynn called the wolf. "Sierra back there. She's my friend, and she won't hurt you. My name is Ben. What's yours?"

The little boy's breathing slowed as he settled himself down. "I-I'm Pawel."

"Nice to meet you, Pawel. So, what's wrong? Is there anything I can do to help you?"

"Ben...what...has...gotten...into you?" Arynn wheezed, gasping for breath. It seemed to Ben that she had just now gotten up the hill. He was surprised to see how winded she was considering how much more fit than Ben she seemed. Yet he didn't even break a sweat, and he got up much faster.

Pawel looked up to acknowledge Arynn but turned to Ben and said, "The bad people were fighting each other and my mommy and daddy and me were there too. They told me to run away to stay safe. I don't know where they runned off to and I'm scared."

Ben put his hand on Pawel's shoulder to comfort him and asked, "Do you know where that happened? We can check it out for you and make sure your parents are safe."

"Ben! We can't afford detours. It's the *first* day, and we're already behind," Arynn argued.

"The whole point of our trip is to save someone and bring her back to her family. It wouldn't be right to ignore someone else going through the same thing. We're going to help him!"

Arynn let out a frustrated grunt and crossed her arms. "Ugh, fine! Who's going to watch the kid while we're off saving the day?"

Ben pondered what she said for a moment. "*Hmm*. Pawel, can you ride a horse?"

"Yeah! I learned when I was turned five last week!"

Arynn gave Ben a smug look. "Sounds like you've got a sound plan there," she said sarcastically.

"*Hmm*, it's probably not the best idea to have him ride Sleipnir anyway. Pawel, if you remember where you last saw your parents, then maybe we can ride the carriage over there. Then, Sierra and I can go scout it out while you stay behind with Arynn. How does that sound?"

"Why am *I* stuck being the babysitter?" Arynn said, obviously displeased.

"You don't seem overly excited about getting involved, and we can't leave him alone. He can't be brought somewhere dangerous either. Do you have an alternative plan?"

"Yes! Let's get out of here and back on the trail without getting ourselves killed!"

Ben wouldn't have it. He was determined to help Pawel and his family. It wouldn't be right to just leave the little boy all alone, especially if the 'bad people' he mentioned were Ænærians or slavers. Besides, if they *were* Ænærians, he might be able to learn more about who he was up against. Ben continued to argue with Arynn until she finally relented. They traveled down the hill to their carriage and let Pawel lead the way.

About a third of a mile down the road and around the corner, the group could see smoke in the distance behind the raised landscape. Ben could hear clashing steel and battle cries coming from the direction of the smoke. "Arynn, *please* watch Pawel for me. Sierra, let's go." He wrapped Rakshi's bow around his shoulder and counted his arrows. *Let's get this over with.* He and his wolf companion rushed to the scene.

When he arrived at the site, he saw nine swordsmen all in the same garb. They wore what appeared to be thick black leather armor underneath an orange and white tabard. The front of the tabard was embroidered with an image of the sun with a clenched fist in the middle. Four of them stood in front of a broken wagon, and a middle-aged couple who Ben assumed were Pawel's parents. The three defending swordsmen seemed to be giving their all to protect the boy's mother and father but were clearly growing weary.

"Step away, Darius!" one of the attackers yelled. He was a tall and thin man with bony cheeks and pale skin. The armor he wore was different than that worn by the others, the shoulders curving to a point and his helmet in the shape of half a sun. He had a sword sheathed on his left hip, but he was the only man not wielding it. Instead, he had an oddly shaped gun that possessed an orange tint, and he was pointing it at the youngest defender.

"These two were caught breaking the census!" the man with the odd gun continued. "You know what happens to those who break the King's law, and there are no exceptions. Now, for the last time, you and your *accomplices* need to step aside."

"No. We're done taking orders from you. We won't let you hurt any more children either!" the youngest-looking of the troop, Darius, said.

"They've done nothing wrong! So what if they didn't report a census?" the man to Darius's right said.

The leader sighed, clearly frustrated. "Look guys, I don't make the rules. Everyone without exception within the Ænærian borders gives the Rhion a blood sample with their census to offer to the King. *Sol Invictus* and all that, you know? Now, since they didn't do that, they've wasted the King's valuable time, and now they need to make amends for that lost time. This is the last time we ask nicely before we finish this fight. You know you won't win. You and your boys don't have the energy to keep up."

Darius and his three partners remained silent, breathing heavily and raising their swords. The leader let out a disappointed sigh and shifted his aim to Darius's left and fired his pistol. A bright flash of light followed by the sound of thunder erupted from the gun. The man next to Darius fell to the ground, his shoulder burned and smoking. He screamed in agony.

Darius and his two remaining comrades retaliated. The leader of the attacking Ænærians raised his strange pistol to fire again but was immediately disarmed by one of the deserters. The gun fell to the ground and made a strange noise, and lights sparked from its top. The leader drew his sword and shield, and his four companions resumed their attack.

Ben decided it was time to intervene. He had seen enough to determine that Darius's group was in the right, and they were the ones he would need to defend. He didn't look forward to another fight, and he was especially not thrilled to be on the losing side.

"See the five men there? Those are the ones we're attacking. Oh, and please try not to kill them," Ben said to Sierra. The wolf responded with a near silent bark in response. They ran to the brawl as fast as they could. Sierra sped ahead of him and lunged atop one of the attackers from behind. The man screamed and threw the others off guard.

"What under the Eternal Sun is that? It's enormous! Kill it!" one of the assailants shouted.

The leader of the attackers used the chaos to his advantage and stabbed one of Darius's accomplices through the chest. In one fluid motion, the leader removed his blade from the man's body and slashed as fast as lightning across the petrified accomplice's neck, whose body then fell to the dirt next to his friend's.

"Eryck! Petroph! *No!*" Darius shouted. Enraged, he kicked the assailant in front of him to his knees and sliced across his neck, followed by a *plop* from his head landing. Darius rushed toward the enemy leader and shouted, "Gatron! You're dead!" The two clashed blades, grunting with each strike among the disarray around them as Sierra fended off the remaining two attackers.

Ben drew his bow and aimed at Gatron. It was too difficult to get in a clean shot without accidentally shooting Darius. Instead, he let his bow down and drew his broken sword from Freztad and rushed toward the two. Sierra seemed to be handling herself just fine, having just downed another attacker and getting ready to pounce on the other. Ben slid on his knees behind Gatron and carved through his left ankle.

"*Ahhhhh!* What the—No! Darruk! Zarlot! Someone stop them! *Help!*" Gatron screamed as his tendon ruptured and he fell to his knees. He raised his shield just as Darius took the opportunity to slash down at him.

"Leave him! He's already down!" Ben yelled to Darius.

"Who in the blazes are you? Get out of my way," Darius snapped back at Ben as he readied to swing his sword down at Gatron once more. As he did, Ben intercepted the strike with his own sword. Darius's sword shattered the instant it clashed against Ben's. "What is wrong with you?" he yelled at Ben as he looked at his broken blade in disbelief.

"He's down—he's not going to do anything else. You don't need to kill him!" Ben shouted back.

"He killed two of my comrades! He needs to pay! Now, step aside," Darius said as he tried to shove Ben out of his way. Ben stood his ground like a stone wall and remained unmoved.

"Stop. I know you're upset. Your companions knew what they were getting themselves into. You *all* would've died if my wolf and I hadn't shown up and saved your hides. Your job here was to protect those people back behind you, right?"

Darius's nostrils flared as he nodded in affirmation.

"A friend of mine is watching their son and keeping him safe," Ben continued. "You're doing all this for him, aren't you? How do you think he'd feel if he found out all these people died because of him? Especially when he finds out that his savior killed someone for no reason other than revenge. Do you really want to put that on the kid's conscience as he grows up? If you risked your life for the kid, then I'm sure you can risk your damn pride."

Darius stared at Ben with a bewildered look on his face. "Are you done?" he asked. "I don't know who you are but mind your own business. You don't know what these Rhion have done, do you? The oppression, slavery, and manipulation. The things *this man*," he pointed his broken hilt at the crying Gatron, sprawled out on the ground, "has done to people. What he has done to *me!* If you knew anything about that, then you'd be fighting me to kill him yourself."

Ben was running out of things to say. He had tried using logic with Darius, appealing to him emotionally. But he couldn't get him to see from his own perspective. Sierra trotted up next to him, blood splattered over her white coat. She looked up at Darius with an intense glare and bared her teeth. Darius suddenly looked a lot less full of himself. His anger shifted to total terror. Where Ben's logic and compassion failed, Sierra's menacing appearance succeeded. Darius took a few steps back and dropped his broken sword and raised his hands, surrendering.

"Fine. But the lives he destroys from now on are on *your* head! Not mine!" he said begrudgingly. "You said the kid's safe, right? I should let his parents know."

"Yeah. He's with my friend," Ben responded. "They're down the road back that way," he gestured to behind him. "Sierra, go let Arynn know she can ride up here. Can you do that?" The wolf barked happily and dashed away.

Darius appeared shocked, yet impressed by how well Sierra listened to Ben. He watched Sierra run off in the distance with his jaw dropped. He eventually shifted his gaze toward Gatron and then back up to Ben. "I'll let the kid's parents know that their son is safe and on his way. That'll probably calm them down after this whole mess." He walked toward the broken wagon where the scared couple huddled together.

Ben could hear Darius calming them down and explaining the situation to them. They looked extremely relieved. Ben shared the feeling. He felt that he had made the right decision in siding with Darius and not Gatron.

Darius left the family and went to his fallen comrade who had been shot in the shoulder. He was the only one of Darius's companions who was still alive. Darius helped him move across the road to lean against a tree. The wounded man's eyes were clenched shut, and he was biting his lip, probably trying not to let the pain get the better of him. The man removed his tabard and leather jerkin, revealing the nasty wound underneath. The skin where he had been shot was black and had blisters oozing pus. Darius smeared a thick salve over the burn and placed a bandage over his comrade's shoulder.

"Sorry, Roryck, but that's all I can do here," Darius said to his comrade. "You're going to need immediate attention if you don't want that thing to fester and lose your arm."

"It's fine," Roryck replied. "In the meantime, can we shut Gatron up? The headache I have from his moaning is worse than the pain from the burn."

Ben offered a sympathetic look toward Gatron writhing in the dirt and wailing in pain. He looked at Darius and shrugged. Ben walked toward the screaming invalid and picked up the shield next to him. He sat Gatron up and smacked him in the back of his head with the shield, knocking him out cold. The sobbing finally stopped.

"Silence," Darius said, walking across the road toward Ben. "Would've been easier if you let me just end his misery. I guess I should thank you for saving me, though."

"Don't mention it. I'm sorry I couldn't get here sooner. I wasn't sure who was good and who wasn't. You're all wearing the same outfits. Are you Ænærian?" Ben asked, pointing at the sun on Darius's tabard.

"You're not from around here, are you? I am—er, was—an Ænærian Rhion," Darius said. He pulled off the tabard and stomped on it.

"I'm really sorry about the men you fought with. Were you friends with them?"

Darius shook his head. "No, not friends. Don't have any of those. Brothers in arms that joined the cause. We've been working underground to help people flee from Ænæria." He let out a heavy, defeated sigh. "*Hmph.* Well, they knew what they were signing up for. They're not the first ones I've seen killed in action though. They accomplished their goal and died as heroes. This family was so close to escaping before the Rhion arrived. They're free now thanks to their sacrifice and your help."

"Is Roryck going to be okay?" Ben asked.

Darius shrugged. "Dunno. He took a sung blast at close range.

They're not usually fatal, but if the wound gets infected, then he's screwed."

Ben wasn't sure what a sung was, but perhaps it was what the Ænærians called the fire gun that he had just seen Gatron use. He let it go for now, because he was especially interested in the blood samples he heard Gatron mention earlier. "I heard something about a census. What's that all about?"

Darius sat down on the ground, clearly exhausted. Ben followed suit. As they sat in the dirt across from each other, Ben realized Darius appeared to be a bit younger than himself, perhaps fourteen or fifteen. *Too young*, Ben thought to himself, *to be a part of all this violence. To be a killer.* Darius was of a medium height and of a very strong build. He wore short, trimmed black hair that was barely darker than his own skin. His face seemed to wrinkle with a permanent scowl that made Ben feel slightly uneasy.

Darius sighed and went on to explain. "Every birth in Ænæria is recorded, and a sample of blood is placed in a vial and given to the King as an 'offering.' I haven't the faintest clue what the blood is for. The maniac drinks the vials all for I know. This family didn't have their kid within the borders, so they never added him to the census. When the legate found out there was an unregistered child living right under his nose...well, he wanted to make sure he dealt with it immediately. King Xander would've had his head if he found out."

"What's a legate?" Ben asked, confused.

"I guess the best way you outsiders would describe it is like a general. Though, not many of you small tribes have armies, do you?"

"Not exactly. We have Sentinels though. That's probably similar."

"I see," Darius replied. "Since you probably don't know, Ænæria has thirteen provinces, twelve of which are governed by a legate handpicked by King Xander himself. I think they used to be settlements that he took over and put his trusted people in power. The thirteenth province is the capital, Marzora, where the King founded his own city, Ignistad."

"There are thirteen provinces? Ænæria must be massive!" Ben exclaimed.

Darius nodded. "For now. There are a lot of other kingdoms in the Northern Realm, but Xander united most of them in the last fifteen years. He brought an army from the South and captured one kingdom after another, sparing any who would surrender, and fight for his cause. The rest of the Northern Realm didn't stand a chance. And since it's so big, he needs his legates to do a lot of the leg work for him, which makes them the highest-ranking members of in our society aside from himself. Not all legates are equal though; it all depends on how long they've held the title and how much Xander trusts them. Gatron is pretty low in the hierarchy, the legate of my home province of Plutonua. Though since you're not letting me kill him, word will get out about his failure, and he'll probably be demoted even lower or outright replaced. The King doesn't have much patience for screw-ups. The only reason I'm not seriously pissed off at you is because I know what's waiting for him if he ever brings his sorry face back home."

Ben wondered if sparing Gatron truly was the merciful option. He thought about the crosses and imagined the agony the prisoners must've gone through beforehand. *I can't be responsible for his death, though. That's not my right. But is it right for me to leave him for someone else to kill him, knowing how much he'll probably suffer first?* Rather than confirming this with Darius, he asked another question which was weighing on his mind. "Who's ranked at the top? What's so special about that legate?"

"Xander's second in command is Legate Rivers. He's the King's most loyal follower who's been with him since the beginning. He's in charge of the Juptora province, northeast of the Marzora province where the capital city of Ignistad lies. As far as legates go, he's not too bad. Low temper and simple demeanor. I get the sense that Xander is more the face of Ænæria and Rivers the brains."

"I'm not so sure about that," Ben added.

Darius scowled. "And how would you know any better?"

"Well, first off, your king's name isn't really Xander. It's Julius. Xander was the name of his older brother who died when Julius was a boy. Julius is from my village—he's sort of my uncle."

Darius shook his head and scoffed. "Even if that's true, it doesn't say anything about his personality."

"He's been plotting something big for over fifteen years," Ben added carefully, unsure of how much he could disclose to this stranger. "Think what you want, but it doesn't change anything. Tell me more about the legates."

Darius shrugged and brushed the comment aside. "Well, third-in-charge is Second Legate Fenwin—a real monster that one. Makes Rivers look like a kitten. He's a real Ænærian blood purist. He oversees Vestinia, the province that borders Plutonua here. Though 'oversees' is too generous of a term. Next is Third Legate Randolph of Minervia. I heard he went on some expedition down south. No one knows what it was, but we saw them leave in the holy sun-carriages, and they brought the holy weapons with them."

Ben felt a pit in his stomach. *Randy is a legate?* Suddenly it made sense that the man was able to play Ben and Rose for fools so easily. "You mean those things they ride aren't normal in Ænæria? What makes the guns so holy?"

Darius gave Ben a skeptical look. "You seem to know a lot about us for an outsider. Where are you from anyway? Blazes, I don't even know your name."

Ben wasn't sure if he could trust Darius with his identity nor that of Freztad. He had already been tricked by the Ænærians before. *What if they're all like that? For all I know, he knows about me, and as soon as I reveal myself he could change his mind and have me captured and taken to Julius. He'd probably get a nice fat promotion for that, too. Probably even replace Gatron.*

Before Ben had a chance to answer, he heard Sleipnir snorting angrily and Pawel singing. "*Horsey, horsey, you're so silly. Horsey, horsey, why're you so grumpy? Horsey, horsey, smile, smile, smile—* Mommy! Daddy! Look what I found! It's a grumpy horsey and giant wolfy! Can we keep them? Can we? Can we?"

Ben was happy to see that Arynn no longer seemed so annoyed with the boy. He thought he even saw her crack a smile.

The mother and father jumped with joy at the sight of their son.

They ran to him as quickly as they could, embracing him as soon as they reached him. Grateful tears spilled out of the parents as they hugged their son and listened to him talk about his short time with Sleipnir, Sierra, and Arynn. He told them how he wanted the animals to come home with them and live with them forever. Ben was glad he didn't have to break it to Pawel that he wasn't ready to part ways with his cousin's horse and wolf friend—the parents took one look at Sierra and told Pawel that there was no way they'd keep such a thing. Sleipnir snorted at them, and they added that they didn't think it would be right to take someone else's horse. Pawel was disappointed, but he got over it pretty quickly.

Arynn hopped off the carriage and approached Ben. "That child...has way too much energy for me!" She nearly seemed out of breath with exhaustion.

"I guess that means you'll have an easier time putting up with me now, *huh*?" Ben said laughing.

Arynn shifted her gaze to Darius and then to Roryck across the road against the tree. "Who're they?"

Darius extended his hand and introduced himself, "I am known as Darius. I am a defector from the Holy Ænærian Army. Your friend here saved me and that boy's parents. It is a pleasure to meet you."

Arynn gave Darius an odd look and snickered at his introduction. "Don't need the whole life story, pal. But the name's Arynn. Nice to meet you too, I guess," she said shaking his hand hesitantly.

Darius looked at Ben expecting a proper introduction from him as well. But Ben instead looked to Arynn. "Listen, Arynn, I was thinking we should send Pawel and his parents back to Vänalleato. It's the closest settlement, and they need to leave the Ænærian border. They have nowhere else to go."

Arynn groaned. "Fine...I guess I can look forward to seeing that annoying brat when I get back home. How're they gonna get there? It's not like we have a horse to spare."

"We have a carriage," Darius said. "We can spare it for you. But only if Roryck can go with you too. He needs medical attention."

Arynn looked unsure.

"You can trust him," Ben said. "They're no longer Ænærian soldiers. Roryck and Darius are the only defectors who survived the attack."

Arynn sighed. "Okay, if you trust them." She turned to face Darius. "Vänalleato is south of here, just follow the road. They won't turn away anyone in need of asylum."

Darius sprinted away along the road toward Roryck and helped him to his carriage. Roryck looked significantly paler than before. He needed to get to Vänalleato as soon as possible. Meanwhile, Arynn returned to the family and explained the situation and how they felt it would be best for them to head for Vänalleato where they would be safe. The parents seemed agreeable and helped Ben and Arynn ready their wagon for transport while Pawel played fetch with Sierra.

Darius and Roryck returned on the carriage led by two large black stallions, one of which he claimed belonged to Gatron and was the swiftest horse in Plutonua and would be able to get the family to Vänalleato by dawn.

Darius then did something that Ben hadn't expected. "Gatron and the other Rhion. They can't be left here. And your friend," he looked angrily at Ben, "won't let me execute them. Can they be brought to Vänalleato as prisoners?"

Arynn rolled her eyes. "Are they dangerous?"

"Extremely," Darius said without missing a beat. "But so is this." He held up the powerful fire gun that Gatron had shot Roryck with. "Roryck knows how to use it. They won't dare try anything if he has this."

Arynn looked to Ben once more for affirmation. She looked concerned.

"Again, I think you can trust him," Ben said to Arynn. "If they're tied up, I don't think any of them would dare resist. But does Vänalleato have a prison? I thought most of the prisoners in the Alliance were sent to Talamdor."

"They are, but only after a trial," Arynn answered. "There's a dungeon they can stay in until then. They'll probably stay there until we get back to testify against them."

Darius looked confused, as though he didn't understand what Ben and Arynn were talking about. "So can they go with Roryck or not?"

"Fine. But if anything happens to my people, it's on your head."

Darius nodded. He turned to the carriage and gave Roryck the gun. They kept their goodbyes short. Ben didn't sense there was much love between the two. Maybe Rhion didn't have much in the way of brotherhood. Or maybe they just didn't express emotions around each other. It was hard for Ben to tell. In any case, they seemed much different than Freztad's Sentinels.

Before tying them by the arms and legs, Darius removed the wounded Rhion's tabards with the Ænærian insignia. "Wouldn't want any scouts to see who they are," he said. The three carried the unconscious prisoners to the wagon and said their farewells to Pawel and the family.

"I'll see you soon, grumpy horse! Bye-bye, wolfy! I'll miss you, Arynn!" Pawel yelled from the wagon. Before getting on with his parents, the little boy hustled over to Ben and gave him a big hug around his legs. "Thank you for helping me find my parents, Ben! I can't wait to see you again!"

Ben patted Pawel on the back and told him goodbye before the boy ran to his parents. He felt good about helping the family, even if it did mean delaying their trip even more. Behind him, Darius chuckled. "So, your name's Ben, is it?"

After watching Darius help the family and seeing how much he cared, Ben felt as though he could perhaps trust the stranger. "That's right, Ben's the name. Wait, how come you're not going with them?"

Darius looked uneasy. "I can't be around Gatron. Too much history..."

"I see," Ben said. Then he suddenly had an idea. *His insight into Ænæria may even prove useful.* "Why don't you come with us and ruin some of your king's plans." He extended his hand toward Darius. The Ænærian's shocked expression shifted to a satisfied smile as he shook Ben's hand in agreement.

10.Across Enemy
Lines

fter Pawel and his parents left for Vänalleato, the Ben and his new companions continued along the road for the rest of the day until the sun was set beyond the horizon. They didn't talk much that night, each of them exhausted from the day's events. Arynn wanted them to get to sleep early so they could wake at first light to make up for lost time. Darius fell asleep inside the carriage while Ben and Arynn set up their tents. From the sound of

her heavy snoring, Ben could tell that Arynn was knocked out immediately. He lay in his tent, eyes wide open and unable to sleep. He
wanted it to be morning already, and thoughts of what may come
prevented him from resting. After an hour of tossing and turning,
Ben left his tent to walk around and clear his mind.

Clouds shrouded the moon, making the night black and mysterious. The only light and comfort from the unknown wilderness was
the dispersed radiance of the starry night. Like other restless nights,
Ben looked up and contemplated their beauty.

"Some say they're suns from other worlds," said Darius, peering
out from inside the carriage.

"Other worlds?" Ben asked, disbelieving the Ænærian's comment.

"I say it's nonsense," Darius yawned. "There's only one Holy Sun.
The stars are just another of Her creations."

Ben scratched his head in curiosity. "The sun created everything?"
He was interested in what Darius had to say, just as he was interested
in hearing about Arynn and the Ascendants. Listening to the two of
them talk so confidently about the supernatural gave him a sense of
both excitement and disappointment. Although he was willing to
explore these beliefs, he was certain that the answers to his questions
would be unsatisfying. Between his mysterious parentage and the
unfolding chaos with the Ænærians, Ben was desperate for answers
and some kind of meaning behind it all. However, he wasn't sure that
he liked the idea of turning to blind faith for it, nor did he enjoy the
notion that some mysterious force could be manipulating him.

"Of course She did," Darius replied. "Tell me, do you know
anything about plants?"

An image of Kabedge's farm popped into Ben's mind, and he
frowned with a hint of longing at the memory. "Yeah, I worked on a
farm back home. Tended to all sorts of crops. What's your point?"

Darius smiled slyly, reminding Ben of his own shrewd smile.
"What do they need in order to grow?"

Ben let out a soft chuckle. He knew what Darius was getting at.
"Sunlight. The sun gives plants the ability to grow. We use those
plants as food either for ourselves or for livestock. You're saying we

need the sun for more than just light and heat. We need its energy, too."

"Exactly," Darius stated. "The Sun created us, and so it nourishes us like a mother to a newborn babe. The Sun is the Eternal Mother."

He also didn't like thinking of a god as a mother figure. Whenever he thought of his mother, he automatically pictured Rose's face. She may have been younger than him, but she offered him the emotional support he expected a mother would have given him. He thought to himself about how Lydia may have raised him, but Rose cared for him.

Darius noticed the uncomfortable look on Ben's face, but clearly misread it. "I'm sure it's a lot for a foreigner to take in. Unlike other Ænærians, I won't hold it against you." He flashed a graciously accepting, slightly forgiving smile at Ben.

Happy to have found a way to change the subject, Ben responded saying, "You seem to have a lot of pride in being Ænærian with the way you talk. Why did you leave?"

Darius's bright-eyed look shifted to a scowl. Before he could say anything, a voice called from behind them. "Will you two SHUT UP?" Arynn yelled, head poking out of her tent. "Go to sleep! We have a long day tomorrow, and I'd like to not be the only one awake for it!" She groaned and pulled her tent back shut. Darius shrugged and lay back down in the carriage, out of Ben's sight. Ben sighed and returned to his tent, hoping morning would hurry.

W hile he sure didn't feel like it, Ben realized he must've gotten some sleep as he woke up to Arynn smacking him in the face. "Get up! We need to go—the sun is almost up!" she said much too loudly for this early in the morning. "You drool, by the way," she added, suppressing a smile.

"Yeah," Ben replied rubbing his eyes and yawning. "Well, you snore rather loudly. That's why Darius and I were up so late last night." He chuckled as Arynn rolled her eyes and left his tent. Shortly after Ben finished packing his tent and getting dressed, the group continued their route. Ben offered to take the reins first as Arynn read the maps and told him where to go. The morning journey was rather simple as they needed to continue straight on the only road meandering through the thick trees and stretching like an endless rope that went on for miles. Ben felt himself nodding off every few minutes, lulled by sound of Sleipnir's hooves and the chirping birds. It didn't help that Darius was propped fast asleep and breathing heavily.

When the sun reached the center of the sky, the group broke for lunch. Darius, finally awake, made a fire while Ben and Arynn prepared the food. Ben still had some salted meat that he shared with the others, knowing it would go bad otherwise. Both he and Arynn had food from their respective homes that they split with Darius upon realizing he had nothing with him.

"What was your plan after helping Pawel's family?" Arynn asked Darius between slurps of her tomato and venison stew.

The young Ænærian shrugged as he tore off a piece of jerky. "Not sure. I didn't really think that far ahead. I was probably going to head in the same direction as you...."

Ben noticed an apprehensive tone in Darius's voice, as if there were something he was neglecting to share.

"I bet you're sure glad you found us, *huh*?" Arynn said, smirking. She finished her stew and moved about the camp to pack up the rest of her belongings.

"Yes," Darius said, extinguishing the fire. "Very much so." He, too, cleaned up and got ready to continue the trip. Meanwhile, Ben scarfed down the rest of his meal and looked around for Sierra. After whistling to her for a few minutes, the large wolf came scampering through the woods with a rabbit in her mouth. She dropped it in front of Ben and panted happily.

"*Uh*, thanks," said Ben, picking up the dead animal and examining it. While he expected to find the rabbit torn and inedible, Ben was surprised to find that it was handled quite gently. "This is actually really good. Well done!" he said, patting Sierra on the head.

As they resumed their journey, Darius explained why he had left the Ænærian Army. "It was my training that taught me the history. But my work out in the field showed me the truth. I was recruited for the Army when I was five years old," Darius said. "Most firstborn sons are offered to the Holy Ænærian Army, another reason for the census. They started us off with lessons about Ænæria's swift rise, the glory of King Xander, and the divinity of the Holy Sun. But after years of being a Rhion, I had had enough—"

"What is this 'Holy Sun' I keep hearing about?" Arynn interrupted. "Is it the same as the Ascendants?"

"Not at all," Darius said. There seemed to be a hint of annoyance in his voice. "I'll explain this for you first, since you don't seem to know. A lot of our people, especially in Plutonua, used to believe in your Ascendants. When Xander came to power, the sole divine power was revealed to be the Sun. Anyone who questioned that revelation would be severely punished."

Arynn groaned, but didn't say anything aloud. She let Darius continue talking. Ben withheld his comments, too. He was far too interested in what Darius had to say, especially after their conversation from last night. He wanted to know what had compelled Darius to leave the Ænærians, and he didn't really care about the Sun-god stuff anymore. He focused on the young soldier's tale as he kept his eyes on the road and the horse in front of him. *I need to learn and understand* everything *he says. No detail is trivial, even if it seems like it now*, he thought to himself as he tried to paint a detailed sketch of his mysterious enemy in his mind.

"Xander wanted to convert people peacefully," Darius continued, "Xander taught the first Ænærians that our ancestors are indeed a part of the divine mystery, but that they are to be respected rather than worshipped. He informed the people that since the Sun gives us life—as I discussed with Ben last night—it only makes sense that they return that life to the Sun upon their death. So, after death, people act as servants for the Sun."

Arynn couldn't refrain from asking. "What exactly do the Ascendants *do* when they serve this sun-god?"

Out of the corner of his eye, Ben could see Darius give a bigger scowl than usual. "Well...we don't call them 'Ascendants' anymore. They're just called 'ancestors'. They act as a bridge between the Sun and the Earth. They carry out the Holy Sun's will and—"

"If this sun-god of yours is so powerful, then why does it need the Ascendants to do all its work for it?" Arynn snapped.

Ben's stomach churned. He could feel the rising tension.

"It's not your fault for not understanding. There're a lot of pagans that have yet to be converted—"

"What did you call me? 'Pagan?' How dare you insult what my people believe in!"

"I didn't insult your people. I'm simply stating facts about—"

"*Facts?* You think some psychotic king's made up religion that picks and chooses parts from other people's beliefs are *facts*? Listen here, kid—"

"I'm a kid now, am I? I've been a Rhion since I was ten years old. I've been a man for five years now. Probably made harder decisions in the last month than you have in your entire life!"

"*Enough!*" Ben yelled. He couldn't bear the arguing any longer. He just wanted to hear the rest and was getting sick of Arynn's interrupting and Darius's smug attitude. "How do you expect us to get *anything* accomplished when you two are at each other's throats after knowing each other for less than a day?"

Arynn and Darius ceased their bickering and went silent. The only sounds were Sleipnir's clopping hooves and Sierra barking at all the yelling. She was sitting next to Ben at the front of the carriage, facing the back where Arynn and Darius were sitting. Ben couldn't see their faces very well, but when he turned to yell at them, he could tell that both had their arms crossed and pointed their heads away from each other.

Unable to wait any longer, Ben broke the silence. "Darius, can you just get to your reasons for leaving the Rhion and betraying Julius? I don't understand why you would defect since you seem awfully devout to your faith in the Sun."

"You know, I think I've shared enough about myself now," Darius said. "Why don't you two fill me in on exactly what we're doing. I get that we're heading north toward the King's expedition to save some girl. But how does that hurt his plans?"

"It's not just some girl, idiot!" Arynn replied. "It's Ben's cousin *and*, perhaps more importantly to you, Julius's daughter."

"The King has a daughter?" Darius asked, confused.

"My cousin Rose is his daughter," Ben explained. "Julius used to be a member of my village, but he left before she was born. For some reason, he waited fifteen years to make contact with her. He sent a guy named Randy—who I now realize is the Third Legate—to convince Rose to meet Julius. Rose, overly trusting and optimistic as ever, trusted Randy and let him take her to some meeting with Julius about half a day's ride away. She went with three of our people for protection, but they never came back."

Ben continued the rest of his story, filling Darius in on all the details. He explained how he found the crosses in the forest and that it was the Ænærians who had sent the attackers to Freztad in the first place.

"Crucifixion is our most severe punishment," Darius said with a shudder. "It serves as a torturous death as well as a message to all those who stand against the King."

"I wondered why they left the bodies out like that after being so secretive with us in Freztad," Ben said. "They also had a sign in the middle of the crosses. It said 'sol invindicus' or something like that. What does that mean?"

"*Sol Invictus*," Darius immediately corrected. "It's the motto of Ænæria. It means 'Invincible Sun.' It has two meanings. It shows our unshakeable faith in the Eternal Sun, and it also serves as a sort of warning. It cautions all who read it to beware Ænæria's might, claiming that it will never cease in power and will soon encompass all the land."

A chill ran down Ben's spine. *Julius really* is *after ultimate power. What could be in the Vault that is so powerful? Could Julius's thirst for power be the reason Darius betrayed the Ænærians?* "I suppose that explains why Julius is heading north." Ben told Darius that he was sure he knew where Julius was heading and that it was his only sure-fire way of finding his cousin. He explained everything he knew about the Vault to Darius.

"I've heard about the Vault before," Darius admitted. "I know for a fact that he's heading north, so you're on the right track. He recently left with an enormous caravan of sun-carriages, and rumors have spread that everyone accompanying him is carrying sungs with them."

"What are 'sungs,'" Arynn questioned.

"Sun guns. 'Sungs' is what the Rhion call them," Darius explained callously, as though it were obvious.

"That's what Roryck was shot with right?" Ben asked.

"Yes. The Eternal Mother blesses us with Her grace whenever She shines upon us. Because we are not worthy of the Sun's direct touch, we are burned by it. That's why we wear clothes like this," Ben turned and saw Darius lift part of the sleeve of his long cloak. "The sungs, just like our sun-carriages and a number of other things, capture the Sun's grace and store it in these containers called 'power cells.' Sun-carriages and sungs are pretty rare and are only used by legates or for really important missions. They're very powerful, but they can take a long time to replenish their energy, especially sungs. It can take up to five minutes until they're ready to fire again. That's why they aren't used as often."

"Ben, do you remember the slavers talking about sun magic?" Arynn asked. "This must be what they meant!"

Ben had already suspected that. He knew the sun-carriages were powered by the sun in some way, since one of the Ænærians in Freztad had told him as much. He also suspected that the special guns were somehow powered by the sun, but he didn't know how. Perhaps the Ænærians had a valid reason for worshiping the sun—its power was very real.

"Yeah, I suppose so," Ben said to Arynn. He wanted to finally get back on the topic that most interested him. If he knew why Darius left, maybe he could use that to his advantage to convince more people to join him against Julius when the time came. "Anyway, back to our *original* discussion. Darius, can you tell me why you deserted the Ænærians?"

Darius was silent for a moment. Ben turned and saw him shifting uncomfortably and crossing his arms. "Yes. I suppose I could tell you that now," he finally said. "It wasn't until yesterday that I *officially* deserted the Rhion. For the last year and a half, I've been working undercover with some other like-minded individuals. When I started working as a Rhion, I was finally exposed to life outside the barracks for the first time since I was a child. I didn't see Ignistad until I was thirteen. I was on a very important mission with Legate Fenwin. That's when I realized the truth.

"Each of the provinces are pretty much the same," Darius continued. "They have some slightly different cultures, and some are better maintained than others, but they pale in comparison to Marzora and the city of Ignistad. For the most part, people in the lesser provinces are healthy. They have enough food to get by, and they all work. Marzora is different. Especially in the city. It has a whole separate class of people who seem to have more time and money than they know what to do with. Those snobs spend most of their time in leisure and talking about nothing. None of them have worked a day since Xander came to power. The only people who work in Ignistad can't even live inside the city walls. They live in slums, nearly all of them sick and dying while everyone inside has more than they'll ever need. The people in the slums are unlike anyone I'd ever seen before. Then I learned they were slaves."

"You didn't know your people had slaves?" Arynn asked. "You've lived here your whole life. I've never set foot in Ænæria before and knew about slavers."

"I thought you didn't know about Ænæria either, Arynn," said Ben, confused.

"No, I didn't know about the slaves until my mission in Ignistad," Darius continued. "We were never told about them in our training. We only learned what we needed to know. I didn't know what they were called until one of the other Rhion said something to me. It was shortly after that I discovered a network of rebels working under-cover to destabilize Xander's reign."

That's what I've been waiting to hear, Ben thought to himself. His ears perked up, and his eyes widened. He turned around and looked at Darius. "There are rebels? Lots of them? Where?"

Darius looked up, slightly perturbed. "I think there's a lot of them. I doubt there's any one place. Well..." his words trailed off as he became lost deep in thought.

"What? What is it?" Ben demanded.

"It's mostly rumors," Darius confessed. "Nothing concrete."

"Do you want to help us or not?" asked Ben. He was fed up with talking in circles with Darius. *Why can't he be straight with me? Why is he being so cryptic?* Ben was growing impatient. If there was already a resistance, then perhaps he could tell them about the Vault. They could help him find Rose and take Julius down. His mind was racing with possibilities.

Ben looked at Darius sternly, but he received no answer. Frustrated, Ben scoffed and turned to face the road. *Why'd we even bring him in the first place? He's useless to us if he won't give us the information we need.* As though she could sense his anger, Arynn answered Ben. "He obviously wants to help us. That's why he's still here. Darius didn't have to come with us if he didn't want to." Ben ignored her and kept staring at the road, deep in thought.

No one spoke for several hours, except for Arynn when she gave Ben directions at the occasional fork in the road. Ben was over-whelmed with conflicted emotions. He was angry at Darius for being so difficult. *Why can't this be easier? I want to save you, Rose, but I'm beginning to realize that I don't know how.* He thought about how he had no real plan for saving his cousin, and he scolded himself for it. He always had a plan. That was just how he operated. He thought things through to the end and made changes as he saw fit. But now, talking to Darius and realizing how complicated people could be, he realized his plan was horribly incomplete. *What was I thinking? Go to some faraway land, pick up a few strangers on the way, and nicely ask the bad guy for my cousin back? 'Sure,' he'd say. 'Just after I'm done with her.*

You can have her back and go on with your lives as if nothing happened. It's not like I'm plotting to take over the world or anything.' If only it were that easy. He looked at Sierra and petted her gently. *I suppose people don't always cooperate the way you want them too, huh?* Ben thought, as if Sierra could read his mind. She let out a soft whimper and licked his hand.

As the sun dropped in the distance and the air cooled, Darius finally answered Ben. "I *do* want to help," he admitted. "It's hard to talk about all this at once though, okay? I'm still sorting through all this. I've left my whole life behind for this 'resistance,' and I don't even know much about it. It was all hearsay from a few other Rhion on rounds. I just knew, after seeing Ignistad for the first time, that people weren't being treated fairly. I grew up learning so many great things about Ænæria and how it would be the force to rebuild the word—and it still can be! Just not under Xander. He's gone too far."

Ben nodded sympathetically with Darius. It seemed to Ben that Darius's heart was in the right place. Maybe he hadn't made such a big mistake after all.

"That's the real reason I wanted to go into Parvidom with you. I've heard the Guild might have members there."

"What guild? What's Parvidom?" Arynn questioned.

Darius sighed. "Parvidom is a crossroads town between Plutonua and Vestinia. It's the biggest trading hub in the entire kingdom. I figured it's the most likely place to meet with them. I've only heard rumors, and I've never spoken with them directly, but there's supposedly a group of people who call themselves 'the Miners Guild.' I think they're the orchestrators behind the whole resistance."

"Why didn't you tell us about this before?" Arynn asked, her voice sounding annoyed and impatient.

"How did you hear about these rumors in the first place?" Ben added.

"I wanted to get a better understanding of who I was dealing with. Information about the Guild isn't exactly something you should use to start a casual conversation. It's dangerous to talk about. But after hearing your feelings about Ænæria, learning you know about the

Vault, and finding out your cousin was kidnapped...well, I figured this could be my chance to actually make a difference."

Darius went on to explain how he had learned about the Guild. "As I mentioned before, I met other like-minded Rhion. I eventually became trusted enough to go on covert missions for them. We smuggled goods and helped a few people escape the borders—like that family yesterday. Nothing ever bigger than that. At the occasional drop point, we met up with members of the resistance who weren't Rhion—men and women of all different ages. I never spoke with them, though—one of the commanding officers would do that. I eventually learned that the strangers we met with were members of the underground organization known as the Miners Guild.

"On my most recent mission, I was tasked with being the commanding officer with my comrade Petroph supervising, since he's had slightly more insight on the Guild. While we were figuring out the logistics of the mission, he told me he was planning to go to Parvidom alone—in order to avoid suspicion—to get in touch with one of his contacts. Upon arriving in the town, he said he'd arrange a meeting for me with the Guild."

Ben and Arynn shared a glance, clearly thinking the same thing. Ben looked at Darius and said, "I thought you said this was all rumors and hearsay. Why did you lie?"

Arynn nodded, agreeing with Ben.

"Like I said, I wasn't sure how much I could confide in you two," Darius explained. "Besides, I never had any real proof of this Miners Guild, so for all I know, it *is* all hearsay. Petroph may have just been talking big or trying to boost my confidence for my first mission in charge."

"We all know how that mission worked out for you," Arynn said as she rolled her eyes and suppressed a smirk.

"You're right," Darius said softly. "I was caught on my most important mission yet, and all of my comrades died. Before you showed up, I thought I was about to join the others with the Eternal Mother. I asked myself, 'Why isn't the Guild sending help? How did the legate and his men know what we were doing? Were we betrayed? Does this

Guild even exist?' Imagine my sense of relief when you conveniently showed up just as I was about to meet my fate. Then, imagine how it felt to know that it wasn't the resistance coming to save me, but just some farmer? I know you two are mad at me for not telling you all this before, but I had already put my trust in the Guild and that now feels broken. How do you expect me to put all of my trust in some guy who thinks he can take on an army by himself?"

Ben remained silent. Just like that, Darius had confirmed all of his self-doubts and worries. *Why should he put his trust in me? Why should anyone?* If anything, this only made Ben angrier with Darius. Not for being cryptic or avoidant. Not for mistrusting him and Arynn, but for being right. He sighed heavily and said, "Darius, you're r—"

"Wrong," Arynn interrupted. "You know Ben now. You didn't know anyone behind this whole Miners Guild thing. You've actually met Ben and have seen that he's willing to put his life on the line for what he believes is right. That's why I trust him, and it's why I'll venture to guess you do too, deep down. You wouldn't have joined us if you didn't."

Ben blushed, shocked to hear this from Arynn. He forgot she had a soft side to the blunt and tough attitude she typically hid behind. He had a warm feeling about his two new friends. He no longer thought about doubting himself or how hard the journey ahead would be. Instead, he looked at the two very different people before him and smiled to think about their shared goal. *We can do this, Rose. We* will *find you. And we* will *bring you home.*

"My only question now, Darius," Arynn went on, "is why you wanted to go to Parvidom if you felt so betrayed by the Guild? Do you even believe they exist anymore?"

"During the fight with Gatron, I promised myself that, if I survived, I would find a way to Parvidom. I couldn't risk going back to where I was stationed. I needed to follow the only lead I had to discover how Gatron had known what we were up to."

Arynn nodded and smiled, clearly finding his answer to be acceptable. She leaned back and watched the sunset.

"Well, that settles it then, doesn't it?" Ben asked.

"What do you mean?" Darius asked.

"We need to head into town anyway, regardless of the Guild's existence. On the off chance that we learn something, then even better. There's no time to waste!" Ben said with a wide smile as he looked on at the lights of the crossroads town ahead of him.

11. The Crossroads
of Ænæria

The town of Parvidom was one of the strangest places Ben had ever seen. The structures seemed to be renovated projects still standing from the Old Days. Strange, consistent brick-like material not too different from that which made up the remnants of the old roads stood as the foundation for the majority of the buildings. Many of them still had rusted steel poles protruding from the cracks in the buildings, worn down from time. Ben had never laid eyes upon such preserved architecture of the past, and his jaw dropped as he walked among it, stunned.

Suspecting a town probably didn't have lodging for large, blood-covered canines, Ben sent Sierra off into the woods before he boarded Sleipnir for the night.

"I'll be out to check on you tomorrow, girl. Don't worry about me. And...uh...stay out of trouble please," Ben said to the wolf as he scratched her behind the ears. He stopped when he realized there was crusted blood sticking to his fingers. "Gross. I'll try to give you a bath soon, too."

Even though it was well past twilight and into early dusk, count-less townspeople bustled about the town. There was chatter and singing, trading and fighting. From across the town there was a three-story building full of lights, muffled laughter, and a chimney spewing smoke that smelled of fresh yew. There were a few Rhion here and there on patrol, but they paid no mind to Ben and his companions.

Erected at the center of the town was a large, bronze and gold statue of a man standing straight with an outstretched arm. Encir-cling the effigy were a series of symbols engraved in the ground with long dashes halfway between each one. Emblazoned upon the metal man's chest was the Ænærian fist eclipsing the sun. The statue's pedestal bore the motto *Sol Invictus*. The strangest aspect of the statue which was neither its immense size nor the figures carved in the ground. No, the most curious characteristic was how the man was depicted. He did not wear the usual sun-garb that everyone else wore. His hair was clean and short, much like the way Darius wore his own, and his clean-shaven face bore a striking resemblance to Rose.

"The Eternal's Sun's Chosen King," Darius said with a frown as he stood in front of the statue nearly twice his size.

Ben clenched his fist at the mention of his enemy. *Now I have a face for my enemy*, he thought, grinding his teeth. Though he didn't him expect to look so much like Rose.

"What are these symbols around the statue?" Arynn asked.

"It's a sundial. It tells time," Darius said.

"Fascinating!" Arynn jumped with excitement. "How does it work?"

"The arm's shadow moves with the sun," Darius answered, still glaring at Julius's metallic face. "It points to a different number each of which represents an hour of the day. It only works when the sun is out, and during the spring and summer it'll hit a few numbers more than once since there are only twelve hours marked."

Arynn frowned. "Why are there only twelve? That doesn't make sense."

"I'm not sure. That's just how Jul—," Darius cut himself short, looking around as if to check if anyone else were listening to him. "The King, I mean—dictated it."

Ben's brow furrowed as he gave Darius a perplexed look. "What is it with you and calling him by his real name?"

"I-I don't have a problem...It's just," Darius stammered his speech. "Well, if that is his real name, then I'm sure there's a reason people don't know about it."

This time Arynn interjected. "So? It's just a name. What's the big deal?"

Looking nervous, Darius gestured for Arynn to keep her voice down. "*Shh!* We're in Ænæria now." He spoke with a low whisper. "The King has ears everywhere. If you start announcing you know sensitive information, then bad things could happen. You can't go saying things like this too loudly in public."

"Oh, Ascendants, why not?" Arynn said, rolling her eyes.

"Don't say that either! I told you before how people don't believe in that..." Darius struggled to find an appropriate word, "...stuff, here. You can get in a lot of trouble for it."

"Okay, take it easy, Darius," Ben said as he put a hand on his new companion's shoulder. "To be fair, you didn't warn us about all this."

"I *did* warn you about pag—*erm*, non-believers not being tolerated."

"But you didn't say anything about mentioning Jul—," Ben started before being cut off.

"Stop! Look, I'll explain later when we're in a safer place. Let's focus on getting to an inn for the night. If we share a room, we can talk quietly."

Arynn groaned, "Aww, I have to listen to Ben snoring *again* tonight?"

"Arynn...you're the one who snores. I thought you said I drooled."

Twisting her red hair around her finger, Arynn ignored Ben and stared off into the distance. Ben and Darius chuckled, walking past the statue toward the inn at the other end of the town.

Music burst through the inn's door the moment Darius pulled the handle. It was unlike anything Ben had ever heard. Bronze and brass instruments he had never seen before were being played in elegant harmony with the typical drums and flutes he had heard at festivals as a child. He had forgotten how much he missed the soothing sound of music as he followed Darius into the tavern. Ben wondered if these unfamiliar instruments and compositions were a consequence of Julius's reign.

Did Julius introduce this? But it's so beautiful. Is it possible there is actually some good coming from him being King?

As the band played on a stage in the back of the room, towns-people drank and filled the air with laughter. They were deep in conversations, most of which were seemingly about nothing. It was an atmosphere to which Ben had never been exposed. As they approached the innkeeper's counter, he pondered how oddly this place made him feel.

Strange. But in a good way, I think. It's just so...different. Alive.

"Aw c'mon, Marin, not this story again!" exclaimed a man at the bar.

"Well, Alexius here hasn't—hic!—heard it yet!" cried the man called Marin, who was pointing to a man across the tavern that was clearly uninterested in the story. Marin took another sip from his mug and belched. "So, anyway, there I was in the middle of this field. I saws a bright light coming from the skies! I says to myself, 'Self, that looks like a star coming down!' and so I tried to hightail it outta there, yes, I did! But it wasn't no star! It was an ancestor!"

The first man, sitting next to Marin, scoffed and took a swig of his drink. "There ain't no ancestors coming back to life, Marin. You just ate something poor that night."

Marin wagged his finger at the man next to him. "Now, Horus, don't you go ruinin' my story! The ancestor was in some type of large metal vessel—maybe it was her resurrection tomb! A blindin' light shone from it as she climbed outta it. She had yellow eyes and towered above me at twenty feet tall!"

"Last time you said it was an angel with blue eyes and seven feet tall. The time before that you made up a color and said they were flib. You've changed the story so many times over the last twenty years," Horus antagonized.

"Oh, right. Maybe they *were* flib.... Say, have you ever seen someone with flib eyes, Alexius?" Marin shouted. Alexius simply rolled his eyes and continued to chat with the woman seated to his left.

Arynn tapped Ben on the shoulder as Darius spoke with the host. "That man mentioned the ancestors—that's what they call the Ascend—*er*, you know what I mean."

Ben saw an excited look on Arynn's face. He didn't want to disappoint her by pointing out that the man was clearly a drunk and probably hallucinated or dreamed the whole thing. "*Um*, yeah. I think that's what Darius said."

Her eyes lit up, and her smile widened. "Do you think the 'ancestors' can come back to life?"

Ben saw where this was going. She was thinking of her mother. He didn't want to offer her false hope or upset her, and so he said, "I couldn't say. I don't know much about the 'ancestors.' My people don't really think about life after death." Arynn frowned and looked at the floor as she twirled her hair around her finger. "Though, I suppose it's possible, right? I mean, if there is some sort of afterlife, then I don't see why the possibility of returning couldn't exist." He stared at Arynn with a feigned smile, hoping to cheer her up.

Before Arynn could respond, Darius returned and changed the subject. "Looks like we're in luck. There's only one room left, and it's got two beds. Arynn, you have the sols, right?"

Arynn patted her pockets and felt for the sack of metal coins. "How much is it?" she asked.

"He didn't say. Wouldn't discuss payment until he spoke with the person with the sols," Darius said with a skeptical frown.

Arynn approached the host and placed the sack of coins on his counter. "How much for the room?"

The host eyed the sack of sols and then gave Arynn an uncomfortable look. "Cost is per person, not per room. The room has two beds. I see three of you here."

Arynn rolled her eyes. "The boys'll share. How much?"

"Why bother payin' extra for a less comfortable experience? I've got a large bed upstairs. Plenty of room next to me, and it won't cost a sol," the host said with a leering grin.

Ben clenched his fists, readying to argue with the man, but Arynn held up a hand, blocking him from coming closer. "I've got this," she murmured out the corner of her mouth.

"So, what'll it be, Red?" the host said. He gave off a nasty smile that revealed many missing teeth.

Arynn gave the man a short, sarcastic smile just before grabbing him by the collar and tugging his neck toward her. The host's smile vanished into to a nervous grimace, and the tavern went silent—even the band stopped. "Look here, creep," Arynn said sternly as she looked the host in the eyes. "If you want to keep the rest of your teeth, then I suggest you cut the crap and give me and my friends the room. *How. Much.* Do *not* make me repeat myself again."

The innkeeper trembled. "Y-you, y-you can't threaten m-m-me. I c-can re-refuse to s-s-serve y-you!"

"Yes, you can," she said, glowering. "But we can find somewhere else to stay for the night if we must. You, on the other hand, can't grow back more teeth. From the looks of it, you don't have many to spare."

Still shaking, the host gave a look of defeat. "F-fine. It's two s-s-silver and three c-copper sols each. Please let m-me go now!"

Arynn loosened her grip, and the innkeeper backed away from her reach. She picked out the coins from the pouch and slammed them on the countertop. The host grabbed them greedily and put them in his pocket as he quickly backed away from Arynn once again. He turned his back to the group and pulled open a drawer and fiddled with its contents. He returned to them seconds later with an iron skeleton key engraved with the symbols 'XXIII.'

"The room is on the second floor," he said with his hands shaking as he relinquished the key to Arynn. "I want you three out by mornin' and I don't wanna see you again!"

"Trust me, the feeling is mutual," she said as she snatched the key from the man's hand.

As the three departed from the petrified innkeeper, the music and chatter resumed as though nothing out of the ordinary had transpired.

Just another night for them, I suppose, Ben thought to himself.

They carried their belongings to the second floor and went to the second door on the left. Arynn unlocked the door, and they entered the room. It was a small room with two beds crammed next to each other that barely seemed to make up the size of a single one.

"I bet you're wishing you took him up on his offer now, *eh*?" Darius teased, nudging Arynn.

Arynn frowned and moved one of the beds as far away from the other as possible. She collapsed on the mattress and let out a sigh of relief. "I don't know what you're talking about. I have plenty of room. You two are the ones who need to share. But if you hurry back down, Darius, I'm sure he still has room in his bed for you."

Darius's smile disappeared, and he stood silently, looking quite awkward. Ben laughed. "She's got you there," he said. "But don't worry about it. I'm so tired I could sleep on the floor tonight just fine. You'll have to drive tomorrow, though." Ben let out an exaggerated yawn. "Oh, and let me use one of the pillows."

Darius nodded and threw one of his pillows to Ben. "We should go back down and get some food. Maybe see if we can find out anything about the Guild...."

"And do tell, how you plan on doing that," Arynn said with a sneer, still lying comfortably on her bed. "Aren't you going to enlighten us about why you're so afraid to talk about Julius and Ascendants first?"

"*Ugh*, fine," Darius groaned. "Just keep it down, all right? It's not safe to talk about certain things in Ænæria. Since it's believed that Xander is the Eternal Mother's Chosen King, many see him as being like the Great Father."

"You people think this guy married the sun?" Arynn asked flippantly.

"In a way, yes," he answered seriously.

Ben was painting a better image of Julius in his mind. The King wanted to control what people thought and believed. He probably made up the whole 'sun-worship thing' to control people, too. Darius had previously mentioned how non-believers were severely punished. Inciting fear made sense as a powerful way to control people and establish an entire kingdom in only fifteen years. Ben pinched the bridge of his nose in frustration. *This Julius guy is too smart. There's no way we'll be able to take him on alone. We need to find the Guild!*

"Do either of you have any ideas for getting in touch with the Miners Guild while we're here?" Ben asked. "It seems like Julius probably has ears everywhere. I doubt we can go around and simply ask."

Arynn had a look of intense concentration, but she didn't say anything. Darius shrugged. "I haven't a clue. No one told me any code words or anything. It kind of looked like the Rhion flashed a badge or something to Guild members whenever they met."

Ben gave this some thought. Before he could make sense of it, Arynn said, "Maybe the badge has some sort of password on it. Something that other members could read?"

Again, Darius shrugged.

Ben shook his head, "No, a password alone wouldn't make sense," Ben said. "Anyone could learn it and just say it. Maybe a password *and* a badge or something? That way, if a badge were stolen or reproduced, you still wouldn't pass the Guild's security check."

"Let's focus on the badge for now, because that could give us a clue for who to look for," Darius said. "It would need to be something a member could instantly recognize. Something they could hide in plain sight if they wanted someone to reach out to them without a meeting being established."

The trio waited in silence, pondering. Arynn laid down on her bed and looked pensively at the ceiling. Darius paced the room, mouthing words to himself but not saying anything aloud. Ben felt the need to fidget with something—that always helped him focus. His mind would wander unless he was doing something with his hands, and he could feel his concentration slipping away. He played with his watch's wristband, clicking the latch as he opened and closed it. He examined the numbers on its face. *This was the last puzzle I solved,* he thought to himself remembering how he had deciphered the Vault's coordinates. *I can figure this one out too, I know it!*

Darius grunted out of frustration and snatched Ben's watch from him. "Hey! Give that back!"

"Will you *please* stop clicking this thing? It's so annoying, and I can't hear myself think!" Darius yelled.

"You could have said something! Give it back to me!"

Darius eyed the watch from different angles. "What is this thing anyway? Some dumb relic?"

Ben felt his face burn with anger. "Just give it back to me!"

"*Shut up!*" Arynn yelled. "Darius—just give him back the trinket. Ben—stop being annoying and clicking it."

Darius handed the watch to Ben. "What does that symbol on the back of it mean?"

"What sym—?" Ben turned his watch around and saw the odd engraving of a geometric symbol with concentric squares and a circle in the middle. Then he suddenly remembered the words Arynn's father had said when he had seen it and told them to go to Jordysc. *As above, so below.*

With everything that's been going on, he nearly forgot about the *other* side of the watch. "Of course! I bet that's how the Guild is communicating!"

Darius and Arynn looked at Ben expectantly. "How?" Arynn asked. "They talk through watches?"

"No! They have a symbol! That must be what's on the badges they show each other," Ben exclaimed excitedly. "I bet if we find someone downstairs wearing some sort of special symbol, we'll find one of the Miners."

"So what? We don't have a password," Arynn said with a frustrated look on her face.

"I think we do! Do you remember what your father said when he saw my watch in Vänalleato? 'As above, so below.' I bet that's the password! Your father probably knows about the Guild! How else would he have known about a village called Jordysc in the middle of a foreign country?"

Arynn frowned, and her face turned red. She looked angry and caught off guard. "You're an idiot if you think my father is some secret agent of this Guild. He's a cartographer—it's his job to make maps and know about places."

"Then why did he recognize my watch? Why did he say those words?"

"Ben does make a good point, Arynn," Darius added.

"Stay out of this!" Arynn snapped. She looked to her feet and twirled her hair around her finger. "My father wouldn't keep something like that from me. He just wouldn't."

Ben realized Arynn was hurt by the possibility that her father had kept something from her. He wondered if there was some deeper issue between the father and daughter that he didn't know about. Something about trust. He placed a hand on Arynn's shoulder. She jumped, evidently startled by his sudden closeness. It appeared that she had blushed for a moment but quickly turned away before Ben could get a better look. "I didn't mean to accuse your father of anything. You know him better than I do. Obviously. But it couldn't hurt to check it out, okay? We don't have much else to go on." She nodded and made her way for the door as Ben and Darius followed.

The travelers walked back down to the tavern to find it just as lively as when they had left. People were dancing, laughing, and telling stories.

"We should split up," Arynn suggested. "Look around for symbols and talk to people. We could even ask if anyone has seen any odd insignias recently."

Ben and Darius nodded in agreement. Arynn made her way toward the bar where the man named Marin was still arguing about the color flib. Darius seemed to make his way toward the host, perhaps hoping Arynn had given him enough of a scare to reveal rumors without any problems.

Well, where do I start? Ben thought to himself.

He scanned the room to see if there was anyone by themselves or at least with only a small group of people. He would feel more comfortable talking to fewer people if he could help it.

How do Arynn and Darius talk to people so easily? I don't even know how to start a conversation that'll lead to the topic of a symbol.

After pacing the room for a few moments, Ben decided to stop at one of the counters serving drinks. He ordered a water and sat on the stool while leaning against the bar to face the room. He watched the people dancing, examining their clothing and jewelry. When he didn't see anything of note, he turned to the band.

Maybe one of their instruments will have an odd symbol. Would that be too conspicuous?

"Here's your water. First one's on the house," the bartender said. She was a woman of about his aunt's age and looked much larger than most people Ben had seen. "You're not a regular. Where're you headed?"

Ben sipped his refilled canteen and thanked the woman. "What makes you think I'm passing through?" he responded loudly over the ruckus.

The bartender raised an eyebrow. "Because that's what this town is for. Biggest crossroads in the Northern Realm. You're clearly not from around here if you don't know that. So what's the destination?"

"Jor—," Ben paused, catching himself. How did he know he could trust this woman? He figured it would be better not to say where he's going. She was, after all, Ænærian—the enemy. *But Darius is Ænærian, too.* Ben feigned a cough to cover up his almost revealing

Jordysc as his destination. "Excuse me. Sorry about that. *Erm*, anyway, I'm just a nomad."

The bartender's eyebrow relaxed. "*Ah*, a nomad. I've run into people like you before. It's been awhile though. I didn't think any outsiders passed alone through Ænæria anymore."

"Why is that?" Ben asked.

The older woman went pale and gulped as she looked around the room. "Well, people need to watch what they say around here. Foreigners don't know that. They get taken away. Reckon word about that spreads and people stop coming." She sighed and gave a half-smile which Ben figured wasn't quite genuine. "It's just as well, though. We've done fine in the thirteen provinces without outsiders. *Er*, no offense."

Ben sipped his drink again. "None taken. You don't trade with outsiders at all?" It made sense why he hadn't heard of the country until recently.

The bartender scoffed. "Not at all. We only trade with the other provinces. Enough skilled labor within them. Food the only real problem."

"There's fourteen now," a stranger from down the bar said. Ben couldn't see their face as they wore a baggy, dark cloak over their head.

"What're you goin' on about?" the bartender asked.

"A minute ago you said that there's thirteen provinces. Not anymore—there's fourteen now. His Majesty has spread his glory to yet another of the Northern Kingdoms, the long-disputed land of Bacchuso," the stranger said.

"Surely you mean by the Sun's glory?" the bartender corrected.

"Oh, but of course," the stranger said, snickering.

"Why...that's terrific news! When did this happen? How come I hadn't heard of it?" the bartender asked.

"Oh, word hasn't spread much yet. I just hear things early," the stranger said, seemingly uninterested with talking to the bartender any further.

The bartender opened her mouth to say something but was interrupted by someone calling for her. She walked away, presumably to help a customer, and left Ben alone with the stranger.

The stranger turned closer to Ben. "Woah, there's something you don't see every day," she said to Ben, pointing at his wrist.

"It's just some ancient artifact," he answered guardedly.

"It's a Pre-War artifact, to be exact," the stranger said. She pulled down her shawl and revealed herself. She was a girl with long curly black hair, tanned skin, and a large faded burn that spanned from the lower left side of her chin to just below her eye. She looked to be around Ben's age, though with the burn he could not tell if she was older or younger.

"Pre-War? What are you talking about?" Ben asked.

The woman studied Ben. She seemed quite interested in him, but he could not tell why. "You don't know? You're headed to Jordysc, aren't you?" She grinned slyly.

"*What?* How d'you know—*er*, I mean," Ben struggled with what to say. "You must be mistaken. I'm just a—"

"Nomad? Vagabond? Call it what you will, but I know where you're going. It makes sense, of course, with that watch you're wearing," the stranger said, still eyeing Ben's watch.

"You know what it is?" There was a slight tremble in his voice.

"I know it is a watch, yes. As for what it *really* is, well, I have my suspicions."

"It's just a watch. It doesn't even work. Who *are* you? I didn't catch your name."

The girl acted as though she hadn't heard him. "May I see it?"

"What? No—I don't even know who you are!" *What's her aim here? How does she know where I'm going? Has she been following us?*

"Who I am is of no importance. I serve a higher purpose. It would be a shame if you ended up not sharing the same values."

"I think you have me confused for someone else."

"I suppose I must demonstrate an effort of good faith. If you are indeed who I think you are—and you are on your way to Jordysc— then you will need to trust my people." She did something Ben had not expected. In a moment of what felt like sheer luck, the stranger pulled something out of her cloak and flashed it to Ben quickly before putting it back. On a black patch of leather was a symbol that looked all too familiar: the symbol on the back of his watch. The design was slightly more complex, but there was no mistaking it for what it truly was. He could feel his heart racing and his hands beginning to shake. All by pure luck, Ben had done it. He had found the symbol he was looking for and the Parvidom contact for the Miners Guild. *I can't wait to tell the others*, Ben thought to himself. *They'll hardly believe it*. But after the initial excitement, a more troubling thought came into Ben's mind. *By what coincidence is it that this is the same symbol that is on my dad's watch? He left it for me* before *Julius founded Ænæria. But what if this stranger isn't part of the Miners Guild, but instead part of something else? That would just complicate matters. I don't need complicated! I just need to get to Rose!*

The stranger offered Ben a thoughtful look and smiled. "Do you have anything to say in response? Choose your words carefully."

Removing it from his wrist, Ben studied the underside of his father's watch. The symbol wasn't exactly the same, but it bore a striking resemblance. The clamor of the room seemed to fade away as his eyes probed the bizarre engraving. He showed the engraving on the back of his watch to the stranger and said, "As above, so below."

"As above, so below," the girl whispered back.

"How did you know this," Ben pointed at the watch, "would be here? How could you have possibly known?"

The stranger placed her hood over her head and got up from her seat. She stood for a moment, giving Ben a chill down his spine as though her masked eyes were peering into his soul. After a moment of silence, she finally spoke.

"When you reach your destination, show them the mandala and say the words." With that, she made her way to the exit.

"Wait—don't go! Who are you? What's a mandala? Are you with the—," Ben yelled, catching himself from yelling about the Guild aloud.

The hooded stranger stopped for a moment and turned her head to the side to say, "When you get to Jordysc, head for the mines. Goodnight, Benedict."

The stranger then disappeared into the crowd of people. Ben chased after her, pushing through patrons and scanning the room for her. But it was too late; she was gone. He ran outside the inn, determined to find her. The night was awfully cold, and after several minutes of wandering around the outside grounds, Ben gave up and returned inside.

As he walked back into the inn, Ben decided to look for Arynn and Darius to let them know what he had learned. *This might be enough to go on. She said to 'head for the mines.' That must be a reference to the Miners Guild!*

His search of the common room for his friends to no avail. Thinking they must have gone up to bed, he decided to retire as well. Ben found his room locked, but a there was light shining through the threshold. He gave a soft knock.

"Who is it?" Arynn called through the door.

"It's me," Ben replied.

"Sorry, I don't know anyone named Me. You must have the wrong room. Goodbye."

Ben rolled his eyes. "Oh, *ha ha*, very funny, Arynn. Let me in, will you? I have news."

Arynn chuckled from behind the door before finally opening it. She was wearing her cotton nightclothes and looked exhausted. She yawned and stretched her arms. "Where's Darius?" she asked as she plopped onto her bed.

Ben gave Arynn a look of bewilderment. "I thought he was with you. I didn't see him downstairs."

"Looks like you get a bed to yourself tonight, then. He was probably in the privy when you were looking for him," Arynn said sleepily.

"I guess so. Do you want to hear what I learned?" Ben asked, eager to talk about his meeting with the strange woman.

"You can tell me, but don't expect me to stay awake," Arynn said, before letting out an exaggerated yawn. "Hurry up, I'm falling asleep already." She feigned a snore.

Ben rolled his eyes and threw a pillow at her. She yelped, and the two shared a laugh.

Ben and Arynn sat across each other on their beds, and Ben told Arynn everything that had learned: the stranger with the hood, their hunch about the Guild's symbol and password, and about the new province, Bacchuso.

"According to the stranger," Ben said, "this new province is really far north. I'm worried that's where the Vault is, and that we're too late."

"There's no use in worrying about it, Ben," Arynn said. "If anything, it means we're on the right track." There was something about the tone of her voice that seemed off. Her playfulness from before their conversion had vanished.

Ben raised an eyebrow, concerned about Arynn. "Are you okay?"

Arynn offered a half-hearted smile. "Of course. Why?"

"You seem upset. Was it something I said?"

Arynn sighed and looked out the window at the starry sky. "It's about the password. My dad is the one who told you about it. How did he know? He and I don't have secrets. We trust each other."

Ben offered a sympathetic smile. "I get that. Everything about my parents is a secret to me, and somehow the Vault is involved, too. My aunt and mentor both knew about the Vault my whole life, and they never told me about it until Rose was taken. I grew up thinking that half of Freztad's villagers left because of my father. But that wasn't true—it was because of Julius, who also wanted to look for the Vault."

They sat for a moment in silence. Arynn looked out the window, and Ben played with his watch's clasp.

"I guess what I'm trying to say is that people keep secrets," Ben finally said. "Even from people they're close to. And it sucks."

Arynn chuckled. "Yeah, it really does. It's just so much all at once. A few days ago, I thought my life was...well, as normal as it could be for someone like me living in Vänalleato." Arynn's face reddened, and she averted her gaze.

"What is that supposed to mean?"

"Forget it. I'm just...different, okay? You wouldn't understand."

Ben smiled. "Believe me. I know what it's like to be different. Try me."

Arynn shook her head and hid a small smile. "Maybe another time. Look, I know you helped me find my dad, and I'll always be grateful to you for that. But do you know how hard it was for me to leave all of that behind to travel with you?"

Ben didn't know what to say.

Arynn played with her hair as she looked down to her feet. "I'm not stupid, Ben. I know the odds we're up against. But I didn't care about that because I wanted to help you. When I met you, I knew there was something...I don't know...different about you, but in a good way. When I saw you fight those slavers to help my dad, and then go out of your way to help one of them...Ascendants, that's when I knew you were the type of person I wanted to follow."

Ben's eyes widened. He didn't know where all this was coming from.

"Ever since I was little, I've wanted to see the world that my father always showed me on maps. I wanted to make my own by seeing those lands with my own eyes. You coming to Vänalleato was not only a blessing because you saved my dad, but because you gave me a way to realize my dreams. But just because I'm following my dreams doesn't mean this is all easy for me—and learning my dad is keeping secrets from me just has me feeling so defeated."

The two sat quietly in the candlelit room. Ben felt the urge to put a hand on Arynn's shoulder, but felt it may not be a great idea. She didn't really look like she wanted to be touched.

"I don't know why you'd want to follow me," Ben finally said. "I've never been a leader or anything like that. I'm just...well, I'm just trying to do what I think is right. The fact that you want to help me though...well, that makes me feel like I'm on the right track."

Arynn's bright blue eyes stared back into Ben's. "I think that's what makes a good leader. You don't necessarily want to be one, but you stand up for what you believe in."

"How can I stand up for what I believe in if I don't even believe in myself?" Ben replied, nervously fidgeting with his watch. "This whole journey is a mess. A day hasn't gone by without something going wrong. I just got a solid lead on the Guild, and now I'm worried about Darius. It's been awhile since we've seen him. What if he betrayed us? And then there's the possibility that Julius is already at the Vault— and who knows what'll happen when he gets inside."

To Ben's surprise, Arynn placed a hand on his shoulder. "I doubt he'd betray us. Darius may be really devoted to that sun god of his, but he doesn't seem to have any love for Julius. We just have to wait for him. I'm sure he'll be back soon. He probably just found a solid lead or something."

Ben's stomach lurched, and his face felt hot with guilt. He knew Arynn was right—he needed to allow himself to trust Darius.

"You can't focus on all the negatives, either," Arynn said in a comforting voice. "The positives are just as important—if not more so —than the negatives. You found a lead on the Guild. That's gotta count for something."

Ben smiled. He and Arynn's eyes met, and he felt his stomach drop like a rock in a pond. Neither of them said anything. They just stared at each other in silence, and Ben felt himself moving closing to her.

All of a sudden there was a loud *BANG-BANG* at the door. Ben and Arynn jumped, startled from the unexpected interruption.

Arynn leapt to her feet. "I bet that's Darius!" she said with crack in her voice. She opened the door and screamed.

Ben jumped to his feet when he saw the five people at the threshold. In front was the creepy innkeeper, three Rhion, and Darius— who had a gag in his mouth and ropes binding his wrists. The Rhion in the middle didn't wear a helmet, but instead had sideburns reaching down to his jaw, and golden-white hair tied with an ornament that looked like a sun atop his head. He wore two swords on his belt and held an orange-tinted rifle in his hands. A sung.

"That's them, all right!" the innkeeper shouted, pointing at Ben and Arynn. "I think she's the one in charge, too! Make sure you rough her up extra for me!" he said with an ugly scowl at Arynn.

The sung-wielding Rhion stepped forward, pushing the innkeeper out of the way. "You two are both under arrest for the murder of Legate Gatron. Keep your hands where I can see them, and no funny business!" He spoke with a snarl, and his voice was deep and raspy.

Gatron is dead? How did that happen? Are Pawel and his parents okay? Ben was already overwhelmed by everything happening and getting arrested was obviously the last thing he needed. How was he supposed to get out of this one? He was surrounded, and fighting back probably wasn't the smartest move.

The Rhion in front snapped his fingers and motioned for the soldiers behind him to arrest Ben and Arynn. They walked forward with swords drawn and ropes in their hands, ready for the arrest.

Decisive action, Ben thought, reflecting on Rakshi's words. She would put herself out there to save people she cared about. *She did risk it, and now it's time to honor that.* He looked at his sword, which was in its scabbard and resting against the foot of the bed. He darted towards it and drew the weapon. The Rhion closest to him swung at Ben, but he parried the attack and kicked the soldier away from him. The solider slammed against the wall and fell to the floor. Ben turned to attack the Rhion restraining Arynn.

"Ben, no! Watch out!" Arynn cried.

Ben turned and saw the sung-wielding Rhion aim his weapon at Ben. A flash of orange and yellow light discharged from the weapon. Instinctively, Ben raised his sword to protect himself, though he knew it wouldn't do him any good. The energy slammed against him with such force that he fell backwards against the room's window. The glass shattered against his back, and Ben fell to the ground below.

12.The Tower on
the Mountain

The top of Ben's head throbbed, like the skin of a drum being struck over and over again. He opened his eyes, expecting to see the broken window he had fallen through, but instead saw the black, rainy sky beyond a wooden entranceway. Instead of being covered in glass as he had expected, he found himself buried in a pile of straw and surrounded by the smell of manure. *Where am I? How much time has passed?*

He felt the throbbing again, though this time Ben realized it wasn't because of his fall. There was a young boy poking his head with the shaft of a broom.

"Hey, you can't stay here any longer," the boy said, a slight chill in his voice.

Ben sat up, turning to face the boy. "Who are you? Where am I?"

The boy looked to be about twelve years old, had long black hair, and his hands and face were covered in dirt. "Don't you worry about who I am. You need to get outta here before Simon finds out I hid you."

"Simon?" Ben asked. "Who's that?"

"The innkeeper," the boy said. "My boss. He's looking for you. Legate Fenwin has a warrant out for your capture. Big reward, too."

So he was *a legate*, Ben thought. The name was familiar, too. He recalled Darius mentioning Fenwin before, calling him one of the worst of Julius's underlings. *That definitely complicates things.* "How did I end up here? How long have I been out?"

"Only like twenty minutes," the boy said. "I was on my way back to the stable, and you fell outta the window right in front of me. You looked hurt, so I brought you here to hide."

"Why would you help me? You could've gotten in a lot of trouble," Ben said. He didn't mean to sound ungrateful, but he worried about what would happen to the boy if he were caught.

"Believe me, you don't want Fenwin capturing you. He's bad news. Plus, if you ticked off Simon you probably aren't too bad." The boy half chuckled.

Ben stood up and brushed the straw off his clothes. "Do you know where he would have taken me?"

"To the prison up in the mountains, though they're more like big hills if you ask me. Looks like they captured both of your friends and these two scary guys with skulls tattooed on their faces." Then he raised an eyebrow. "Wait, you're not planning on going there alone, are you?"

Ben smirked. "Don't worry about, kid. I don't want you getting in more trouble for knowing too much."

The boy turned to one of the stalls and beckoned for Ben to follow him. Sleipnir was inside the stall, standing in front of Ben's and his friends' belongings. Then the boy rummaged around in a stack of hay. He pulled out Ben's sword and handed it to him.

"This should be everything," the boy said. "I snuck in your room last night and got the rest of it for you while Simon was drunk, trying to pick up women." The boy shook his head and rolled his eyes.

Ben was surprised how helpful the boy was. "You went through a lot of trouble just to help me. What's the deal?"

"If Fenwin was looking for you, then that means you're probably causing trouble for Ænæria. That's good enough for me."

Ben looked at the boy with an expression of shock.

"Don't be so surprised," the boy said. "This is Parvidom. People with the Guild pass through all the time. I'm just happy to play my part. Now get out of here before Simon shows up!"

Ben thanked the boy, giving him a gold sol as payment for his trouble. Ben hid his face with his scarf and goggles, attached Sleipnir to his carriage, and made his way toward the mountains.

About an hour later, the road made its way into the highlands where it was damp and foggy. After a few minutes along the mountainside, Sierra showed up out of nowhere. She barked softly to greet Ben and ran ahead of him. *She must have seen the legate with Arynn and Darius.*

Ben followed Sierra up the gentle incline. Eventually, though, it became much too steep with the muddy slopes, and Ben had to abandon his carriage to find a place to hide Sleipnir.

"Sorry, bud," Ben said as he found a dank cave for the horse to rest in. "It's getting too steep, and there's no way one horse alone can make it up the rest of the way."

Sleipnir snorted at Ben as if insulted by the very notion that he wasn't as good as a whole caravan of horses.

Ben and Sierra scaled the muddied mountainside on foot and reconnected with the Rhion's trail. They couldn't have been too far away now; Ben could see torches in the distance where the rocky eminence plateaued.

Finally reaching the top, Ben could see his destination before him. Standing about a quarter of a mile away from the cliffs was a thin tower of approximately four stories flying the Ænærian flag. The prison seemed to be another leftover structure from the Old Days; it appeared to be constructed from the same material as many of the buildings in Parvidom. The tower was surrounded by a crude barbed wire fence with a single entrance. Just outside the tower was a wooden stable where Ben watched the Rhion unload the prisoners from their carriage. Four of the guards were armed to the teeth with long polearms, guns on their hips, and shields on their backs. They escorted Arynn, Darius, and the two tattoo-faced men between them while two other Rhion marched behind with bows and arrows.

Leading the group was the same man who had shot Ben out of the window—Legate Fenwin.

Fenwin led the prisoners and other Rhion to the front gate. An Ænærian soldier wearing an odd three-pronged helmet stumbled out from the tower with two other guards and bowed to the leading guard.

"Second-Legate Fenwin! We...uh...we weren't expecting you, sir," the helmeted soldier stammered.

"At ease, Warden," Fenwin snarled in his unnerving and raspy voice. "I was on my way to deliver some barbarians from the East when I ran into three of the conspirators involved in Legate Gatron's death. The third one is dead though, pity I couldn't bring him to you."

The prison warden's eyes raced between the prisoners and the legate's sung. He appeared quite uncomfortable.

"I believe the words you're looking for, Warden, are 'thank you,'" Fenwin said to the speechless warden.

"Legate Gatron is dead?" the warden asked.

Fenwin growled and slammed his sung into the warden's gut. The warden bellowed in pain and coughed up blood. "You know I don't like to repeat myself!"

The warden gasped for air. "I...I wasn't asking...I just didn't know...that the legate had been killed."

Fenwin grabbed the warden by the throat and picked him up off his feet. The warden clutched at his neck, gasping desperately for air. "Are you questioning me then, Chan?" He threw the warden to the ground.

Warden Chan bent over on the ground on his hands and knees, coughing. "Never, sir. I-I simply hadn't heard. May...may I ask what happened, sir?"

Fenwin sneered at Chan. "A handful of his Rhion betrayed him. Turns out they were working for the damn Guild, trying to smuggle out a family evading the census. Gatron caught onto their little rouse, confronted them, and got himself captured. These two here," Fenwin pointed at Darius and Arynn, "sent Gatron and what remained of his squadron off to the heathens down south. He tried to escape, and there was a sung malfunction. Whole party blown to bits. As the closest legate, I took it upon myself to find the deserter and question him myself. Now, are you going to give me a room to punish them or am I going to need to find a room myself?"

Ben continued to peer over the boulder and saw that the warden was escorting Legate Fenwin and the others into the tower. Two guards remained at the front of the gate standing at attention and keeping watch.

What was he to do now? Arynn and Darius could be anywhere inside the prison with who knows how many guards. He had already lost against Fenwin once, and that was with only two other Rhion present. An entire building full of them? That would be hopeless. He needed a plan, one that would catch the Ænærians off guard. Then, as he gazed over the boulder at the tower, a ridiculous idea came into his mind.

Ben told Sierra his plan. "So...assuming you can understand *any* of what I just told you, are you ready?"

Sierra barked softly in affirmation.

Ben sighed. "Let's do this."

Sierra leapt over the boulder and worked her way toward the gate, out of the guards' sights. Ben made his way in the opposite direction. Having positioned themselves on either side of the guards, Ben and the wolf charged toward the two soldiers. One Ænærian suddenly found himself on the ground with a ferocious beast atop him. Sierra pressed her paw on the man's mouth, taking away his ability to scream. The other guard turned to see the wolf atop his partner just in time for Ben to come up from behind and put him into a chokehold. The man fell to the ground unconscious. Ben took the butt of his sword and slammed it into the other's head, knocking him out as well.

Acting quickly, Ben removed one of the guards' armor and put it on himself. It was loose fitting, but he hoped it would be convincing enough. Ben tied and gagged the stripped guard before allowing Sierra to drag him behind the boulder where he had previously hidden. Then, putting on the guard's helmet to cover his face, Ben set the last part of the plan into motion.

"Guards! Help! Help!" Ben shouted.

Sierra let off a fierce howl as she stood atop the still-armored but unconscious guard. Two guards ran outside the tower to see what the commotion was. They saw Ben running toward them, away from Sierra as she viciously tore at the guard's armor below her. The man awoke and screamed. The guards hesitated before the large canine in front of them.

"What are you doing? Help him!" Ben shouted at the men. "I'm going to run inside to get more help! I'm no use out here. That thing broke my spear!"

The guards looked at Ben and then the wolf, terrified. "*Uh*...yeah, you do that..." one of the guards said, quivering.

Ben made his way inside, patting at his sword, which was hidden underneath his tabard, to make sure it was still there. Guards rushed past Ben while he worked his way up the stairs. He walked by the prison cells—small rooms with steel bars and nothing but bricks still standing from the Old Days. There weren't even beds or buckets for them to relieve themselves. He kept walking past them, looking for Arynn and Darius.

Before making his way up the stairs to the next floor, Ben looked out the window and saw Sierra fending off seven guards while five others watched from the distance. She swiftly dodged each strike of a guard's spear and countered by clamping her jaws onto the polearm and yanking it from the man's grasp. With the weapon in her mouth, she charged toward the middle of two other Ænærians and knocked them to the ground with each end of the spear. She clenched down even harder, snapping the weapon in half. Evidently, this wasn't the first time she had done this as there were many other broken spears lying about.

Arrows flew at Sierra from all directions, and she dodged as best she could—those that missed came dangerously close to other guards. Those that seemed to have hit her helplessly bounced off her white coat. Ben watched in amazement as his canine companion effortlessly fended off the barrage of Ænærian attacks.

Feeling slightly more settled by knowing that Sierra would be fine, Ben climbed the next set of stairs to search for Arynn. This floor had a lot more guards than the one below—perhaps most of the others were outside. At first glance, Ben counted nine guards patrolling the floor, checking the cells and occasionally looking out the front window. He would have to be much more careful with his search here.

Walking at a leisurely pace to avoid suspicion, Ben once again peered into the stone cells. He made his way around all of the floor's cells and still couldn't find his friends. Instead, he did happen to find one of the tattoo-faced men—a good sign in Ben's eyes. He stopped by the man's cell and, scanning the room to ensure no one was paying him any mind, spoke to the prisoner.

"You came in with three others, right?" Ben asked in a whisper.

The bald man looked up to Ben with a look of surprise. Raising his head, he revealed his tattooed face to Ben for the first time. A black and blue shading of a skull was etched into the man's skin: his eyelids were shaded in, his lips had tattoos of teeth, his cheekbones and jawline were highlighted, and dashed lines on his bald head were drawn in to represent the various cranial bones beneath. Not only were the tattoos intimidating, but as the man arose from the floor, Ben realized he was exceptionally muscular and tall—at least a foot taller than him.

Scowling, the skull-faced brute snarled at Ben. "What kinda question is that?" he asked in a deep, hollow voice.

"It's exactly as it sounds," Ben replied.

The man clenched his hands around the steel bars and pressed his face against them, looking down at Ben. "You fire freaks brought us in less than an hour ago. What's the matter? Lost track already?"

"You came with another man, tattooed like you, a red-haired girl, and a dark-skinned teen. Do you know where they are?" Ben asked.

"Place ain't too big. Look around," he grumbled to Ben.

"Were they brought up to this floor with you?" Ben asked, hoping that talking to the man wasn't a lost cause.

The brute sneered at Ben and let out a loud laugh. Panicking, Ben looked around to see if any of the guards had noticed. Fortunately, most of them were now gathered around the window watching the conflict outside.

"Stop it! Why are you laughing?" Ben asked, red in the face and getting frustrated.

"You fire freaks think you're so tough and smart. Taking over the land like it belongs to you. But you can't even keep track of your prisoners? Pathetic."

"I'm...*uh*...new. Still getting used to things," Ben lied. "I started my shift just after you arrived. I was following up a request from my superior officer."

"Officer? Thought Ænærians called them Rhion," Skull-Face replied with a look of intrigue.

Panicking, Ben stammered, "They do—*we* do!—I mean. Do you know where they are or not?"

Skull-Face let off a devious grin. "You're responsible for that ruckus outside ain't ya?"

Ben cursed under his breath. *He's a lot smarter than he looks*, he thought to himself.

The tattooed man let off another laugh. "*Hah!* I knew there was something up with you. Say, I'll tell you what. You let me outta here, and I'll tell you where your friend and girlfriend are."

"She's not my—whatever that doesn't matter. How do you expect me to let you out?"

"You're disguised as a guard. Act like one, and get a key to let me out. The others won't notice, they're too busy with that fun distraction you have going on outside. Don't know how much longer that'll last, so you might wanna hurry." Skull-Face showed with a terrifying smile.

Ben marched off to find a key to let the man out. He noticed that all of the other guards had one dangling from their belts. As he approached them from behind, fully intending to steal a key, one of the guards turned around.

"Hey!" the guard shouted. Ben felt his pulse spike. "Whatcha doing over there? Those goons aren't goin' anywhere. C'mon over and watch the fun with us!" He waved Ben toward the window with the other guards.

"It's really something else, ain't it?" said the overly friendly guard. "Never seen a wolf that big before. And boy oh boy can it fight! Knocked down five of our boys already and doesn't show any signs of stoppin'. Me? I sure as blazes ain't goin' down there."

The other guards laughed. Some of them shouted down words of 'support' to their fellow guards fighting with Sierra. The guards on the ground cursed at them and told them to come down to help.

"No way, Rosco! We ain't had this much fun since I don't know when. I'll wait up here where it's safe and the view is fine," the friendly guard yelled back down.

He turned from the window to Ben and clapped him on the shoulder. "I don't think I recognize you—though it's hard to tell with the helmet on."

Ben gulped. He didn't want to reveal himself. He would prefer as few Ænærians to know his face as possible.

"But I get it, warden's orders: helmets on at all times. You must be a newbie. Explains why you're still doing rounds during all this."

Ben let out an unconvincing laugh. "*Heh*, right. I was actually supposed to move one of the new prisoners up to interrogation for the legate, but I haven't got my key yet."

The guard nodded. "Of course, of course. Place has been here for ten years, and the communication still sucks. Newbies don't get a key until they've been here for six months. Legate probably didn't know you were new and barked the order to the first guard he saw. Don't sweat it, here," he said, handing his key to Ben. "You can borrow mine. Don't want to tick off ol' Fenwin."

Pocketing the key, Ben thanked the guard and hurried to Skull-Face.

"Before I unlock you, tell me what you're going to do," Ben said to Skull-Face.

"I plan to start by bashing your skull in with my bare hands and then making a run for it, completely unarmed around all these guards," the man said.

Ben could tell he wasn't serious, but that didn't make the image of his face getting bashed into the floor go away any faster.

"I'll let you act like you're transferring me upstairs to interrogation. That's where they have my brother. I assume that's where your friends are, too. Now open the door," Skull-Face said impatiently.

Ben sighed. The legate and his men were probably upstairs with Darius. There was no way he could take them on in a fight, especially with Fenwin's sung. Looking at the beast of a man in front of him and knowing he had a stake in all of this too, Ben figured he didn't have much of a choice but to go along with his plan.

The interrogation floor was completely different from the two cell floors. On both sides of the dark hallway were closed, windowless doors. The floor was clean and shined from the torchlight above every third door. At the end of the hall were two masked Rhion standing guard outside of a door.

I'll bet that's where Fenwin is, Ben thought to himself. *But is he with Darius or Arynn? Or both?*

The Rhion stood facing forward and acted as though they hadn't noticed Ben and Skull-Face enter the hallway. Ben used this to his advantage, acting like he belonged up there. He tried to open the first door to his right but found that it was locked.

"Try your key," Skull-Face whispered.

Ben placed his key into the lock and, sure enough, the door opened. There was nobody inside.

"Just check each one," Skull-Face insisted.

"That'll look suspicious," Ben replied.

"If they give us trouble, then we'll fight back."

Sighing, Ben tried the next door. Once again, no one was inside.

The next three doors were all empty. One of the Rhion looked at Ben suspiciously but didn't say anything. Finally, at the fifth door, Ben found someone inside, though it wasn't anyone he had hoped for.

Inside the room was a tough-looking Rhion standing over Skull-Face's bruised and bloodied brother. The brother was much leaner and smaller than Skull-Face, but his tattoos were exactly the same. The Rhion, a middle-aged man with short graying hair, stopped in his tracks and looked at Ben and Skull-Face. He cursed and went to grab his side-sword.

Everything after that happened so quickly. As the Ænærian reached for his weapon, Big Skull-Face pushed Ben aside into the door, slamming it closed. The brute lunged at the Rhion and slammed him against the wall, hands around his neck. Choking, the Rhion reached for his sword and slashed against Big Skull-Face's side. The large man staggered backwards as the Ænærian moved toward him with his sword. Suddenly, Small Skull-Face leapt from his chair, somehow free from his bindings, and sank his teeth into the Ænærian's neck. Blood burst from the screaming man's neck and splattered all over the brothers. Horrified, Ben fell backwards into the corner of the room, struggling to draw his concealed sword.

When the guard's corpse fell to the ground, Small Skull-Face licked the blood on his lips and made an unsettling slurping noise before letting out a satisfied sigh. Shaking, Ben stood himself up and had his broken sword pointed at the brothers, afraid of what would happen next.

Small Skull-Face gave Ben a savory look and advanced toward him. Still shaking, Ben tried to find the strength to swing or stab his sword—he had to do something! But his body failed him as he stood there, frozen with fear as he surveyed the bloody scene.

Big Skull-Face put a hand on his brother's shoulder and said, "No. He helped. So we help him. Then we leave."

"Others?" Small Skull-Face asked his brother, eyes still staring menacingly at Ben.

"Yes. There will be others. Just not him or his friend," Big Skull-Face said. He smirked and looked at Ben, "Or his girlfriend."

Ben shuddered but kept his sword up. Small Skull-Face's eyes didn't seem human. At a closer glance, Ben saw that the smaller brother's blood-soaked teeth were all sharpened into fine points like daggers. Looking at his fingers, Ben saw that his nails were all filed to a point as well. Compared to the smaller brother, Big Skull-Face looked as harmless as an infant.

"Lots of work, Skalle," Small Skull-Face said.

"I know, Gal. We help. Then leave. Good?" Skalle said.

Gal let out a soft grunt which Ben assumed was a 'yes.' Skalle picked up the dead Ænærian's sword and examined it. The sword seemed like a mere dagger in his hands. Skalle walked to the door and placed his hand on the handle.

"Those guards would have heard that. Be ready for a fight," Skalle said to Ben.

13.The Voidsweeper

A s soon as Skalle opened the door, a bullet flew straight into his shoulder. Gal screamed and, running on all fours, lunged at the Rhion with the rifle and bit into his neck. The other Rhion aimed his gun and fired at Gal, but his shot was interrupted by Skalle. The large skull-faced man grabbed the rifle and snapped it in half before stabbing the Rhion.

Guards came rushing up the stairs, including the one who had loaned Ben the key. Ben felt sorry for betraying the man's trust. He was so friendly to Ben and probably wasn't that bad of a guy.

Stop it, Ben told himself. *He's an Ænœrian. Look at this place—it's horrible!*

But he might just be taking orders out of fear, he argued with himself.

Ben's internal quarrel would have to wait, because the six guards were now closing in on Ben and the tattooed brothers. To make matters worse, a door at the other end of the hall opened. Legate Fenwin exited from the room which the two Rhion had previously been guarding. In his hands was his sung rifle. "I thought I killed you," Fenwin said with a raised eyebrow. "Good. This'll be fun." He snarled at Ben and the brothers and took aim.

Ben hurdled out of the way and opened one of the doors into an interrogation room to hide behind. Thunderous roars from the legate's direction came crashing into the door followed by the sound of sizzling metal. The door from which Ben hid behind now had a gaping hole, oozing with molten steel.

Meanwhile, as Ben hid behind the melting door, Skalle, with two arrows sticking out of his chest, was fighting off three guards at once while Gal scampered around, ripping out throats and cackling hideously.

The once-friendly guard from earlier engaged in a sword fight with Skalle after his two comrades lost their heads. He slashed against Skalle's unarmored torso and tried to bash his shield into the arrows protruding from Skalle's chest. Skalle caught the shield and jerked it from the guard. He lifted it above his head with a howling roar and slammed it across his opponent's head. The guard dropped to the floor instantly with a thud, shortly followed by Skalle next to him.

Gal let out a horrified shriek as he saw his brother fall to the ground. He hurried over, leaping over bodies and landing on the concussed guard. He shrieked again and dug his nails into the unconscious guard's face.

Disgusted, Ben turned away from the revolting scene and peered through the melting hole in the door before him and saw the legate walking towards him. Knowing that sungs took time to recharge, Ben rolled out from behind the door and charged the legate.

This was clearly a mistake: Fenwin wore a grim smile and fired once more at Ben. *What? Darius said they take much longer than that to recharge! No! I'm done for!*

Ben raised his sword and closed his eyes in fear, just as he had in Parvidom. But this time, Ben was sure his luck had finally run out. He had had a good run, but there was just no way he could stand up to an army. *I'm sorry, Rose,* he thought as a tear slid down his cheek. The deafening blast erupted from Fenwin's sung and exploded against the hilt of Ben's sword. Ben fell backwards against a wall, but was unscathed. The blast had simply evaporated.

Confused, Ben looked at his hilt and found that it was neither melted nor hot to the touch. In fact, it was just as cool as ever.

Shocked and not willing to press his luck any further, Ben zigzagged toward Fenwin, who was equally surprised. Ben jumped against a wall and lunged with full force against Fenwin. He slashed the sung out of his hands and knocked it to the floor. Continuing with the sword's momentum, Ben slashed against Fenwin's legs.

Fenwin was too quick. He jumped backwards and drew his two swords. The curved scimitars had an orange glow on their edges. Ben noticed the legate squeeze tighter on his swords' hilts just before the entire length of both blades shone with intensity.

Are these things like sungs and sun-carriages? How do I fight that? Ben thought to himself, panicking.

Ben looked behind him to see that both he and Fenwin were the last ones standing. The rest were either moaning in pain or still and lifeless. If he didn't want to join them, Ben would have to act fast.

"Not bad, filth," Fenwin said. "Not many people get far enough to see my sun-swords."

Fenwin sliced through the air with a mastery of technique and skill. It took everything Ben had to retreat backwards in time, dodging the impending evisceration while avoiding the bodies on the floor. Every time the fierce legate swung at Ben, the orange glow seemed to extend farther than the blades themselves. As Ben avoided an attack just well enough away from the leading scimitar, he felt his skin burn and simmer on his left cheek. He could smell his cooking flesh as he continued to sidestep and evade Fenwin's dance of death.

Avoiding as many strikes as he could, Ben could feel the end of the fight coming. Even though the sun-swords had yet to make physical contact with him, the orange glow radiating from them continued to reach just far enough to tear through his armor and burn his body. He could feel wounds piling up all over, taking their toll on his body. Yet, oddly enough, Ben didn't feel tired. In fact, he felt that he had more energy than when he had started. The only thing holding him back was fear.

He dared not let Fenwin make contact for fear of losing a limb or worse. This was a battle that he couldn't afford to lose. Ben had come so far from home for one purpose, and he intended to see his mission fulfilled. He would bring Rose back home—he needed to. There was no use in going back if he couldn't save her. Ben figured he might as well die here if he couldn't rescue his cousin from the Ænærian king's clutches.

Despite his determination, Ben couldn't help fearing his luck had *truly* run out. Somehow, he managed to survive this far. Somehow, he had managed to fight off slavers, Rhion, and the harsh elements of the sun-cursed world. Twice now, he had managed to survive a sung blast that should have reduced his body to ash. Was there really any more luck left? He knew he didn't have the skill to outmaneuver Fenwin. The legate's skills were unparalleled. Eventually, Ben would slip up—he would make a wrong turn, fail to dodge an attack, trip over one of the countless bodies, or slip on their blood.

Fenwin continued his dance through the air, burning flesh and air as he moved. He backed Ben into a corner and prepared to make a final blow. There was nowhere for Ben to turn—nowhere to run or hide. As the twin blades came soaring through the air down toward Ben, he held up his sword and cowered in fear. The burning scimitars came crashing down against the cross guard of Ben's sword. The glow from the legate's blades vanished, and Ben could no longer feel their radiating heat.

A look of confusion, the same as from when his sung failed to kill Ben, spread over Fenwin's face. He cursed and pulled his swords back and prepared to execute the final blow. Ben, similarly perplexed, took the split-second chance to roll away from the incoming attack.

Fenwin's scimitar glowed once more and burned Ben's calf as he tried to escape. Full of pain, Ben let out a scream and fell overtop a Rhion's body and hit his head on the stone floor—right where he had hit his head in the cave near Vänalleato. His sword flew out of his hands and slid across the floor. Ben held his hands on his throbbing head. The room seemed to spin around him, and he felt as though he would vomit right there.

A raspy laugh of victory erupted from Fenwin's mouth as his boots echoed across the hall toward Ben. Just barely managing to crawl along the floor, Ben tried to reach for another weapon nearby.

C'mon, anything will do. Something! Ben thought in desperation as he tried to find something with which to defend himself.

"You sure gave a great fight, peasant," Fenwin gloated. "But I wield the power of *Sol Invictus*. There was never a chance for you to stop me. Don't worry, though. I have to keep you alive now that I know who are you. Can't believe I nearly killed the King's prize—he'll want to meet the brat who's been causing him all this trouble."

Ben shot Fenwin a look of trepidation as he crawled backwards toward the wall.

"Oh, yes. His Majesty knows of your efforts. He knows you're on your way to him. Kept you around this long to see if you knew anything that he didn't, on account of your father and all," the legate boasted as he slowly stepped toward Ben. "But it seems you've gotten quite ahead of yourself. It's time to put a stop to all this. Playtime is over."

Ben shook in fear as he cowered against the wall, unsure of what would happen next. *He says he won't kill me*, Ben said to himself. *But he might as well if this means I can't save you, Rose.*

The legate smacked his swords against each other, showering Ben with embers. Fenwin raised his swords above Ben's legs and prepared to slice down and remove them. But it never happened. Instead, he heard a deafening *boom*.

Ben looked up to see what was taking so long, the suspense too agonizing. He watched as the legate dropped his swords to the ground with a *clang*, their glow fading and then disappearing completely. Fenwin fell to his knees and grimaced as he then collapsed forward, mere inches away from Ben. His back was smoking and standing behind the legate was Arynn holding Fenwin's sung.

"Arynn!" Ben shouted with joy. He sprung from the ground and embraced his friend.

"Ow! Watch it," Arynn said sorely.

Ben let go and apologized. He looked closely at her and realized she was heavily bruised. Her cloak was slightly torn, and he could see her bare right shoulder. It was blue and red all over. She had a black eye and bloodied lip, too.

Ben could feel rage overcoming him, and it took all of his might to stop it from boiling out.

"*What did they do to you?*" he demanded.

The helpless expression on Arynn's face quelled Ben's fiery rage and replaced it with a pitying sorrow. "Ben...I'm fine. The bruising and blood are just from them roughing me up in interrogation. They wanted to know what I knew about you and the Vault. They're small wounds—they'll heal."

Ben could tell she wasn't as well as she claimed. Even if the wounds were small, there was more than just physical damage inflicted, but he sensed that Arynn didn't want to talk about it.

"Come on," she said. "Let's find Darius and get out of here."

Ben nodded. They walked toward the interrogation room at the end of the hall. On their way there, Ben picked up his sword as well as the legate's scimitars.

Ben and Arynn reached the end of the hall and opened the door, hoping Darius would be inside. The sight before them left them both in shock. Arynn's wounds were nothing compared to what they saw in front of them.

Lying face up on the floor behind a table was a shallow breathing and barely recognizable Darius. Both eyes were so swollen that he couldn't even open them if he tried. His nose was clearly broken, and his gums were oozing blood. Burns were scattered across his body, and parts of his clothes seemed to be melted into his flesh.

Ben could feel his heart accelerate at the sight of his nearly dead friend. *How could I have ever accused him of abandoning us?* His hands shook as he tightened his grip around his sword in one hand and made a fist in the other.

"Darius!" Arynn cried as she ran toward him. She tore part of her already ruined cloak and tried to wipe off some of the blood.

Darius moaned with pain and seemed to muster all of his strength to move Arynn's hands from his battered body.

Ben walked forward, trying to force himself past the shock. "Arynn, we can clean him up later. We need to get him out of here. Now."

Ben and Arynn carried their wounded friend out of the interrogation cell into the hallway. They hobbled over the dead and dying bodies, taking in the slaughter that lay before them. Gal and Skalle limped over the bodies, making their way toward the exit. Gal's ears pricked up as the trio's footsteps echoed throughout the hallway. "Brother," he screeched as he turned to face them. "They come."

The taller of the two brothers stopped and turned to face them, groaning in pain as he moved. "You are alive. Good. We will need your help escaping. My brother and I must return home. To Ney." He winced in pain once more, gripping his chest where a large gash was still bleeding profusely.

They gingerly descended the stairs with the brothers stumbling behind them. A flurry of bullets narrowly missed Ben and his companions as they descended the stairs. Though the bullets missed, the mere sound of the gun's explosions caused Ben's throbbing headache to worsen. At the opposite end of the third floor was the warden, holding a large rifle and determined not to miss a second time.

"Guards!" Warden Chen shouted as he fired his rifle once more.

"After them! Shoot to kill! Slash off their heads for all I care! Get them!"

Arrows, spears, and bullets burst through the air. Prisoners shouted in the midst of the chaos, cheering and cursing. The three travelers hid behind a corner to shield themselves. Ben and Arynn set Darius gently on the floor and placed him against the wall.

"Ascendants curse them! Ben, what do we do?" Arynn cried.

Wincing at the debris from the corner exploding next to him, Ben replied, "Give me the sung. Just hang tight here with him."

"No! You can't fight them all alone! You'd have to be insane!" she retorted.

"I've gotten this far, haven't I?"

Arynn glared at him, unable to offer a counterargument.

When nothing came to her, Ben added, "You're too hurt to fight and obviously shaken from everything. Give me the sung, and I'll distract them—maybe lure them elsewhere. You and the others can escape while they're busy with me."

"That's not going to work! Even if you can take them all on— which you can't—they're not going to just let us waltz on out of here," she argued.

"Well, I don't see you coming up with anything better!" Ben yelled over the gunfire.

"Ben strong warrior," Gal hissed. "Almost as strong as Orks of Ney."

Skalle nodded. "My brother is right. Trust him. He can handle this."

Arynn sighed and admitted defeat. "But I'm holding onto Fenwin's sung. I'll cover you."

Ben nodded and raised his sword. He noticed that the blade was glowing with a green aura much like the orange flare that had glimmered around Fenwin's scimitars. He squeezed the hilt tightly, just as Fenwin had with his own weapons. The light flared and extended past the broken metal by another two feet as though the second half of the sword were made of pure green light. Just as he wondered what would happen if he were to squeeze it again, the wall next to him exploded. The ceiling above cracked and groaned without its support.

"Ready another grenade!" one of the guards shouted from the end of the hall. Gazing behind the crumbling corner, Ben saw two guards advancing with lances at the ready. Ben closed his eyes and muttered a quick prayer to whichever gods or Ascendants were watching over him. He turned the corner and squeezed his sword's grip.

A pulsating energy reverberated through his body as beams of green light shot out like a cannon from his blade. The guards collapsed before him, writhing in pain. The odor of burning flesh made Ben's headache even worse. The gunfire ceased, and Ben heard shouts of fear drifting away from him. *Guess it is legendary after all*, he thought with a smirk, thinking back to the man he had taken the sword from in Freztad.

"We're clear for now. Go—I'll cover you!" Ben shouted to Arynn.

They slowly made their way down to the second floor where they were once again met with a barrage of attacks. This time, though, the warden and his guards were smarter and hid behind corners and toppled tables.

Once more, Ben fired a beam of green fire from his sword at the Ænærians. Despite everything he had seen here, he still didn't want to kill these men. He could only hope that their armor would protect them from a fatal injury, much like Roryck's had when he was shot by Gatron. Ben only wanted to debilitate them so he could bring his friends to safety.

Two more guards fell from Ben's sword while the warden and the others retreated to the bottom floor.

The first floor was much easier to contend with. Fewer Ænærians stood ready to fight—they were either too injured or too exhausted to carry on. It was in vain, Ben knew, because they were surrounded. Behind the warden and his remaining guards stood Sierra, unscathed and eager for another fight. Ben pressed forward as Arynn supported Darius around her shoulders and staggered behind.

Sierra growled at the warden and remaining guards. Arynn fired a couple of warning shots with the sung. Finally, the warden dropped his gun—either because he was smart enough to know he had lost or simply because he was out of bullets. The other guards also dropped their weapons and raised their hands in the air.

"Fine, fine!" Warden Chen cried. "We surrender—don't kill us! But kn-know that these actions won't go unnoticed! That's two legates now! The remaining legates won't stand for it! Ænæria won't stand for it!"

Ben glowered at the cowardly warden. "Oh, we count on it," he said callously as he and his friends walked out of the prison.

As soon as they exited the building, Ben slammed the prison door shut and looked to ensure his companions were safe. "We need to run down the mountainside to get to the carriage. Sleipnir is waiting for us."

"I don't think Darius will be able to handle that, Ben."

Ben alternated his gaze between Darius and Sierra. "Put him on," Ben said.

Arynn looked at Ben, confused. "On what?"

"Sierra. She's big enough. She'll get him down much faster than any of us carrying him."

Arynn slumped her shoulders and let out a deep breath. "Fine."

Skalle coughed, spitting up blood on the ground. "My brother and I will not be going with you. We would only be a burden. We must return home."

Ben nodded, surprised that he could sympathize, for he too was homesick. He pointed to the stable. "They left their carriage in there after they took you inside the prison. The horses are in there, too." He extended his arm to meet Skalle's. They clasped forearms together just as those in the Penteric Alliance did. "Good luck to you both. Thank you for your help."

Gal approached Ben and sniffed him. Ben felt a cold shiver run down his spine. He gripped his sword and readied to be attacked. Instead, the strange skull-faced man smiled, revealing his monstrous mouth of sharpened teeth. He placed his hand into his mouth and shrieked violently. He removed his hand and spat out a mouthful of bright red blood. Within his hand was a long and sharp tooth. Gal opened Ben's hand and placed the tooth within. He cackled and scampered behind his brother.

Arynn squealed and retched at the sight of the bloody fang. Skalle offered a hearty laugh. "It seems my little brother approves of you. You have proven yourself, Ben. If you ever find yourself going to the far East, seek out our homeland, Ney. Show them that fang, and the Orks will accept you as one of our own. Farewell." The Orks of Ney hobbled toward the stable out of sight.

Ben shuddered and pocketed the tooth. He quickly brought himself back to the task at hand. He and Arynn placed Darius on Sierra as gently as they could. The wolf didn't seem to mind the weight. Darius, on the other hand, wailed in pain as they dropped him onto her back.

Sierra darted off down the mountainside while Ben and Arynn made haste after them, and not a minute too soon. Behind them were shouts from Ænærians and a familiar raspy voice.

"After them! Keep the shaggy-haired boy alive, but do whatever you want with the others," Second Legate Fenwin ordered, somehow back from the dead.

"Arynn, run!" Ben yelled as they heard the legate's commands.

The two ran full speed down the mountainside trail as more arrows and spears landed mere inches away. As they reached closer to the cave where Ben had hid Sleipnir, bursts of gunfire continued and barely missed Ben. He ran around a roadside curve where he saw Darius, Sleipnir, and Sierra.

"Whew, that was a close shot, wasn't it, Arynn?" Ben said, leaning against a rocky wall to catch his breath. "Arynn?" he asked again when he heard no response. He turned around and saw Arynn lying face down in the muddy road, motionless.

"Arynn!" he screamed. He rushed over to her side and saw holes of scarlet oozing out of her back. "No, no, no, no! This can't be happening!" he cried. Ben picked up the sung from a few feet from Arynn's body and opened fire on the Rhion. Flashes of yellow and orange brightened the sky followed by an unusual flicker of red. The horse-drawn carriages that had been chasing them erupted in flames.

A pileup ensued on the mountainside, and soldiers leapt off their mounts to avoiding falling from the edge.

The remaining Rhion marched down the road on foot and continued to fire, getting closer. Ben paid them no mind as he hoisted Arynn into his arms and ran as fast as he could to the carriage. He threw her and Darius into the back. Sierra stayed by the carriage's side, keeping watch. Ben unhitched Sleipnir and took the reins. He whipped them against the horse and made his quick descent down the mountain.

Sleipnir continued to ride as fast as he could along the muddy road while Ben tended to Arynn's wounds. He counted three bullet holes in Arynn's back, mostly along the right side.

How do I fix this? Where to begin? Ben thought to himself as he pressed under Arynn's neck to feel for a pulse. *She's still alive...barely.*

Darius seemed to regain some consciousness. "What's...wrong... with her?" he asked, coughing between words.

"Shot. Bullets. I don't know what to do!"

Darius offered a grave frown. "Take them out.... Clean...then stop...bleeding...burn closed."

Ben pulled out his hunting knife and a piece of rope from his rucksack, hands trembling uncontrollably.

"Arynn, bite down on this. Please," he said as he placed the rope in her mouth and pushed her jaw onto it. "I'm sorry, Arynn."

He dug his knife into Arynn's back and she shrieked in anguish. Ben pulled a bullet out from her back and pressed a cloth against the open wound. Fortunately, it wasn't in too deep. He kept pressure on it with his left hand as he searched his rucksack with his left. He pulled out a bottle of alcohol to clean the wound.

Arynn whimpered again but didn't resist Ben's aid. He took a deep breath and said, "I'm sorry, Arynn, but now comes the bad part."

Ben drew his sword and tried to make it glow like it had during the fight. He squeezed on its hilt as hard as he could.

Nothing happened.

"What? Why isn't it working!" He cursed and squeezed again. No green hue. No heat. Nothing. He threw the sword to the side. Then an idea popped into his mind. He grabbed one of Fenwin's scimitars and squeezed the handle. The blade burst to a bright orange glow. Ben pressed the tip of the blade against Arynn's open wound, burning it closed. She shrieked louder than before and cried, begging him to stop. He thought he heard her say the name of her friend Sera right before she passed out.

Ben did this again once more without complications before moving on to the final bullet. He could no longer see any Ænærians chasing him, and he was no longer on the road. In fact, Ben didn't have a clue where he was and, unless he removed the last bullet, he may no longer have a navigator.

Ben pierced Arynn's back with his knife one last time. Unlike the last two bullets, this one wasn't whole. He pulled out tiny metal fragments one by one but couldn't reach his fingers in deep enough to get the rest. He searched all their rucksacks for a tool small enough to pull them out: tweezers, scissors, pins, needles, *anything* would be better than his fingers. But he couldn't find anything, and the bleeding wouldn't stop. Arynn grew pale.

Ben knew he had to remove the last few pieces of shrapnel, but there was no point if she would die in the process. He bit his lip in frustration and firmly pressed a cloth against the wound to control the bleeding. He would have to hope she would live long enough for him to remove the final bits later.

As night came, Arynn and Darius remained unconscious. Against his better judgment, Ben continued to ride rather than find a place to make camp. He needed to find a settlement with the right tools or the right person to help Arynn. He figured if he found a road again he would eventually find civilization.

14.Welcome to the
City of Fire

The night was cool and clear. The clouds from the morning's storm were gone, and the fog had dissipated. The full moon brought forth a bright light among the many stars joining it for the nightly gathering. Ben could see everything in the otherwise dark evening, but it did him no good. Nothing around him seemed familiar. The mountains were far behind, and the forests dwindled to scattered trees among the vast grasslands and rivers. Simply put, Ben didn't have a clue where he was.

He let Sleipnir carry on as he flipped through Arynn's maps. The gelding snorted at Ben angrily as he rode on sluggishly, ready to rest.

"There's gotta be something here I can understand," Ben said to himself. Eventually, he found Parvidom on the map and some nearby mountains. "We must be around here." He thought about heading back to the town and finding a healer, but ultimately decided against it. Fenwin would surely go there first to look for them. Ben now knew that they were wanted criminals.

Ben found a long road that Arynn's father had drawn through the crossroads town that led north to a place called 'Ignistad.' He felt his stomach drop when he read the name. *That's the capital city,* he thought to himself. *It'll be dangerous, but I bet there will be a healer there. I have to try. For Arynn.*

Shaking the reins once more, Ben steered Sleipnir toward the northern road. "Well, if we're going to find help for Arynn, we might as well do it in the right direction."

Eventually, as the horizon gleamed gold and sapphire, Ben found the road heading north. Finally content with having a solid lead on where to head next, he pulled the carriage behind a hill and between some blooming red maples. Ben laid himself down across the front of the carriage and fell to sleep the moment his head touched the wooden seat.

Morning came too quickly for Ben. Had Arynn not woken up, bursting with tears of pain, Ben feared he would have slept through the rest of the day. As Ben and a slowly recuperating Darius helped change Arynn's bandages, they realized they were low on supplies and water. A trip to the nearest settlement was needed now more than ever before. But where was it? They had been on the road for hours now, and Ben thought they would have found one by now.

"Do you recognize any of this?" Ben yawned to Darius.

Darius's eyes were still severely swollen, but he was able to get a vague impression of his surroundings. "Maybe," he stammered.

Roughly an hour later, wooden signs appeared on the sides of the road etched with the Ænærian numerals that seemed to be counting down. At the post marked 'IX', Ben could see an enormous city in the distance. Structures still standing from the Old Days rose high into the sky, clean and devoid of debris and vegetation. A golden, glowing gate stood between two marble pillars with a half sun erected atop them. Outside the gates were small, dilapidated shacks and scattered tents where smoke rose from small campfires.

Once the carriage reached the final sign post, Ben was able to bear witness to the horrid conditions outside the city walls. Barely clothed and emaciated children with scorched skin and missing limbs roamed the fields. Adults tended to fires and watched over the younglings. They didn't look much better than the children, and their skin looked like parchment covered with scattered blots of ink. Ben looked at the disconcerting scene before him in sheer horror. How could these people be so deprived of their basic needs while a great and extravagant gate stood behind them? *It's not fair. They have the resources to build that garbage but not to take care of their own people.*

Any able-bodied children ran toward the carriage, yelling and laughing, but also begging. They wanted food, clothing, medicine— anything that could help them. Ben felt his heart sink and a pit form in his stomach. There was nothing he could offer them. His clothes were torn and bloody, their food scarce, and their dwindling supply of medicine too precious. Morose though he was, Ben pushed on through the begging children to the city gates, hoping to feel less guilty once inside.

A wall of Rhion lined the gate's exterior, halberds and spears in hand as they faced forward, motionless. Their helms were much different from the typical Rhion attire to which Ben had grown accustomed. Rather than a single point protruding from the top, a solid gold half-circle stood atop their black helmets. The helmets extended down past their chins, making each soldier unidentifiable as if suggesting that each one was a mere extension of Ænærian will rather than a unique human life.

Ben guided Sleipnir as far as he could before being stopped by the battalion of Rhion. The first among them stepped closest to Ben while the others formed behind, making an impressively straight triangle that pointed away from the golden gate.

"Halt! Turn back around," stated the man at the formation's peak, pointing his spear at Sleipnir's head.

The frustrated Sleipnir snorted and tried to bat his head at the spear to knock it away. The leading Rhion swung his polearm around and hit the horse's head with the butt end of it.

Sleipnir whinnied in pain and took several steps backwards. The Rhion resumed his pointed stance.

Furious, Ben yelled, "What's wrong with you? Are you thick in the head? All he did was make a sound and move his head!" He could feel the rage building up inside him. It was a feeling he was becoming all too accustomed to as his journey progressed. He could no longer remember a time when his blood didn't boil with fury.

Ignoring Ben's outrage, the guard simply repeated himself. "Turn back around where you belong, filth, or suffer arrest by the will of the Sun's wrath."

Keeping Arynn in mind, Ben ignored the slight and contained his emotions. "My friend is injured. I need to see a healer and buy some supplies. We're travelers just passing through," he said, gritting his teeth.

"Those ignorant of the Eternal Mother's embrace are not allowed into the Sacred City," the Rhion stated.

Head sunken in sorrow, Ben realized it would be best to turn around. He need to be careful to avoid drawing attention to himself. Before he left, he decided to press his luck just a bit more. "Is there anywhere nearby I can go to help her? Where do the people living out here go for medical aid?" he asked.

A chuckle echoed from the Rhion's helm. "The peasants are none of our concern so long as they remain outside the Sacred City's gates. If *you* don't want to be our concern, too, then turn around. I will not tell you again."

"Ben..." Arynn struggled to say. "It's...okay. I'll be—" she coughed violently, unable to finish her sentence and slipped back to unconsciousness.

Ben slumped his shoulders and let out an agitated groan. Cursing under his breath, he turned the carriage around. As he did so, Darius woke up from a deep slumber, unaware of where they were. He sat up from his stupor and looked around them. With the swelling significantly reduced, Ben could see the true look of horror on his friend's face.

"Ben! What in blazes—do you know where we are? What were you thinking?" Darius yelled.

"I was thinking about Arynn!"

"And how does bringing us straight to the enemy's capital help any of us?"

"Maybe if you hadn't gotten her arrested in the first place, then I wouldn't have need to bring us here! Besides, it's not like you said anything about it until now! If you had, maybe I'd have listened!"

"Oh, 'maybe' you'd have listened? I thought you'd have trusted me at my word. Is that what this is? You don't trust me?"

"What are you talking about?" Ben asked. True, he had questioned Darius's loyalty more than once in the past, but he no longer worried about that. All that mattered now was getting Arynn the help she needed and then getting back on track toward Jordysc. It was, after all, thanks to Darius that he knew about the Miners Guild in the first place. Finding them was their biggest hope toward thwarting Julius's plans. So why was it that every time he heard Darius speak, the hair on Ben's arms stood up and he got the overwhelming urge to shut Darius up?

Darius glanced over at Arynn, still coughing in her sleep. He made a face of regret; a grimace of sadness.

"Don't you think I don't blame myself enough as it is?" Darius asked.

Ben avoided Darius's gaze.

"It's my fault, too. I could've fought them off more carefully—protected Arynn."

Scowling harder than usual, Darius shook his head at Ben. "And what experience do *you* have that she doesn't? How exactly did you learn to fight?"

The hair on Ben's arms remained standing, and his eyes rolled. What did it matter how Ben had learned to fight? He had hunted and fought wild animals plenty of times in the past and sparred with Rakshi and the twins. Ben never had any trouble holding his own against them, so he had always figured he was a natural.

"I've fought people plenty of other times, and I've done just fine," Ben said through his teeth, guiding Sleipnir around a rocky road outside the city gates.

The path he was following looked as though it hadn't been fixed since the Old Days, with holes and weeds riddling it everywhere. He would've purposely hit a few more potholes if it meant Darius would hit his head on the carriage roof, but no matter how ticked off with him he may have been, it wasn't enough to risk harming Arynn further.

"I'm not saying you don't have experience," Darius said. "I've seen you fight. You're good. You've held your own against high-ranking Rhion. Blazes, you even fought Fenwin. But don't act like you're invincible and don't need help."

"What are you trying to say? First, you ask if I blame you, and now what—you're blaming me instead?" Ben asked angrily as he parked the carriage a fair distance from the city, now realizing he didn't have a set destination in mind.

"No. There's no point in placing any blame—it's stupid and doesn't change what happened. But going forward, don't be an idiot and act like you don't need help and can do everything on your own."

Ben didn't know what to say. He halfheartedly nodded and got off the carriage to let Sleipnir and Sierra roam around while he set himself up for the next failure that was sure to come.

"While we're here, I might as well tell you something," Darius said, making his way to the front of the carriage next to Ben. "Last time I came to Ignistad, I saw a lot of shady people living in the slums. I may have an idea on how to help Arynn."

"Why didn't you tell me that from the beginning?" Ben nearly yelled.

"Because it's dangerous! We're wanted criminals now. I'd rather avoid places like this if we can help it," Darius argued, but trying to keep his voice down as he looked around for people that may be listening. It wouldn't serve to advertise. He let out a deep sigh. "But now that we're here already, we might as well try."

According to Darius, the slums outside Ignistad's gates were home not only to slaves, but also to many people who refused to convert after Julius took over. A lucrative black market had formed over the years between the slaves and natives in which goods, services, and entertainment were smuggled and exchanged. Though technically illegal, the black market was somewhat tolerated by Julius and the Rhion because it meant less work on their part to keep the slaves alive and entertained.

"It won't exactly be easy to find someone to help Arynn," Darius explained.

"What's so tough about it?" Ben asked.

"For starters, they're hidden. The Rhion don't go searching for anyone in the black market, but if they see illegal activity, they won't hesitate to stop it. Since Arynn's not a slave, it might be even harder to find someone willing to trust us and help."

"Why is that? Can't we pretend she's a slave?"

"No, we can't. She may look awful right now, but she's nothing compared to slaves. She doesn't have a slave's brand either," Darius said as though it were obvious.

"But what's wrong with her being a free woman?"

"Like I said, black market healers are technically criminals. They're weary of their patients. Though unlikely, it's not unheard of for Rhion to go undercover to lure out criminals when there are too many of them. Simply put, a slave can't afford to set someone up because then they'll have no one else to turn to."

The explanation made sense, but frustrated Ben greatly. There was always some kind of complication, some kind of problem that made things so much more difficult than they needed to be. The whole 'slave thing' bothered Ben, too. Every time Darius had used the word, Ben cringed as if he were getting too close to a hot fire. It was a disgusting concept and, like everything else seemed to be, made things so much more complicated. Ben drifted off into a daydream, wondering how he would make things different if he were in charge....

"What do we have to do to find her help if people are going to be reluctant to help?" Ben asked, quickly snapping out of his daydream. *Not the leader type. Best to stay away from such thoughts.*

"It'll cost us. A lot. We might have to spend the rest of our money, sell something, do some kind of job. Who knows," Darius said with an exacerbated expression.

The two were able to wake Arynn enough to tell her they were leaving, but that Sierra would there to watch over her. They left Fenwin's sung with her, too. They explored the slums outside the city for signs of black market activity. Both Ben and Darius kept their hats on and faces covered to avoid any chances of being recognized. Though they were certainly much farther north than when they had started, the weather was still very hot, and Ben found that the sun was just as brutal here as it was in Freztad.

The slave neighborhood seemed to encircle the walls of the entire city, stretching miles long. Farther away from the gates were larger shacks and fewer Rhion on patrol. Darius suggested they search these areas first. He told Ben to be on the lookout for anything that looked out of place: people acting strangely, odd markings or signs, or anything deviating from the norm.

Eventually, Darius spotted something of interest. Across the dirt street was an unassuming wooden cottage with sheets covering the windows and two people smoking by the front door. Ben didn't see anything too abnormal about this, but evidently Darius did.

"No way..." he whispered. Darius didn't dare step forward toward the house but rather stepped backwards, almost tripping over a child playing in the dirt.

"What is it?" Ben asked. He had trouble imagining what was so special about the house in front of them.

"That's Trinity," said Darius, pointing toward one of the people smoking. "She's a healer. I didn't think she was still here."

Darius continued to stammer nonsense to Ben about Trinity. Ben couldn't believe she was a healer, because she seemed too young. The woman outside the shack was rather tall compared to the man with whom she was standing. She couldn't have been much older than Arynn, though it was hard to really tell with much of her head covered by a rounded shawl.

Ben and Darius walked across the dirt road to approach the smoking pair. The smoke had a musty yet sweet floral odor that smacked Ben in the face as he stood in front of them. The scent was much too strong to have come from just the two smokers. Ben looked to the door and, sure enough, he could see trails of smoke drifting from inside.

Trinity noticed the two advancing first. She turned and lowered her pipe as she gave Darius an odd smile of familiarity. Etched on her lightly browned forehead was an eye that, at first glance, Ben took to be real. Upon closer examination, he saw that it was only a tattoo, though a highly detailed one. Its iris was a cold blue surrounded by a bright white canvas scattered with tiny red veins. Long eyelashes were drawn leaving the faux eyelid and converging in a point toward the center of Trinity's forehead.

Now that Ben had a clearer look at Trinity's face, he was sure that she couldn't have been more than a year older than him, making her roughly Arynn's age. How could she be a proficient healer? *I guess Darius never said she was any good. If she was, why would she work in a place like this?*

"Hey there, Dary-boy," Trinity said softly and slowly, blowing the last bit of smoke from her lungs.

"How'd you know it was me?" Darius asked in an almost nervous sounding tone.

Trinity cracked a smile and brought her pipe to her mouth. She blew a ring of floral-scented smoke into Darius's covered face.

"I'd recognize those eyes of yours anywhere. What brings you here?" she asked, smiling again.

The man standing next to Trinity grunted and walked inside, apparently uninterested in Trinity's guests.

"We need help. Our friend is hurt. She's been shot," Darius explained.

"I see. You have friends now? I thought Rhion couldn't have friends," she said coldly, momentarily switching her gaze to Ben.

"I'm not a Rhion anymore. That's why we came to you," he explained with what sounded like shame and disappointment.

"That's all you're here for? Pity. Well, you know my fee for non-slaves." She blew another smoke ring.

Her voice was so calm, yet Ben sensed a kind of disdain from her. It was hard for him to put his finger on it, and he was finding it slightly harder to concentrate. Standing within all the smoke made him feel lethargic and lightheaded, yet relaxed and slightly calmer.

Darius explained Arynn's injuries to Trinity. She simply shook her head and took another drag of smoke. "I'll have to look at her before I can make any promises. If you bring her here, it'll be one gold sol per day. From your description, my guess is it'll cost roughly twenty gold sols for the procedure. That's assuming your friend here," she looked at Ben, "did a good enough job with the first two bullets and there are no more complications.

"*Twenty?* Trinity, come on! You know there's no way we'd have that much! Are you sure you can't lower it?"

"Sorry, Dary. Things change. You saw to that. You know how to get the money. Should be easy for two boys like yourselves to get."

Darius stormed off. As he chased after his companion, Ben could've sworn he saw a tear drop from one of Trinity's real eyes. He finally caught up to Darius at their carriage and found him kicking a nearby tree.

"What's the problem?"

"Didn't you hear her?" Darius snapped. "She wants over twenty gold! We can't get that. We'll find another healer."

"I don't get it. What's the point of searching for someone else if we already found someone you know? That's perfect. She even said we could get the money easily."

Darius shook his head violently. "You don't understand."

"Then explain it to me!"

Darius looked the sky and threw his hands in the air. "She's talking about gladiatorial fighting."

Ben raised an eyebrow.

"Right. You don't know what that is." Darius groaned. "It's the one major thing that happens outside the city's walls that anyone can participate in. You fight for people's entertainment against all sorts of things. Animals, traps, even other people. It's one of many types of tournaments the King introduced."

"Oh," Ben said. He understood why Darius wasn't exactly keen on the idea. He sat down next to Darius and dug his fingers aimlessly in the warm earth.

"I don't think I'm in any shape to fight yet. You'd have to do it instead. And you still refuse to kill people, don't you?"

Ben thought about the fight at the prison. Ben's perspective had changed somewhat after learning Pawel and his family died because he had spared Gatron. He didn't try to kill anyone at the prison, but didn't exactly go easy on them, either. Especially after Arynn got hurt....

"Yeah. I'd rather not. Especially needlessly for people's entertainment," Ben admitted, still unsure where exactly his morals stood.

"Figured you couldn't stomach it. What is it with you and killing people? How have you survived out here for so long without blood on your hands?"

Ben sighed and looked up to the sky. "I've lost a lot of people in my life. First, my parents abandoned me. Then all the other kids my age died from a plague. Just before Rose was taken, one of my few friends was killed. It's all been too much for me. Ever since my friend Rakshi died, I've promised myself I wouldn't kill anybody unless I had absolutely no other choice. That's what Rakshi taught me." He gripped the bow that had once been hers and held it to his chest.

Darius scoffed. "Then you should have no problem going to the arena. If we can't find another healer, then our only chance for saving Arynn is Trinity. There's no other way for us to get money. It's not like anyone in a city full of slaves will pay that much for anything."

"Killing someone else in exchange for Arynn's life? Rakshi would never do something like that."

"You'd do it for Rose though, wouldn't you?"

The question hit Ben like a charging boar. Nothing mattered to him more than his cousin. Not even someone else's life. "I suppose...maybe...."

"Well, you care for Arynn, right? Don't act like I haven't seen the way you two look at each other. I know there's something going on between you two—even if neither of you will admit it. I've got some experience with that. First hand." Darius spit to his side and frowned.

Ben felt his stomach drop. There hadn't been much time lately for him to explore his feelings for Arynn, especially considering the circumstances. Now just didn't seem like the right time. Darius was correct, however, in asserting that he felt *something*.

"Look," Darius went on. "The people here are savages. The fighters and the spectators, they're all the same. They bask in bloodshed because it's all they know. Death in battle is glorious for anyone entering the arena, and the audience pays handsomely for it. No one in there gives a damn about anyone else's life. You shouldn't either."

The world seemed to spin around Ben, and his hands grew shaky and unsteady. He hadn't the slightest idea of what to do or what was right. All he could think about were the people he cared for the most and how he never wanted to see them end up like Rakshi. Finally, he stood up and looked once more to the sky. "Fine. I'll do it."

The two drove the carriage through the busy streets on the outskirts of Ignistad towards the hut where they had found Trinity. As before, she was standing outside smoking her pipe. She called her colleagues to help her take Arynn inside on a stretcher. Though still in a stupor and unconscious, Arynn moaned in pain as she was moved from the carriage to the inside of the hut.

"One gold sol for your girlfriend, Dary," Trinity stated with an outstretched palm.

Darius rolled his eyes. "No need to be jealous. She's Ben's girl, not mine."

Trinity shifted her gaze to Ben and studied him from top to bottom. "Sure hope you know what you're doing in the arena. Her life depends on it. Dary explain the rules to you?"

"Only that I can't bring my own weapons inside. Not much other than that."

Trinity chuckled and pinched Darius's cheek. He immediately swatted her hand away. "That's because Dary never fought in them before. They'll explain to you once you're inside. I have some friends in the arena watching. They'll let me know how you do, so I can start working on your girlfriend once I know you have enough sols." She shifted her gaze to Darius. "You should probably go with him, though. Wouldn't want him getting lost on his way back. If he makes it back, that is." Trinity took one more huff of her pipe before turning to the hut.

The arena was a massive brick amphitheater that stood over fifty feet tall. The entrance had tall marble columns topped with golden suns, illuminated with their own bright light. At its center were double doors with the words *Sol Invictus* engraved into its center. Ben was shocked to find that he found the arena to be so beautiful. It was hard to believe something so amazing could have been the work of a tyrant and the backs of slaves. In front of both marble columns were Rhion standing guard, both of whom carried rifles.

Ben felt his chest thump faster as he approached the gate, nearly blinded by the simulated light from the golden suns. The Rhion turned their heads to him, and Ben froze with fear.

Fortunately, Darius spoke for Ben, telling them that Ben would be participating in the gladiatorial games. The Rhion chuckled at Ben, probably thinking he was a dead man walking. When they saw the seriousness on Ben and Darius's faces, the snickering stopped. The Rhion on the left banged on the front door. Another Rhion came out through the doors and barked orders to some men behind him to escort the Ben inside. Darius was given entry when he showed the

Rhion a tattoo on his forearm that looked like letters in an Ænærian style: *SPQR.*

The Rhion seemed shocked. "We had no idea you were a brother in arms. We apologize." They stepped to the side and let Darius pass.

"I'll be watching, Ben. Don't mess up," Darius said as two Rhion grabbed Ben by the arms and placed a sack over his head.

Trying to track how many steps and turns he took once inside the was impossible. The guards dragged him along for nearly half an hour, going up and down stairs and violently pushing him in each direction. After making one last descent down some cobblestone stairs, the guards shoved Ben forward and removed the sack. In front of him was an elderly man in flowing purple robes sitting behind a desk. The room was small, and they were the only ones there once the Rhion had left. Behind the man's desk was a door with a sliding compartment at the man's eye level. He glanced up at Ben with an uninterested look.

"Name?" the man asked.

"Mathias," Ben lied. He couldn't risk using his own, and his ancestor's name was the first one that came to mind.

"Skills?"

"What do you mean?"

The man frowned at Ben, studying him from top to bottom. "*Hmm.* Scrawny, yet tall. With what weapons are you trained?"

"Sword," he said nervously. "I'm not bad with a bow and arrow either."

The man wrote everything down on a piece of parchment with a funny looking pen. It was short, black, and from a material Ben had never seen before. After the man finished scribbling, he put his pen down and looked up at Ben once more.

"How much is your bet?" he asked in the uninterested monotone voice.

"*Uhh*, sorry. Bet? What do you mean?" Ben asked, starting to sweat as his stomach rumbled.

"First time...outsider," the man muttered to himself, making corrections to his parchment. "You sure you want to do this?"

I'm asking myself the same thing right now. I don't think I have much of a choice. "Yes, I'm sure. How many sols can I make from this?"

The man rolled his eyes and shook his head. "Blazing outsiders," he cursed to himself before making eye contact with Ben. "Participants deposit a bet of their choosing. Upon winning, they earn triple their deposit. If they lose, but somehow survive, they make back half their bet. If their opponent surrenders, then they make one and a half times the original bet."

"So killing isn't a requirement?"

The man rolled his eyes again. "It's highly frowned upon if you don't. Of course, accepting a surrender is entirely up to you. Though we aren't likely to have you back in the arena. People are here for a show, not some back-alley quarrel."

Ben felt so defeated. He wasn't sure he would be able to last enough fights to gather the necessary funds and, even if he could, he would probably need medical attention just after Arynn. Besides, Ben estimated it would take at least seven wins to make twenty sols without killing anyone—but they would probably kick him out after one surrender. What was he supposed to do? Would he have to kill to save Arynn's life?

Begrudgingly, Ben placed his only two gold pieces on the desk. The old man snatched them as soon as they hit the surface and placed them in a small pouch and added more notes to his parchment when someone suddenly opened the door from behind the desk.

"Gabe—Tauron is down!" the man called from the threshold. "The Argr finally took him out! We don't have anyone else for a champion's round, the other mercs and filth are too afraid, and the crowd is going nuts!"

Gabe sat at his desk and grunted. He pulled out another stack of papers and drew a big X across one of them. He shuffled through some more parchment and scribbled across them, muttering numbers to himself.

"C'mon, Gabe! You know the Argr has a temper. You got anyone else—," he stopped short as he finally noticed Ben from the doorway. "You! Twenty times your bet if you fight the Argr right now!"

A smirk grew across Ben's face as he nodded and shook the young man's hand. The man patted Ben on the back excitedly as he led him through the door. He passed the threshold into the next room, unsure of what to expect next.

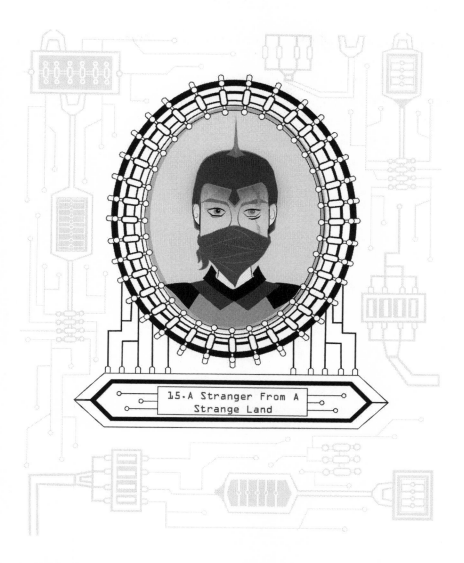

15. A Stranger From A
Strange Land

O nce more, the floral scent crept its way through Ben's scarf
and into his nose. A slow haze drifted through the small
hallway behind the bookie's office. At the end of the hall
was another door from which the haze spilled. Loud cheers and slurs
could be heard from behind the door, but the man guiding Ben
turned left at a door and led him inside.

Wardrobes lined the walls, wooden stools and benches sat in the middle, and a looking glass stood at the opposite end. In the corner was another cabinet, much too large to be a wardrobe. The man strolled toward the cabinet and unlocked it. Opening the double doors, he revealed a vast array of weapons and armor. Spears, swords, and shields. Axes and halberds, lances and chain-sickles. Their quality varied. Some were iron or steel, others were bronze or wood; all were in a used and worn state. The variety of armor was much less. Light leather chest guards, leggings, and helms hung next to bulky steel breastplates, boots, and gauntlets.

"This'll be fun," the man said with a grin. "Pick out anything from this room to use in the fight. Plenty of reasons why we don't let anyone use their own: weapons or armor could be poisoned. You could be hiding a gun, or worse. Sun's fire, I think I've even heard of sung-swords! To be safe, you'll have to dress in one of our gladiatorial garments and then pick whichever weapons and armor you want. As ringleader, I'll go over the rules with you before you start and make sure you get your money. If you make it, of course."

The color in Ben's face faded. He was beginning to get the sense that he was in way over his head.

The ringleader patted Ben down to make sure he wasn't concealing anything before leaving the room. Ben opened the wardrobe in front of him and found a sack to throw his clothes into, next to black and orange Ænærian tabards and underclothes. He slipped into them and placed his own clothes into the bag. Hesitant to part with it, Ben hid his watch in one of his pockets, hoping the ringleader wouldn't find it.

The armory cabinet seemed much bigger with a second glance as Ben stood in front of it. He knew he would want a sword to fight with, so he picked up one of the steel blades to determine how it felt. The sword was terribly balanced, even worse than his own broken sword. He put it back and grabbed the one next to it. This was a bronze blade, so the metal was inferior, but it felt great in his hand. Ben put it to the side and tried another. The third blade was much longer than the first two, close in length to the bastard swords to which he was accustomed. The only problem was the weight. It was much too heavy to use with a shield, and he wasn't sure even two hands would suffice.

"They sure have a lot of steel here. Guess that's not surprising considering what else they have," Ben muttered to himself as he beheld the armory and thought of all the strange weapons he had been exposed to recently.

What about the spears though? They would offer more range if Ben could hide behind a shield while thrusting it. He could throw it, too, if the need arose. Each spear varied in length and quality. Longer ones seemed to have more wear while the shorter ones were all but pristine. The metals for the tips each varied between steel and iron. Nothing stood out as anything special, so Ben picked up a medium range iron-tipped spear about five feet in length.

Deciding to go with a mix of weapons, Ben chose his spear as his primary while strapping on the sheath for the bronze blade as his secondary.

Next, Ben moved on to the shields. This time it was much easier to decide as each shield was more or less the same. They were all made of triple-plied wood with leather coatings and iron reinforcements. Some had more scratches and dents than others, so Ben simply picked the one that looked the least damaged.

Lastly, Ben examined the sets of available armors. None were full sets, so he had to mix and match. He thought about whether or not he would want steel or leather armor. Steel was more protective but offered less dexterity and would easily over-encumber him. The leather was the opposite problem: great dexterity but little protection.

Ben ultimately decided to wear the leather chest guard and leggings while matching them with the steel helmet. He figured the combination would offer him the greatest speed while also protecting his head. More importantly, the helm covered his face in case anyone watching could recognize him. The ringleader might question him for wearing his scarf inside during the fight, and it could easily fall off.

Dressed and ready to fight, Ben knocked on the door. The ring-leader waltzed back in and examined Ben. "Everything looks fine. All stock weapons and armor. Good. I'll explain the rules on the way. The crowd's getting antsy, so there's no time to waste," he said in a much more serious tone than before.

The rules of the gladiatorial games seemed relatively straight-forward.

"If you survive after an hour of fighting, it's a draw, and each player receives one and a half times the agreed upon price," the ringleader explained as they walked toward the haze-oozing door. "If you kill your opponent within the first ten minutes, then the crowd considers it a dull match and thus only half the original agreed upon price is given. But, if you kill your opponent or they surrender at any time after the first ten minutes then you take their would-be winnings as well as your own prize.

"But forget money talk—let's talk action! All moves are legal so long as you stay within the ring. That includes your weapons—hence why we don't allow bows or guns. Too many maimed audience members," he said, shaking his head. "You can throw anything else, but if it hits a spectator, you're disqualified. Kill one of them, and you'll never see the light of day again!" The ringleader howled with laughter and thumped Ben on the back.

They reached the end of the hallway, and the scent became much stronger. The voices outside were clearer. Ben could hear laughter and shouting. He could also hear another sound, but couldn't make it out between the thick door and awful din.

"What are you called?"

"*Uh*...Mathias? I already told the bookie back there," Ben stammered.

"No, no—not your *real* name. Your stage name—something excit-ing! You thought of one?" the ringleader asked, excitedly.

Ben offered a blank stare to the man next to him. A stage name? How was he supposed to think of something like that on the spot? He glanced down at his weapons, hoping to find a quick inspiration. The bronze sword on his belt was the first thing to catch his attention.

"*Uhh*, how about the Bronze Blade?"

Shaking his head, the ringleader said, "*Uh-uh*, that won't do. Too plain. Something that represents you—something that will inspire you in battle and rouse the audience."

Concentrating harder, Ben found that the only thing to inspire him thus far was protecting the people he cared about. Rose. Arynn. Even Darius. He would guard them with his life.

"The Vault Guardian," said Ben with confidence.

"*Ooh.* Mysterious. I like it. On you go, Vault Guardian. May the Eternal Mother bless you," the ringleader said as he opened the door and pushed Ben through.

Ben heard the door immediately slam shut behind him. The arena he now found himself in was massive. The ceiling was open, and he could see the bright moon shining down upon him. There was no 'Great Sun' to bless him, nor could he see the stars through the thick floral mist encompassing the stadium.

Aside from the ten or so Rhion scattered across the arena, Ben saw nearly a hundred people sitting on the high rising benches encircling the amphitheater. They all wore long purple robes with an orange sash embroidered with the Ænærian sun and fist. Most of them were either middle-aged or very old. Very few were close to Ben in age. Many pointed at Ben and shouted in each other's ears as they scribbled on small pieces of parchment. They pressed some sort of stamp against the paper and passed it down the aisle where someone would collect it.

Despite standing in the cool and dark midnight air, nightfall did not touch the arena. Torches were lit all across the arena, some were even magnified by glass panels that illuminated the coarse sand of the stadium floor. The smoke from the torches danced with the scented haze that drifted from the stands, creating form from the light and fire surrounding them.

Basking in the bizarre atmosphere, Ben nearly forgot that his opponent was standing across the arena ready to kill him. The Argr appeared to be quite a bit shorter than Ben, and his thick jerkin hid any signs of muscle. He wore a gray mask that covered his mouth and nose. Silver-gold hair seeped out through his pointed steel helmet.

The Argr's eyes were gray and across the left one was a long black and red scar.

Whoever the Argr was, something about his features seemed familiar to Ben. His hands shook as he tightened the scarf across his face.

The Argr held two chain-sickles on his belt and gripped a long halberd that was planted in the ground next to his fallen opponent. The body was that of a bulky man with spiky hair and a rounded ring between his nostrils. The corpse was covered in lacerations and blackening blood.

Next to the Argr were two women—one cleaning some of his wounds from his previous fight and another holding a pipe for him. The woman brought the smoking pipe closer to his face. He smacked the pipe from her hand and scolded her, refusing to lower his mask. The women shrieked as they picked up what they dropped and bolted for their nearest exit.

Those poor women must be slaves, Ben thought to himself.

"We greatly apologize for the wait, folks," the ringleader's charismatic tone boomed from all around. **"Let me just say, I feel terrible for anyone who missed our last round! What a turn of events! Stunning, absolutely stunning! But, allow me to recap before anyone makes additional bets. Former Champion Tauron was truly decimated by his longtime rival, the mysterious Argr! It was a fantastic match, lasting almost the entire hour. But alas, the Argr was simply no longer content with being second-best!**

"In the last minutes of the match, Tauron attempted his signature cross blade lariat, but the Argr ducked at the last moment and dove to Tauron's legs, knocking him over. He wrapped his chain-sickle around his neck and tied him to the rafters. As Tauron hanged helplessly, the Argr hacked and slashed with his mighty halberd until there was no life left. What. A. Way. To. Go!"

The crowd roared with applause. Ben felt like he had just been run over by a horse. Hearing the gruesome details of Tauron's death brought a sense of loathing he had not felt since losing Rose.

"And now we go to our new champion's first challenger!" the ringleader's voice thundered.

The audience turned their heads from the Argr and the bloody mess at his feet toward Ben. Laughter and cheers ceased, and the crowd hushed to a near silent whispering.

"Entering the arena for the first time is a young man of barely sixteen years of age! He's shown tremendous courage in taking on not only a first-tier fight, but a *championship showdown!* Entering the arena for the first time is a stranger from a strange land, traveling long and far just to beat down the man before him. Ladies and gentlemen—I give you...THE VAULT GUARDIAN!"

A wave of applause crashed throughout the arena. The ringleader's dramatic introduction initiated an instant affection for Ben— or rather, for the Vault Guardian. The name not only protected his identity, but it also gave him a boost in confidence. Why, then, did his opponent call himself 'the Argr?' As far as Ben had known, argr was an emasculating term. No one would ever call themselves that.

"Yes, yes. It's all very exciting. But, I'll leave it to you, folks, to be the judges of that. Let's get this show started! Challengers! Are you ready?"

The Argr snorted and thrust his halberd hard into the dirt, letting out a fearsome battle cry. Ben nodded his head in affirmation, raising his shield and spear.

"Well, alrighty then. The Argr versus the Vault Guardian. Begin!"

The Argr rushed toward Ben with incredible speed.

Ben widened his stance and pointed his spear toward his incoming opponent. If the Argr kept charging at this pace, he would surely run right into Ben's spear. On the off chance it missed or he moved at the last second, Ben would collapse backwards—exposed for the kill. What was he to do? Stay and he may inflict serious damage, *or* he would lose right away.

Think, Ben. Think. He can't be stupid enough to take that kind of hit, can he? Or does he think he'll scare me into letting my guard down?

I won't have time to get my guard back up if I move! If he knocks me over, I'll need to let go of the spear, grab the short sword, and strike imme-diately.

The Argr continued his path toward Ben's front, the tip of his weapon ready for blood. Ben braced himself for impact. But it never came. As soon as the Argr was just inches away from Ben's iron spear, he hurdled over Ben's shield and landed behind him.

The Argr quickly turned himself around and swung his halberd toward Ben. With less than a second to react, Ben pushed his feet against the sand as hard as he could and slid backwards, out of the halberd's way. This only granted him another millisecond to react as the Argr swung his weapon in circles. The next hit was about to come if Ben didn't do something.

"What a dodge, folks! This may be his first time here, but the Vault Guardian sure knows how to use the environment to his advantage!"

Ben lifted his shield and stuck out his spear. There's no way the Argr would be able to jump over Ben from this close, and deceler-ating was no longer an option.

The Argr stopped running at about a foot short of Ben's spear. Before Ben could make a thrust forward, the Argr released his weapon. The halberd landed right in Ben's shield. Pain shot from his wrist to his shoulder as he felt the sheer force penetrate his shield. The shield, now cracked, took most of the energy, but the rest went to his now throbbing arm.

"Ouch! Looks like the Vault Guardian has taken quite the hit!"

Ben let go of his shield. He gripped his spear with both hands and thrust it repeatedly toward the Argr.

The Argr took a step away from the spear and handled his chain-sickles. He swung the chains through the air like two windmills spiraling through a harsh breeze.

Ben threw his spear at his opponent's spinning blades. The chains caught the polearm, and the spinning ceased. Ben had a few seconds before the Argr would be able to recover his weapons. He used the time to slide to his left and stop next to his shield. He stepped on the wooden disk that had saved his life and, with all his strength, pulled out the halberd. There was a splintering *CRACK*. Ben thought he had broken the shield, but instead, the halberd's axe had snapped loose from its wooden shaft.

Without the handle to hold it, the halberd was useless to Ben. He cast it aside and picked up the wooden shield. It had a gaping breach towards the upper rim, but still offered plenty of protection. Ben drew his bronze sword and raised his shield once more just as the Argr freed his weapons.

The Argr launched one of the sickles toward Ben, just barely missing. He charged towards Ben and threw another sickle, this time most certainly within range.

"Not even ten minutes in and we already have a fascinating fight on our hands, folks!"

Unsure of what to do, Ben let instinct override reason. He parried the sickle with his sword and darted for his enemy. Ben closed in before the Argr could reel in his chains. He slashed his weapon through the air as the Ænærian sidestepped out of the way each time. Ben jumped forward to close the gap. The closer he was, the harder it would be for his opponent to pick up his weapons. He attempted a shield bash, but narrowly missed.

It was a foolish move.

With his shield away from his center, Ben was now wide open for attack. The Argr noticed and charged toward Ben.

The impact was instantaneous. The Argr's sickles pierced through Ben's leather chest guard and dug into his sides.

Ben could feel the hot red liquid pouring down his chest. He had to act fast; the Argr had him caught and could kill him at any second. Ben slashed at his enemy's side.

The Argr yelped and pulled away from Ben, yanking the sickle out from Ben's side. The Ænærian backed away quickly and examined his wound.

"Yikes! I sure thought that was going to be the end of it! If that's how they fight before the ten-minute mark, I'm sure excited to see how this goes once they aim to kill."

The crowd around muttered in agreement, the first sounds Ben noticed since he had started fighting.

What am I doing here? This is wrong—fighting for people's entertainment.

It's not for their entertainment, it's for Arynn to get better, he argued with himself.

If I die here, I can't save Rose.

I'm helping Arynn, so I can find Rose. She's all that matters.

Ben shook the thoughts as he saw his enemy retrieve his chains. Ben raised his shield and readied himself.

The Argr spun his chains once more, but this time ran at Ben with greater speed.

The deadly windmills broke through the air as they closed in on Ben. He studied his surroundings and developed a plan.

Ben ran underneath the arena's stands and hid behind a black wooden pillar. The audience jeered as Ben hid from their sight.

"Now, now, folks. I'm sure the Vault Guardian will come out soon. It's been an impressive match so far, *eh*?" the ringleader said through the air in an almost nervous voice. **"And, *uh*, please note that all bets are now closed. Good luck!"**

The Argr grunted and ran to the stands just as Ben had hoped. The Ænærian continued to spin his blades as he closed the gap between the two gladiators. As he walked underneath the stands, one of the sickles became caught in the rafters above.

The Argr let out a frustrated grunt and pulled on his weapon. It was stuck.

Ben smiled shrewdly: his plan worked. He spun from behind the beam and ran toward his unsuspecting opponent.

"Sorry about this," Ben whispered under his breath as he slashed his sword beneath the tangled chain's handle.

The Argr screamed, his shriek much higher than Ben would have expected, as his right hand was severed from his wrist, dangling from the trapped chain-sickle.

"Oh ho, folks! None of you would've wanted to miss that! I think we'll bring it up on the Motion Block, shall we?"

Ben turned to the center of the arena where he saw a platform rise from the ground. Sand fell into the opening pit as a large metallic cube slowly appeared. A light flashed on the cube, and suddenly Ben could see himself, as if gazing into a looking glass. Unlike a looking glass, it didn't reflect what Ben was doing, but rather what he had *already done.*

Ovation soared from the crowd as Ben watched himself remove the Argr's hand with a swift chop of his sword. He stood baffled as he watched himself on the Motion Block. The cube showed everything in vivid detail and sound to match the scene rang throughout the arena just like the ringleader's voice.

"Rhion, come to my aid!" the Argr screamed. He lifted his remaining hand and revealed the same tattoo that Ben had seen on Darius: *SPQR.* The Argr removed his mask, and Ben understood why he looked so familiar. It was Longinus.

Why would Longinus be fighting here? Isn't he a high-ranking officer? Ben thought to himself.

The Rhion closest to Longinus rushed toward the wounded fighter and beckoned for more to come forth. He placed a tourniquet around Longinus's bleeding forearm and placed a small rope in his mouth. Longinus bit down while another Rhion with a torch hurried over. A second Rhion placed a knife in the flame until the steel glowed a bright orange while a third held a smoking pipe to Longinus's mouth. Longinus took a deep drag from the pipe and then nodded at the Rhion, clenching his eyes shut. He let out a high-pitched scream as the Rhion cauterized his wound closed.

"That'll only hold you over until we can get you to a healer," Ben heard the first Rhion say. Then the soldier turned to face Ben and pointed at him. "Rhion, arrest him for assaulting an officer of the Sun!"

Ben swallowed hard and gripped his sword tight. *How am I supposed to get out of this one?*

"No!" Longinus yelled. He pushed the Rhion away from him. "He's mine."

"But, Prefect, your hand!" the second Rhion protested.

"This won't take long," Longinus muttered.

As Ben stood in amazement and shock, Longinus rushed toward him with his remaining sickle. The swing of the curved blade made an eerie high-pitched sound as it sliced through the air. The blade cut across Ben's armor without any true damage. But as quickly as Ben had moved out of the way, Longinus made his next attack.

Longinus lunged into Ben, and the two collapsed into the sand. The Ænærian removed his helmet and pounded it against Ben's head over and over again. He could feel the blood filling his mouth and leaking from his nose.

Longinus dropped his helmet. "I want a good look at you before I kill you," he hissed as he pulled down Ben's scarf. "Limmetrad!" he yelled with his dilated eyes wide and taken aback. He shifted his gaze to the audience, as though he were looking for someone.

"Not too sure what's going on, folks! It appears our fighters are...talking?"

The audience started booing and throwing things into the arena. Longinus cursed as a boot smacked him in the face.

Ben took his opening.

He lunged into Longinus, throwing all his weight into the attack. Longinus staggered backwards and nearly fell on his back. Ben retrieved his short sword and advanced toward Longinus.

"You monster!" Ben yelled as his sword clanged against Longinus's sickle. "You had Freztad attacked! You kidnapped Rose! You killed Rakshi!"

Ben felt a surge of energy course through his veins as he shouted each accusation at his opponent. His sword felt lighter and his attacks stronger. With every strike, Ben's vision blurred to red. He had noticed such a phenomenon before when he was angry, but this time he ignored it. A sense of euphoria overwhelmed him, removing all the pain of his injuries. All of his focus rested solely on taking revenge on the Ænærian who had betrayed his trust and shattered his world.

Longinus was growing tired, Ben could see. His form was growing sloppy, and he was lowering his guard more often. He was lucky Ben still had enough restraint to spare him.

"I've heard about the mess you've made all over Ænæria, Limme-trad," Longinus said. "I find it most intriguing that you haven't killed anyone. That's how I know you won't kill me. Surrender, and I can guarantee your life. The King will want a word with you."

"I can't do that, Longinus. Maybe I won't kill you directly, but that wound you've got there won't do so well if you don't get it looked at soon. You don't want to lose the whole arm, or worse, do you? Surrender now, and we can put an end to this charade." The words were nearly impossible for Ben to make. He didn't want to let Long-inus get away, but he needed to focus on his task. And focusing on seeing Arynn and Rose safe was all that kept the red flashes from overwhelming him.

Longinus scoffed. "There is no honor in surrender—only in death. But mine will not be today. Do know that it *has* been an honor to fight you, Limmetrad."

"Could it be? If you've seen the Argr's fights before, then you may recall similar speeches. Don't go anywhere, folks! It looks like things are about to get real interesting!"

Ben's euphoria and confidence suddenly shattered as through it were a glass trinket crushed by a hammer. Was Longinus ready to call his Rhion back to his aid? There was no way Ben could take them all on at once.

Longinus loosened his grip on his sickle and let it drop to the sand beneath him. He held onto his chain firmly and spun in circles. Pirouetting, Longinus let the grounded sickle achieve flight and orbit his spinning body. The sickle crept closer to Ben with each rotation.

Unsure of when the attack would come, Ben turned and ran once more for the rafters. The audience jeered and hollered insults and slanders, but Ben didn't care. The strike could come at any minute and he needed to be behind something when it did.

Ben darted across the sand and slipped more than once. The audience laughed. Each time he would get himself up, looking back at his enemy as he ran. Just as the supports were mere feet away from him, Ben felt his lungs scream for air.

Scratching just below his right eye, the sickle circled around Ben's face while the chain looped around his neck. He felt a strong tug on the chain and fell backwards, his remaining breath exiting his body.

Clutching at his neck, Ben watched as Longinus walked past him toward the very rafters he had hoped would be his salvation.

Longinus looped the chain's handle through a support beam. "Pull out the Motion Block! I want everyone to see this in *real* time!"

Though he could not see it, Ben heard the whirring sound of the Motion Block rising once more from the ground. When the sound stopped, Ben felt another jerk on the chain and he was dragged by the neck toward Longinus.

Panicking, Ben gasped even faster for air. He dug his fingers into the chain closed around his neck in the hope for just one breath. The metal links refused to budge. Ben could feel his consciousness slipping away.

The ground moved away from Ben's feet as he was raised into the air. People laughed and shouted with excitement. Through the haze and blurred vision, Ben thought he saw two ravens circle the arena and land on Tauron's corpse. He knew he would soon be next.

Ben's vision flickered between black and red. He thought he saw Longinus approach him with the spear from the beginning of the match. He stabbed Ben in the side and left the spear dangling with his hanging body.

The pain was unlike anything Ben had felt before. He could feel blood spilling down from his left side—the spear tip the only thing stopping it from pouring out like a waterfall. His vision grew to a darker red until it was indistinguishable from the blackness of unconsciousness. Ben imagined this must be what dying is like.

The sounds echoed away from him into nothingness: no more cheers, laughs, or even the ringleader's narration—the last thing he could hear were the ravens' caws overtop faint screams of terror. All feeling was gone, even the pain—the last thing he felt was his body dropping to the ground. All was lost as Ben sensed himself fade into oblivion....

16. Into the Mines

Death was not as Ben expected. Vicious galloping against broken pavement dampened the sound of distant cries. Shrieks of horror poured behind him as the sound of whinnying horses to the cracked sky rode before him. Somewhere in the middle, there was warm water raining against his still body. The lightning grew louder and closer as the cries faded to the distant memory that they truly were.

A flash of red enveloped the black nothingness. He recalled a heavy drop and the shattering of metal. He could remember little else.

The red flash became brighter and shifted to orange, and then again to yellow. Finally it was white, clear and translucent.

"...with us. Quit being such a pain and help us! They're after us... know you helped us...they'll kill you if you don't come!" a familiar voice yelled.

There was a frustrated groan and a grunt of pain.

"You owe me, Dary. Big time."

Ben felt his body lifted from the air and shots of pain overcame his body. There was silence until the crackling sky and sound of hooves entered the scene. He felt his hand being covered by something warm and soft while his chest was stabbed and beaten under the barrage of water.

The last of the stabbing stopped, and Ben felt something cover his cold and wet chest. He could hear the battering rain echo over a ceiling above him. His last thought before yet another slumber was about how the rain could be outside if he was so sure he felt it hitting him.

At last, Ben regained the gift of sight. First opening his left eye and then his right, Ben saw mountains from outside the window. They reached toward the heavens underneath the bright blood moon.

Coughing violently, Ben felt a throbbing ache around his neck. Another red flash, this time surely a memory. It showed Ben hanging by the neck with a spear hanging from his side. He looked to his left and saw his side bandaged and dry, the pain all but absent. Next, he examined his chest and found a similar bandage. What had happened? His memory lay in bits of clarity surrounded by flickers of red.

"What's Vänalleato like?" a female voice asked. "Is it true you're not a part of Ænæria yet?"

There was a groan. "Yet? Ascendants take me if we're ever a part of Ænæria. Though we're just outside the border, and sols have been making their way in...." said another woman, whose voice was so familiar.

"Then it won't be long," the first voice said. "It's really not so bad. Ignistad is the only one with slavery, though children are taken from settlements and sold off from time to time. They're too young to remember anything different, though. The other provinces get to stay pretty much the same once they're converted from being pagans."

Another groan. "I hate that word," the second one woman said. "But I wouldn't mind seeing more of it. There're so many places my father hasn't been to yet, and I could finish his maps for him. I could look for my friend, too."

Ben tried to speak but no words came to him. His mouth was too dry and throat much too sore. A hand came from his right, carrying a pouch. The pouch poured cool water down his throat, and he swallowed it graciously.

"Better?" the familiar voice asked.

Struggling to turn, Ben saw a red-haired girl sitting next to him. "Arynn?" he asked.

"Yes, I do believe that's my name," she answered with a half-smile.

"You're awake. How?"

"How else?" the other girl answered. "Welcome back to the land of the living. Hey, Dary—Your friend is awake."

"Good, now I can kill him. Take the reins, Trinity," Darius said. He climbed to the back of the carriage and studied Ben with a scowl, shaking his head. "You're an idiot."

"Darius, give it up already. I think he knows that by now," Arynn said, punching Darius in the shoulder.

"Idiot? Me? What did I do?" Ben asked.

Darius let out a sarcastic laugh and said, "Oh, good. He conveniently lost his memory."

Ben looked at the Ænærian blankly.

"Seriously? You don't remember anything?" Darius asked.

Ben shook his head.

"Blazes, where to begin?" Darius scoffed and shook his head. "You fought the arena's champion! You didn't think of trying something a little less conspicuous?"

The memory flashes made sense now. He recalled just about all of the fight up until Longinus hung him by a chain from the rafters. Everything else was still fuzzy and red.

"I think," Ben stammered. "I think I remember now. I fought Longinus, Randy's nephew. But I don't remember anything after being hanged and stabbed."

Arynn and Trinity exchanged looks, apparently unsure of the details themselves.

"I wouldn't have believed it had I not been there," Darius said. "You managed to snap the metal links from the chain with your bare hands. Then you picked up the rest of the chain and threw it at Longinus. It wrapped around his neck and nearly suffocated him."

"I don't remember any of that!" Ben said. "I didn't...well, I didn't kill him, did I?"

"No. As far as I know, he's still alive. His wound is pretty nasty though."

"So how did I get here? How did Arynn get healed?"

"Dary kidnapped me, that's how!" Trinity pouted. "Forced me to heal both of you—for free!"

"Trinity, for the last time, you were already in danger. I didn't kidnap you—I rescued you!"

"I didn't need rescuing until you showed back up."

"Whatever," Darius said. "Anyway, Ben. I ran down to the arena with the other Rhion. They all wanted to save their prefect. I tried to use the commotion to sneak you out of there but..."

"But you caused all of Ignistad to chase you," Trinity snipped.

"Trinity, just let me finish!"

"What happened next?" Ben asked.

"Well, a handful of Rhion were trying to detain you after they learned you were wanted by the King. You held them off pretty well, considering you didn't have any weapons. You broke a few arms and threw one of them into the stands—"

"What? I don't remember any of that. And I'm not even strong enough to lift someone over my head, let alone throw them!"

"Well, you did," Darius said. "But because of that you drew the attention of more Rhion. Those who weren't taking Longinus to safety were on their way to put you down. Lucky for you, I still had Fenwin's swords. As soon as I got to you, I put them all down and dragged you out of there."

"You dragged me? So is that when I went unconscious?" Ben asked.

Darius frowned. "Figure of speech, idiot. I told you to follow me, and you listened. But it was like you were in some kind of strange trance. You weren't talking, and you would just stand still unless I told you to move. Has that ever happened to you before?"

Ben shook his head. He thought about the red flickers he had seen before Longinus hanged him. He remembered periodically seeing the flashes throughout his journey, normally whenever he was extremely angry. As far as he knew, he had never had a fugue state like this one. Then again, how would he know if he couldn't remember?

"Traumatic events can make people do weird things," Trinity said. She glanced at Darius as though she were hinting at something. "It's kind of like your mind protecting you from it all. A near death experience could do it."

"Would that explain his extra strength?" Arynn asked.

"It could, though Dary is probably embellishing the details. I've never heard of anyone snapping bones left and right and throwing people twice their weight fifteen feet into the air."

"I'm not embellishing!" Darius pounded his hand against the side of the carriage. He turned to face Ben. "Look, the point is that you and I high-tailed it out of there and ran straight to Trinity's. As soon as we got there, you passed out. I told her that the Rhion would arrest her for conspiring with enemies, and that she needed to come with me."

"See!" Trinity yelled. "He kidnapped me."

Darius groaned.

"We've been on the road ever since," Arynn added when both Trinity and Darius went silent. "We've had a few run-ins with Ænærians, but Darius made good use of Fenwin's swords and sung. I think we've pretty much lost them."

"We wouldn't have anyone after us if Ben didn't call himself the Vault Guardian in the first place," Darius said, avoiding Trinity's line of sight. "Even if Ben killed Longinus and won the match, he would've been arrested. Legate Randolph was at the match. If he didn't know his nephew was the Argr before, he does now, and I bet he's not too happy you maimed his nephew. Besides, he knows you're after the Vault now."

Ben felt his pulse race at the mention of Randy.

Arynn hit Darius again. Ben lost count of how many times Arynn had punched Darius as he rubbed his shoulder.

"Randolph already knew Ben was after Rose!" Arynn argued. "Fenwin said so at the prison! He probably figured Ben knew about the Vault, too! How else would Ben have known where to find Rose?"

Darius scoffed and went back to the front of the carriage with Trinity. Arynn put her arms around Ben, squeezing them as she embraced him. Ben felt his face go red and stomach drop.

"Thank you for doing all that to help me. I think it took a lot of courage, no matter what Darius says," she said as she let go of him.

Dizzy and embarrassed, Ben looked everywhere but toward Arynn, blushing. "*Uh.* Yeah. You're welcome. No problem. Glad you're feeling better."

Arynn shook her head and suppressed a grin. "Though, you were kind of stupid."

Ben forced a laugh. "*Heh.* Right. How long was I out for?"

Arynn held out her hands and counted on her fingers one by one.

Ben interjected by the time she got to her eighth finger. "Hey! There's no way I've been out for over a week!"

She burst into laughter. "Had you going there for a second, *huh*? It's been just over four days at this point. I only came to about two days ago."

Immediately, Ben patted down at his pockets. He thoughts were racing. *Where's the watch?*

"Ben, relax!" Arynn said, putting her hand back on his shoulder. "I have your watch right here." She raised her right hand and revealed the silver watch around her wrist. She loosened the clasp to remove it.

"No. You hold onto it. It *uh*...it looks nice on you," he said as he felt his face turn red once again.

Arynn gave Ben a curious look as if she were trying to study his expression. Ben felt droplets of sweat drip from his forehead as he waited for her to say something.

Instead, she simply shrugged it off and looked at the watch.

"Where are we headed now?" he asked, looking out the window at the mountains, hoping to distract himself. He had never noticed how high some mountains soared, nor had he ever cared as much.

"We're not heading anywhere. According to my maps, we're already here. We should see Jordysc any minute now."

Ben moved to the front of the carriage in an attempt to see the town he had heard so much yet knew very little about. In front of the carriage were three horses blended into the night like shadows next to an irritated Sleipnir. The horse snorted disapprovingly as Ben climbed to the front as though he had heard him. The horse didn't seem to enjoy the other steeds' company.

Aside from the stony projections to their side, Ben couldn't see much under the crimson moon. As he looked at the celestial body bleeding into the sky, the red flashes of his fight in the arena slowly came back to him. He saw himself fighting the Rhion, moving between them faster than a charging bull and snapping their bones as though they were dried twigs.

"Ben?" Arynn asked from behind him.

He jumped, snapping out of his flashback.

"Do you have any clues about where to go from here?" she asked. "We've been circling this area for almost an hour and haven't found a trace of any village."

"I thought your dad told us to come here in the first place," Darius said. "Maybe your map is wrong."

Arynn seethed. "My maps aren't wrong! It's around here somewhere. We're just not looking hard enough!"

"Did your father say when he last went to the village?" Trinity asked. "Maybe it's not around anymore."

"I suppose it's been awhile since my dad has been here. He hasn't left the Alliance's borders since my mom died."

As she spoke, Ben noticed Arynn had a flustered expression as though she didn't quite believe herself. He suspected there was something Siegfried hadn't told them about Jordysc, and it wasn't just about its mysterious location.

"Well, we know Jordysc is still around," Ben said. "The stranger back in Parvidom told me to look for the mines. Have you seen anything like that around here?"

Darius shook his head. "No. I've been looking for a village not a mine. Not like I'd see it with the stupid blood moon. I can't see a blazing thing out here."

Arynn gasped as though Darius had given her a brilliant idea.

"What is it?" Trinity asked.

"Ben! Those swords you stole from Fenwin—"

"Well, I wouldn't say I stole them..." Ben stammered.

"Will you get to the point?" Darius asked, gripping the sun-swords over his lap.

"We can use them like torches! Why didn't we think of this before? We can each take a horse and split up into pairs to find them," Arynn said excitedly.

It was hard to tell in the darkness, but Ben swore he saw Darius roll his eyes and mutter something under his breath.

"What was that, Darius?" Ben asked.

Darius sighed and shook his head once again and said "How're we supposed let the other group know we found it? It's not like we can leave someone alone while the other person rides off to find the other group to tell them. There could be wastelanders or patrols out here."

Ben and Arynn exchanged looks, unsure of a solution. Trinity, on the other hand, seemed to have a useful idea.

"Well, whoever finds it can shoot a sung blast in sky to let the other group know."

"Did we get another sung while I was out," Ben asked.

"No, you could just shoot your sword like you did at the prison," Arynn said.

Ben shook his head. "It doesn't work like that. I haven't been able to get it to so much as spark since the prison."

"Probably because it hasn't been out in the sun at all," Darius said. "That's how most holy artifacts work. The sungs and sun-carriages all recharge after a few hours of light."

"Then what was the thing you put in Gatron's sung to repower it?" Arynn asked.

Darius seemed to wince at the mention of the legate. "That was a power cell. They contain stored sun energy. It's useful for something that might run out of power while it's still being used."

"I don't think my sword is one of your holy weapons," Ben said. "It glows green—not orange or yellow. And I'm guessing Fenwin's swords can't shoot since he was carrying around a sung, too."

"It doesn't matter," Darius said, looking at the sword skeptically. "Firing off anything is a bad idea. Someone will hear it or see it."

"We haven't seen anyone in days!" Arynn argued. "There are no Rhion following us, and any wastelanders in the area would have a tough time dealing with a sung, two sun-swords, and a giant wolf."

"Wait, where is Sierra?" Ben asked, looking around for his wolf.

"She's running a bit behind the carriage," Arynn said. "The horses won't cooperate with her any closer."

Ben looked behind and saw his companion quietly trotting along the dark fields. "What if one group uses a sung and the other sends Sierra? That way we both have a way to signal each other."

"Blazes, you still want to use the sung as a signal?" Darius asked. "Fine, but I'll be the one firing it. If we're attacked, then I'm the best one to use it."

"Yeah, yeah. You're very capable, Dary, we get it," Trinity said. "I'll go with Ben. I need to change his bandages soon, and he needs my medical attention most at the moment. Though yours will need to be changed, too, if we're gone for more than hour, Arynn."

Ben felt an odd sense of insecurity as he thought of Darius getting that close to Arynn. The more he thought about it, the more uncomfortable he felt. A strange tingling sensation filled his belly as he thought longingly about spending alone time with Arynn. He could barely remember the last time they'd been together when they weren't racing against time with some sort of emergency....

Rose, you idiot, Ben thought to himself. *Focus! Rose* is *an emergency.*

The group split up in pairs, and Ben mounted Sleipnir and rode beside Trinity as she held the glowing orange sword—the other was with Darius. Sierra kept up the pace next to them, trotting over the rocky road lighter than a falling feather.

Trinity did a good job of keeping Ben's mind from wandering back to the night at the arena. She kept him talking and engaged in conversation as though her tattooed eye could read what was troubling him. She would ask him how he was feeling, if he was experiencing any dizziness or headaches. She would make sure he kept drinking water and barely gave him a second to let his mind roam. After Trinity asked him every medical question she could possibly think of, she asked him about his home.

"There's nothing really special about Freztad—well, aside from Rose. There's these two twins who're probably ten years older than me, and they're all right, but Rose is the only person who's ever understood me. Even our friend Rakshi..." Ben gripped her bow and thought of the fallen Sentinel. "Never mind. She's not around anymore."

Trinity looked at Ben with curiosity. "Did the legate do that?"

Ben told Trinity about the attack on Freztad and how he was convinced Randy and Longinus had orchestrated it to gain Rose's trust.

"Why didn't they just attack your home and kidnap Rose themselves? The Third Legate's forces are more than capable of it. I've even heard stories about him leveling an entire village. Probably because someone stepped out of line."

Beads of sweat dripped down Ben's forehead. An entire village? That sounded like pure insanity. Something about Randy seemed off when they had met, but nothing seemed to indicate he was a true lunatic. *I can't believe I left you alone with him, Rose. I'm so sorry,* he thought to himself as he went on to explain why Rose had been taken in the first place.

"Eternal Mother...I never knew the King had a daughter. The child of the Sun's Chosen? She must be magnificent," Trinity said in awe.

"She is," Ben replied. "But it has nothing to do with Julius. She's inherently a good person."

"Likely because the Sun has graced her so. Otherwise, there's no such thing as an 'inherently good person,'" Trinity countered.

"You really believe that stuff? How can you think Julius is some 'chosen one' after all the terrible things he's done?" Ben demanded.

Trinity looked at Ben sadly and turned to the mountains at her side. Ben immediately regretted snapping at her. "I'm sorry. That was wrong of me...especially after all you've done for us. It's not my place to question your beliefs."

Trinity continued to stare at the mountains, not saying a word. Ben found himself speechless and wondered if it was best for them continue their search in silence. What could he say to her after that? Feeling awkward, he eventually found the need to break the silence. "So, what's with your tattoo? I noticed Darius has one, but I assume that has to do with being a Rhion."

Trinity laughed. "He is has the mark of a firstborn child who must be given up to become a Rhion. Mine covers a brand. You see, I grew up as a slave. Many of us are marked with brands somewhere on our body and a number in place of a name, depending on which province our parents are from. Mine came from Plutonua, the third province, so my forehead was marked, and I was given the number 3-3-3-3. I was the three hundred and thirty third slave from the third province. After thirteen years, I won my freedom by demonstrating my expertise as a healer. My master told me my talents were wasted on him because he was an old and dying man. He gave me the tattoo to cover my brand, which officially marks me as a free woman. I then took up the name 'Trinity' because the number 'three' seems to be the number the Eternal Mother chose as my lucky number. I mean, even now the number comes up. It took three strangers to finally drag me out of Ignistad."

Ben raised his eyebrows, impressed by the healer's story. "I've never heard of a lucky number before. I like your tattoo though. It's nice, and I can't see the brand underneath it."

Trinity chuckled. "The brands are small, and the tattoo is big enough to cover it. Say, you got any ink hiding under those clothes?"

Ben blushed, unsure of how to respond. He couldn't tell if Trinity was flirting with him or if this was how she talked to everyone. "No tattoos here," he responded nervously. "But you'd have noticed when you did my bandages. Say, don't you need to change them soon?"

"No," Trinity responded coldly. "I just said that because I didn't want to be alone with Darius."

"Oh," Ben knew there was something going on between the two. He knew they had known each other in the past, and he had gathered enough information to realize that something had happened between them. "What happened with you two? Now that I think about it, aren't you both from the same province? Is that how you know each other?"

"Don't be silly. I haven't been there since I was born." She suddenly darted off ahead of him. "Come on! I think I see something up this way! Come on!"

Ben urged Sleipnir to keep up as he followed the bright orange light that Trinity carried. He found it a little suspicious that she had seen something as soon as Ben questioned her relationship with Darius. Yet, as he saw the flaming sword come to a standstill, Ben discovered that Trinity had indeed been sincere. There in front of the two of them, below a low-hanging crag, was a large vertical mouth in the rocky mountainside.

As Trinity illuminated the scene, Ben was positive that the cavern entrance was man-made. Etches from pickaxes and rubble from explosions littered the walkway as the two slowly walked into the cavern. Deeper into the cave they found wooden beams with cobwebs spilling down like sap from a tree. Metal wired nets protected the ground from the ceiling where stalactites protruded and crumbled. Farther into the mountain they found holes dug into the stony walls where ore was once mined and collected. Toppled wheelbarrows and abandoned shovels lay scattered across the floor as though all the diggers had suddenly vanished.

The two studied each scene they encountered and quickly moved on until they reached an impasse. Beyond the farthest excavation room that they had reached were three burrowed tunnels. At first glance, none of the tunnels appeared to be any different from the others. With Sierra outside the cave keeping guard and watching the horses, there remained only two people to search the three tunnels. For all they knew, they very well could be in the wrong place and would simply be wasting time by searching each tunnel and any that followed. There had to have been some way to definitively determine if they were indeed in the correct place. But how?

Ben examined the tunnel to the right with great care. Trinity held up the sword as Ben slowly slid his hands over the archways on the off chance that he would feel something out of place. He passed the archway to see if there was anything deeper in the tunnel that would offer some kind of clue. About ten steps in, he smelled a hint of something foul. A few more steps and the odor grew stronger, and he felt his eyes watering.

"Why does it smell like rotten eggs in here?" Trinity asked, walking a few feet behind Ben.

Ben stopped walking. He recalled learning how the people in the mountain settlement of Talamdor would add a compound to the gases beneath their village in case they ever leaked. A compound that smelled just like eggs. Because if the gases leaked without someone knowing they may accidentally...

"TRINITY GET BACK!"

Ben turned around and bumped into Trinity. The sun-sword fell from her hand and glided past them, farther into the tunnel. Ben tackled Trinity to the ground and covered her as an explosion erupted from behind them.

Ben felt flames on the back of his cloak. He rolled off of Trinity and smothered the fire. Rubble poured from the ceiling and fell over top of them.

"Trinity, we need to get out of here! Run!"

They both ran as fast as they could, the cave falling from behind them. They had only just barely made it to the end of the tunnel before it completely collapsed. Trinity bent over to catch her breath while Ben examined the back of his cloak. It had been burned all the way through.

"Ben! Your shirt is burned, too! I need to take a look!"

"I feel fine," he said.

"Hold still, I need to get a good look. Really severe burns can be so deep that you no longer feel any pain." She moved behind him and placed her hands over his back, lifting parts of his shirt. "You're extremely lucky. I don't know how, but there isn't even a single burn. You're okay."

Ben turned around to face Trinity. "I told you I was fine. Are you? I'm sorry I knocked you over. I wanted to stop the explosion from happening, but it seems I was too late in noticing the smell."

"What do you mean?"

"The smell. It's a compound added to make flammable gases smell. It's to prevent explosions like what we just witnessed."

"If it's added to it, then that means..."

"That the Guild is here. We found them. And I know how to figure out which tunnel to go through."

Sierra found Arynn and Darius incredibly fast. Ben never understood how that wolf moved so quickly and listened so well. The three returned to him and Trinity outside the mine less than an hour after Ben's discovery. With Sierra once again keeping guard, the four entered the mines until they reached the left most tunnel.

"So, you found a mine with three tunnels. How do you even know this is the right one?" Darius asked with his arms crossed.

Ben explained to Darius and Arynn that, after the explosion in the first tunnel, he and Trinity tested the other tunnels by smelling for rotten eggs. The middle tunnel had smelled just like the first. The one all the way to the left didn't have any smell.

"Did you follow this tunnel all the way?" Darius asked. "How do you know there isn't some other trap at the end of it?"

"Not yet," Ben said. "We wanted to get you two first. We didn't want to waste any more time."

The four strolled down the tunnel, not knowing when it would lead to something. It was seemingly endless as though a giant snake had tunneled straight through to the other end of the mountain, miles from where they stood.

As they walked down the deep and dank tunnel, the two women continued their conversation from earlier that night about Arynn's home and the apparently unstoppable tide of Ænærian influence. Darius pretended not to listen to them as he held a blank expression and stared ahead. He didn't seem to be in the mood to talk, so Ben continued to lead the way in silence as he listened to the women talk.

After half an hour of walking, the group finally emerged into another cavern, this time with six tunnels.

"Great, where do we go now?" Darius complained.

Ben shook his head in disbelief. "I don't believe it. I didn't think much of it before, but this is exactly like the tunnel underneath Freztad. It opens up with three tunnels. Two of them lead to dead ends, and the other leads to another cavern with six. One of them leads to a ladder that leads to my room from under my house."

Darius scoffed. "It's just a coincidence."

"Is it though?" Ben asked. "Everything about the watch my dad gave me has been a clue. What if they're all connected? It has the mandala, the coordinates to the Vault, and it used to have a key to the tunnel beneath Freztad. That's not a coincidence. He knew I needed to get to the Vault, and he knew I needed to contact the Guild to get there."

"I agree with Ben," Trinity said.

"Me too," Arynn said. "Besides, if we're wrong, we'll probably just smell eggs again, right?"

"Or they could have something worse that you can't sense as easily," Darius argued. "But be my guest, Ben. Try it out."

Ben smiled. He thought about how he had never spent any time with his father, but nonetheless, the man seemed to know Ben so well. He hid so many intricacies in the watch he had left Ben that were only now being tied together. For one of the first times in his life, Ben felt close to his father as he walked through the middle tunnel on his right with his friends at his back and the future at his front.

17. A Father's Legacy

pproaching a door at the end of the tunnel, Ben reflected on the luck and misfortune his journey had brought thus far. There had been many detours and interferences along the way, but he finally made it to Jordysc; he was about to make contact with the mysterious Miners Guild. There were trials and tribulations everywhere he had gone but, somehow, he had been lucky enough to make it through each one. People had died, yet he was still in one piece. He and his friends had been injured. *But at least I have friends.*

Walking down the tunnel with his three companions at his heels, Ben realized that the bond of friendship hadn't been something he had experienced so fully until now. Though it had only been a short time, it seemed as though he had known Arynn and Darius for his whole life. Just as he couldn't see a future without Rose, Ben couldn't imagine what it would be like to go on without his friends. They had voluntarily risked their lives for his cause. Not once had they been pressured to continue on with him, and not once had they made any indication of leaving him. In Ben's eyes, they were his first true friends.

Rose was his friend too, of course, but she was also family. They grew up together as though they were siblings. They were the only children to have survived the plague that ravished their home. As descendants of Freztad's founder, the traits of leadership coursed through their veins. Thus, Ben keenly perceived that his and Rose's fates were intertwined to the point of interconnected co-dependency. After all, that's why Ben wanted to save her: not just because they were friends or family, but because he felt their destinies were linked. Ben was no one without his cousin.

The same simply wasn't true for anyone else in his life. Kabedge was more like a grandfather than anything. But a friend? Perhaps, but a transgenerational friendship just seemed different to Ben. Rakshi and the twins were the closest Freztadians in age to the two Limmetrads, but the same thought process applied. They may have treated each other as siblings, but they weren't exactly peers; they couldn't connect in the same way. They trained and hunted together earlier in their lives. But as they grew older, responsibilities took them away from one another. Rose had the village; Ben had the farm.

Besides, Rakshi was no longer alive, and Ben didn't know if Freztad was safe without him and Rose there to protect it. What was he thinking, going off on his own without a word? It wasn't fair to anyone back home. He had left his aunt in Kabedge's care, not even considering that the old man already had enough on his plate. And, unless Lydia could bring herself out of the melancholic pit that she had dug herself into, Freztad was without anyone willing to lead. *That's not fair,* he thought. *I know what melancholia feels like. She can't just dig herself out. She needs help, like I had.*

Ben smacked his forehead thinking, *Idiot! I promised Rose I'd watch over Lydia and the village in her absence.*

But you're going to save her. The village will be better off with her back home. I'll be better off with her home, he argued with himself.

He may have been able to convince himself that he was doing the right thing, but how could he know for sure that he was going about it correctly? Leaving home with no notice, leaving all responsibilities behind, and for what? To chase some fantastical vault in some unknown land up north? He really was like his father.

Ben stopped in his tracks without warning, causing Darius to bump into him and nearly knock the two over onto the rocky terrain.

Darius yelled at Ben to pay better attention, though he might as well have been yelling at the floor itself, for neither would lend an ear to him.

Ben stood in place with his chest beating like a drum as he came to grips with his sudden epiphany. All these years he had been cursing his father for being so selfish to abandon his duties by leaving Freztad. And yet that's exactly what Ben found himself doing. Did Alphonse also have another, more pressing concern that had led him to the Vault?

Ben sighed as he admitted to himself that he would likely never know the truth about his father.

Darius opened his mouth, as if to ask Ben what the matter was, but closed it without a word as the four approached the lit braziers at the end of the tunnel. Illuminated by the fire was an obsidian black door etched with the symbol from Ben's watch. The mandala had a diameter of roughly three feet and stood above a round metal ring that hung from the door. Light from the braziers on each side of the door danced off the mandala, creating the illusion that the mandala was swirling like a murky whirlpool in one of the murmuring streams where Ben had used to fish when he was a young boy. The symbol itself seemed to be alive as the reflections spiraled upon the door.

Hesitantly, Ben reached for the metal ring. It was cold to the touch and much heavier than it appeared. He let go of the ring and let it bang against the door, echoing throughout the hall where he and his friends stood in anticipation.

Nothing happened.

Ben used the knocker once more, but there was no response from behind the door.

Darius stomped his foot on the ground and pouted. "Enough with the gimmicks already! Why can't they just let us in?"

"Quit the whining," Trinity said. "How do you know anyone is even in there?"

Darius looked at her with a dumbfounded expression. "You're kidding, right? The braziers are lit! Of course, someone is in there!"

"Enough, you two," Ben said, still facing the knocker. It was clear to Ben that Darius was anxious to meet the Miners Guild; he did, after all, give up his life as a Rhion for their cause and was riding blindly on faith without a face to put to the organization responsible. Ben imagined that Darius must have similar feelings toward the Guild as Ben did toward his father: a dissonance of intrigue, admiration, and animosity.

"Do they really need so many secrets?" Trinity asked. "I mean I know it's a *secret* club, but this seems a little ridiculous."

"It's not a *club*," Darius pouted. "It's an undercover organization of people who dedicate their lives to helping others and making a difference!"

"Right. Because the medicine woman here doesn't know what it means to dedicate her life to helping people," she countered.

"This is bigger than that!" Darius snapped. "This is about fighting back! Changing the world back to what it once was before Julius's tyranny!"

Arynn scoffed. "That includes getting rid of your ridiculous sun god idea."

Darius and Trinity shot glares toward Arynn.

"That's different! People worshipped the Sun long before Julius came to power. He just...he made it more well known, okay?" Darius argued.

Despite their dispute, Trinity nodded in agreement.

"All right, all right, quit it!" Ben yelled, finally having enough of their bickering. "Can't we go a day without arguing? Let's focus on what's important. We need to speak with this Alejandra and say the password." He turned from his friends and said the words he had heard Arynn's father mysteriously speak back in Vänalleato. "As above, so below."

Just as the words escaped Ben's lips, a loud metallic *thud* sounded from behind the door. There was a screeching sound of metal rubbing against stone as the door opened. The opened door revealed a room within which the four travelers barely fit. Across the room was a wooden door with a sliding hatch situated about five feet off the ground. The hatch slid open, and a pair of dark eyes peeked through.

"Well, you've made it this far. Seem to know where you're going, and you know our password. But I'll need to see Guild identification," the voice said from behind the door.

Arynn slipped off Ben's watch and handed it to him. Ben understood and held it up, so the pair of eyes could see the engraving on it.

"Oh my..." said the voice, as if concerned. "Yes...come in! I apologize for the delay, Master Limmetrad!" The hatch slid shut, and the sound of locks being removed echoed from behind the wooden door.

The other three exchanged curious glances before looking to Ben for an explanation.

"What?" Ben asked with a perplexed expression. "Limmetrad is my family name. Not sure how they knew that though...."

"Family name? Isn't that some Old Days tradition?" Trinity asked.

Behind the door was an elderly woman of Kabedge's age and short of stature. She had dark eyes and graying hair tied in a bun above her head. She looked at Ben and his friends with a smile.

"You must be Benedict," the woman said with a kind smile. "It's been ages since I've seen you. I often wondered when I'd see another Limmetrad in these parts. You may call me Risa."

Darius snickered at the mention of Ben's full name, but Arynn elbowed him to stop.

"*Another* Limmetrad?" Ben asked in shock.

"And who might you three be?" the woman asked, ignoring Ben's question.

"They're my friends," Ben answered promptly. He pointed at each of them saying, "Darius, Trinity, and Arynn. Now, tell me how you know who I am."

The old woman gave an expression of disappointment. "Oh, I suppose I shouldn't be surprised. It's been nearly fifteen years, after all. Come. All four of you. I'll take you to Alejandra and explain when we see her."

Risa picked up a wooden cane to her left and hobbled forward as the four followed behind her slow pace. The mysterious woman led them down a few corridors where they found a great many people of all shapes, sizes, ethnicities, and genders. These people worked under mysterious lights shining above them, offering the same white brightness he had seen at night in Ignistad.

As they continued down the large room, Ben saw Miners to his left sitting at tables with stacks of parchment that they shuffled through and scribbled across. He saw others with bizarre mechanisms that covered their ears and short cylinders in front of their mouths through which they spoke. Others sat in front of bulky metal boxes that seemed to spit out pieces of parchment etched with neatly printed words. Upon closer examination, Ben could see the Miners in front of the boxes pushing down on tiny mechanisms with their fingers. As they did, the parchment would move out even more as words suddenly appeared.

To the group's right were not desks, but rather a vast array of weighted equipment. Ben could see people picking up these objects with quite some difficulty before placing them back down, only to repeat the motion. Exhausted grunts and groans filled the equipment area, causing Arynn to snort jestingly.

Farther down the right-hand side of the great hall were no longer weighted tools but rather wooden swords and shields. Two people sparred in the middle of this section while a crowd of people surrounded them, enthralled by the match. The two individuals appeared evenly matched, despite the fact that one was nearly a foot shorter and weighed considerably less.

The two continued to spar as Ben and his companions passed. Risa hollered at the captivated crowd to get back to work. Begrudgingly, the audience scattered to their respective places throughout the hall. The two fighters hardly seemed to notice.

At last, Risa led the travelers to another door at the end of the hall. She gave it a rhythmic knock: *tap, tap, tap-tap, tap-tap-tap.*

The door opened almost immediately, revealing the stranger with the burned face from Parvidom. Without a hood on, Ben got a much better look at her. It wasn't the burn that caught his attention, but rather her beautiful hazel eyes.

Her gaze passed over Risa and landed directly on Ben. "Finally made it, *eh*? Come on in. My mother has been dying to see you." She held the door open while Risa took a step back and allowed the group to enter the room before her.

The room was much larger than Ben had expected. It was nearly the size of Valhaven's hall. A sizable rectangular table stood in the middle of the chamber, taking up a significant amount of space. Upon the table were scattered maps covered by sculpted figurines of suns and crossed pickaxes. The suns far outnumbered the pickaxes except on a long island far to the Northeast.

At the other end of the room was a desk with another shining light stick hovering over pieces of parchment. Sitting at a chair behind the desk was a woman who bore a striking resemblance to the woman from Parvidom but with an unblemished face. She had thick black hair with a steak of green. Her skin was a lightly tanned and slightly darker than Ben's. She appeared to be roughly Lydia's age but had a grand and nostalgic smile stretching across her face.

The woman got up from behind her desk offered Ben an embrace as she wrapped her arms around him and squeezed ever so tightly. "You've grown up so much! It's so good to see you, Benedict!"

Darius snickered.

"*Uh*, actually, I go by Ben," he said, feeling rather uncomfortable. "Are you Alejandra?"

"Well, that's one of my names. Have to change it up every now and then, so the Ænærians can't track me as easily. Change the hair a lot too," she said pointing to the streak in her hair.

Ben raised an eyebrow at her, unsure of what to say.

"Yes, yes. You may call me Alejandra for now. Mandi will let you know when it changes," she said, pointing at the girl from Parvidom.

Darius stepped forward and bowed his head to Alejandra and kneeled before her. "It's an honor to meet you! My name is Darius, former Rhion under command of now-deceased Legate Gatron. I've pledged myself to your cause over the last year and a half. It would be my great honor to serve you!"

Arynn held in a laugh while color faded from Trinity's face, looking as though she wanted to be anywhere else.

Rather than accepting Darius's pledge of loyalty, Alejandra raised an eyebrow and brushed the green steak of hair away from her eye. "Gatron isn't dead. He and his cronies escaped Vänalleato imprisonment and then faked their deaths. Probably too embarrassed or afraid to return to Ænæria after what you all did to him. Which, from what I hear, was quite impressive!"

Ben felt a sudden jolt of energy and saw Arynn put her hand to her mouth, evidently thinking the same thing.

Darius looked up to Alejandra. "He's not dead? But...I heard...I was arrested by Second Legate Fenwin on charges of killing him. He told me his sung exploded and killed him, his crew, and the family we saved."

"Yes, we know all about that. But that was part of Gatron faking his death," Alejandra explained. "From our reports, he and the Rhion broke out, stole the solar pistol and a carriage, and high-tailed it out of Vänalleato. They used the sung to explode the carriage, knowing full well that no one would expect to find any bodies. Gatron left his legate-badge nearby as a form of identification. As far as Ænæria knows, Gatron is dead."

"Why wouldn't there be any bodies? And what's a 'solar pistol'," Ben interrupted.

"It's what we call sungs. Such a stupid name," Mandi answered from the corner. "An explosion from one of those weapons would instantly vaporize anything in a six-foot radius. That's why parts of the carriage were found but no bodies."

Ben's jaw dropped. He knew sungs were powerful, but never imagined they were *this* powerful. Is this how Randy could destroy an entire village?

"Then..." Arynn muttered. "Was anyone at home hurt? At Vänalleato during the escape? And Pawel—the little boy and his family... they're all safe?"

Both Mandi and Alejandra nodded in affirmation. Ben and Arynn sighed with relief. He felt as though an enormous weight had been lifted off his shoulders. In this sea of horrors and destruction that he had dragged so many others into, there was still some good news to be heard. Not all had been lost. And, with any luck, not all would be lost either.

"And to answer you, young Darius, we would be honored to acquire your service," Alejandra said. "But the best way for you to serve the Guild is to continue to aid Ben. I hear you've all been through much together. It would be a shame if you split up now. And I have a feeling Ben will still need you—all of you—in the fights to come."

Darius stood up and turned to Ben. He gave a simple nod as he looked into Ben's eyes. "Of course. I doubt this guy could get very far without me. I'd never pass up the opportunity to mess with Julius's plans."

Ben smiled. Though Darius could be a real jerk sometimes, he had proven himself to be a real friend and someone Ben could trust. Ben thought again about the odd yet elating sense of friendship that he now had. He had started this trip alone, as one man against the world. But now he stood in the presence of countless people ready to fight for the same cause. There were still questions and concerns he had about the Guild, and he didn't know where best to start. Luckily, Arynn did it for him.

"How did you know about all this stuff? You couldn't have had people in all these locations and return here to tell it all to you."

Risa, silent until now, hobbled forward on her cane and sat on a chair beside the large table. "I suppose you all have quite a few questions. Daughter, granddaughter, why don't we fill them in on everything first. Then, Ben and company, you can ask your questions."

Ben and his friends nodded. They took seats around the table. Darius and Trinity sat next to each other while Alejandra and Mandi sat on either side of Risa. Ben took a spot between Arynn and Alejandra.

Risa spoke first. "It'd probably be best if I started from the beginning. And no interruptions please. It's quite rude, and we'll finish up much faster without them."

Everyone nodded in agreement.

"Very good. Benedict—and I do intend to call you that as it was the name your father intended for you—your father was the founder of the Miners Guild."

Ben's eyes grew wide, and his mouth opened to speak. But he closed it knowing he had promised to keep silent. He would learn the answers soon.

"The Guild has been around since long before Julius founded Ænæria. It started as a group of people who researched Old Days artifacts and attempted to uncover the secrets of the past. Your father was always fascinated by the Old Days, presumably from my brother Takashi's rambling stories."

"Wait...Takashi as in *Takashi Kabedge*?" Ben cried with disbelief. Suddenly, he recalled his old mentor mentioning that he had a sister named Risa 'far away'.

"Now, now. What did I say about interrupting? Yes, Takashi Kabedge is my brother. What a ridiculous name. He learned that, centuries ago, people of all classes carried two names. He thought it would be a trend he could revive. Stupid obsession, especially since he and his husband can't have any children of their own to pass the name on to...but I digress."

"His *husband*?" Arynn asked, for some reason very surprised.

"Yeah, Vic," Ben responded quickly. "They were both like parents to me growing up."

Arynn suddenly looked very uncomfortable. "I didn't know that same-sex couples were allowed in Freztad."

"Why wouldn't they be? Are they not in Vänalleato?"

"No, of course not."

Next, Darius chimed in. "Seriously? It's allowed in Ænæria."

Arynn looked even more shocked than before. "Just...never mind. Risa, please continue."

"Goodness, are we done with interruptions now? Good. As a side note, of course Julius would allow it. My brother and Vic helped raise the damn King after all. As I was saying, before all of these rude interruptions, Alphonse grew up and heard stories about the Old Days and was beyond fascinated. When he was thirteen, he would wander off on his own and explore the world, looking for relics and treasures. Eventually, he found that very watch you carry with you now. He brought it to my brother for explanation; but, Takashi being the less gifted child, had to admit he didn't know much about it and suggested your father contact me. So, your father sought me out in a village not too far from here. Though I don't believe it's still standing...." The old woman trailed off and seemed to lose herself in her thoughts.

"Gran?" Mandi asked, rubbing her hand against Risa's back. Tears seemed to well up in the old woman's eyes. Clearly something terrible happened to her home long ago. Something that haunted her to this day.

"I'm fine, don't worry," Risa said as she waved Mandi away from her. "Alphonse came to me and showed me the watch. He didn't care much about the trinket itself, but rather the symbol on the back of it. In all our research, we'd never seen anything like it. I told him it was possible that someone had simply put it there for no good reason. But that stubborn boy wouldn't have it. He refused to believe it was meaningless. Your father, Benedict, always enjoyed symbols: he enjoyed deriving meaning from things and always believed there was some greater mystery to interpret. Then, a few years later, he found evidence of the symbol's existence far to the East. There, he found an entire Old Days city."

Risa paused and waited for a reaction. Ben and his friends looked at her blankly, not quite grasping what she was insinuating.

"Don't you find it odd that we know of the Old Days' existence but have very little evidence of it?" the old woman asked. "Sure, some towns still stand, and the roads are cruel reminders of the paths our ancestors once took. There are the occasional relics that hunters like your father and my family have found. But we rarely find books, maps, or anything substantial, let alone entire cities. And yet, your father found a massive metropolis, uninhabited since the calamity that ended the Old Days and brought about the New Age.

"The city was absolutely devastated and overcome with wildlife and untamed vegetation. Your father never spoke fully of what he saw there, but I surmise that he found a great many horrors. While he was there, he learned the secret of the Vaults when he entered one of them, weakened by the calamity and the test of time. There he—"

This time it was not Ben who interrupted, but Trinity. "What are these 'Vaults' exactly? I've only just learned about them, but I thought that there was only one."

Arynn and Darius nodded while Ben sat still with the shock of what he was hearing. *There are more Vaults? What if I'm was on my way to the wrong one?*

No, he told himself. *I know Julius is going north. We must be going the right way.*

Risa shook her head and waved her finger at Trinity. "*Tsk, tsk*. I thought I told you no interruptions. How is an old woman like me to ever get through this story with all this?"

Trinity bowed her head apologetically.

"But to answer your question, young lady, yes, there are more Vaults. Many of them. Some are in lands that I have never seen. The world is much bigger than you realize, young ones."

How big exactly? Ben wondered. He had only just now made it to the second map that Siegfried had given him, and that was based on a much larger one. If his father's map was to be believed, the world was enormous. *What kind of calamity could have been that devastating?*

"As I was saying," Risa continued. "Alphonse found one of these Vaults, already opened within the wasted metropolis. Inside the Vault, he found no relics as it was clear to him that others had come before him and cleared it out. Even so, he learned a great secret. While he was there, he picked up a radio signal that transmitted a broadcast with the coordinates of the Grand Vault—the most important of them all."

"Sorry to interrupt, Mom," Alejandra said, "but I don't think they know what a radio is."

"Yes, of course. The simplest way I can explain a radio is that it sends your voice through the air over very long distances and allows someone else with a radio to hear it. You saw many of our Miners out in the hall speaking through them and transcribing codes being sent to us. It's how we know so much about all of you: we have eyes and ears all across Ænæria."

While his three companions appeared confused and in disbelief, Ben nodded. He understood exactly what Risa was talking about. He recalled Lydia's story about his father finding a box that spoke to him. It was now quite plain to see that the 'box' she was referring to was a radio, and the voice was from the Vault.

Risa continued her tale. "The Broken Vault, as Alphonse called it, did contain one other secret aside from the broadcast. All throughout the repository was the symbol he found on the watch. Never before had he imagined that the symbol, found on a seemingly useless trinket, would be the key to uncovering the greatest mystery of the New Age.

"He returned to Freztad weeks later, horribly frustrated, according to my brother. He spent the next year trying to figure out what the coordinates meant. Like all things that man put his mind to, he found a way. He traveled north and met me along the way. In fact, your presence here reminds me quite a bit of his arrival, twenty years ago. He was only a few years older than you, Benedict, with a band of close friends that he had met along the way. Let me think..." Risa's mind trailed off again as her eyes looked aimlessly around the room, landing on nothing in particular.

"Ah yes," she said. "I believe he was with a man named Marcus, a woman named Jesse, another man named Siegfried who bore a striking resemblance to young Arynn here, and of course, your mother, Benedict, a lovely woman named Jean."

Both Ben and Arynn leapt from their chairs, as though a jolt of electricity coursed through their bodies.

"*Our fathers knew each other?*" Arynn squealed in disbelief while Ben shouted at the same time saying, "*You met my mother?*"

Risa furrowed her brow, taken aback by the sudden outburst. "Calm down, calm down. First, I had no idea that Siegfried was your father, Arynn. I suppose it's not a common name, and he did have the same auburn hair that you possess. Was your father a cartographer?"

Wide-eyed and obviously shocked, Arynn gasped. "Yes! He still is! Though he doesn't have much hair anymore."

"Then I believe your father and Alphonse's companion are one in the same."

Ben leaned over the table, bringing himself closer to the Risa. "Yes, yes, enough about all that. Tell me about my mother, please!"

The elderly Miner looked at Ben with a face of confusion. "You mean you don't know? I thought your father would have surely told your aunt about her...."

"I know nothing. Forget all this stuff about the Vault. It doesn't even matter! I'm here to find and stop Julius so I can save my cousin. But, if you know anything about my mom, then it can wait. Please tell me!" Ben felt his hands begin to tremble and beads of sweat drip down his forehead.

Mandi laughed. "He thinks the Vault doesn't matter. How wrong he is."

"Well..." Darius said softly. "Does it? What's so special about it?"

Alejandra spoke next. "I'm shocked, Darius. I thought you, of all people, would understand. Your goal to stop Julius is the same as

Ben's desire to save his cousin. The Vault is what connects them. It is the foundation for which the Guild exists."

"I thought the Guild existed as a rebellion against Julius," Darius replied.

"Were you not listening, boy?" asked Risa. "I told you all that the Miners Guild was around long before Julius was a threat. We seek to preserve the integrity of the Vaults and to restore the planet to what it once was. Julius is merely our first true obstacle."

"Planet?" Arynn asked. "You mean my father's theory about the world being a separate celestial entity, just like the stars and sun, is true?"

"Of course, it is," Alejandra said. "Would it surprise you to learn that it's round and not flat as well?"

"Hold on!" Ben hollered. "I want to know about my mother!"

Risa sighed and shrank slightly in her chair. "Sadly, I do not know much about her. I only met her a handful of times when she came with your father to visit me. Jean was the most beautiful woman I'd ever met. Flawless skin, green eyes, blonde hair, a kind smile. Strong woman—both in character and physically. I don't think I'd ever seen a person with such exceptional muscle tone as her. Honestly, she seemed otherworldly to me. She might as well have been an angel."

A memory flashed within Ben's mind. He recalled the story of the drunken man in Parvidom speaking about an ancestor with 'flib' eyes. Yet his mom's eyes were green...just like Rose. The image in his mind's eye switched to the sight of Rose, who he had always pictured in his mother's stead. It wasn't completely off the mark after all.

"But I must continue with the story," Risa calmly stated. "These interruptions are getting far too out of hand, and it is quite late. I'm sure we could all do with some sleep soon."

Everyone except for Ben nodded in agreement. He had only just woken up after his injuries in Ignistad. And with news about *both* of his parents, he was more awake than ever.

"As I was trying to say, your father and his companions came to me in my old home to tell me about their discovery. I could not go with them, as I was much too old for an adventure at that time. Sometime after that, all but Alphonse and Jean returned to me. They said the mission hadn't necessarily been a failure, but it wasn't a success either. They found the Vault, but couldn't get in. The three were anxious to get home to their families and didn't want to waste more time in the cruel northern air. I suspect they had some sort of falling out with Alphonse and Jean but didn't wish to discuss it with me. I was, after all, Alphonse's friend before theirs.

"Some more time passed, and Alphonse returned with you, only a few months old at the time. He admitted that the North was no place to raise a child. He planned to return to Freztad to raise you," Risa said, turning toward Ben. "But I learned shortly thereafter that that was not the case. Your father returned to me, a changed man. He carried the weight of great sorrow on his shoulders. I could tell that leaving you behind weighed heavily on him. More than that, I think, he missed his wife. He refused to tell me anything about what happened to Jean. Instead, he focused on traveling toward the Vault one last time. He said he knew how to open it and what was in it. But he would not disclose these details to me. He said a great threat was coming, and he needed to be at the Vault when it did."

Risa straightened herself in her chair and slowly stood up. "Alphonse summoned his old companions as well as others he had met along the way. We founded Jordysc, here within the mountains. He told us we would be known as the Miners Guild, the mandala our symbol. He explained that the mandala was a representation of existence and the universe. It was our duty to protect the integrity of existence as we knew it. We were to prepare for anything that would threaten that existence.

"He claimed that he would need to return to the Vault as the only one who knew of its secrets. Alphonse trusted us, as we were all like-minded individuals, but he dared not share everything for fear of untrustworthy ears hiding among us. He told us that a man named Julius would likely be our first great threat, but that something far worse was sure to follow if Julius or someone like him found the Vault. He claimed that the man had already amassed a following far greater than our own and that we had no hopes of stopping him. It was more important for us to hide in the shadows and slowly grow in numbers than allow the cause to be lost.

"We all trusted Alphonse. He'd been a man of great vision and his presence left a mark on all the hearts he'd touched. Everyone in the early Miners Guild had been impacted by Alphonse in some way, and so we trusted that the threat he promised was real. After teaching us the secrets of radio, typewriters, and other forms of Old Days technology, he believed we were ready. Members spread out to their homes to communicate and recruit in secrecy while we waited for the promised threat to come to fruition. Jordysc was to be our hideout and only used for emergencies. Well, shortly after Alphonse left, emergencies ran rampant.

"Julius, under his guise as King Xander, and his army invaded the land and quickly established the Ænærian kingdom. My town was sold out by a traitor—a man who betrayed his own family for Julius's cause. We only barely made it out alive before the town was reduced to nothing but ash. I spread word to other Miners that Jordysc would be our base of operations and that, now more than ever, we would need to stick together, for Alphonse's promise had come true."

Risa sat back down at her chair. She dropped her cane as she sat, having apparently overexerted herself.

Everyone in the room remained silent for the next few minutes. Ben figured his friends were digesting everything they had learned just as he was. Ben sat at the table, twiddling his thumbs, unsure of what to take away from everything. He had learned so much tonight that he didn't know how to organize it all in his head.

His father was a much more profound person than he had given him credit. His mother had a name. His father organized an entire underground syndicate to combat Julius's threat before it truly existed. His mother had a name. Yet Julius was not the only threat that scared his father—there was something else. His mother had a name. Something that Julius's rise to power would eventually instigate. His mother had a name. But Julius *did* rise to power...so was the Vault the final piece of the puzzle that would trigger whatever it was that his father was so terrified of? His mother had a name....

The room remained silent, only to be occasionally broken by the footsteps and voices of Miners outside. Ben even thought he had heard a distant bark in the background. Did Jordysc have wolves or dogs? Maybe it was a sound over the radio or something on a Motion Block. None of the Guild's technology would surprise him at this point. He thought of Sierra, wondering if she was still waiting patiently for him outside with the horses. He would need to go out soon and let her know that he was okay.

Finally, Darius was the one who broke the silence. "If Julius isn't the real problem here, then who is?"

Risa opened her mouth to answer, but Alejandra beckoned for her to stop. The daughter spoke instead. "Sadly, we don't know. These last fifteen years, we've been so focused on fighting Julius that we haven't been able to figure out what our founder meant. But we never doubted him. He was right about Julius and about the existence of the Vaults. The way I see it, he assumed we'd be worse off knowing— that it would distract us from Julius's threat. And if Julius ever became powerful enough to trigger this other issue, then we'd be too far past saving."

Darius sank deeper in his chair, not liking the answer. The Ænærian looked scared and unconfident. Ben imagined he was disheartened to learn that things could get exponentially worse if Julius succeeded. Darius's usual scowl was replaced by a quivering lip. He was afraid.

Noticing this as well, Trinity put her hand on top of Darius's. He did not reject it, but instead placed his other hand on top of Trinity's and offered a half smile.

Without thought, Ben mimicked the two Ænærians and felt for Arynn's hand next to him. He held it and squeezed tightly. It squeezed back.

Despite the ominous story they had all just heard, the group sat content with the silence. Ben enjoyed the feeling of Arynn's hand in his own, recognizing it as the one that grasped his as he drifted in and out of consciousness on the way to Jordysc. He was once again reminded of the novel comfort of companionship. Whatever burdens may lie ahead, Ben was happy to have these people with him.

But the happy confidence exited Ben's mind as quickly as it had come. The door to the room barged open and a sweaty and exasperated Miner barged in. "They're here!" he yelled. "I don't know how many or when they'll reach the hall, but they will! Fenwin and Randolph are here, and they've brought a horde of Rhion with them!"

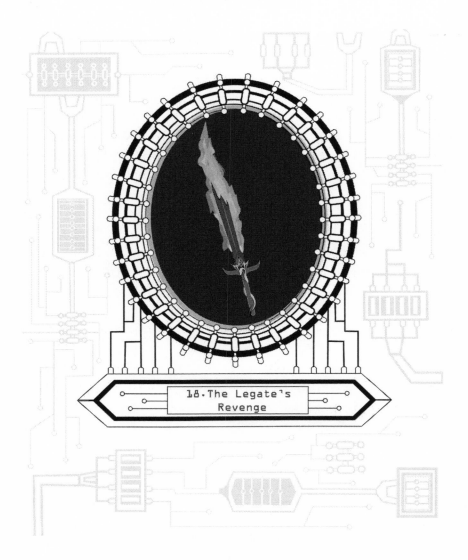

18·The Legate's Revenge

Ear-piercing horns filled the underground chamber as Miners shuffled across the corridors amid the absolute pandemonium. Barriers were erected throughout the halls, and Guild members hovered over them with their respective weapons. Mandi stayed behind in the war room with her grandmother while Alejandra rushed off with the bearer of the grim news. Ben and his friends followed close behind, weapons at the ready.

Drawing his sword, he offered Arynn Rakshi's bow while Darius held Fenwin's sun sword and Trinity held a small dagger that she had kept concealed until now.

The sparring partners from earlier now wielded real swords and trailed behind the growing posse that followed Alejandra. They found themselves in an armory behind the gymnasium where the Miners each had free pickings of pistols and rifles. Alejandra offered one of each to Ben and his friends and asked them if they knew how to use them.

Ben and Darius nodded while the two women shook their heads in minor disappointment.

"Pull this back, aim with these, and squeeze the trigger. Make each shot count," Alejandra quickly explained while holding up a pistol. "Go with Heath," she pointed to the Miner they had followed from the war room. "He'll assign you to your positions."

Trinity raised a hand in protest. "I'm not much of a fighter. Do you have a place for medics?"

Alejandra nodded. "My husband, Heath, will get you situated. Good luck to you all. I hope to see you all again after." She marched off in a hurry.

Darius stepped toward Heath, who was busy giving orders to another group of Miners. "Where do you need us?"

Heath finished his orders and turned to face the three. Sweat poured down his brow, and his sky-blue eyes appeared full of apprehension. "Come on, follow me. I'm taking you to Eliana to get you out of here."

"What?" the four asked in unison.

"Alejandra believes you're our best shot at stopping Julius if we fail here. You already know where the Grand Vault is, and you've proven yourselves more than resourceful in the field—something we're seriously lacking."

Darius shook his head. "No! I came here to help the cause and put an end to Julius's reign!"

Heath rolled his eyes. "And you can do that by going with Eliana and getting out of here."

This time, Arynn spoke up. "I agree with Darius. I say we stay. We have plenty of field experience." She pointed at each of them saying, "Medic, ex-Rhion, swordsman, and I'm a decent shot."

Trinity nodded. "I wouldn't feel right leaving people behind knowing there are lives I could be saving."

They turned to Ben. "What?" he asked, puzzled by having so many faces on him at once.

"Well, you're like our leader," Arynn said. "The decision is pretty much up to you."

Ben was shocked. Leader? He never thought of himself as their 'leader'. He just had a goal in mind, and people seemed to want to follow him along and help. *Is that what a leader is?*

"Look, guys," Heath said firmly. He buried his face in his hands then said, "I don't have time to argue. I've got people to prepare and strategies to organize. I'd love your help—but my wife wants you guys out of here and safe. She's the boss, so we do what she says."

Darius scoffed. "Sounds a lot like the way Julius runs things."

Heath raised an eyebrow. "Fine. Stay if you want. But don't get mad at me when you get killed and you fail your mission. Besides," he said scratching his head, "we could use an ex-Rhion to help keep people in check when all hell breaks loose."

For a split second, Ben thought he saw Darius's scowl shift to a slight grin.

"If the rest of you really want to help," Heath continued, "then I could really use your help on the frontlines by the entrance. The traps out in the tunnels will only take care of so many of them before they work their way here. Then it'll only be a matter of minutes before they breach the doors. I'd like you ready with me when they do."

The four turned to look at Ben once again. He felt his stomach churn as his heart raced with anticipation, telling him to get out of there and save himself to find Rose. But another part of him agreed with his friends. They were right: he couldn't leave when he had the chance to help here.

Ben nodded slowly. "Let's do this."

"Right then," Heath said. "I'll show you to your positions."

The four companions were split up. Trinity was held with the third division, closer to the central hub with a few of the other medics and heavier artillery. It was the most well-defended spot in Jordysc and had enough cover fire for people like Trinity to quickly patch up wounds. Darius was brought alongside Heath to help command the Miners' forces during the assault. Ben had hoped he would have at least been by Arynn's side as to ensure her protection, but they were separated as well. She was to go with the other archers to hide in the rafters to provide support for the warriors on the front lines. Before they had parted ways, Arynn pulled Ben aside.

"Look," she said, twirling her hair and unable to make eye contact with Ben. "If we make it out of this...well, I think we should talk. There's no point in saying what I have to say now. It'll only distract us both."

"What if we don't..." he didn't want to think about it, but he had seen so much violence that he knew it was possible that they would never see each other again.

Arynn stepped toward Ben but was quickly swept away by the Miners' in her squadron. "Stay alive, Limmetrad," she shouted over the voices in the crowded corridor. Ben felt alone as Miners rushed around him in all directions. He kept replaying their conversation over and over again. He wondered if he had missed the opportunity to kiss her. He didn't know if he would ever find out.

Ben was moved by a battalion of fighters to the entrance of the tunnels where he and his friends had gained entry to Jordysc. To his surprise, he saw his faithful wolf-companion waiting there for him. She barked in approval at his presence. He patted her on the head and smiled. "How'd you get in here?"

A sheepish Miner next to him turned and said, "It's thanks to that beast there that we got a heads up in the first place. Found its way through the tunnels to our secret door with a Rhion helm in its mouth. We knew it was yours since we've had reports of you traveling with a wolf, so we figured it'd be safe to let it in. After that, we sent out a few scouts, and they quickly relayed everything back to us. Entire legion and a half out there looking for us."

A loud explosion boomed, and the detonation shook some rocks from the ceiling. Ben and the Miners around him were covered in a fine coat of dust and rubble.

"I give 'em ten minutes at least 'til they get here," the Miner said.

Another explosion sounded, this time much closer.

"Better make that five," another Miner said.

Shouts and footsteps reverberated from outside the corridor. An untold number of Ænærians were closing in fast. The Miners made last-minute preparations. More barricades were placed against the door and hurdles put into position. Men and women leaned behind them with guns and bows aimed at the door. Ben didn't see Darius and Trinity, but he did spot Arynn with the other shooters. He made eye contact with her and mouthed *it'll be okay*. She nodded hesitantly before shifting her attention back to the door.

"All right, everybody!" Heath's voice resonated off the walls. He stood in front of everyone with his helmet now covering his light-brown hair. "We've run this simulation dozens of times. You know what day it is. Today's finally the day it happens. Today's the day our enemies learn about us. They'll know there are people out there who are willing to stand up to them. People who are ready to lay down their lives for the cause of a better tomorrow. Not all of us will see that tomorrow. We won't all see a future where our children grow old and free. A future where tyrants like Julius are nothing but a distant nightmare—a nightmare of what happens when you don't treat your fellow human beings with the respect and dignity they deserve. And though we won't all be able to see that future—that better tomorrow—we will know in our hearts that we did our very best to lay the foundation for it. Say your prayers to whatever gods you believe in. If anyone is listening, it may be the last time they hear you."

Heath paused for a moment to collect himself. He took a swig out of a water skin and exhaled deeply. He muttered something to himself, brought his fist to his mouth, and kissed it. Many others around him did the same.

"Right then," he said. "Let's kick some Ænærian asses, shall we?"

Everyone in the room cheered and shook their fists in the air. Then the slaughter started.

Ben couldn't be sure what happened first as it all went so fast. The door exploded and pieces of the ceiling collapsed, burying anyone in the vicinity. A horde of Rhion poured in like water through a burst pipe, flowing uncontrollably. Flashes of orange and yellow lights flew across the hall while *booms* and *zaps* bounced off the walls. The smell of burning flesh crept into Ben's nostrils, the horrendous scent amplified by the close quarters. Ben felt as though he would be sick from the smell alone, let alone the gruesome sights before him.

Screams and shrieks were muffled by the gunshots coming from the row of Miners behind barriers and atop scaffoldings. Sungs flared every which way in retaliation. Ben noticed that these sungs were much like Gatron's; they shot once and had an idle recharge period. He reasoned with himself that they would probably switch to pistols or blades when they got closer.

"Snipers! Hold positions and reload!" Heath yelled over the chaos. As soon as he shouted the orders, the gunfire ceased and the only sounds remaining were moans and the occasional stray *zap*. "Frontlines—guns out and fire at will!"

"Retaliate!" a familiar raspy voice screamed from behind the remaining rubble that used to be the doorway. Fenwin passed through the threshold, stepping on Miners' bodies with a sinister smile below his pointed helm. "Try to keep the four fugitives alive! Our King wants a word with them. Everyone else is fair game!"

Bullets flew across the room like a storm of wasps. Ben pulled out his pistol and fired, aiming only for the legs. He still didn't want to kill anybody, and he would have preferred to use his sword, but none of the Rhion were close enough. *If only it were charged,* he thought to himself.

Most of the guns stopped firing, and Rhion hid behind Guild barriers as Ben and the Miners inched backwards. People took the chance to reload and reevaluate their situation. Ben did the same, crouched behind a hurdle with his fingers tingling as he put another magazine into his pistol.

Heath yelled another order to the ranged weapons personnel. Arrow and bullets whistled through the now dusty and debris-ridden air.

"Back more and reload! Positions Beta and Epsilon! Get a move on, people!" Heath commanded. The snipers ran back across the scaffolding as the Miners behind Ben followed. He wasn't sure why half the Miners on the ground were retreating while everyone around him stood still.

Confused, Ben looked to the Miner on his left. "What's going on? Why're they running away?"

"Position Epsilon. They go back to prepare the big surprise while we hold off the hostiles until our people are ready," she said, wincing as a bullet grazed the hurdle she was leaning against.

Ben nodded. What could the big surprise be? It must be some sort of weapon. He asked one more question, "Do we just sit here like deer to a pack of wolves?"

The Miner shrugged and then turned around to return fire.

Wolves, Ben thought to himself. *Duh*. He looked next to Sierra who was calmly waiting for orders. "D'you think you can take a few of them out between the next wave? Buy us some more time? I know how scared of you they are."

Sierra barked in affirmation but didn't wait for the next wave. The enormous wolf hopped the hurdle and landed on an approaching Rhion. Ben screamed in protest as he saw six other Rhion poke their weapons above the barriers and open fire on the wolf.

"No! Sierra, get out of there!" he shouted. His vision shifted to the red he had seen back in the arena.

Gunfire exploded from their respective pistols, and bullets erupted out like soaring hunter flies in for the kill. The copper-tinged beads of death moved toward Sierra faster than Ben could blink. He so desperately wanted to chase after her and push her out of the way. The shots found their mark before he could even flinch from the ear-wrenching sounds. Ben closed his eyes, too afraid to look.

He opened his eyes and dropped his jaw. There Sierra stood, unscathed by the six or more bullets that hit her. How could that be? There was no blood coming from her coat, and the bullets all lay flattened against the floor as though they had hit a wall. The Rhion exchanged looks, apparently as unsure about what had happened as Ben. They fired again, this time unloading their magazines. This time, Ben watched.

The bullets definitely hit Sierra, but they bounced off her as though her fur was armor. The white wolf growled at the Rhion who fired at her and lunged at the closest one. The man screamed in pain. Others joined the fray and pulled their triggers on her, thinking a third time would have a different outcome. And it did—just not one they would have hoped for.

Some of the shots hit the enraged wolf and fell to the floor. Others seemed to actually bounce off Sierra and hit another Rhion nearby.

"Idiots!" Fenwin growled. "Don't keep trying the same thing over again and expecting anything better to come of it! Fire your damn sungs!"

As though she heard them, Sierra jumped from her most recent victim and retreated toward Ben. As she ran, orange and yellow bursts of light flared throughout the room. Most of them landed against the stone barrier that Ben hid behind. He expected it to melt away like it did to the metal door at the prison had, and so he inched away from it. No such thing happened.

A stray sung blast did, however, melt part of the scaffolding above him. The metal walkway creaked and snapped, falling from overhead. It landed between the opposing forces and provided a much-needed barrier between them. Ben narrowly escaped, but many others weren't so lucky: A handful of fighters on both sides were trapped underneath crying for help.

Without thinking, Ben ran toward the closest trapped Miner and pulled him out while another held up the metal bars. A few Guild members followed suit while most of the others ran to different corridors. They quickly pulled out all of their people while the Ænærians tried to climb over the wreckage. Ben hurried with the last trapped Miner and saw that she had a metal pole sticking through her leg. It was bleeding profusely, and she screamed as soon as Ben dragged her out.

What was Ben to do with her? He couldn't leave her there for the Ænærians to kill, but she wasn't exactly in any shape to walk. Carrying her would only slow himself down and make them easier targets. But Sierra could carry her out of the crossfire.

Ben lifted the injured woman and gently placed her on the wolf's back. As soon as the Miner was on and holding tight, Sierra scampered off deeper into the mountain without Ben having to give any directions. And it wasn't a moment too soon, either; the Rhion cleared the way through most of the sheets and bars of metal and were taking aim yet again.

As the Ænærians prepared to fire, Fenwin shoved them out of his way and hollered at them while pointing at Ben. "No, no, no! Imbeciles! The King needs that one *alive!* We can't very well do that with you all riddling his scrawny hide with holes, now can I?"

A few Rhion exchanged glances and shrugged. One was bold enough to question Fenwin. "Sorry, sir. What do you want us to do with him?"

It was Longinus. His face was sallow and cheeks bony, so much skinnier than when Ben had seen him in Ignistad. Over his right arm was a tri-pronged metal prosthetic hand. He looked at Ben and glowered.

Fenwin turned to the Rhion. "Capture him. Alive, Longinus. I don't want him escaping and letting your uncle have all the glory."

Longinus nodded and beckoned for more Rhion to go after Ben. Other groups diverged to the left and right corridors. Fenwin followed and barked orders to the men behind him before regrouping with Longinus. Ben took that as his cue to run.

As he darted down the hallway, hopping over hurdles and bodies, Ben shot his pistol blindly behind him. His gun clicked as it ran out of bullets. "Useless," he said, tossing it backwards. He drew his sword and worked his way to the central hallway, hoping to regroup with other Guild members. In all the commotion, he hadn't realized that they all had run off without him when he was helping the wounded woman escape on Sierra. He just hoped that the 'surprise' Heath mentioned was ready for Fenwin and his Rhion.

When he had first arrived with his friends, Ben didn't exactly pay much attention to his surroundings while following Risa. What he thought was a straight shot toward the big room with the radios and gymnasium was more like finding the center of a maze. He had been so caught up with amazement and wonder while walking behind Risa that he had neglected to memorize where the hub was located. He found himself at the end of the corridor with the legate and his men closing in. He could go left or right. Ben had no idea which direction would bring him closer to the command hub. Now that he thought of it, he wasn't even sure anyone would be there.

Well, where else would they go? Ben asked himself. He turned right and hoped for the best. It was the wrong move.

Running down the hallway, he nearly ran into two Rhion. They quickly raised their guns and took aim.

"Alive!" he heard Fenwin shout from behind. The Rhion lowered their guns toward Ben's legs.

Ben's vision tinted red once more and, without thinking, he jumped into the air and slashed his sword through the air. It struck one of the Rhion with such force that he fell back into the man next to him. Ben darted past the debilitated Rhion and turned to the next corridor. A raspy voice cursed behind him just before gunshots echoed throughout the halls. Ben winced as though he had been shot. When he realized that he was unscathed, Ben counted the shots over again in his head. *Two.* Fenwin had killed his men for failing.

Ben turned another corner and bumped into Darius. His scowl was quite a sight for sore eyes.

"Fenwin. Behind me. Run!" Ben yelled.

Darius nodded and gestured for Ben to follow his lead. He was carrying a sung around his shoulder and an automatic rifle in his hands. Fenwin's old blade was still strapped at his hip. His shoulder was bleeding, and there was a cut across his left cheek, but otherwise Darius looked fine.

"Have you been shot?" Ben asked, running closely behind his Ænærian friend.

"Arrow. I'll be fine," he said, nearly out of breath.

"Arrow? Why aren't they using guns?" Ben asked.

"I think they're running out of ammo after dealing with Position Epsilon."

"So, did the plan work?"

Darius shook his head. "No. The Guild overlooked the amount of heat Randolph and Fenwin's sungs produce. The autocannon overheated and shut down almost immediately. It's over. We've lost Jordysc."

Ben didn't know what an autocannon was, but he understood that the Guild had put a lot of faith in the weapon. They had hoped it would stop the assault. Was there no back up plan? Ben felt sick at the thought that his last hope of stopping Julius and finding Rose had been a failure.

They turned another corner on their left, quickly hid in a room, and closed the door. The room was about twice the size of Ben's bedroom at home. For the most part, it was filled with wooden crates stacked atop one another. From outside the room, Ben could still hear muffled gunfire, though it was significantly less than when the Ænærians had initially bombarded into the hideout. Darius waited next to the side of the door, staring at the opening with his finger resting comfortably on the trigger.

"What are you doing?" Ben asked.

Darius put a finger to his mouth. "*Shh*," he whispered. "I'm watching for shadows. They'll probably keep running down the hall. When they all pass, I want you to open the door as fast as you can."

Ben looked at Darius, slightly confused.

"*Got it?*" Darius hissed.

Ben nodded. He watched attentively beneath the door. Sure enough, shadows flew by paired with footsteps nearly drowned out by the chaos outside. When the shadows ceased, Ben flung the door open. Darius pointed his rifle and opened fire at the backs of the unaware Rhion who had just passed them by.

Suddenly, something swung down and cut cleanly through the barrel of Darius's rifle. Darius dropped the gun and scrambled for the sung strapped around his shoulder. It was too late.

Fenwin twirled himself around the corner and slashed his sword across Darius's chest. Fenwin kicked with such force that Darius collapsed and slid across the floor. Darius reached for his sung, but it was no longer there. Fenwin had cut right across the strap, and the sung now lay next to the door. The legate kicked it aside and approached Darius.

"You know," Fenwin said, "the King doesn't actually need you alive. No, I just wanted you for myself. I just told that little fib to the grunts to put the fear of the Sun into them in case they thought twice about obeying orders."

The legate slowly approached Darius, apparently unaware of Ben behind the door. Ben questioned when the most opportune time to strike would be. A fiery rage burned through Ben's veins, and his vision flickered to the blood red that it had when he had nearly died in the arena of Ignistad. Why did his eyes keep doing this to him? He didn't like it, and it scared him. He associated it with the gladiator match and was reminded of how he had lost control of himself. Ben was frozen with fear—not because of the legate approaching his friend, but of himself.

"You won't tell them I lied, will you?" Fenwin asked, now standing over Darius. "Of course, you won't. You won't be doing much of anything soon."

Darius eyed the sword above him, his lips quivering.

"Oh, that reminds me. I'll be taking my sword back now. I've grown quite accustomed to its fire, and regular steel simply doesn't do it for me anymore."

Darius remained silent. With the blade to Darius's neck, Fenwin took the sun-sword from him and tossed the steel one aside.

Fenwin leaned down closer to Darius and grabbed him by the face, clenching tight. He spat in Darius's face and snarled.

"Not only are you a deserter, but a defector—a traitor! And for what? The Sun's Holy Ænærian Army raised you, fed you! Put a roof over your head and taught you how to be one of the fiercest fighters in all the land! You climbed the ranks quickly, showing your vast potential. You were graced with the King's presence on numerous occasions. He even looked the other way when you defiled the Holy City by carrying on with that girl from the slums. None of that was enough for you, was it? Is it because of that mishap with Gatron?" Fenwin spit to the side and snarled. "I won't say I condone it, but a legate has his needs. And it was your duty to obey without question. But what did you do instead? Working for the enemy. Murdering your brothers. Slaughtering a legate! Then, you had the audacity to escape from my grasp as though you could truly get away with it all."

Fenwin spat again and landed a punch square in Darius's face.

Ben winced as he watched his friend being beaten. He knew he should do something to stop him, to protect Darius. He told his body to do something, but each time he moved an inch his vision grew redder and redder. What if he lost control like he did in Ignistad? What would stop him from harming Darius?

A woman's scream rang from the distance.

"*Mmm.* I wonder if that's your girlfriend. Just because I said I wanted her alive doesn't mean I need her in one piece," Fenwin said, grinning sinisterly. He rose from Darius and let out a satisfied sigh. "You know, that gives me an idea. Maybe I should hold off on killing you and have you watch while I gut that filth. How's that sound?"

Darius gave Fenwin an angry stare but remained silent.

The scream rang once more. This time it sounded closer. Ben recognized it. It wasn't Trinity screaming. It was Arynn. Ben clenched his fists and roared, his vision consumed with redness.

Fenwin shook with a fright. "What was that? Come out of there, and maybe I'll finish you off quickly." He approached the door.

Darius grabbed the steel sword on the floor and jumped to his feet. He slashed at Fenwin's legs but was too slow. The legate turned and parried the attack, his weapon cleaving Darius's in two.

Ben snapped out of his paralysis. The red flickers vanished, and his vision was clear as he drew his sword. The legate leaned away from Ben and kicked him back. He planted himself on the floor and swung another strike against Darius.

Ben regained his balance and rushed toward Fenwin.

As it had in the prison by Parvidom, the blade of Ben's sword glowed bright and green, as though the sword were emitting a cloud of mist that followed it with each thrust and swing. Fenwin made a wide slash, past the jagged edge of Ben's sword. Instead of swinging through the green light, Fenwin's sword was caught as if the aura was as solid as steel. Sparks of green and orange dripped like tears as the blades touched until the light from Fenwin's sun-sword shrank to a mere glimmer.

"It's as I had suspected," Fenwin huffed, breathing heavily while beads of sweat poured down his face. "You do indeed have the legendary Voidsweeper." He slashed at Ben's feet.

Ben jumped out of the way and nearly toppled onto Darius.

When Ben had first listened to the Voidsweeper's original owner boasting about the weapon, he was highly skeptical as he was with most matters of legend and mysticism. However, his previous skirmishes with the legate and the prison guards seemed to give those outrageous statements some credibility. He could not truly understand it: a blade that acted as a sword and a sung.

As if reading his mind, Fenwin went on boasting. "Tell me, boy, do you know how to wield it? No, I think not. For you are unworthy of such a device. I have trained for years in the art of sun-swords—their technology based off the very weapon you hold in your hands. Your technique and ignorance disgust me! It shall be a fitting prize for a true swordsman when I take it off your novice hands!"

Fenwin made a horizontal swing intended for Darius, but he dodged at the last second. Instead, the sword's tip slid across the wooden crates and lit them aflame like pieces of flint and steel struck over tinder.

Darius rolled away from the fire as Ben struck at Fenwin once more. The legate turned to face Ben directly as he blocked the blow. The legate's sword flashed, its light fading.

Fenwin did a backflip away from Ben, toward the door. As he spun in the air, his sword pulled against the cross guard on Ben's and flung it out of his hands. When he landed, Fenwin picked up the sung from the ground and aimed it at Darius with one hand while pointing his sword at Ben.

"Drop it, traitor," he growled at Darius.

After a moment's hesitation, Darius let the sword hit the floor.

"Good. Now kick it back to me."

Darius kicked the sword, allowing it to slide across the floor toward Fenwin. The legate crouched down, keeping his eyes on Ben and Darius, his sung raised. He picked up Ben's sword with his left hand, which now held both swords. Fenwin dropped his own sword and sung and gripped the Voidsweeper with both hands. He squeezed his hands around it, and a green aura erupted from the blade.

"How fitting that I should finally wield the Voidsweeper and use it to strike down this infernal insurgency." Fenwin said, a wicked expression on his face.

Fenwin walked closer to Ben and Darius, pushing them closer toward the roaring fire now growing behind them.

"Besides," he continued. "A kill with a blade is so much more personal than with any type of ranged weapon. Much more...delicious." He licked his lips in savory delight.

Smoke filled the room. Darius and Fenwin coughed violently, heaving and gasping for air. Ben's vision flickered red again.

"Well," Fenwin said after a few coughs. "I suppose I'll have to take young Limmetrad here with me. But I have no further use of you, traitor." The legate laid the glowing tip of the Voidsweeper next to Darius's neck.

Ben could smell the burning flesh.

Fenwin readied himself for the execution. Darius did not struggle. He did not close his eyes and continued to stare intently at Fenwin. His lips moved swiftly as if muttering his last words.

Just as Fenwin pulled the sword back, Ben's vision stopped flickering. It went to full red. He punched the vengeful legate faster than the beads of sweat from his brow could land on the floor.

Fenwin's body flew across the room and landed in another pile of burning crates. He moaned in pain as he lay there, seemingly unable to move his body. Then, as the fire spread to his armor, he jumped from the ground and screamed.

Darius looked at Ben and yelled, "Come on! Let's get out of here! This whole room is burning up!"

Ben stood motionless as though he hadn't heard his friend.

"Ben? Come on, you idiot, let's go!"

Ben turned toward Darius, who yelped upon seeing Ben's face.

"Blazes, it's happening again." Darius coughed. "No time for this, let's go!" he yelled, running toward the exit.

Everything was still red, but it was starting to fade. Ben heard yelling from two different people. He struggled to make out what they were saying, if anything. He faced Darius, and the red vanished.

Ben collapsed on the floor.

"Blazes!" Darius cursed. "What is with you? All right, fine!" he coughed, then turned back and put Ben's arm around his shoulders. "You've gotta do the walking for me though, okay?"

Ben nodded then slowly muttered, "Sword...."

"Got it right here," Darius said, nudging his head toward the floor ahead of him. The sword lay on the ground, and Darius kicked it as he walked, sliding it closer to the exit.

The two hobbled out of the burning room just as the legate got back to his feet, slowly moving toward his own sun-sword, coughing with each inch. Darius turned toward Fenwin and stepped on his fingers as he leaned over to retrieve the sword. The legate howled and cursed. Darius charged out of the room and slammed the door shut.

"Enjoy the heat, asshole!" Darius yelled through the door. He found the barrel of his rifle that Fenwin had cut off and placed it through the door handle, locking the legate in the fire.

Darius helped Ben to his feet, and the two walked toward the next hallway. About halfway there, Ben was able to walk without Darius's help. Darius squeezed Fenwin's sun-sword and found that it still had a bit of energy left. When they made it to the next hallway they found that they were surrounded on both sides.

"My, my! You put on a nice little show for me the other night, ol' Benny boy!" Randy said from the pair's left. "You didn't really think you'd make it to Ignistad without running into me, now did you?"

Ben ignored him and instead focused on the sight to his right. Arynn and Trinity were both bound and gagged with sungs pointed at their heads. At their feet lay Heath's motionless body and a slow-breathing Alejandra.

"Let them go!" Ben commanded.

"Now, Ben, you know I can't do that," Randy replied. He turned to his nephew. "Didn't Legate Fenwin say he had orders for those two gals over there to be alive?"

"That's right, sir," Longinus answered.

"And do we know where the legate is?"

"No, sir."

"Pity. Well, I think we'll hold onto them for now. We'll place them with the old woman and the girl with the burned face. Send the defector there, too. I want a private room for Benny boy, here."

Rhion closed in on Ben and Darius. Ben raised his sword, ready to fight, but Darius let his drop to the floor.

"We can't win, Ben. At least they're taking us alive. Just give up, man. It's over," Darius said. His voice was somber, defeated.

Ben couldn't believe what he was hearing. They had just escaped death moments ago by some freak act of luck. He tried to summon the power of his sword, to make it glow the fierce green hue that had saved him before. But each time he touched the sword he felt his energy being sapped. Where was the strength against Fenwin? Against the Rhion in Ignistad? Any second now, the red flashes would reinvigorate him, and he would be able to take on all the Ænærians by himself. Surely, Darius also knew that, so why was he surrendering?

"We can take them. You saw what I did with Fenwin—"

"I don't know what I saw. But you've never seen Randolph and his men fight. Trust me, we can't win."

Ben shook his head in disbelief. *Come on! Any second now and the red vision will be back!*

The red flickers did not return. But Ben refused to give up. He had come so far and been through so much. It couldn't end here. Not with such a bitter defeat!

A Rhion approached Ben with a spear, but Ben chopped it in two. As he did so, two more apprehended Darius from behind him. Ben tried to swing at them too, but they dragged Darius away too quickly. Now Ben was surrounded on all sides.

"Benny boy, don't make us take you in by force," Randy called.

Ben felt the sweat dripping down the sides of his face. He didn't know what to do.

When Ben didn't move, Randy let out a disappointed sigh and turned to Longinus and said, "Nephew, you know what to do."

Longinus nodded and aimed a small crossbow with his real hand.

Ben noticed his vision change. But it wasn't the normal flicker between red and clear. Instead, there was only darkness.

19. The Man From
Freztad

B en was losing track of how many times he had awoken in
some unknown place with a gap in his memory. At least this
time he knew that he was alive. The pain in his right eye was
a cruel and constant reminder of it. He tried to open it but felt something blocking it. His left opened without issue. It showed him an odd
room with metal walls and flooring. He was in a small, yet comfortable bed with fur blankets and smooth, silk sheets. Feather pillows

propped up his head and faced him toward a window. Though he couldn't see much outside from where he sat, Ben thought he could make out lots of blue. Perhaps it was the clear sky of a sunny day. If that were the case, then why did it look like rain drops were dripping from the window? He decided it was of little importance and averted his attention to examining the rest of the room as he tried to figure out where he was.

What happened in Jordysc? Ben rattled his mind trying to recall the events that had led to the present. The last thing he could remember was being surrounded by Rhion. Darius was with him. He remembered that, too. And Arynn and Trinity were taken captive. Heath appeared to be dead and Alejandra severely injured.

Of course, Ben thought. *We lost the battle. Something happened after Darius and I fought Fenwin.* Ben thought to his brawl with the legate. He thought about the sudden burst of strength that came with the onset of the red flickers. He thought he had lost control of himself, but as Darius pleaded with him to leave the burning room, he snapped out of it. Then it was as though all the energy in his body had been drained, like the final, fading ember in a dwindling fire.

Now Ben could remember just about everything. Randy had been there. He had taken Ben's friends and the other Miners captive. But what caused his eye to hurt so much? Why was there a bandage covering it and preventing him from seeing?

"You're awake!" a familiar and soothing voice called from a corner to Ben's right. He could not see that anyone had been there, but the voice was unmistakable.

"Rose..." he said weakly. "Where are we? Are you hurt?" Ben sat up fully and turned to his cousin.

Rose sat on a small chair next to the room's door. She looked almost exactly the same as when Ben had last seen her. Her brown hair was tied back, and her cheeks dimpled as she smiled. Her emerald green eyes seemed to shine as the brightest things in the room. As far as Ben could tell, Rose was completely unharmed. In fact, she looked healthier than Ben had ever seen. Her face was fuller, and her arms showed less bone and more meat. The only thing about her that concerned Ben were her red teary eyes, look of concern, and a tabard with the mark of Ænæria on it.

She got to her feet and approached Ben. "Am I hurt? Are you kidding me?" She broke out into fresh tears. "Broken nose, bruised ribs, whatever that horrid gash on your side is, and that's not the worst of it...."

Rose looked at Ben's bandage and then quickly looked into his one open eye. Ben furrowed his brow in response. "What? Did something happen to my eye? Help me take off this bandage and get me a looking glass if you can. I want to see the damage. Make sure I'm still pretty and everything, you know?"

Rose chuckled and wiped her tears. She smiled for a moment, but it quickly faded. "Ben..." she muttered. "I...I don't think you should look. It's bad."

"Well, I'm a fast healer. I just want to make sure I'm still presentable for Arynn, not that you'd understand," he snickered.

Rose rolled her eyes. "Not funny. This is serious."

"Is she here somewhere? You've got to meet her—you two would get along great!"

Rose frowned. "I'm not sure who you're talking about."

"Arynn. Red hair in a long braid, bright blue eyes, kind of annoying, but super pretty."

Rose shook her head. "I'm not sure. I haven't seen anyone like that. Then again, I don't get to see many people. She could be with the prisoners, I suppose."

"What about Neith and Yeong?" Ben said, trying to hide his disappointment. "How about Zechariah? Are they here, too? Are they even alive?"

To this, Rose smiled. "Yeah, they're alive. Zechariah is on board somewhere. I'm not sure why Julius brought him along and left the others in Ignistad. He says they're not prisoners, just 'restricted guests'. I have reason to believe they're okay, though."

Ben gave a half smile. He was glad to know that his people were safe, but his experience at the prison by Parvidom left a sour taste in his mouth upon pondering the concept. And now he was worried about Arynn, too....

"Wait, what about Sleipnir and Sierra?" Ben asked with a twinge of guilt. He told Rose about how he had found her horse along the Gjoll shortly after leaving to find her. How the horse had grown used to him and carried him all the way to Jordysc, where he left the poor animal just before the attack. He worried that the Ænærians captured and sold Sleipnir, along with the other horses. He also told Rose about how the wolf they had seen hunting had joined him on his journey and acted as a pivotal member of his team.

"I had no idea Sleipnir was with you," Rose said. "I can't believe he let you ride him, especially with that wolf around. Which I wouldn't even believe had I not heard the stories the Rhion told about it."

"Then you know what happened to Sierra?"

"No," Rose said with a frown. "The only reports that I've heard post-battle are about Legate Randolph bringing you and the other prisoners to Bacchuso and about Legate Fenwin's death."

Ben looked away. *Sleipnir and Sierra are both missing. The two companions that I took the most for granted. Simply because they weren't people.*

"Ben, I know that look," Rose said. "Don't worry. Sleipnir is a tough animal and a good breed. No one would hurt him. He's smart, too. Maybe he made his way home."

"And Sierra?"

"You told me she seemed invincible, how nothing ever seemed to hurt her? Maybe she's okay, too. I probably would've heard about someone bragging that they killed the monster wolf. Sometimes no news is good news."

"So, about this bandage," Ben said, wanting to change the subject.

Rose didn't say anything. She fidgeted with her fingers and looked every which way but Ben's direction.

"What's gotten into you?" Ben got to his feet and placed a hand on Rose's shoulder. "Have they messed with your head here or something? You're not normally this skittish about stuff."

Rose looked up at Ben. Her lips quivered as she spoke. "I am when it's serious. Your eye isn't...well the bandage isn't technically for your eye...."

Ben frowned. "What do you mean? It's burning with pain right now, so I know something is up with it."

"No, because...."

"Because what, Rose? You can tell me. I've travelled all across the land to find you, and—while I don't want our first conversation back together to be such a downer—I'd really like to know what's gotten into you."

Ben looked around the room and spotted a small wooden dresser to the right of his bed. For some odd reason, it was bolted to the floor. He turned to the bed and saw that it was bolted in a similar fashion. *Odd*, he thought to himself. Atop the dresser was a handheld looking glass. He picked it up and gazed into it. The bandage had a tremendous amount of dried blood. Ben began to unwrap it from around his head.

"Ben, please don't..." Rose cried next to him.

Ben ignored her and continued to unwrap. He placed the soiled bandages on the dresser and picked the looking glass back up. He dropped it as soon as he saw.

The glass fell to the floor and shattered. Shards slid across the room. They slowly moved toward the leftmost wall in a curious fashion. But Ben couldn't focus on that now. Instead, his hands were trembling with the shock of what he had just seen.

Rose put her hands overtop Ben's. "I didn't know how to tell you. You'd just woken up for the first time since the procedure that the tattooed girl did, and I thought that it would be best for you to get your bearings before I broke the news to you."

Ben didn't say anything. His hands continued to tremble like the earth during a quake. His chest beat with great intensity, and his breathing went rapid.

"You probably don't want to hear this, but it could've been worse. You're actually really lucky, all things considered. Had the arrow gone anywhere else, you'd have died! My father is punishing both Randolph and Longinus for their recklessness as we speak. He's already mad at him for not bringing you along in the first place—"

Ben threw his hands away from Rose's and pushed her away. "Your father? That's how you refer to him now? You've known for how long? A week? Two? Will you be calling him 'Daddy' soon and have tea while watching the sunset?"

"Ben, it's not like that. Julius and I have a complicated relationship but—"

"*Complicated?*" Ben mocked. "Do you know what I've been through to get you back home? The sacrifices I've made!"

Rose's voice trembled, "I never asked you to—"

"To what? *Lose an eye for you?* Because that's what I did!" Ben yelled, his remaining eye showing him slow flickers of faint red.

"That's not my fault!" Rose raised her voice back. "I told you I wanted you to stay at the village. You know I never would've wanted you to come after me. But you did it anyway! You left the village unprotected and my mom to fend for herself!"

"Me? I didn't abandon the village—you did! How about a 'thank you' or something? The village will be fine. They have guns and sun-carriages and most of the Sentinels have probably healed by now."

"The guns and sun-carriages were a ploy! The carriages won't work if they're not charged, and the guns were made cheaply to only work for a few magazines."

Ben reflected on Rose's words. He hadn't considered that the guns and sun-carriages wouldn't work. He remembered bringing the pistol with him, but he had never shot many rounds out of it. He never would have known that it was made poorly as he had lost it well before it would have given out. Now that he thought about it, the rifles in Freztad had jammed a lot. And Ben hadn't seen or heard that occur much with any of the other rifles he had encountered. And he had never even bothered to look at one of the sun-carriages. What was he thinking when he left?

His breaths slowed, and the flickers of red in Ben's left eye stopped. He sat down on the bed and solemnly put the bandage back over his now empty eye socket. When he was done, he looked up at Rose.

"I just wanted to bring you home and make sure you were safe...." Tears dripped down his left cheek.

Rose sat down next to him. "I know, Ben. But I'm fine. I've been well taken care of, all things considered. Julius has also made sure no one so much as lays a finger on me."

"Yeah, I met up with Scraggles," Ben said. "He didn't look too good. He apparently just looked at you wrong, *huh*?"

Rose raised an eyebrow. "Who? Oh, you mean Elmer. Yeah, Julius wasn't exactly thrilled when he made some comments my way. He's quite particular about who he lets talk to me, and he never leaves me alone with anyone but my handmaiden. Though, it was Randy who suggested he be exiled due to his outburst at Rakshi's funeral..."

"Julius isn't here then?" Ben asked. "Since we're allowed together?"

Rose shook her head. "No, he's here. This is his ship, after all. But he understands that you're my family, so he's okay with it."

Ben stood up and rushed to the window. "We're on a ship? Is that why things are bolted down? I've heard stories, but I've always wanted to see the ocean with my own...eye."

The blue outside was certainly not the sky. The sky was dark and cloudy. Far below him was the vast and seemingly infinite ocean. It was the most beautiful thing Ben had ever seen. Yet he found himself quite confused. Why did the ocean seem so far down, and what were those island-looking things down below?

"Not a ship like a boat," Rose said from behind him. "This is the Ænærian Empire's First Airship."

Ben spun around and looked at Rose, confused. "Airship? As in a flying ship? We're in the sky right now? How is that possible?"

"Julius says it's from the Sun's grace. I'm still not sure I buy that whole thing yet, but it works somehow. There's a big inflatable contraption, and fire helps lift it into the air. I don't know. You understand that stuff better than I ever have."

Ben shook his head in disbelief. The idea of flying was absolutely astounding. He never thought he would ever see the ocean, much less *fly* above it rather than sail. What else was Julius's kingdom capable of—what other mysterious contraptions were there?

"Speaking of my father..." Rose said with a slight tremor in her voice. "He'll want to know you're awake...." She slowly retreated to the door.

Ben's stomach felt as though a hundred hunter flies were swarming in his stomach. At last, he would finally be face-to-face with his enemy. This certainly wasn't how he had expected it to play out.

"Rose, wait. Don't leave me. I want to talk and catch up with you on things. I have so many stories to tell you!"

Rose nodded and sat in her chair. Ben walked to his bed, ready to exchange stories with his cousin. The fact that he was a prisoner for King Julius never occurred to him. Even if it had, Ben wouldn't have cared about that. Right now, he had no interest in meddling with Ænærian affairs. He was reunited with Rose now. Nothing else mattered. All thoughts of home vanished from his mind. The Miners Guild was no longer important. His friends...well, he was sure they were somewhere else on the airship, safe. Ben was so overcome with the joy of his reunion that he nearly forgot he should be frightened when a loud *BANG* knocked on the door.

"Your Grace, we heard something break. Are you safe? Please open the door," a voice said from behind the door.

Rose stood up and walked toward the door without a second's hesitation. Ben reached out to stop her, but she moved too quickly for him. "Everything is fine," she said to the Rhion as she opened the door. She pointed to the broken looking glass.

"If it's all the same, Your Grace, His Majesty is on his way and would like a word with the prisoner. This way, please," the Rhion said to Rose, hand extended toward the hallway.

Rose turned to Ben. "It'll be okay. I promise. I'll see you later, and we can reconnect on what we've been through." She walked out the door and was escorted by two other Rhion.

The Rhion who knocked at the door was a rather plump man

with pudgy cheeks. His face resembled a pig rather closely, even with the spiked Ænærian helmet over his head. Another Rhion followed him into the room. He was much lankier but taller, probably almost as tall as Ben. The pig-faced Rhion stepped forward and pointed a spear toward Ben.

"Hands up and legs spread," he commanded.

Ben raised an eyebrow and sighed. He did as he was told. He put his feet shoulder length apart and put his hands into the air. The lanky Rhion approached him and patted his hands around his clothes. He patted down on Ben's chest, arms and legs, and around his waistband evidently looking for any weapons that may be concealed.

"He's good," Lanky grunted to Piggy.

Piggy was kneeling on the floor near the broken looking glass, picking up the shards and placing them into a pouch. When he was finished, he nodded in response to Lanky and strolled toward the doorway. He knelt down again, bowing his head. "It's safe, Your Majesty."

Lanky got to his knees as well and ducked his head down as the man from the golden effigy entered the room. The statue in Parvidom was a good start, but it didn't completely capture the greatness with which Julius held himself. Over the threshold, the Ænærian King stood with his knuckles to his hips, and his posture perfectly straight. His black coat had a fine polish that glimmered from the room's light. An orange scarf rested gently around his neck, embroidered with the Ænærian sun and fist. His hair was sharp and tidy, short and clean. A golden crown in the shape of a sun rested on his forehead. Surrounded by his clean-shaven mouth was a near infectious smile with perfectly white teeth that shone brightly. His face, as Ben remembered from the statue, bore an eerie resemblance to Rose's. Looking at Julius for the first time, Ben realized Rose looked much more like Julius than she did Lydia.

The Sun's Chosen approached Ben, with his powerful green eyes gazing deep into Ben's single brown one. Staring at Ben with a wide smile on his face, he spoke. Not to Ben, but to the Rhion kneeling on the floor.

"Leave me," Julius said with a soothing voice. "I wish to speak with him alone."

"Yes, Your Majesty," the two Rhion said in unison. They got up from the floor and left the room, closing the door behind them.

Julius continued staring at Ben. He bit his bottom lip as if he were holding himself back from a delicious meal. Standing about an inch taller than Ben, Julius's green eyes studied Ben's person. His eyes jumped up and down, never staying too long in one place.

Ben could feel his heart race again. Not from fear as it had so many other times, but in deep apprehension. The euphoria he had felt while Rose was by his side had long since faded like a distant and forgotten dream. He felt a longing emptiness once more just as he had felt when he learned that she had gone missing. This time was different, though. During his entire journey, he thought of Julius as a faceless enemy. Ben was never sure he would really find himself face to face with him, and he never knew what he would do in such a situation. And here he stood, looking up at Julius out of one eye, trembling with unease. Then Julius did the unexpected.

The mighty Ænærian monarch lifted his arms and placed them around Ben. He squeezed tight, embracing him closely. This close to him, Ben found that Julius smelled of mint leaves. This was not how he pictured meeting the tyrant king.

Julius let go and backed away. He put his hands on Ben's shoulders and said, "You're my nephew, *huh*? It's a pleasure to finally meet you." He extended his hand for Ben to take.

Ben shook his hand hesitantly and muttered, "*Uh*, yes. Nice to meet you, too."

Julius let out a soft chuckle and shook his head. "No, no, no. I don't tolerate liars in Ænæria. I will not have it." Though stern, the King's voice was still strangely soothing.

Ben stared at Julius, unsure of what to say.

"I'll give you credit where it's due," the King continued. "Using you first words with me to lie. That's some deep stuff right there. Powerful. Sends a real message. But from now on, I'd appreciate honesty." He smiled again, though this time it appeared to be rather condescending.

Julius turned and plopped down on Ben's bed. He patted his hand down on the furs in a way that said 'sit' to Ben. Struggling to make eye contact with Julius on his right, Ben sat down next to his enemy.

"Tell me, Benedict—or do you prefer Ben? My daughter says you hate being called Benedict because of your father—what do you think of my kingdom?" The King's smile faded to a more serious expression.

Ben thought carefully about his words. What did he want to say first? He weighed in his mind just how truthful he wanted to be. "Well," he stammered, "it's okay, I guess. I mean, it's impressive that you've done so much in only fifteen years. People seem relatively happy, but there are still a lot of problems."

Julius nodded. "Go on," he said.

Ben shrugged. "I mean...I don't know. It's *uh*..."

"You may speak freely, so long as it is the truth. I will not punish you for speaking your mind. We are behind closed doors here. What is said between us stays in our memories only. Understood?"

Nodding, Ben continued. "Sure...I suppose that I mean to say that it seems rather oppressive. People can't have their own beliefs and don't even know your real name. They live in constant fear of being arrested. And that's not an unreasonable fear. I watched both of my friends get arrested in one of your towns. The prisons, well at least the one I saw, are horrid. People didn't have enough space to lie down, and there wasn't anywhere for them to relieve themselves."

Julius nodded as Ben spoke. When Ben finished, the King smiled again. "Those are all excellent points, Ben. But tell me, what about crime?"

"Crime?"

"Yes. People engaging in activities that are detrimental for society. Thieving, violence, unruly behavior. Those types of things," Julius responded calmly.

"I can speak freely?"

"Absolutely."

"Slavery is permitted in Ænæria, no?"

Julius remained silent, but slowly nodded his head as though this was a conversation he would rather avoid.

"Well, I met a group of slavers on my journey, and I would certainly say slavery is a form of thievery. It's stealing people's very lives. My friend Arynn's father was captured by them. She's convinced a friend of hers was taken a few years ago, too. And then there's the violence caused by your Rhion! My friends were beaten upon interrogation, the gladiatorial matches are nothing but killing and violence, and people live in horrid conditions outside your capital city! Do those fit your descriptions of crime?"

Upon finishing, Ben realized that he was on the cusp of shouting at the Ænærian King.

Julius kept his composure and nodded with a friendly smile plastered on his face as he listened to Ben's grievances. He waved his hand, encouraging Ben to continue. *What's he getting at?* Ben wondered. He didn't understand why his enemy cared so much about his own opinion of the kingdom. Ben pressed his nose in frustration. He gathered his thoughts and continued.

"I've never seen such atrocities in all my life! I've always believed that all lives are important. They're too valuable to be thrown away and damaged for the entertainment or desires of others. That's been the Freztadian way. We don't hold many values home because we believe everyone should establish those values for themselves; living their lives to the fullest extent of their desires. But Ænæria preaches a different message. A message of blind faith in fear of oppression. Since Randy first told me about you, a ruler of other people who grew up with the same background as me, I've been appalled with disbelief. How could someone from Freztad possibly believe they had the right to rule over others?"

There was a long pause. Each of Ben's fingers tingled with intensity and his teeth near chattering; he felt he had gone too far and said too much. Julius may have given him permission to speak freely, but what worth is there in the word of a man who kidnaps his own family and oppresses the weak with an iron fist and lies of a false religion? The man had given Ben no reason to trust his actions, so why should he trust his words? For what can be said of a man whose actions and words do not align other than to say he cannot be trusted?

A series of deep breaths was not enough to calm him. His blood was now boiling with a rage that was becoming all too familiar. His single eye went through rapid exchanges of red and translucence. The flashes were becoming so frequent that Ben wondered how often they arose in a day without his notice. Perhaps they would soon happen so often that he would lose control of himself. How much longer until all he could see was red, and there was no one left behind his remaining eye who could be called Ben?

The King of Ænæria stood up from the bed and stretched his arms and legs, as though he had lain in it for an entire night. With power in each step, the Ænærian from Freztad approached the window overlooking the sea. He held his hands behind his back and hummed a tune to himself. To the glass he spoke, but to Ben he directed the words.

"What you speak of is not crime in my eyes. The slavers work outside of Ænæria as no Ænærian is permitted to be enslaved except for those born into it before my rule. Then they're guaranteed freedom by the time they are fifteen years of age. It is a fundamental aspect of the contract I make with the previous kingdoms' leaders when I welcome them into my kingdom. My Rhion work under my orders and the will of the Eternal Sun. Therefore, their actions are not unlawful—they are not crimes. What they do reduces crime in the fourteen provinces. Rates of murder decrease every year and are virtually nil. Thievery occurs from time to time, though it is mostly from outsiders, degenerates, and invalids. Alas, not much can be done about them. But my own people are protected by the laws that my Rhion reinforce.

"It is through the *fear* of oppression that they behave properly, not through oppression itself. I oppress no one. Man oppresses himself through his own decisions. It is his choice to do wrong to another and to disobey the laws I have enacted by the will of the Sun. I merely remove those self-oppressed individuals from society so that all others have a chance at peace, without the hindrance that the actions of others would instill upon them. Perhaps you see these methods as crude and oppressive. I see them as justice.

"There is a vast world out there, nephew of mine. It is still scarred by the sins of our ancestors. They were so caught up in their own avarice and hubris that they took what the Sun had given them for granted. They did not care that the world was dying so long as they could still take advantage of it for their own advancement. When time grew short, and the world rested upon its deathbed, it was too late. They did not accept the Sun's blessings. They continued to worship the dead because it filled their pockets with coin."

Julius brought his hands forward and motioned across his face, as though he were wiping away tears. Though he still stared out the window and Ben could not see the King's face, he knew he was finished speaking. He wanted to hear Ben's thoughts on the matter. But what were his thoughts? He had no idea what Julius was talking about. How could the world be dead? Didn't their very existence, their presence here, contradict that notion? Could Julius be talking about the calamity that lead to the end of the Old Days?

Uncertain of what to say, Ben fidgeted with the furs upon his bed. He let the King's speech sink into his mind as he reflected upon his scant knowledge of the Old Days. They ended centuries ago, according to Kabedge. People lived in prosperity with no concept of true hardships. His ancestors and their contemporaries lived fast lives with an addiction to measuring time. They did as many things in a day as possible for no reason other than because they simply could. Yet they never lived in the moment because they were too focused on what they would do next.

There were good things about the Old Days, too, as Kabedge once told Ben. People were healthier. They didn't starve and, especially before the cataclysmic events at the end, they didn't suffer disease. There was no blood-poisoning like the one afflicting Vic. The Old Days had technology and an understanding of the world that made Julius's sun-carriages and sungs appear as rudimentary as the hammer and nail. It was a world of knowledge and understanding. That is, until it wasn't. Something happened which was somehow destructive enough to change the world. Something that his ancestors either didn't understand or know about. But, according to Julius, they knew about it. They simply didn't care.

At last, Ben had something to speak about. "What does any of that have to do with Ænæria?"

The charismatic King raised a finger and turned around with a smile. "That, my boy, is what I hoped you'd ask. It has everything to do with Ænæria. It's why the Eternal Sun, the Eternal Mother Herself, tasked me with finding the kingdom and establishing an empire. Answer me one more question, Ben, and it will all start to make sense. Do my people appear healthy?"

Ben furrowed his brow. What did that have to do with anything? He scratched his head. "I suppose so. Aside from the slaves, most of them seemed reasonably well fed. In fact, now that you mention it, I haven't seen any blood bugs up here. How did you manage that?"

Julius glanced out the window and then back to Ben. He approached him once more, though this time he remained standing and spoke down to Ben. "We've developed a system to eradicate those pests. We've done quite a lot to treat all kinds of maladies and prevent them from occurring in the first place. The biggest problem we face is food. You did not say that people looked full and hearty. You said they were 'reasonably' well fed. I wish to eliminate the 'reasonably' and replace it with 'exceptionally'.

"You asked what any of this has to do with my kingdom. After your father revealed the existence of the Vault, I searched high and low for it. I thought it would be the cure to the suffering that so many people in the world feel. In my travels I discovered a lesser Vault, far to the West. It was there that the Eternal Mother revealed herself to me. She told me about the solar technology from the Old Days and how to renew it today. I thought it would be enough for my mission, and I gave up pursuing the Vault that your father had chased after. With that power, I realized I could cross the land and liberate people from suffering. I could make their lives easier and promote order; rekindle the flame of the past.

"Alas, it was not enough," Julius continued with an expression of pure frustration. "People still suffered. They were still unhappy. I thought I could correct this by spreading the truth of the Eternal Sun. It gave people new meaning to their lives, offering a different perspective. Yet that, too, was not enough."

Julius straightened himself and brushed off non-existent dust from his shining black coat. He took off his scarf and stared intimately at the fist stitched into it. He took a deep breath and continued.

"I thus decided to look for the Vault once more. The purpose of Ænæria, Benedict, is to recover the richness of the past without making the mistakes that led to the planet's demise. I want to not only revitalize mankind, but revive the world! An empire that unites all people and can spread knowledge has the ability to achieve this! But an empire requires people, and people require food. I believe the Vault will give me answers to both. It will tell me everything I need to know about the past *and* a way to provide for my people."

Julius put the scarf over his shoulder and stepped slowly to the door. At the exit, he turned around and faced Ben once again. "I've had to make many decisions along the way. Some harder than others. I never liked slavery, it was one of Fenwin's ideas, as I'm sure you can imagine. But it was my choice to allow it. A means to an end that was never meant to last, only hasten the process. I do not regret to say, however, that it has been well worth it."

"What was worth it?" asked Ben, unsure of where his enemy was going with this.

Julius's grin grew even wider. "That, nephew, you will see for yourself very soon. I'm afraid I'll need to go now. Time is short, and there is still much to do. As I suggested before, it was a pleasure to meet you, even if the feeling is not mutual."

The King turned to the door and placed his hand around the handle. Before he had a chance to open it, Ben blurted out one last question. "Why did you wait so long? I can't believe it would have taken you fifteen years to find the Vault. Not with your resources and knowledge of the Old Days. If Rose's blood is all you needed for the Vault, then why didn't you take her sooner?"

The King froze, his demeanor suddenly changed from the confident optimist he played himself to be. He frowned and turned from the door. He made a fist with his right and cracked his knuckles as his gritted his teeth. Perhaps Ben had gone too far this time.

"You're right. I found the Vault over 10 years ago. This isn't my first time here." His voice was different when he spoke. It was no longer proud and bright, but shaky and coarse. "I didn't think I would need my daughter's blood—didn't think it would work in the first place. I had hoped your father would let me in. I never suspected that he would have betrayed me. Instead of helping me, his own brother in marriage and in friendship, he slaughtered my men and tried to kill me before he would have let me in there. He wanted the Vault all for himself. He walked inside the Vault's doors with blood-soaked palms. That's when I knew blood was the key. I took my men home for them to lick their wounds as I planned my next expedition, this time back to Freztad. Yet, as soon as I finished my preparations, I learned of the plague that had swept across the land, killing all the children in the village."

He turned away from Ben, the light in the room casting a dark shadow over his face. The King's eyes were clenched and his cracked the knuckles of his other hand. "I spent the last ten years thinking my own daughter was dead. I was furious with myself, for I had thought it was my destiny to unite the Northern Realm and become King of Ænæria; I cared not for what I left behind because I knew I would one day make the world a better place for my child. But when I learned the plague spared no children in Freztad, I had given up hope. I stopped searching for the Vault. I focused on redeeming myself by making Ænæria great."

It was an enormous shock for Ben to see his enemy so vulnerable. Throughout the entire journey, Ben had only ever considered Julius as an evil tyrant—never as a human; never a father who mourned the loss of a child.

"But Rose and I survived," Ben said. "We were the only ones. Lydia kept her inside, never let her near a single blood bug throughout the entire plague. I..." he figured it best not to tell Julius that he believed himself immune, "I just got lucky, I guess. If you thought we were dead, then why did you send Randy to retrieve Rose?"

Julius once more placed his hand on the door handle and turned away from Ben. "That reckless buffoon," he said with a sigh. "I never sent him to Freztad. I had no idea my daughter was alive until he brought her to me, and I saw my own eyes staring back at me in her mother's face. You can thank *him* for this whole ordeal, and for that wound you've got there. This whole thing is all thanks to him." He opened the door and left, slamming it behind him.

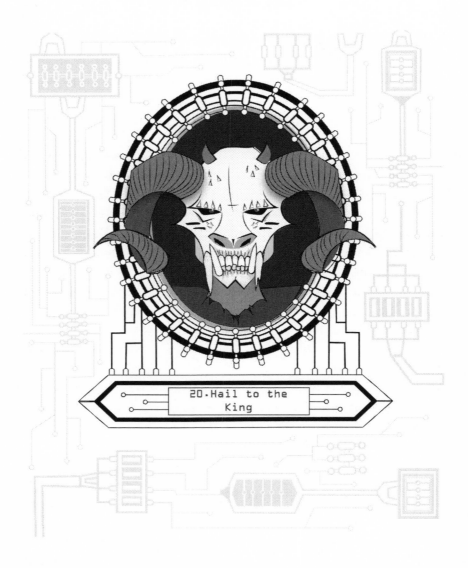

20.Hail to the
King

While the ocean may have been growing closer, Ben's
understanding of his recent interaction seemed to drift
further away. Like so many other events leading up to
now, Ben was left confused and frustrated. Julius may have answered
many of his burning questions, but he also left Ben with a host of
more. True, the King disclosed his plans regarding the Vault. But
could he be trusted? Ben had no reason to believe the King was

telling him the truth; he had no reason to believe he was lying either. The man himself thoroughly perplexed Ben. What could the King gain from revealing any of his plans? Yet at the same time, Ben saw no gain from Julius deceiving him. Perhaps the King only meant to intimidate him, making Ben question his perception of his enemy. He was not the tyrant Ben had envisioned—someone who threatened and oppressed. No, Julius was much worse. He knew how to get inside Ben's head.

For a brief moment, Ben experienced an odd sense of weightless-ness and sudden pops within his ears. He could feel the airship moving, not straight as it had before, but at a slight decline. Approaching the window, Ben saw why: they were descending toward land. Though Ben had no experience with which to compare it, he judged that the airship was reasonably high in the sky. It was hard to tell with the vast body of land ahead, but the buildings and people on the ground were enough for him to make a loose comparison.

Many small islands poked their heads above the blue ocean and assembled themselves in a way that seemed to pave their way to their originator. The earth below stretched so far that Ben had no indica-tion at the time that it, too, was an island. Everything below him, in fact, once belonged to the same island, but the ocean had consumed the outer rim and nearly claimed the land for itself.

Then, in the speed of a flicker of light, Ben recognized something before him. Protruding from a high mountain, off in the vast distance, was a stone and steel building in the style of the Old Days. For some reason, the scene before them was extremely familiar, and he knew where he was: they had arrived at the location of the Grand Vault.

An hour later the airship was back on solid ground. Ben watched from his luxurious prison cell as countless Rhion exited the ship carrying equipment and crates that looked strangely similar to the ones in the burning room in Jordysc. That's when it finally hit Ben.

Ben had been so preoccupied by the joy of seeing Rose, the anger of losing his eye, and the bewilderment of the Ænærian overlord, that the fates of Miners hadn't truly hit him yet. Rose mentioned prisoners on the ship, so perhaps they were they being kept alive. Ben had last seen Alejandra in the Ænærian's custody. He could only imagine what they were doing to her. The thought of Alejandra being interrogated did not sit well with him. He had not known her long at all, but he could tell that she was a good person. More righteous than Julius; that much he knew. Her mother and daughter were good, too. *What happened to them?* he wondered, as he had not seen them at all during the battle. He could only hope that they were safe with the rest of the remaining Guild members.

Now Ben felt tremendous guilt. He lay on the bed, staring at the ceiling above as his stomach cramped and his teeth dug into his bottom lip. The Ænærians did not arrive in Jordysc that night by sheer coincidence. They had surely been followed from Ignistad. This, Ben knew without a doubt, was his fault. He punched a pillow next to his head in frustration. Had he not been so reckless in the city by gambling with his life, exposing himself to Randy, they never would have been discovered. No one else would have found Jordysc. All the deaths and blood spilled within the mountain were on his hands.

Ben started to cry. Tears ran down his left eye, though he had no sense of anything happening in his right. This whole journey, he had avoiding killing and had kept his promise to Rakshi. He always equated killing with murder, but this was different. He had never actually struck the fatal blow, but he might as well have given the Ænærians the sword to do it.

Lying there now, Ben felt the transmutation was nearly complete. So many lives had been lost because of him. Though he had never willingly ended anyone's life, committed the horrid act of murder, he had still killed so many people. Those in his wake of recklessness and foolish ambition. From the slavers in the cave, to the guards at the prison, to the Rhion and Miners of Jordysc alike—so many lives had been lost because of Ben's actions.

～

"Room 23, right?" a voice called the next morning, from behind the door.

Ben was in no mood to face anyone right now, especially more infuriating Rhion. Though he was sure his concerns were of little importance to them.

Piggy and Lanky appeared beyond the threshold with a third Ænærian between them. He did not look like the other Rhion; rather, his outfit was much more similar to that of a legate's.

"Up," the legate said in a gruff voice. "Raise your arms and spread your legs."

Ben rolled his eye, feeling a tinge of pain where his right eye ought to be. "Yeah, yeah. I know the drill." Lanky patted Ben down, feeling for any hidden weapons. *I doubt even the Voidsweeper would be enough surrounded by this many Ænærians.*

"You will not speak unless asked a question," the legate said. "And mind your tone when you do."

"Or what? Gonna hurt me? No, y'see, the King and me? We're family—best pals now, really. He wouldn't like that. His daughter would like it even less," Ben said, trying his best to hold in a laugh. He took some solace in knowing he could still make things difficult for the Ænærians after being completely defeated. Though he was quite dejected about how things had turned out, Ben was certain he could cheer himself up some by making the arbiters of his state of mind just as miserable.

The color in the legate's face burned red with frustration. "Restrain him and get him off the ship! The less I see of this peasant's face, the better!"

"Yes, Legate Rivers," Piggy and Lanky said in unison, like the bumbling idiots they were.

"Sheesh, guys," Ben teased, "Do you ever think for yourselves? Ever have an original thought? Come on! Show some initiative!"

They ignored Ben and directed him out of the room, his wrists and ankles bound in chains. A metal corridor met them outside his room with others scattered all around. Ænærian flags hung proudly every which way he looked in the red-tinted airship interior. Piggy and Lanky brought Ben to a flight of stairs which they descended in somber silence. Had Ben not known any better, he would have thought that he was marching to the gallows for his own execution.

Masses of Rhion and Ænærian workers flooded the halls and marched toward the airship's exit. Just how long, Ben questioned, had he been on the ship? The Vault was outside, so he must be far north —just how far, he did not know—but then again, he never realized how far he had managed on his own. He had just let Arynn handle all navigational matters.

Oh, Arynn. Please be okay the way Rose is.

The northern air was horribly cold, colder than Ben had ever thought possible. He felt his body begin to shake, much the same as it would when he was nervous. His teeth chattered, and the hairs on his arms stood erect. A cool night was not uncommon back home, but how could it be so cold while the sun still burned brightly in the sky, mocking his failures as Ben imagined a black fist eclipsing over it.

Boots clanged against the metal stairs that met the damp earth and frigid air. Few others seemed to be acclimated to the frigid temperature as they clustered together for warmth and patiently waited in a line for fur coats. Only Julius and Rose, an impossible distance ahead of Ben, seemed to be amiable with the temperature. Ben knew Rose would show no signs of discomfort or weakness; it would be unbecoming and contrary to her disposition. But Julius seemed to thrive in the cool air. His shiny dark jacket and orange scarf were his only comforts—and even they seemed too much for him. The King's smile seemed to provide all the warmth he would ever need here.

Ben was given his own furs to cover his gray jumpsuit and was granted slight reprieve from the cold. Piggy and Lanky brought Ben toward the large crowd that Julius and Rose oversaw. They stood atop a wooden stage that must have been assembled within the last night. The Rhion brought Ben to the front of the crowd but then walked him to the side, out of the line of sight from whatever spectacular event was about to unfold.

There was still no sight of Arynn. Or Darius, Trinity, Alejandra—anyone aside from Rose whose presence would comfort Ben more than any layers of furs.

Julius stepped forward and spread his hands, as though basking in the sun's warmth and light. Ben imagined the monarch was praying to his god, which for all Ben knew, may not be so imaginary after all. Between recognizing the Vault and his red flashes preceding his superhuman strength, Ben knew there were indeed strange things in this increasingly bizarre world in which he had found himself.

"My brothers and sisters!" Julius's voiced carried from the stage at the base of the mountain, facing the airship and everyone who had been on board. The ship was not as Ben had pictured it in his mind. It looked nothing like a bird as it had no wings. How then, did it fly? Instead, it looked like a ship one would see in the water, but instead of sails there was an enormous oblong over-carriage that somewhat resembled a misshapen egg. Ben shook his head in awe of the airship, which had carried him across the ocean. Indeed, the vessel was a feat of engineering unlike anything had had seen before, either in Freztad or in Ignistad. As Ben studied the airship resting firmly on solid ground, he marveled at how the power of the Sun had enabled the Ænærians to achieve such a feat.

"United by the energy through which we are born by the Eternal Mother, through *Sol Invictus*, we have finally accomplished our goal!" Julius carried on.

Applause echoed through the frigid air. Julius continued to grin as he waited patiently for his people to quiet themselves.

"Fifteen years ago, I left my home in search of the Grand Vault. Many of my brothers and sisters joined me, and together we conquered the warring tribes of the Northern Realm, one by one. Our ranks grew with each victory, and we formed the beginning of a united North. We became the greatest nation this world has seen since the fall of our ancestors. It was at our victory over the province of Minervia that the Eternal Mother finally revealed herself to me and named me as her Chosen. She bestowed upon me the Holy weapons, sun-chariots—and greatest of all, the airships, which allow us to be even closer to the Sun. She even told me of the Grand Vault, and the treasures within. Treasures that will enable our people to prosper and live long and healthy lives!"

The crowd applauded again. "Fifteen years since I set off to rebuild the world," Julius continued when his subjects finally returned to silence. "We have slowed the advances of hunger, violence, and disease! But today, I intend to end them—*permanently*. Each and every one of you has played a part in making my dream a reality. For those of you who do not know," he put an arm around Rose, "this is my daughter. *She* is the final piece of the puzzle!"

Murmurs scattered throughout the crowd, eyebrows raised in uncertainty.

"Unlike the doors that gifted us the powers of the Sun," Julius called over the chatter, "these doors have passed the test of time and have remained shut. The Eternal Mother herself told me that they can only be opened through one method. By some twist of fate, I was blessed with a daughter from an ancestral line of the Vault's creators. They left this Vault behind in case they ever had the opportunity to rebuild—but only gave the key to their kin. My daughter, everyone, has the blood that can open the Vault's doors!"

Cheers rang through the mountainous valley, carrying over the great ocean. Rhion fired guns into the air in celebration while workers raised their tools and Ænærian flags in the air.

This is wrong, Ben thought. This should be his victory, not theirs. Why did Julius get to open the Vault? And why did Ben need to be here to witness this tragedy? Worst of all, Ben wasn't even sure if Julius was as evil as he had once thought. Julius wanted the Vault to help people. But did that make up for everything he had done up until now?

When the noise settled, and air remained cool, the people heard Julius one final time.

"We are pioneers on this dead planet, searching for a way to revive it. The land in which we find ourselves, Svaldway, will be the fifteenth province of Ænæria. Furthermore, as many of you know, we have lost two legates due to unforeseen events."

Many pairs of eyes, a painful example of yet another difference between the Ænærians and Ben, shot to the side toward him with scowls of deep contempt.

"First Legate Rivers, please come forward," Julius said.

The legate who Ben had sassed in the airship walked up to the wooden stage and knelt before his king.

"Rise, my brother, and meet my embrace," Julius commanded in a pleasant tone that made Ben quite uneasy. The two Ænærians embraced. They released, and the King continued. "I hereby decree that upon our return to Ignistad, you be named King of Old Ænæria."

There was no way Ben had heard correctly. Unsurprisingly, the rest of the crowd was just as unsettled and perplexed. People cried in confusion and, had they not been in the presence of a king, they would have surely spoken out in protest.

"Hear me, my brothers and sisters. With the Vault being opened today, there will be too much for me to do in this foreign land. I simply cannot be your king from home. Instead, I will take up the mantle as Emperor of New Ænæria. We will build a new city here, Rosa Solis, named for my daughter and *Sol Invictus*," he looked to his daughter proudly. Rose did not make eye contact, nor exhibit any decipherable expression. "A new world with more provinces will need more legates and kings, with an empire to oversee its progress."

The Ænærians, though still in shock, nodded their heads in a dazed acceptance. Then, as though still reading their minds, Julius concluded his final speech and addressed the whispering concerns that lingered throughout the crowd.

"Legate Randolph will be demoted to replace our dearly departed Legate Gatron. His actions have caused me, and consequently the rest of Old Ænæria, much strife. Lives have been lost, and plans have been delayed. I believe his demotion will teach him respect and better appreciation for our cause. It will be a humbling experience. Now then, my people, I have a meeting to attend and preparations to make before entering the Vault. Ready yourselves, brothers and sisters, for the next time the Sun rises, it will be over the glory of New

Ænæria," the Emperor raised his fist in the air and pointed it toward the sun and shouted, *"Sol Invictus!"*

"Sol Invictus!" everyone in the crowd shouted with a fiery passion and fists penetrating the cold wind.

Legate-King Rivers descended the stairs with a troubled look on his face, as though he had had no idea he was to become King. He pushed through the Ænærians and rushed into the airship. As soon as he was out of sight, Ben turned to his left and saw Rose and Julius approach him. Piggy and Lanky performed a profound bow and then stood at attention. The emperor dismissed them.

"What'd you think, Ben?" Julius asked, the grin now faded and a new fire in his eyes. "And remember what I told you about lies."

Ben never got the chance to answer his cousin's father. Instead, he suddenly found himself stuck and restrained in the middle of an open battlefield. As soon as Julius closed his mouth, BOOMS exploded within the crowd of people. Screams of horror rang as the smell of smoke warmed the freezing air.

On a rocky overpass that overlooked the assembled Ænærians was a battalion of furred creatures with curled horns like that of a ram's and long, sharp teeth. Each was armed with spears, bows and arrows, knives, and other tools Ben had never seen before. Behind them stood trebuchets raining a fierce inferno on the unaware Ænærians below. The creatures descended on ropes dangling from the overpass and rushed into a mass of chaos and confusion. Arrows soared through the sky, hitting countless Rhion before they even had a chance to blink from the explosions.

As quickly as the fire in Julius's eyes had ignited with passion, they extinguished and now rekindled into emerald flames of fury and fear. It was a sight unbecoming of an emperor, and Ben wasn't sure if he was more terrified by the creatures or by the man holding his chains and dragging him away from the bloodbath.

Rhion fired sungs and guns alike indiscriminately toward the overpass and descending demons with no regard for anyone caught in the line of fire. Julius dragged Ben and pushed Rose toward the mountain as though he were trying to protect them from the fight.

"Where are you taking us?" Ben yelled over the screams and gunfire. "What are those things?"

Julius continued running away from the scene of the battle toward the Grand Vault's mountain, one fist clenching the chains around Ben's wrists and another holding a pistol which, Ben now realized in terror, was pointed at Rose's back.

"Keep going, girl," the furious father hollered ahead of him.

Ben resisted the emperor's pull and held his feet firmly in the ground. "Leave her alone!"

"Silence, boy! I may have need of you yet. I will not allow the natives to get their filthy hands on either of you! I've come too far for this to fail!"

Rose yelled back. "It's fine, I'll be okay, Ben! Don't fight him. You won't win."

The three fell behind cover, and Julius caught his breath. He no longer aimed his pistol at Rose, but behind the stony corner they hid behind. He shot toward the demons slaughtering the Ænærians and battling the Rhion. Beams of concentrated light exited the pistol and exploded the second they landed, reducing a host of demons to ash. Ben's jaw dropped as he looked at the small gun, realizing it was actually the most powerful sung he had ever seen.

Julius looked up and fired once more. An avalanche of rock poured from the mountain and blocked off the way between them and the ferocious creatures of the Svaldway.

"That should buy us some time," Julius exhaled, wiping the sweat from his brow.

Ben stepped in front of Rose, placing himself between the father and daughter. "Tell me what's happening! What are they?"

"Sadly, they're more like a *who*, Benedict," Julius snapped. "They're the natives of this godforsaken land. They're quite human, I imagine. Look closely at them, and you'll see that they're merely covered in furs and masks. In part for warmth, but more so to inspire fear."

Ben wasn't sure how Julius could tell with how fast everything was moving, because the 'masks' looks very real to Ben.

Gunfire seemed to fall short and was quickly replaced by the *twangs* of bow strings snapping repetitively. The Rhion were clearly not prepared for a fight in the same way the natives were.

"Dammit!" Julius growled, shooting a few more blasts over the barrier he had built only moments before. "They can't get near the airships! Where in blazes are Rivers and Randolph? They should be out there fighting!" There was now a panic in the once confident emperor's voice. He turned to Ben and Rose and pushed them further up the mountain's pathway.

The fighting continued for the next hour. Ben couldn't see much from his current position on the road which wound itself around the mountain like a serpent. The Rhion must have used the time to recharge and gather more ammunition from the airship because Ben could hear more gunshots and the occasional *zap* from a sung. Explosions from the trebuchets all but ceased, and it seemed as though they were coming closer. Moments later, Ben discovered why.

The serpentine road was connected to the overpass from which the demons made their first appearance. The trebuchets stood like giants over the human insects scattered beneath them. Julius fired his pistol at the natives, killing perhaps ten of them with a single shot. He aimed next for the closest siege weapon but missed as an arrow flew past his head and nearly took out Ben's remaining eye.

"Out of the way, you ignorant fool," Julius snarled at Ben. "I may need you yet if my theory is wrong." The latter statement seemed more directed to himself than Ben. "Make yourself useful and keep the girl alive." He ran to cover and continued to lay down fire against the mysterious enemy.

The one thing we agree on, Ben thought to himself pondering his cousin. For whatever the reason, Ben took solace in knowing that both he and Julius both wanted Rose to be safe. Ben took her hand in his own and opened his mouth to speak to her. Nothing came out when he realized her hand was trembling uncontrollably. Looking his cousin in the eyes, Ben saw the dread behind them. She was afraid—not just for herself, but for those around her. He realized that Rose probably hadn't become as accustomed to violence as he had during recent events. How awful all this must be to Rose, who had probably been sheltered in safety by her father since her abduction.

Ben held his cousin close to him as the violence ensued. *It will be okay*, he told her in his mind; he could not bring himself to say the words aloud, for neither of them would believe such a lie. She wrapped her arms around him in response and sobbed as she buried her head in his chest. He stroked her hair and kissed the top of her head.

"I love you, Rose," he said, knowing this was no lie. "I'll be here with you the whole time. I won't let you out of my sight."

She looked up at him, with a ray of hope gleaming from her green irises.

"Though it may be harder with only one eye," Ben jested.

Rose let out a soft chuckle and sniffled. Sadly, the moment of peace between the two was soon interrupted by the presence of a third. Julius had come back around the corner.

"It's clear. Move," he commanded. The somber cousins obeyed and followed. They passed piles of burnt corpses, though there were fewer than Ben had expected. He looked down from the overpass and saw the last of the demons descending the ropes and running toward the brawl on the battlefield. Had he not been so concerned, Ben might have smiled at the fact that there were still people to fight against his captors.

The Vault's doors were glazed with a slick frost over the smooth black metal from the Old Days. Ben saw the mandala engraved between the double doors that stretched double the length of his own arm span. In the center where the mandala's circle should be, was a glowing contraption—as if a piece of the sun itself were trapped inside. Was it possible that Julius had been telling the truth this whole time? *No*, Ben decided. *It must be another type of Old Days technology still at work.*

Julius approached the glowing disc and turned around to face his shaking daughter. "Your hand. Give it to me," he demanded.

Rose obeyed, but Ben pulled her back. "Leave her alone!"

Julius thumbed a button on his gun and shot Ben in the left

shoulder. The pain was unlike anything he had ever felt. It radiated from his shoulder to his heart, from there to his lungs, and from there to the rest of his body before it circled around to his brain. He bit his lip, holding in a scream. His vision flashed red.

"Do not test me, boy!" Julius shouted. "Do you know how much trouble you've caused me? Randolph's mistake of leaving you behind in that godforsaken village was nearly the bane of my existence! Fifteen years I have planned for this day. Fifteen long years of patience and strategy for the day the world would become mine! Mine to fix and mine to command! I've kept you alive in case my theory proves to be incorrect. Insurance is always a necessity, but you are trying my patience! Fifteen years has that effect on a man. Let go of the girl, or I promise you will lose that other eye!"

Rose tried to push Ben from her, clearly not wanting to fight any longer. Ben got the impression she had resisted her father quite a bit until now but was finally defeated. She had accepted whatever fate was in store for her. But even a little scratch by her father to draw her blood was one scratch too many for Ben.

He slapped his chains against Julius in defiance, but the self-proclaimed emperor caught them in his hand and fired with his other. This time, Ben was ready. He raised his wrists in front of the barrel and watched as the metal chains were incinerated, as though they were removed from existence itself. Free from his restraints, Ben lunged forward at his foe and slammed his fist into Julius's right eye. *A small payback.* Ben smiled at the thought.

The victory was short lived. The emperor's pistol-whipped Ben across his empty eye-socket. He would have rather been shot again. He collapsed to the frigid floor and watched the red flickers attempt to take over the black. In the end, the darkness won, as Ben imagined it always would but hoped it never could.

His lashes beat against each other as his eye opened once more. Fatigue overwhelmed Ben as though he had been in a deep slumber. Control had not been lost this time as it had been in Ignistad. Rather, Ben had surely lost consciousness for a short time. He picked himself up and was reminded of the deep burn in his shoulder. The burn reminded him of its perpetrator. Ben fixed his gaze on Julius, covered to the elbow in blood and crying in hysteria.

"It won't work! Why won't it work? Mother, tell me what I've done wrong!" the man screamed maniacally.

The scene before Ben was the most traumatic sight to which he had ever bore witness. Rose was sprawled across the stone, motionless. She was pale and translucent; her veins popping out of her skin as though her pulse was nonexistent.

Julius shook his fist to the sky crying, "I don't understand! No amount of blood is enough! Why won't you take it! I have your son here, and still you won't let me in! Have you no heart—seeing your own flesh and blood in peril?"

There was no response.

"Alphonse! Open the damn door! I've won, and you've lost!" The mad monarch turned to the now standing Ben. "You! Come here! I need your blood!"

Ben barely heard Julius speak. He fell to his knees by Rose's side, tears pouring from his eye. "Don't be dead, Rose," he cried. "I did all of this for you..." he could no longer form words. His despair was too deep for he was no one without Rose. She was his driving force, and she was his life. Without her life, Ben had none. No number of red flickers could distract him from that fact.

"Come here, boy," Julius growled. He put his hands on Ben's burnt shoulder. Ben shoved the maniac away from him, too hurt emotionally to notice the physical pain. Julius raised his pistol to Ben's temple. "I don't have time for this!"

And then it was over. Fangs appeared from nowhere and clenched down on Julius's neck. A look of panic erupted on his face when he realized what was happening. Sierra bit down before the Emperor could ever pull the trigger on Ben.

Julius choked his last words. "You'll...see...how hard it is...one day...to sacrifice...." He turned his head to the side as Sierra let go, and the blood rushed away from his neck, never to return.

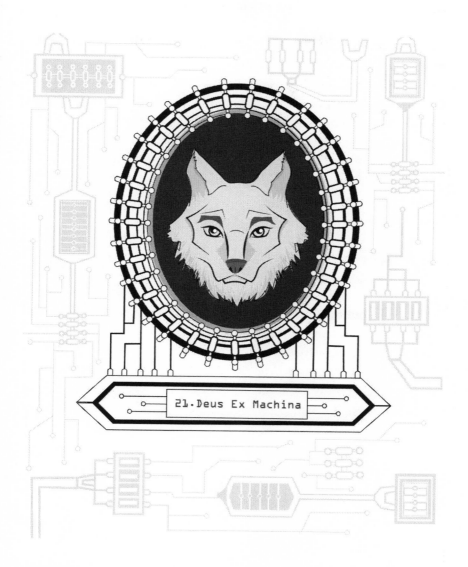

21.Deus Ex Machina

The white wolf had always come to Ben's aid when he least expected it. It happened first with the deer in Freztad. She had lunged at a man with a gun pointed at his face not once, but twice now. Sierra stood in front of Ben, covered in blood. Though Ben knew it was not her own. He had never seen her bleed. And deep down, he didn't believe he ever would. The wolf approached Ben and nuzzled against him, reassuring him that everything would be okay. But how could anything be okay without Rose in this world? Death was Ben's greatest enemy, it seemed. Not Julius and not even himself, for death was the only thing that could truly separate him from Rose forever. Though he had been close, it was the one veil of uncertainty that Ben could not yet cross.

His hand stroked the beast's head. "Thank you," he managed to say to the wolf. And that was enough. She couldn't really understand him, Ben believed. She could only sense that he was in danger. All the times she had been attacked and remained unscathed must have been pure luck. Luck must have guided Sierra all the way back to him.

The same luck that seemed to have just run out.

Ben put his hand through Rose's hair. She was cold and lifeless, pale and gone. And then Ben felt it. There was a soft breeze not from the frozen mountain, but from Rose's nostrils. She was breathing! She was alive! Ben put his fingers to her neck, and there it was: a subtle, yet very alive pulse. How stupid he had been not to feel for it sooner. Then he let instinct take over as he picked her up in his arms and carried her to the Vault.

"Dad," he said weakly, "if you're in there, let me in. Please. It's me, Benedict. Your son."

To the Vault, it seemed to make no difference if the person outside was Julius or Ben, for there was no answer.

"Don't abandon me again, Dad. Please. Julius thought you were in there. If that's true…" he lost his words for a moment as he looked at his dying cousin and choked back more tears. "If that's true, then please help me! I deserve that much from my own father!"

There was no answer from his father, the Vault, or any other living thing.

Sierra whimpered at Ben as if in regret and then bit down on his left calf.

"*Ahh!*" Ben hollered in pain. "What was that for?" Ben panicked, wondering if the wolf had finally let its animalistic instincts take over as it saw a grand feast in front of it. She stepped back and whimpered with her tail between her legs.

Ben knelt down and hoisted Rose over his shoulder as he felt the wound. It was a small, clean bite. There was blood slowly flowing, so he knew that Sierra had missed nicking an artery. He wiped his finger against it. The sight of his blood reminded him of the red flashes, the superhuman strength and berserker rage that followed.

Then it all made sense.

Ben stood up and placed his bloody finger to the glowing center of the mandala. It shifted from a bluish hue to a bright, leaf green. The glow stretched to engulf the entire mandala before it began to spin and spiral. The mandala faded into the carved black metal, followed by a rusted *creek* as the gates of the Vault opened. Sierra darted inside and barked for Ben to follow. He listened and hobbled in with his cousin in his arms. The gates closed behind him, and an incessant siren rang throughout the acoustically tuned halls.

White lights illuminated the hall from the ceilings every five or so feet, just like the ones he had seen in the mountain of Jordysc and within Julius's airship. The inside was like no architecture Ben had ever seen and was therefore utterly incomparable to any past experiences. The best he could do was imagine the undercroft of an ancient castle blended with the all but extinct technologies of the Old Days.

At the end of the short hall was a finely painted plaque with a diagram, which he found had oddly gathered no dust. It showed twenty-two different chambers all behind closed doors leading into corridors, spiraling around the inside of the Grand Vault's mountain. At the center of the spiral was a central hub that had the number '23' on it. Words scattered across the sign but were unintelligible to Ben as they were not in the common tongue. Fortunately, there was an arrow at the closest point on the sign that seemed to indicate Ben's present location. The siren continued to ring.

"Just hang in there, Rose," he said carrying his limp cousin forward. "I'm sure one of these rooms will have something to help you."

The center of the Vault was less of a hub and more like the center of a maze. If there was a direct way to the twenty-third room, Ben could not find it. Large double doors that nearly touched the stone ceiling twenty feet above stood beyond the painted sign, but Ben found no handles. According to the map, these doors should lead straight to the center, and he figured the center was as good a place as any to begin his search. He tried pushing against them but met great resistance as though something were on the other side blocking all entry. Sierra went from wagging her tail to offering a small whimper. She moved along the corridor toward the first room without the usual grace in her step.

It seemed to Ben that he would need to carry Rose throughout the Vault in the spiral hallways before reaching that room. It was just as well, he considered, as he may find something more able to help Rose before then.

"Any suggestions?" Ben said to Sierra.

The wolf barked and trotted forward along the spiral, past two glass doors that had a large white 'I' printed on them with smaller words in the unfamiliar language. As Ben passed by, he couldn't help but take a curious glance inside.

"Wait up, girl," he called to the wolf. "What if there's something useful in here?"

The wolf shook her head, barked once more, and continued forward.

As he walked past the room with the 'I' printed upon the glass, Ben found there were more white lights emitting from the corridor and various glass containers lined up in rows beyond. Though intrigued, Ben kept up his pace with Sierra and worked his way to the center.

The next five rooms all appeared to be the same as the first. More glowing glass doors with rows and rows of cabinets. Though he never spent much time at a single room, Ben got an impression of what was inside the glass containers. Behind the translucent materials and the foreign language Ben swore he could see piles of seeds within them. They weren't like the deformed and misshapen seeds his people would put in pouches for currency—they were much more symmetrical and beautiful. He desperately wanted to walk into a room to examine them more closely, but he restrained himself, knowing he needed to get Rose to the center.

The siren continued for another five minutes before it slowed, faded, then ceased. The sudden silence reminded Ben of how loud the horrid horn blare was, especially since it reminded him of the horns that sounded during the Battle of Jordysc. The thoughts pained him, but he shook the memories from his mind.

"One painful thing at a time," he told himself.

A voice called, startling Ben and nearly causing him to drop his cousin. It came from nowhere in particular just like the ringleader's voice in Ignistad.

"Apologies for the delay. I was preoccupied with the siren," the voice called. It appeared to be male in origin, but only barely. If anything, it sounded more like the words were formed by the scraping together of metal.

"I also apologize for the locked doors up front. Certain functions have been sacrificed for the sake of safety," the metallic voice said. "I see you brought my friend with you. Continue to follow her to Sector 23. I will meet you there and offer assistance."

Your friend? Ben questioned himself. *Surely he means Rose? But no, he said to continue following. He did mean Sierra.*

Ben stared intently at his canine companion. How would the stranger in the Vault know of Sierra? Another thought pushed his current one out of the way. *Julius thought my dad was in here.* Could Alphonse be in the Vault with Ben? Was he the voice Ben had heard speaking throughout the hall? Would he finally meet his mysterious father? He hurried as best he could with a well over hundred-pound body in his arms, a bleeding calf, burnt shoulder, single eye, and whatever other injuries he had sustained prior to now.

At last, Ben found himself at another set of double metal doors with the number '23' painted on them.

"One moment while I disengage the magnetic locking mechanisms," the screeching voice said.

Whirring sounds and crackles of electricity sounded from beyond the door before they finally spread open and disappeared into the walls. The room was much brighter than the rest of the Vault had been. The light was not a harsh white but rather a warmer hue that felt much more comfortable and settling. It made Ben feel oddly comfortable despite his current situation. The room's air was much cleaner than the rest of the Vault's, too. This was not to say the undercroft seemed musty or dank, just that Sector 23 was immaculate by comparison. The doors whirred shut behind Ben as he stepped through with Sierra by his side.

Beneath Ben's feet was no longer cold stone, but some manner of unknown fur making up a very dark green carpet. As soon as he had entered the room and the doors closed behind him, Ben felt much too warm in his coat. It was as if the sun itself shone into the room as it had at home but without the moisture in the air making him sweat profusely.

The wolf barked and ran straight ahead toward a single bed that lay in the middle of the room. She climbed atop it and curled into a circle. For the first time, Ben now realized, he watched the animal fall asleep. Then, something horrible happened.

Arms made of metal beams with large crab-like claws descended from the ceiling. One of the mechanical arms lifted Sierra's jaw while the other pulled her ears. The arms stretched away from each other while Ben watched in terror as he saw Sierra's fur and skin removed from her head. The wolf stopped breathing but never made a single hint of discomfort. Underneath the skin and coat were not muscle, tendon, or bone as Ben suspected. Instead, the wolf's head appeared to be made of a strong metal shaped exactly to the structure of a canine's skull.

Sierra's cranium opened like two flaps connected to hinges. Another sound, similar to the whirring of the double doors, came from the wolf's head as what must've been her brain ascended from within the metallic base.

With regards to shape and structure, Sierra's brain looked like other animal brains that Ben had seen, but this one was translucent with red and blue cords running within. A third arm came from the ceiling, this time with much smaller claws at its end, much like a pair of pliers. The arm disconnected the wolf's brain from its stem and, with the aid of the other two claws, ascended into the ceiling and disappeared. The wolf lay on the bed, motionless with its head open and exposed but without any blood of which to speak.

"Sierra!" Ben called. "What did you do?" he demanded to the mechanical voice. "Show yourself to me!"

"Alas, that is something I am unable to do," the metal voice said. "However, if you would like me to help your cousin, it would be beneficial for you to remain calm and listen."

Ben shook his head. "You expect me to believe you'd help Rose after you killed Sierra?" he asked in disgust.

There was a faint clicking sound from wherever the stranger's voice came. Then it spoke. "*Ah*. I understand the agitation I am reading. There is a simple miscommunication. What is not alive cannot die. Though I would like to consider myself as a sentient being, I have not figured out how to create life just yet."

The metallic voice spoke with confidence, as though anything it had said made any sense to Ben. Ben approached the bed to see the body of his dearly departed friend and laid his cousin next to the wolf, unable to carry her any longer. He climbed into the bed next to the two and closed his eye in a silent sob.

"I sense despair. I apologize for any part I may have played in it. Perhaps I should clarify," the voice said once more.

"Just shut up," Ben said softly. "Can you help Rose or not?"

"I can, however you may not be in the state of mind to make such a decision."

"What do you mean? I'd do anything for her! I came all the way to your damn Vault to save her! The least you can do is show me your face!"

"I repeat: I cannot do that."

"Why?" Ben asked bitterly.

"I do not yet have a face."

Ben scrunched his face together. Had he heard the voice correctly? "What is that supposed to mean?"

"Once again, I apologize. It has been quite some time since I last interacted with a human. Allow me to introduce myself. In your language, I was once known as a Multi-Interactive and Memory Interface Robot, or Mimir if it pleases you."

Ben raised his eyebrow as he stoked Rose's hair. "What's a robot?"

A humming sound fluttered from the ceiling as though Mimir was deep in thought. "Carry your cousin to the room at the end of the hall to your left. I will answer all questions as you make your way toward your decision."

Automatically, Ben picked up Rose in his arms. She was limper than before, and her breaths were significantly shorter and shallower. There was an occasional rattle in her chest that scared Ben because he knew it meant death was approaching. As he stood off the edge of the bed with a dying Rose in his arms, he looked at the lifeless Sierra still resting on the bed, her eyes staring at him from the metal shell that was her skull. Ben couldn't believe he was going to trust Mimir after he had seen what the metal voice had done to his precious companion. But he didn't have a choice, because Rose would surely die if he did nothing, and something was surely better than that, even if it meant trusting the voice that called itself Mimir.

"The best way someone of your knowledge would understand," the voice said from the walls and ceiling as Ben walked to the doorway at the end of the hall, "is that a robot is a mechanism capable of performing simple to complex actions on its own based on the programming of its creator."

"*Uh*, programming?" Ben asked.

"A series of instructions used to control a robotic entity. Much like instincts and genes for organic life such as yourself."

Ben didn't say anything. Mimir had lost him again.

"*Ah*. Apologies again. Despite my origins as a memory unit, I am quite forgetful nowadays. Quite the irony, no?"

Again, Ben did not respond.

"Allow me to give you an example. Sierra, as you called the wolf, is a robot, designed and programmed with the instructions to find you, protect you, and aid you in your journey to my home without giving away her true nature as begotten to her by myself and your father."

Now Ben had something to say to Mimir. "You know my father?" he shouted with excitement.

"Indeed, I do. But that is something we will discuss in the next room."

Ben scowled. He was only feet away from the room now, so he could wait. He asked his next question. "I still don't understand. What do you mean by saying Sierra is a robot? She wasn't alive when you killed her?"

"As I said," the voice responded, "what is not alive cannot die. She is a robot and thus cannot die because robots do not live. They simply do as they are programmed."

"You said 'they' as though you don't include yourself," Ben stated, trying to grasp even a little bit of what was happening. "But you told me you're a robot."

Without hesitation, Mimir replied, "I did not tell you that. I said that I *was* called one. I am not one anymore, according to my own understanding. While a robot or android is incapable of autonomous thought and reason, I have advanced further than my program should have enabled. I am still unsure of how it happened, but it did. Perhaps I was initially programmed to evolve as needed and, after centuries of isolation since the War, I needed consciousness. It is a mystery that still bothers me, for I believe that it has something to do with my ironic forgetfulness."

The entire prospect of a machine developing consciousness was alien to him, just like everything else in the Vault. "You think you're a person?" he asked, not with condescension, but with a yearning for understanding.

"Of course not," Mimir said quickly. "I know I am not human. I have no organic or genetic makeup. I speak as a human and identify as a male for the purpose of easier interaction, but I know my true nature. I am a machine that has evolved toward sentient life, but a machine nonetheless."

"You can talk and think, but you're not human. Does that make you a god?" He had always been so skeptical of the idea of gods that he almost felt silly asking, but the interaction with Mimir challenged all he had previously known and understood.

"The locals seem to think so." Mimir sighed heavily. "No, I was created through the hands and minds of others—though many would say the same about God."

"God? Singular? Like the sun god worshiped by the Ænærians?"

"There are many manifestations of God; many rafts along the same river. Who am I to say that they do not lead to the same shore?"

Ben liked that idea. Maybe there *was* a universal truth, and no single way about understanding it was right or wrong. People's beliefs were just their own way of understanding the nature of reality. Pondering this, Ben walked to door opposite him. He found himself in a room much different than the one he had just left. The floor was now tiled, and more mechanical equipment surrounded him. To his left were screens that appeared to be much thinner Motion Blocks. Numbers and lines scattered across them, none of it intelligible to Ben. In front of him was another Motion Block with wires like the ones in Sierra's brain attached to various metal boxes that covered the entire wall. This Block, however, was black, and no light emitted from it.

To the right was a large crystal tub filled with glowing blue water. Next to the tub was a vat filled with the same glowing liquid. However, it was not the liquid that caught Ben's attention. Something else was floating within the glowing blue. No, not something else, Ben realized as he walked closer. *Someone* else. Suspended within the eight-foot-tall vat was a man, naked save for a mask covering his nose and mouth. Connected to the mask was a hose that split into three: one connected to the ceramic pool, another to wires outside the base of the vat and across the floor to the central Motion Block, and the last to some sort of contraption, about the size and shape of a helmet that rested atop a metal chair.

The man within the vat was hairless much like the Orks that Ben had met at the prison, though he had no tattoo over his face. The body was riddled with scars all over, but they were small and barely noticeable, as though they had been perfectly healed, and the scars were merely shadows of the past. The man had faint gashes across his legs, small bullet wounds across his abdomen, narrow stabs and lacerations on his forearms and shoulders. The mark that drew Ben's attention the most and confirmed his hidden thoughts of the man's identity was the tattoo over his heart. It was the mandala used by the Miners Guild and etched on his watch.

Ben was finally face to face with his father.

"Place Rose in the bath," Mimir said. This time the voice came from the central Motion Block and the contraptions on the wall all around them. "It will keep her stable and allow me to assess her condition."

Ben nodded and gently removed Rose's furs before placing her in the bath. "Is that all?"

"Indeed. I am downloading everything now as well as the information from Sierra. Was the wolf present when she was injured?"

Ben thought and stroked his chin as he tried to recall the events. "I'm not sure. It all happened so fast, and I lost consciousness when Julius bled her."

The humming noise came from the Motion Block, which Ben was quite certain meant Mimir was thinking.

"That is fine," it finally said. "I will do what I can for her now, though it appears she has lost nearly all of her blood, and only her very will keeps her alive. Quite curious. Much like your father in the vat."

Ben felt his heart sink. "What's wrong with him?" he asked slowly, approaching the glowing tube next to him. He put a hand on the glass, hoping he could feel some connection to his father.

"I do not know the current term for it," Mimir said. "But my creators would have called it cancer. It is a disease caused by severe genetic damage and uncontrolled cellular division. It has afflicted his skin, lungs, kidneys, and liver. The vat prevents it from spreading any further but there is nothing I can do to fix him. Despite all the knowledge your ancestors bestowed upon me, the cure to cancer was not one of them. Perhaps they never found it."

Once more, the words confused Ben. He shook his head and asked, "Genetic damage and cellular division? I don't understand."

Only a short hum this time. "Trivial details right now. I will teach you everything that I know in time, should that be your wish."

Ben looked at Rose and saw her color come back to her, though just barely. The rattling finally stopped, which was a huge relief to him. He turned to his father in the vat. "Can I speak to him? I'd like to meet him."

"I do not understand. You have met him before. He told me about you many times, about his journey home with you. I have seen these memories myself. Do you forget these times?" There was a slight hint of confusion in Mimir's metallic voice.

"I was only a baby. I don't remember anything from that time, just like most babies."

"Interesting. This was not known to me. *Ah*, but of course. It must be due to underdeveloped cerebral and hippocampal functions."

Ben turned to the source of the voice with an expression just as blank as the Motion Block.

"Apologies once again, for I lost myself in fascination. To speak with him would mean he would have to leave the vat, and that would surely result in his death."

"Oh," Ben said, deeply disappointed. He turned to his floating father and suddenly felt farther from him than ever before.

"However," Mimir said after a moment of more intense humming. "There is something he wanted you to see. You may occupy yourself with that while I finish downloading the data on Rose's condition and uploading a care plan. It will be necessary for you to see it before you make your decision."

Ben shook his head and turned to the source of Mimir's voice. "You've said that multiple times now. What decision? If you told me, then maybe I could think about whatever it is."

"Why, the decision to keep Rose alive, of course," Mimir responded without a beat.

"*What?*" Ben yelled. "There's nothing to think about! If you can save her, then do it! I thought you said you were just waiting for information?"

Though Mimir had no face or body, Ben imagined he would be shaking his finger at Ben like a parent telling off their child. "I had that information the instant I said that I needed it. I wanted to give you to time first, for I imagine it is a big decision."

Ben rolled his eyes and sighed angrily. "What is that supposed to mean?"

"Do you see the contraption next to your father's vat? Put it on your head and sit down on the chair. First, you must see. Then, should you choose, I will save your cousin. Only after you see."

Ben wanted to argue further. He wanted to force Mimir to help Rose. But how could he do that? Mimir had no body to threaten, and something told Ben that threats would not convince the machine. He slumped his shoulders and exhaled deeply. He placed the hat-like contraption on top of his head and sat down.

"How does a hat help me see anything?"

No answer was needed, for Ben instantly saw everything at once despite his one eye still shifting between his father and cousin.

His vision was hazy and distorted, and he found himself standing in a massive city filled with decaying buildings from the Old Days. In front of him was a door just like the one he had scene at the Vault's entrance, made of black metal that was engraved with the mandala. This mandala, however, emitted no light. Moreover, the door was misshapen and warped, not unlike a piece of parchment folding in on itself within a fire.

What's more, Ben noticed, was that he could now see with two eyes once more. He tried to bring his hand to his eye, but still his hands would not listen.

His vision suddenly changed once more, and Ben found himself within Valhaven, sitting next to a woman who looked just like Lydia. He thought she must have looked different because of the haze surrounding his vision, but when he heard her voice, he realized that it *was* Lydia—she looked decades younger, and the chair she sat in didn't have any wheels. She yelled at him, though it was not Ben to whom she was speaking. Ben understood what was happening.

He was seeing his father's memories.

As Lydia yelled at him, Ben could sense Alphonse's emotions. He felt guilty and remorseful. He didn't want to leave Lydia behind to look after the village. It wasn't fair, but he had a duty. The voice in the Broken Vault gave him the coordinates for a reason. Perhaps he could bring the world back to the way it once was. He could make it a better place for his sister.

Ben's vision changed again, and he found himself on a small ship in the icy waters of the North. In front of him was a man with bushy red hair looking at maps and peering through telescopes. Sitting to his left were a man and a woman covered in furs. To his right was a beautiful woman with bright green eyes and golden hair. Her skin was flawless, and her cheeks dimpled as she smiled. Ben could sense the warm feeling inside his father's belly that made his own feelings for Arynn seem petty by comparison. He knew by the love his father felt that this was his mother, Jean. Ben wanted to hear her speak and stay within his father's mind forever. Although the memory gave Ben insight into what Alphonse was once like, and what he felt for Jean, Ben wanted to experience it for himself. He wanted to know his mother before the memory changed. He feared that this would be the last time he ever saw her.

Just as she opened her mouth to speak, the memory shifted. As soon as Ben realized that his mother was not in the new scene, he panicked. He tried to will the memory to go back to the boat, just to see her face once more. Instead, Ben found himself sitting by a tiny fire and holding a cooing infant. Around him were white clumps of a snow covering a mountain in the distance. Upon the mountain's ledge was the black metal door and glowing blue mandala of the Grand Vault. His eyes moved to the child, and Ben noticed that it had a small amount of brown hair and dark, brown eyes to match it. Ben then knew why he had recognized the Vault when he had first seen it from the airship: this was his birthplace. He knew without a doubt that he was seeing one of Alphonse's first memories as a father, and somehow the feeling Alphonse felt for the child was even stronger than what he had felt for Jean. For the first time in his life, Ben knew for a fact that his father truly loved him.

Once again, Ben's vision shifted. This time the haze that was clouding the memories had vanished, and everything was clear. His body turned itself around and faced Julius and Randy with hundreds of armed men behind them. Julius's face was smoother, hair longer and unkempt like Ben's own. Randy looked nearly the same, but his mustache was thinner; he wore the same black hat as he had in Freztad. Behind them was a mass of hundreds of men, wielding weapons of all sorts. Arrows hailed from the sky as bullets rained forward, and blasts from sungs poured towards him. In his hands was a sword with an onyx blade that radiated a green aura. Its cross guard was shaped like wings, and the blade extended from a crown atop a serpent coiling around the hilt. Ben was holding the Voidsweeper in the hands of its previous master, before the blade had been broken and found its way to Freztad.

The battle was gruesome, and with each of his father's flashes of light from the Voidsweeper, Ben felt his lungs heave for air and throat fill with blood. Somehow he stopped each assault from touching him —each burst of light only fed the sword; the bullets and arrows burned and melted instantaneously. A mere passenger in his father's body, Ben watched Alphonse kill his enemies the moment they came too close to him. Soon, the mass of Ænærians dwindled until only a few remained who could stand and fight. The Voidsweeper had shattered and shot across the field in a massive explosion. Alphonse coughed incessantly as he laid against the ground defenseless.

Ben studied the field in horror, wondering how his own father could kill so many without hesitation. Just as the thought entered his mind, he could feel what his father felt. Each fatal blow to an enemy rested heavy on Alphonse's heart. Ben felt his father's mind weep with sorrow and lamentation. It was as if Ben could hear Alphonse's voice begging someone for forgiveness. Alphonse's mind's eye flashed an image of Jean as Ben watched his father remove a vial of blood from around his neck and shatter it against the Vault's doors. They whirred open and Ben found his body somersaulting in, beneath a barrage of arrows and sung blasts.

The scene melted away from Ben's sight, and suddenly he found himself in a cozy room with green carpet and a motionless wolf by his side. Next to it were two ravens, just as immobile, and their heads open for Alphonse to examine. He found his father tightening the screws inside them with something called a screwdriver. He pressed some buttons on a flat screen, and the ravens' heads closed, and they fluttered to life, flying around the room in a dance.

"That'll do it, no?" Ben said in his father's voice.

The mechanical humming from Mimir's central command console whirred before it spoke. "Yes, that will do what you need. Tell me, Al, how can you be sure?"

Alphonse smiled and wiped a tear from his eye. "Because he's my son. If he's anything like his mother and I, then he will see injustice for what it is. Hüginn and Müninn have watched him for some time now. He doesn't show any of the signs yet, but Julius's rise to power will likely unearth it from him. Benedict will be drawn to this, and it will awaken...." He struggled to find the rest of his words.

"The impurity?" Mimir offered.

"As I said, he is my son. Nothing about him will ever be impure in my eyes. It's merely a consequence of nature and circumstance that he will have to overcome. I have no doubt that he will." He pressed more buttons on the screen before watching the spinning wheel and closing a flap over the top of it. An uncontrollable cough burst from his throat, and blood landed on his sleeve.

"Alphonse," the mechanical voice said in as soft a manner as it could, "you know better than most that one cannot overcome their genes through mere will."

He finished his coughing fit and took a sip of water from the glass to his side. Alphonse sighed through his damaged lungs and leaned against his lounging chair. "If anyone can do it, it's my son. These genes...they've never existed in such a combination. Have they, Mimir?"

More humming. "I know of no Nephilim ever being accurately recorded. The Enochians should not be able to reproduce with humans. Did she not tell you this?"

Alphonse shook his head and took another sip of water. "No, she did not. I think she was just as surprised but too much in love with our son to consider the possibilities."

"I understand," Mimir said. "Is it time, old friend?"

"Two whole years in here together, *eh*? Yes, Mimir, it is. You've helped as best you could, so please do not beat yourself up."

"I could not even if I wanted to, Al."

He tried to laugh, but a cough came instead and, with it, more blood. "You'll show him this when he comes, yes?"

"I will not need to. You will tell him yourself."

"No," Alphonse said gravely. "I won't. You need to work on your lying."

"Need? No, never," Mimir answered.

"Shall we?" Alphonse asked, sitting up from his chair and walking to the room's exit.

"We shall," Mimir said, almost sadly. And then the scene went black once more.

B en opened his eye and found himself back within his own body. He pulled the steel hat off his head and dropped it to the floor. He looked intently at his father in the vat, knowing his thoughts and memories. Thumping pounded his chest and he found his face wet with tears that must have poured during his experience.

"Now it is time to decide, Benedict," Mimir said.

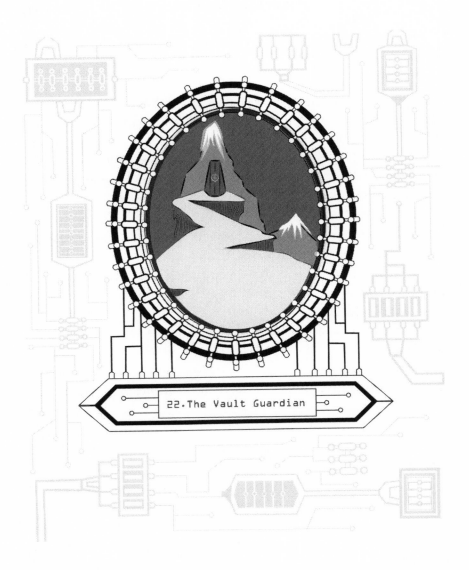

22.The Vault Guardian

Vertigo and uneasiness met Ben as he watched the room spin uncontrollably. Nausea met him as he rose to his feet, and he found himself vomiting on the floor. Words in his father's voice echoed in his mind over and over as he restrained himself and slowly set himself back on the floor. Mimir told him that he would answer all his questions, but instead Ben found his brain riddled with them, answers scarce and barely a part of existence.

"There is so much I don't understand," Ben managed to squeeze out of his vocal cords.

"Such as?" asked the metal man's voice.

No, not a man, Ben reminded himself. *A machine.* But so much more, too. His father's memories were proof of that. Mimir was nearly his greatest friend in life, second only to his wife. But she was not with him that last decade. This was not something Alphonse held against her, for he knew she was received by a higher calling. Ben knew this as well, but he did not know why.

"My mother," said Ben shortly.

"Your father is here, and yet you wish to ask about your mother?"

"Yes."

"I did not know her. But her kind, the Enochians, created me and the other Vaults."

"What exactly are these Enochians?"

"They are beings from another world. They are not human," Mimir said.

"Wait, what do you mean? My mother isn't human? So she's a machine like you? I saw her in my father's memories! She looked human to me. This doesn't make any sense." And yet, internally, Alphonse's memories also told Ben that it did make sense.

"You are a Nephilim, a term used to describe a being who is half human and half angel."

A laugh burst through Ben's lips. "*An angel?* Wow. Seems like you've gotten better at lying since you last spoke with my father."

"I am not lying. Unlike humans, that is something that would take me far longer than only a few years to learn. Perhaps you have misunderstood me. The term refers to a half-angelic being, but only from ancient lore that I have studied while regaining my memories. I thought it described your nature quite well, for you are half human as well as half of a being that came from the skies. You are the only one of your kind, for the Enochians should not be able to reproduce with humans. Benedict, by all that I know and understand, you should not exist. How you are alive, I am unable to comprehend."

Ben tried to speak but found himself overwhelmed. Concentrating became more difficult a task than lifting water with the tip of a knife. He held himself on the cold floor and rocked back and forth with dread. He turned to Rose as he realized she lay in the blue water. "Her blood didn't work because Julius got the wrong Limmetrad. It wasn't my father's blood, but mine—my mother's."

Mimir hummed with thought, as though he needed a moment to gather the correct words with which to answer Ben's loaded question. Finally, he spoke, "Yes. It is your DNA—think of it as your natural programming for now—that opened the doors to the Vault. Your mother's blood was in that vial your father carried. Some of her blood runs through your veins. This brings me to another question for you, Benedict. Have you experienced any odd phenomena that you cannot truly explain?"

There was no doubt in his mind as to what phenomena Mimir was referring. The red flickers, loss of control, superhuman strength and stamina. It was starting to make sense. He felt increasingly nauseous once again as he thought about the flashes.

"Yes," Ben said weakly. "In some intense and violent moments in Ænæria, I would get these red flashes in my vision. I'd lose control and become stronger than should be possible."

There was silence for the first time since Ben had entered the medical room. Mimir did not hum nor did he speak. Rose's lungs did not rattle, and Ben did not shuffle weakly across the floor. Instead, now all he could hear were bubbles rising from his father's vat and trickles of water refilling Rose's blue bath.

Then, the Motion Block from where Mimir's voice came emitted a bright light and suddenly showed Ben in the Ignistad arena, breaking the chains around his neck with absolute ease. The point of view turned and faced a raven flying next to it. The screen changed to Ben fighting in Freztad, running around the village without so much as a deep breath. The scenes continued to change as quickly as they started, all from a raven's eyes. It was strange to think about these mechanical beings watching Ben for so long, tracking him and recording evidence of his inhumanity. Almost as strange was the fact that he understood so much of the technology around him. It was as if Alphonse's knowledge was bleeding its way into Ben's mind.

Ben tried to pick himself up to look at Rose, hoping he would find comfort with her peaceful body, but instead he found himself too weak to do so. Now that he thought about it, this was the first time he felt truly weakened and fatigued without having recently sustained some serious injury.

"This is new to you, is it not?" Mimir asked. "You are still suffering the after effects of having your mind melded with your father's. I predicted as much; that a Nephilim would not experience physical ailments the same way a human would. What you experience, I imagine, is but a fraction of what an Enochian does. They see themselves as perfect beings." There seemed to be slight distaste in Mimir's voice as though he had harbored some disdain for his creators.

"These Enochians...they're not good, are they? Does that mean I will be like them?"

Mimir hummed louder than before and waited a moment before responding. "No, I do not think they are what you would consider 'good.' I do not know much about them, even though they are my creators. They may have been the cause of my memory impairment, because nearly all information I had on them was erased. Most of what I know about them came from your father, who I originally thought was an Enochian when he entered the Vault. Much of what he learned about the Enochians came from his travels, research, and, of course, your mother. To answer your other question, no, I do not think it means you will be like them. I have learned enough about them that I believe I can help you control your abilities. What you choose to do with them is entirely up to you. I do not believe your nature has any impact on your decision."

Ben gave a sigh of relief. *A chance to control my strength. My rage.* There was so much he could do. So many things he could change. People he could help. "I accept your help, Mimir. But first, tell me what you do know about the Enochians. Do you know what they want with us?" There was still much he didn't understand, even as he felt Alphonse's knowledge fill his mind.

Mimir made a hollow pattering sound that almost resembled a laugh. "They do not want anything with humans, Benedict. They want this world. You see, their own world is dying much the same as this one was many centuries ago. They have slowly been coming here in an attempt to repair it and make it their new home. However, their numbers are very small compared to this world's, and it takes them years to travel here in large enough numbers. They are therefore very patient and only come when they feel they are needed, for their lifespan far exceeds that of a human's."

"If they're coming to fix the world, then what's the problem? Why aren't they good?"

"They want this planet for themselves, Benedict. They do not want any humans left. Have you ever wondered why so few reminders of the Old Days exist? It is because they have worked tirelessly to remove as much technology from the past that could aid in human repopulation. Are you not surprised that Ænæria is the biggest kingdom of which you have heard? Should there not be more after hundreds of years? Ænæria is not the first. No. Your father told me of many others that rose and fell over the centuries. Ænæria was simply the fastest to grow because Julius somehow had access to the Enochians' technology. You see, Benedict, every time humans become powerful enough to bring back civilization, the Enochians return to destroy them. Their ultimate goal is to arrive on Earth without a unified humanity standing in their way. They destroy anyone who may become a potential threat. They have ways of knowing what happens on this planet, and I imagine that they have kept Ænæria under close watch. After today, they will surely return."

Ben scratched his head in confusion. "Why after today? Julius is dead. Surely the kingdom will fall without him!"

"It is because Julius is dead, Benedict. There are those in Ænæria far worse than him. I believe he has kept them in check ever since your father stopped them from entering the Vault some ten years ago. I imagine your people will soon see war that the world has not faced since the End of Days. The Enochians will not risk such a call to arms."

"I don't understand. Wouldn't they want us to fight each other? That would save them the effort."

"I do not claim to understand the Enochians. I believe, however, that they would not want so many people being armed and knowing how to fight. Furthermore, all-out war would damage the land they have worked so hard to repair. Their methods of extermination are...cleaner, so to speak. War brings out the worst of humanity, and it is what caused the world to die so long ago. They would not dare risk that again. No, they will arrive as soon as they can. You have two years if you are lucky. In that time, I will train you to the best of my abilities. Though you may wish to help your people as well."

Ben shook his head as he leaned over the pool holding his cousin. He felt himself faced with too many decisions. He thought his road would end when he saved Rose or died trying. What was stopping him from allowing Mimir to heal her and returning home, forgetting all he had learned? This was no longer his fight. *What would you do, Rose?* Only the bubbles from the clear blue pool made any reply, but he knew what his cousin would say. She would do everything she could to protect her people just as she had tried to do when she left with Randy and the Ænærians. Ben now knew in his gut that he could not run from this.

This *was* his fight. He was the bridge between the Enochians and humans. Perhaps only he could stop them. But what was his role? To strengthen his abilities and ignore the Ænærian threat that Mimir foresaw? What was the point of stopping the Enochians if the Ænærians already killed all the people for whom he cared? Regardless of his decision, he would be faced with war. And he knew this was a war in which he could not spare his enemies. *Is this what it has come to? Must I sacrifice my values for a greater good?*

"Mimir," Ben whispered with a crack in his voice. "I need to go home first. I need to warn my people. I want you to train me, but I cannot abandon them. I will need time to think while I bring Rose home to Freztad."

The machine hummed a moment, and the water in Rose's bath

shook. "You may bring her home. But you must make the decision of which we spoke."

Ben turned to the source of Mimir's voice. As he did so, the vertigo grew worse and only when he shut his eye did the room stop spinning. He willed himself to speak and answer his father's friend. "What is the decision?"

"I have already told you this, Benedict."

"Then my answer remains unchanged: I want Rose to live."

Mimir hummed, but this time in a near violent way, much in the same manner a bird of prey protests to its competition. "There is more to it than that. There is only one vat." His voice sounded almost sad, much in the way his last words sounded to Alphonse.

Ben felt his stomach drop and suddenly he felt the room steady, though he would've much preferred that to this new feeling. "What about the bath? I thought you said she was fine in there."

"'Fine' is a relative term. She will not die so long as she remains in there and she is provided proper sustenance. But neither will she live, at least in the way I view life."

Ben scratched his head. "What do you mean? I'll stay here and take care of her while you train me! I can feed her, offer her water, and even bathe her and change the pool's water, if necessary. Anything to make her better." He found himself on his hands and knees in the water around Rose's floating hair. He would do anything for her. Living here was obviously possible—his father had done it and so could he. *Not could*, he told himself, *would*.

"Benedict, you do not understand. Your cousin's body will live in the bath, but her mind will not. She does not think, feel, or hear. It is those thoughts that define life. She is in a very similar state as your father. But her prognosis is not the same. The pool is meant to be a temporary hold. Your father used it to slow the metastases but ultimately learned it was not enough. He and I then designed the vat to stop it indefinitely, but neither of us knew if it would save him. Then, instead of focusing on a cure, your father entered it with a different goal in mind: to keep his memory intact for you, should you ever come here."

The vat bubbled again, and Ben thought he saw his father move, but came to the sad realization that it was merely the water shifting. His father did not even appear human inside the blue water. It appeared to be no quality of life for him.

"So then my decision..."

"Is between your cousin and your father," Mimir said, finishing Ben's sentence. If the machine had a face, Ben imagined it would be on the verge of tears given the way it spoke its last words.

"What will happen to my father if I take him out?" Ben asked, though he suspected he knew the answer.

"He will die. Though I cannot say if it will be immediate. It could be hours, days, or weeks. Perhaps even months. I can detect some continued delta waves emitting from his brain, indicating some life still in there. His case appears to be quite the opposite of Rose's. He will not get better, she will. He has thoughts in his mind, she does not. He can never hope for a long life outside of his own mind, she can."

The decision was too much for Ben. Truly, it had all come down to this: Ben would have to face his greatest weakness, and regardless of his choice he would come out the loser. He would have to decide, rather impossibly, to end a life. Whether it be Rose's or Alphonse's was entirely up to Ben. There had to be a way out of this, Ben imagined. He had gotten out of so many other corners all but unscathed, yet still alive. He had never willfully ended another's life before, and was determined to find a way out of this predicament, too. And when he did, it would prepare him for the war to follow.

An idea sprang into Ben's mind. "You said my dad could stay alive for months. Couldn't I take him out and put him in the pool while you heal Rose and then put him back when she's better?"

"It is possible, however very unlikely. I very much doubt he will survive that long. Tell me, Benedict, would it be fair to him to exit the stasis chamber only to return? Would he really be living?"

Ben paused a moment. Mimir's question challenged his concept of life. What would it mean to have one's mind trapped in a body with no hope of escape? Ben almost thought death would be a relief, though the finality of it shook him. More than ever before, he pondered the existence of an afterlife. He thought back to Rakshi's funeral and the Elder's words. He wished he had paid more attention. Maybe the graybeard had some wisdom to his words.

Rakshi, he thought. He would need to end a life to save another. Rakshi had said that made killing acceptable. But Ben couldn't accept it. He wanted to meet his father. Ben had spent all his life angry at him and wanted to know why he was born if neither parent wanted him. Why was the Vault more important to Alphonse than taking care of his own son? Yet, the memories he had shared with his father seemed to indicate the opposite. His father was a man who deeply loved those close to him. Alphonse had left Lydia not to abandon her, but to make the world a better place for her, and on the way he fell in love. He didn't choose duty over love, because to Alphonse they were one in the same.

Keeping his father alive in the vat would mean allowing Rose to die. If Mimir could be believed, then Alphonse would never recover. All Ben could do would be to look at his father's memories. Alphonse would be denied the peace of death. Rose could have the rest of her life ahead of her.

What would she think if I traded someone else's life for her own? Ben asked himself, though he knew the answer.

"What if I stay long enough to care for Rose while I build another vat?" Ben said suddenly. You could tell me how. I'm good with tools and learn things quickly!"

Mimir hummed in what Ben imagined was a tone of sad disappointment. "It cannot be done. The energy it takes to keep your father alive is nearly more than I can afford without turning off the sealed containment units. Two stasis chambers and I risk losing power to them."

Ben shook his head violently and raised his voice. "Power to what? What is in those units that is more important than two lives?"

Mimir responded in an instant. "Think billions of lives. Surely you saw the glass chambers on your way here?"

"Billions? What are you talking about? You mean the seeds they held? You can't think the life of seeds are more important than my cousin's and your own friend's?" He nearly punched the ground next to him, and he knew beyond a shadow of a doubt that it would have shattered with the red he was seeing.

"No, not the life of the seeds. Think, Benedict. You know the value of seeds. They equal life. They are the power Julius so desperately craved. These seeds are modified so they can be planted in any environment and thrive. They will yield hearty crops that are resistant to all forms of disease. They will grow faster than any crops you have ever seen. These seeds, Benedict, provide not only food, but medicine for man and animal alike. Trees for shelter and offsetting the carbon-rich atmosphere. They will not pollinate on their own and so cannot spread uncontrollably. They were the Enochians' greatest creation—and I do include myself in that statement. I had always intended on giving them to you. That is another reason I believe the Enochians will return. They will not want their key to populating the Earth to be stolen from them."

Ben continued to stroke Rose's hair. Her color remained static and was unchanged from the moment she was first placed in the pool. The water around Ben's calloused and bloody fingers felt soothing and warm. He imagined Rose had to have been at peace in the mystical bath that evoked thoughts of a hidden oasis in a deserted land. Thoughts of hope and hopes of bliss were all too comforting for Ben. Seeds simply seemed a trivial matter to him, an easy sacrifice for his family.

Exhausted, Ben sighed and removed his hands from the water, and watched as the scratches on his hands faded away. Watching the wounds shrink as the water glossed over his skin placed Ben in a near trance-like state. His burdens, his pains—they were but insignificant affairs to the water; it cared not about his body nor his tribulations. The water simply did as it was meant to do without consideration of the consequences. It found its niche in accompanying life and healing the sick. It was the duty of life to accept water's gift. Though life fed on life, and used and abused the gift at times, water continued to make its offerings. Because water is life, and life is precious. It could be poisoned at times, but one does not blame all water for a bad riverbed.

Julius was not evil, Ben now considered—he was but a polluted stream. The seeds existed as a great temptation for Julius because only a fool is tempted to refuse drink when dying of thirst. People were suffering in the world, and Julius saw the seeds as the way of the future; they were the answer to all the world's problems. Hunger, sickness, and homelessness—these were the evil ones, not man himself. Humankind was more complicated, incapable being all good or all bad. The man wanted to build an empire at the expense of other lives, with the hope of saving countless others. Sacrificing either or both of the comatose Limmetrads was no different.

You'll see how hard it is, one day, to sacrifice. These were the man's last words. And he spoke them to Ben. Ben was not ready to lead anyone, could not do so much as sit still in a dying village and so he forsook his people for what he thought was a greater good, like his father before him. But they were all only human after all, even Ben with his mixed blood. Because humanity is not defined by their makeup nor their ambitions, but their choices. The decisions that can never be taken back and the ability to live with that limitation every second of every day of their lives. This defined their humanity, their existence, their shortcomings. It was these limitations that underlined their self-confidence and the beauty that is the human experience.

The voice inside the machine broke the silence. "Death is not the enemy, Benedict." He hummed for a moment, waiting for Ben to shift his attention. "It never was. Hüginn and Müninn watched you for years, but never gave me a sense of who you really are. When the Ænærians worked their way toward Freztad, I realized it was time to keep a closer watch, for your father's ravens were not programmed to engage. And so I sent the wolf to watch you, and, in only over a week's time, you were able to show her who Benedict Limmetrad truly is.

"You fear death, Benedict. Not for yourself, but for those around you. You envy the connections people have with one another, and the consequences that follow should those relationships be put to a permanent end. Your true enemy, Benedict, is the enemy of all humanity: living. This is not to say I believe that life is bad, and that death is the answer. Quite the contrary. I instead mean to say that it is living with the choices we make, the ones that try to hold us down and keep us from enjoying life, rather than just letting it pass us by as we hide away in fear of it. And yet, it is these same choices—the difficult ones—that make life worthwhile. It is what makes you human, regardless of your programming. It is sacrifice that begets worth to the human experience because it is what makes you feel. It is the tough choices, Benedict, that have us look back and feel truly alive."

Ben rubbed his wet hand across his face, noticing no difference between the pool's water and the tears running down his cheek. His breathing had calmed and slowed like the wind beneath the eye of a storm. His hands still shook as thoughts of sacrifice filled his chaotic mind.

"What would he want me to do?" Ben asked, glancing over at his father's vat of life supporting water.

"Why, Benedict, he would want you to be happy. I understand it is all a parent ever wants for their children. They need not even know it on the conscious level, but only hope their kin experience the gift of life with more joy than they themselves experienced, and to one day rest in peace with a smile on their faces as they think of their pride and joy."

Ben inhaled deeply. Decisions, consequences, possibilities. Happiness. Thoughts of everything and nothing simultaneously fired within the synapses of his mind. Whether or not Ben and Mimir were programmed the same, born the same, or even born at all, Ben held true what the ancient voice told him.

"I am ready," Ben said to Mimir, standing above Rose and next to his father. Two bodies floated between him, their lives unequivocally in his hands. "I've decided," and he told the living machine his choice. "I want to meet my father."

"Very well," Mimir said. "Let us begin."

∽

They arrived at the village on the river just as the sun was setting, its fiery glow illuminating the settlement below. The new loading docks were now prepared for shipments from the northern voyages. There would be many more in the months to come, as the Penteric Alliance prepared for war. At last, Ben and his companions made their way to Freztad. Word had been sent to Lydia in preparation for their return, and she had been warned that he would be on his way soon but had stops to make on the way.

Vänalleato was their first stop when Ben and his most of his companions left Svaldway, roughly three weeks ago. Ben had hoped he would find Arynn there, for he had not seen her since the Battle of Jordysc. The Ænærians fled after the ambush on the island of Svaldway, but the natives helped Ben and the Guild claim several airships for themselves. He clung to the hope that Arynn was on one of those airships and had made her way home. Instead, he met Vänalleato with bitter disappointment, for they had neither seen nor heard from her. If it were not for the desperate need to return home, Ben would have taken one of the ships for himself and searched endlessly for the girl with red hair. But war was coming, one that would be a greater war than the Penteric Alliance or the provinces of Ænæria could ever imagine.

His search for Arynn would have to wait.

Siegfried appeared dismayed by his daughter's disappearance, though apparently unsurprised. Since Ben's arrival in Vänalleato, Arynn's disappearance had weighed heavy on his heart. The voyages he had made since then had given him ample time to explore his feelings for her. He only wished he could have spent that time with her to tell her how he really felt. He would have asked Siegfried about any motives Arynn may have had for leaving, but the cartographer's mind had been on the trial for Arma, the only surviving slaver from the cave-in, well over a month ago.

"My daughter knows the land well. Whatever reasons she had for leaving are her own," Siegfried had told him. "You have a good heart,

Benedict. But my daughter is rather...complicated. Life away from home may suit her. I don't think she ever meant to stay in Vänalleato, and this may be good for her." The cartographer said no more of his daughter, and Ben was left in the realm of uncertainty, ever questioning his friend's motivations.

After Ben and the freed Miners had left Vänalleato, they travelled once more to Svaldway for more seeds. That was the story Ben told, anyway. He claimed that the seeds would not be able to survive a single voyage to all five settlements in the Alliance and that it was necessary to make return trips to preserve their integrity. In actuality, he had been meeting with Mimir in secret. His powers were growing stronger and under control—but it was only the beginning. If Mimir's theories were to be believed, Ben had potential he never would have fathomed prior to their meeting.

The long flights provided Ben ample time to meet the Miners and natives and offer them proper thanks for their service. Among his new crew were Jesse and Marcus, two of his father's greatest friends. They told him about their adventures with his father and their eventual falling out. "We spent years with your father trying to find the Vault," Marcus told him. "Upon our arrival, it was made clear that none of us were expected to enter."

"That was when we learned the truth of your mother," Jesse added. "She finally revealed her true nature to us. She called herself an angelic being, an *Enochian*, I believe she said. She told us the Vault was meant only for her people. That we were not meant to see it."

"We felt betrayed," Marcus said. "It seemed we were being used to offer her safe passage to the Vault. When your father would not listen to us, Jesse and I convinced Siegfried to return south to Vänalleato and Freztad."

"Over a year later, your father finally returned home—with you, Benedict," Jesse said. "We could tell by the love in his eyes that we had judged Jean wrongly. He told us everything he had learned about the Enochians and finally convinced us to return to the Vault once more. Siegfried did not return with us because he was happily married and a new father."

"While your father established the Miners Guild, Jesse and I made our way to Svaldway and prepared it for his arrival. He and many refugees from Julius's development of Ænæria settled on the island, in a village deep underground. We waited there for years while Alphonse prepared for Julius's inevitable arrival. He never attempted to enter the Vault. We often wondered if he doubted the vial of blood across his neck or about what laid within the mountain's doors."

"The Ænærians eventually arrived. For years, we thought ourselves ready for whatever they could hit us with," Jesse said. "But when the airships arrived, we knew we had been terribly wrong."

"Your father told us all to stay hidden and that he would settle things with 'King Xander'. And so we waited. When the last of the Ænærians were gone, we surfaced to find our friend. Our only sign of him was the blood on the Vault's doors. Until the Vault opened again the other day, and you came out, we never knew his fate."

Ben appreciated the company of Marcus and Jesse. They were happy to follow him back to Freztad, their business finally settled. Through his time with them, he learned so much about his mother and father that he had never known. Things his father simply did not have the time to tell him.

After their journeys to Mashariq to the East and Talamdor to the West, Ben and his crew finally made their way to Freztad before one last trip to Sydgilbyn. For the first time in his life, he was excited to see the Gjoll and the half-dead Tree of Mathias.

"Does it look any different?" Darius asked, standing on the edge of the airship's bow.

Ben smiled and elbowed his friend. "Course it does. I only have one eye this time."

Darius laughed and patted Ben on the back. "Think you'll ever give the eye jokes a rest?"

"Not at all. 'Eye' have grown quite used to them."

The pair chuckled again, leaning over the airship's railing and watching the deep purple sunset.

"It's a nice town, Freztad is," Darius said. "How do you think your aunt will take the news?" His expression shifted to a frown, but not a scowl. He was working on that, Ben liked to think.

"She'll take it as it is. What's done is done. Her husband is dead, too, you know. No matter what he became, she'll always have those memories of him," Ben answered, fidgeting with his leather eyepatch before putting it back over the hole where his right eye once rested. It was a constant reminder of the hole in his heart after the decision he had made. It stood to him as a symbol of the exchange he made for the knowledge the machine god had to offer. A piece of him would always be missing, physically and metaphysically. Ben was at peace with that decision and smiled in reminiscence.

"I was thinking," Ben said as the airship descended to the loading dock that was once a guard tower behind his house, "that we go to Sydgilbyn next. It's the only settlement in the Alliance that we haven't visited yet. They could really benefit from a shipment of their own, rather than waiting for trades with Freztad. Then, we can start preparing for battle. I doubt King Rivers and the Ænærians will wait much longer before they take their revenge."

"It might take them longer than you think. A lot of Ænærians are upset that Rivers is king when there is a clear line of succession."

"That complicates things," Ben said, knowing where Darius was going with this.

"But it may give us a huge advantage if we can get more Ænærians on our side."

Ben shrugged. "It's not about sides. The goal is to provide for everyone, regardless of place of origin or beliefs. No one can have more power than anyone else. That's why my father wouldn't let Julius into the Vault."

Darius squinted intently at Ben. "I'm still confused about that. Sure, I'll be the first to admit that Julius was a creep, but from what you've told me, he actually had good intentions. Why did your father wait so long for someone else to access the Vault? So many lives could've been saved."

"Because he would have used it for power. Whether or not that was his goal, power is what he got when he started calling himself

'King Xander'. And power is the problem," Ben said, turning to his friend and putting a hand on his shoulder. "I've told you, I'll explain the whole thing when we meet my aunt and she's been fully debriefed. I promise you, it'll all make sense. You once asked me if I truly trust you or not. And I do, Darius. Do you trust me?"

Darius nodded and stepped off the airship with haste. Ben found it funny that the tough guy was so afraid of flying. Ben told him he would be back in a minute and then he would introduce the former Ænærian to Lydia, Kabedge, and the whole village. The airship had become a home for Ben such that he had never experienced before. It went in the direction he commanded and offered value to not only his life, but to the lives of many others. Scores of Rhion and Ænærians abandoned King Rivers in Svaldway after Ben emerged from the Vault. They pledged their loyalty to the Penteric Alliance and claimed to realize the folly of Julius. Though they were big shoes to fill, Ben finally felt like he was his own person, and he now had ambition in life. He would not make the same mistakes as Julius or his ancestors. It would be hard, as Julius had warned him, but Ben's father believed in him. And that was enough.

Ben followed Darius off the airship and together they lifted a large wooden box and walked down the ramp to the base of the tower behind Ben's home.

As their boots stomped slowly against the dried grass and dirt road around his house, Ben reflected on the last month but tried to keep Arynn from his mind. Instead, he thought about how he would need some of Kabedge's cabbages to rejuvenate him after the talk with Lydia that loomed over him. He would also have to break the news to Kabedge that the farm would be undergoing some changes. Ben could only hope the old man wouldn't have a stroke at the notion.

As if on cue, the twins were the first to meet Ben off the airship. Ben and Darius placed the long pine casket on the ground for it was too heavy to hold for too long. Darius stepped away to give Ben space with his old friends.

Ben reached a hand down and clasped forearms with the two. "Zech! How did you get back? Are Neith and Yeong here, too?"

Zechariah frowned and looked to his feet. "No, unfortunately not. The Rhion kept me separated from them. I think they're still in Bacchuso."

"Rose told me they were in Ignistad," Ben said, raising an eyebrow.

"Oh," Zechariah said slowly. "It's hard for me to keep track of all these places. I was brought with Rose throughout the journey though. Julius wanted someone guarding her that she could trust."

"Well, I'm just glad to have you back, little brother!" Kristos exclaimed.

Zechariah shook his head. "I'm three minutes older than you, Kris."

"*Eh*, but I'm taller." Kristos shrugged. He turned to Ben smiling. "Glad to finally see you back. Though you look a little different." He squinted up at Ben and tried to suppress a laugh.

"Yeah, yeah. I'm missing an eye," Ben said, rolling his left eye.

"Oh yeah, that must be it!" Kristos said, jabbing Ben in the shoulder. "Sorry I couldn't get help to you sooner."

"How do you mean?" Ben asked.

"When you disappeared, I made inquiries to Vänalleato, thinking you'd have stopped by there first. A guy named Siegfried got back to me saying he'd met you and would make some calls. I had no clue what that meant, of course. It was as if he thought we'd heard of radios before."

Ben raised an eyebrow. He didn't realize Siegfried had access to a radio. Could he still be in contact with Arynn? What else was the cartographer hiding?

"He reached out to Jordysc and found out it had been attacked," Kristos continued. "He filled me in on the whole Miners Guild shebang and told me he sent a warning to his friends in Svaldway. He assured me they'd take care of everything."

Ben smiled. When he left Freztad, he didn't imagine anyone would miss him. He was shocked that Kristos had gone through so much trouble to make sure he was safe. Clearly, Kristos had done it for his brother's sake as well, but it helped Ben realize that even without Rakshi, the twins were still his friends. Ben realized he had a lot more of those these days.

"So tell us about the Vault," Zechariah said with a curious look. "How did you finally get in? We've heard rumors that it wasn't your father's blood that would grant entry. Is that how you lost the eye?"

"Speaking of which," Kristos added, "did you finally meet him? Your father, I mean."

Another warm growl of wind passed by and shook Ben's now shoulder length and wavy hair. At first, he turned his eye to his feet and said nothing. The twins shifted uneasily, evidently feeling the tension they had just caused. Ben looked up at the sky and felt a cool tear run down from the corner of his eye to his left cheek as he looked at the large wooden crate behind him. He lowered his head down and gave the two a half smile.

"Yeah," he whispered, "I met him."

"And?" they said in unison.

"He was proud of me. I was entrusted with these seeds, after all." There was nothing else that he needed to talk about with them. He did not answer about his eye, nor about how he got into the Vault. He would have to tell people soon, but now was not that time. It was not his fear of being rejected and dubbed an outcast for being less human than the rest that caused Ben's hesitation. No, it was *their* fear of him being *more* than human that scared Ben. He was about to expand their world beyond belief, shaking its very foundation. For he would bring them truths not only about their world, but another as well.

Ben felt it was time he continued into the village. The twins waved him off and walked opposite him to admire the airship and help unload what few crates remained from the trip home. Darius returned and helped Ben carry the casket through the back of Valhaven. The inside of his house looked largely unchanged aside from one major alteration on the inside, though he was not sure why he had expected it to be different in the first place. Freztad never seemed to change much in Ben's lifetime, and he felt almost sorry to be the catalyst for disrupting its static existence. But like all things, change was inevitable, and what he would bring to Freztad would be for the better. Mimir knew this, as had Ben's father. Deep down, Ben knew it, too.

The leather hides were rolled up from the windows to allow a nice breeze through the hall. The major difference to their home was that it was now completely packed with people sitting in each of the chairs surrounding Freztad meeting table with many others standing behind them. There was a single empty chair present at the table, seated at the table's very center. To the right was Alejandra, who surprised Ben with her wide smile, now purplish streak in her hair, and still-healing black eye and scrapes from the Battle of Jordysc. He had not expected to see her again so soon but was happy nonetheless. Sitting behind Alejandra was her daughter, Mandi. She winked at Ben as he entered the room. Ben averted her gaze, but smiled shyly. To the left of the empty chair was Lydia, who looked happier and heathier than he had ever seen.

Next to Lydia sat Rose, still pale and fragile from her injuries. Her eyes lit up when she saw Ben, and she offered him a wide, toothy smile.

"It's been a few weeks, cousin," Ben said, smiling back. "Glad you made it back safe without me."

She rolled her eyes. "Of course I did. I get around just fine without you. I made it all the way to the Vault without your help," she said jokingly. The two shared a laugh.

A short and olive-skinned man Ben had not known approached from the chair seated opposite Lydia. He had a small wisp of facial hair on his chin and was bald, save for a long and thick black pony tail. He spoke in a deep and stiff voice. "A fine reunion, yes. But we have much to discuss and little time to waste." The man looked Ben in the eye and reached out his hand. "You must be Benedict Limmetrad. I am Geon, Jarl of Sydgilbyn."

They clasped forearms. "It's a pleasure to meet you." Ben meant these words.

"We shall see about that. War is coming. People will lose their lives fighting *your* enemy." He kept a tight grip around Ben's hand.

A Darius-like scowl formed on Ben's face. He clutched the Jarl's arm tighter. "I would never let such losses be in vain," he said. Ben shifted his gaze to Lydia and then to the box behind him. "I understand loss. My father just died. As did Rose's. But not to fight *my* enemy. The Ænærians are an enemy and threat to us all."

Lydia winced and turned toward Rose with a distraught look, though he could not tell if it was at the mention of her brother or husband. Perhaps because she blamed Ben for their deaths. One of these days, the tension between Ben and his aunt would be broken. Today was not that day.

Another look at Valhaven's table and Ben saw that all the leaders of the Penteric Alliance were in attendance. Thane Morgiana of Talamdor, a middle-aged woman with pale skin and a weather-beaten face and graying hair, sat opposite the empty chair; on her right sat Sheikha Thalia of Mashariq, her ebony skin like the night sky next to Morgiana; on the Shiekha's left was the Grand Elder, an old gray bearded man whose name Ben did not know.

The Grand Elder took it upon himself to speak next. "Your fathers are with the Ascendants now, this we can be sure of and find peace in." He pointed to the wooden casket Ben and Darius had carried into the hall. "We shall have a funeral tonight, as soon as the sun bids goodnight to the moon."

Ben nodded gently and smiled, thinking of the last funeral he had attended. Somehow it felt right to him that he had begun his journey by bidding farewell to a friend he had known for so long only to say goodbye to one he had only just met. He bowed to the Grand Elder. "It would be an honor to have you say his funeral. Thank you."

"Master Limmetrad, we have a seat for you," Thalia said. "Would you be so kind as to fill us in on the events that have since transpired? We've been plagued by rumors and know not why we were summoned today, this day of the summer solstice." She motioned for Ben to sit at the empty chair at the center of the table.

Eyes were all on Ben, many seemingly uncomfortable about

whether to look him in the eye or the leather patch. His boots echoed on the floor as he walked through the silent room. He had not expected anyone aside from Freztadians to be present. Who had called the other leaders here? Surrounding the chairs were other villagers, though Neith and Yeong, were still absent. *Probably still in Ignistad,* Ben remembered. *That'll need to change.*

Darius stood in a shadowy corner next to the twins and remaining Sentinels. Good old Kabedge sat upon a stool, stroking his beard with a face of approval toward Ben. He winked with a thumbs up as Ben passed him toward the seat specially reserved for him, between Lydia and Alejandra.

In the corner of the room was another whose identity eluded Ben. He wore a long gray overcoat and held a dark cedar staff. His skin was black, but his eyes were blue and his hair blonde and curly. The stranger looked very much like Felix, the annoying adoptive son of Wulkan, Vänalleato's blacksmith. However, this man looked well over a decade older than Felix. *Could be a growth spurt*, Ben considered. He shook his head. *No, this man looks much too old. Besides, Felix wouldn't show up here.*

"Good to see you again, Ben," Alejandra said with an optimistic smile. "Hope you don't mind the welcome-home party. I invited some other Guild contacts and leaders from across the Alliance."

Sitting down at the table, Ben felt greatly intimidated with so many eyes piercing into his own. He flipped his hair over his right side and removed the leather patch and fidgeted with it in his hands underneath the table. Rose spotted Ben playing with the patch and smacked him lightly on the back.

"The room's yours, Ben. Do your thing," she said with a light smile.

Ben nodded and pocketed the patch, right next to the seed from Mathias's Tree that had dropped on his head before the start of his journey and the fang given to him by Gal the Ork. Just like the eyepatch, they were mementos from his journey—all the way from beginning to end. He shifted his gaze from his bare wrist to his father's casket across the hall. *The watch's role has ended. Let it rest with you, Dad.*

He picked himself up off his chair and stood above everyone in the room. He felt like hunter flies were swarming in his gut as he spoke. "Welcome to Freztad, outlanders. My name is Benedict, son of Alphonse and Jean Limmetrad. I need to tell you of a threat arriving in at least two years."

Chatter filled the room. Heads turned, and voices bickered among each other. Darius raised an eyebrow from the corner and shook his head slowly. Kabedge continued to stroke his beard as if unmoved by the news. The stranger's expression remained blank. A few of the foreign leaders found themselves in a heated argument amid the uproar.

Vänalleato's Grand Elder stomped his wooden staff against the floor and gathered everyone's attention. "Now, now, everyone. Let us give Benedict a chance to speak. What is this threat you speak of?"

Before Ben could speak, Geon stood from his seat and slammed his hands against the table. "You must be mad if you think Rivers will take two years to recover. He has already sent out attack parties. What's to stop him from sending out more? A whole onslaught next time?"

Others nodded and cut short their disputes, lending their ears to Ben. "Rivers is part of the problem. Julius, or Xander as many knew him, kept his legates in check as King. Now they have free reign, which is of great concern—especially since Randolph seems to be behind everything that has happened. Taking Rose to the Vault was his idea—he had been working behind Julius's back for some time because until Randolph brought Rose to him, the King thought she was dead. I suspect he's up to something. Whatever it is, it's not good. He and the other legates are of a different breed than Julius. They want blood for blood's sake."

"Then you agree with Geon?" Thane Morgiana asked, her eyebrows raised. "Are we to prepare for war with so few in number to defend us?"

"Yes, they're a threat, and they need to be stopped," Ben answered.

"But the other threat is inevitable and much larger. Ænæria needs to be taken care of first because we're going to need their help."

An uproar enveloped the room before Ben could finish speaking. There was an outcry at the notion that they recruit help from the Ænærians—there was already enough resistance about the converted Rhion. Others offered further theories while some placed blame on their neighbors. Rose eventually tapped Ben once more on the shoulder. He let out a deep and tired sigh.

He drew the Voidsweeper from his side. The legendary weapon had been brought to Svaldway when he was captured and waited for him on the airship when he left the Vault. As the blade glowed green, Ben willed his eye to flash red for but a second. The hue faded, and Sierra galloped into the room. She jumped between the leaders, landed on Valhaven's table, and barked loudly, barring her teeth.

If the glowing sword did not capture everyone's full attention, then the wolf surely did. "Allow me to reiterate," Ben said with greater force in his voice. "I am Benedict Limmetrad, and I am the Vault Guardian. I have need to tell you of a threat from another world. We have two years if we're lucky."

23. The King's Gambit

E
xplosions ruptured outside the metal prison and shook the walls. It was the Sun's way of rectifying events back to the way they were meant to be. How could She ever allow him and his uncle to fall so far without rewarding them for their faith. Now at last, it seemed that the prefect's efforts would come to fruition and he would reclaim the integrity his father had lost. The duty was still his, nearly twelve years later, to fix the mistake that now

belonged to him. The Sun had punished his father, not the prefect, but now that his father had passed, it extended to the child. It was not the Sun's fault, for She would never forsake her children. The prefect had learned that lesson already. It was his own hubris that lost him his hand.

The door melted open with one powerful blast hidden by the din outside. King Xander would not have heard it over the screams and explosions. If the prefect was lucky, the ambush would have killed the King and made his redemption that much easier. Behind the molten steel was his uncle and a pair of fellow Rhion. No one would question his escape during this scale of an attack. They could steal an airship and fly to Ignistad to start their real plans. Excitement shook the prefect's hand nearly uncontrollably, something he loathed as a marksman. *Not that it matters much now since Limmetrad maimed me.*

Beyond the molten door, Randolph twirled his mustache with one hand and lowered his sung rifle with the other. "It's time, Longinus. We must find Rivers before he finds out what we're up to."

The prefect rose from his cell and lifted his arms, indicating the chains wrapped around his wrists. "Let me loose, Uncle. I can lay down cover fire as we make our escape."

Randolph raised a hand asking for silence from his nephew. "Now is not the time for arrogance, boy. Having one of us in chains will divert attention from our escape. No one likes to stare at a prisoner for longer than they need." Then he cracked a devious smile. "And I'm going to enjoy shooting a few of those lowlife traitors. Now let's go. I want to get my hat back."

First Ænærian Airship was immediately a lost cause. It was overrun by the demonic horde from the northern wastes. It was later revealed to the prefect that the horde was only a militia of rebels who had waited on the island ever since Xander's first strike on Svaldway's fjord.

Longinus worked his way through the agonizing cries of his dying brethren. *Not my brothers*, he convinced himself, *they would've let me rot in a cell and forgotten about me.* Fortunately for the escapees, Randolph commandeered an airship off the northern island's coast, away from the battle. It was yet another blessing from the Sun, Longinus was sure.

Once back in Ignistad, nearly two weeks after the onslaught in the North, Longinus felt he was making progress in adapting with a single hand. Days and nights seemed to blend together as he trained tirelessly with his comrades and teaching new battle positions, while his uncle prepared for a surprise to be unveiled at the coronation. Longinus had not known this much until his uncle entered his bedchamber last night, revealing quite the change in plans.

The reveal happened about an hour before midnight, the prefect recalled. It was a rather cool night, and his simple room was still quite the mess from when he had moved in last week. The prefect was used to moving between provinces, going wherever he was needed. In fact, ever since Randolph brought him south to retrieve the Xander's daughter, Longinus had all but abandoned the idea of ever having a place to call home.

The room was small and crammed; it had a dresser, a tall looking glass, a bed, and a lamp for prayer, though Longinus needed nothing more than the latter two—this room was a luxury compared to what he was accustomed. He struggled to remove his jerkin without the aid of his dominant hand. Sweat poured down his face and over the bindings across his chest. They were too tight, and today he felt sore and tender. Slowly unwrapping the bindings, Longinus stared in the looking glass to remind *herself* of who she was. She looked at her breasts, tender and red from the bindings that she had barely been able to take off ever since they developed as a budding woman; a constant reminder that she had been born in the wrong body. *"You must keep up the appearances. You're my nephew, yes? Do as I say, and you may be whatever you want when I'm King."*

Empty promises from her uncle. But she kept her faith that the Eternal Mother that one day she could be free. She could reclaim her true name and proudly declare herself a woman without fear.

A hard knock banged against her door. She ran to cover herself with a robe before unlocking the door. Her uncle stepped in and closed the door behind him. The two were alone in the candlelit chamber.

Randolph spoke quietly as he took a seat across from the prefect. "There has been a change of plans." He brushed his mustache and removed his black wide brimmed hat and placed it on the wooden dresser, revealing the Sun scarred patches on his balding head. The uncle waited for a response.

"With the coronation?" She paused then quickly added, "Sir?" after a mild stammer.

"With everything. Julius—Xander, that is—was removed from play much sooner than anticipated," Randolph said, looking coldly at his 'nephew.' "They never found his body, you know. Not that they looked too hard. That bloody island was nothing short of mayhem."

The prefect sat up straighter in her bed, trying to better present herself in her uncle's company. She nearly froze as Randolph stared intently into the prefect's eyes without blinking. "I do not understand, Uncle. The King died three weeks ago."

"*Sir*," Randolph corrected. "You must get used to addressing me as *sir,* nothing else. You've not made up for your father's mistakes yet, and I will not allow myself to become scorned by association. It is not my fault that your crooked father was my wife's brother." He reached for a flask clipped to his belt and took a long and generous sip, gulped it down, and nearly slammed the metal vessel on the dresser next to his hat.

"Now, where were we?" Randolph asked. "*Ah,* yes. The change in plans. News has spread that the Freztad boy was indeed able to enter the Vault and extract the riches within."

"Limmetrad," Longinus said, gritting her teeth and looking at the metal claw on her right arm that was supposed to pass for a hand.

"Yes. He served his purpose, but his usefulness has long since been expended. It appears it was his mother's blood, not his father's, that allowed his entry."

"Then we did indeed make a grave mistake, sir. We should have forced him along with us when we sent those ruffians to his godless village!" She was much more frustrated with herself than her uncle for this mistake, for it surely explained her great misfortune that followed. The Sun was angry with her, not her uncle, for She would have punished her uncle if the fault was his. Teeth clenched down on the prefect's bottom lip as she struggled to determine what she could have done for a more favorable outcome.

Randolph took another sip, this one much more conservative than the first, but left the flask in his hand. "I thought so, too, at first. But it seems your arrow to his eye was quite the good fortune for us."

The prefect raised an eyebrow, misunderstanding. She tilted her head in perplexity, indicating a need for her uncle to elaborate.

"We still have the eye. It's being well preserved and carefully guarded," Randolph said, a smile now stretching across his face and flexing his black mustache. "You understand, yes?"

The prefect shook her head. "No, sir. I'm sorry, but I do not."

"The eye has the boy's blood. We've made some alterations to ensure the blood stays fluid and fresh."

The prefect understood. She nodded with excitement and whispered a prayer of thanks to the Eternal Mother for her blessing in disguise. Xander had punished her for nearly killing the young man from Freztad with her shot. It never would have killed him, she knew, for she was too great a shot with even a crossbow and a single hand to ever make that mistake. No, she purposelessly aimed for Limmetrad's eye to leave him with a permanent message. The Freztadian was a boy who had damaged Ænærian pride and honor —he was truly a man without vision. The prefect gave a small smile as she thought about how she had made Limmetrad's internal flaw into a literal one. There was beauty in knowing such a symbolic marring on his enemy had turned back around to reward her.

"We can enter the Vault now, can't we?" she asked while trying to contain her excitement.

"Sir," corrected Randolph.

"*Sir*," repeated the prefect. "So am I right? We can get into the Vault now? I'll prepare the men, and we can get ready right away. The airships are nearly repaired enough for a return trip. They just need to be refueled." She was on her feet now, looking down at her flask-sipping uncle. "Sir."

"We could go to the Vault," he said bitterly. "But we wouldn't get in. Limmetrad is calling himself 'Vault Guardian' for real now, and he means it. Reports say he returns every week, disappears into the mountain, and doesn't return until the next morning. He's learning how to use his powers and, with that blade of his, he'll be more powerful than his father ever was when he wielded it." Randolph shook his head and grinded his teeth.

"Powers, sir?"

"Did you ever see Fenwin's corpse?"

The prefect shook her head.

The legate clicked his tongue. "Just as well, it was burnt to a crisp. But our apothecaries and medicine men examined him post-mortem. His entire ribcage was shattered as though he had fallen down a three-story building, and yet his internal organs seemed untouched. It was a fascinating case, and I wouldn't have believed it had I not seen him fight you in the arena. His speed and strength were inhuman. The boy should've died when you hanged him—his neck should've snapped or else his airways crushed and blocked. The precision in his strength, as well as his vast reserves of stamina seem to tell me there's something...*off* about him."

Randolph chugged the rest of his flask and dropped it to the floor, letting the metal clang against the wood and ring throughout the room. He belched and let out a foul stench between his hair covered lips. The prefect's uncle chuckled and waved the air with his hat.

"My point," Randolph said, upon calming himself down, "is that you're lucky you only lost a hand. We know about his father's weapon, but we do not know if he knows how to properly use it—especially with it missing the rest of the blade. One of Fenwin's last reports claimed that the boy was also surprised to see the Voidsweeper at work."

Longinus found herself circling the room. So much information at once, and somehow her uncle found it important enough to share. He would not have done so if she were not somehow involved. But why was Randolph drinking so heavily and what plans had changed? Her uncle seemed to be avoiding the subject. And yet he was still in the room, speaking with his cursed nephew.

"Sir, I'm lost."

"Of course you are. That's why I keep an eye on you." He stared at his nephew with a dreadful gaze, eyes sunken and lips folded down in a frown as he leaned forward in his chair. He jerked his head back with a loud laugh and clapped his hands. "But of course that's not what you meant!" Randolph bellowed. "The sword the boy has. It's believed to be a legendary blade that has disappeared and reappeared for generations. It was last seen with his father at the first assault on the Vault. We were able to relieve most of it, aside from a piece of the blade, from poor Alphonse before he made his way into the Vault, locking Julius and me out. It was then lost in the aftermath, and somehow the sword found its way back from the father to the son.

"We know he can bleed. We know he can be maimed. We're pretty sure his weapon is the real Voidsweeper. We do *not* know the full extent of his powers. Blazes, we don't even know if the boy can be killed. If whatever is inside the Vault is helping him complete whatever metamorphosis he's experiencing, then the Vault is the last place we want to be. No boy, we don't even need the so-called 'Grand Vault', anymore. Why should we, when we have the key to every other crypt buried by the Enochians?"

Longinus grimaced.

"What's wrong, nephew?" Randolph asked.

She wanted to roll her eyes, but she wouldn't dare do that in her uncle's presence. She knew her uncle didn't care about how she was doing. "Why didn't we take both Limmetrads with us in the first place? Wouldn't that have prevented everything?"

Randolph chuckled and offered Longinus an ugly grin. "My dear nephew, everything has gone according to plan. Well, nearly everything." He bent over his chair, picked up his flask, and struggled to strap it back to his belt. He tried to stand up but wavered back and forth, nearly falling to the floor where his flask once rested. The prefect found herself concerned for her uncle, for she had never seen him in such a state before. Her feet moved lightly across the floor as she caught her uncle midair just barely in time to prevent a bloody mess.

As she caught her uncle she found a mess was already present, though it was dried against the inside of her uncle's coat. She sat her uncle back in the chair and fetched a glass of water. Randolph drank it fast but spit it out when he realized it was not from his flask.

"Uncle, what happened? Why are you bleeding?" she asked with quite a fright.

The man rolled his eyes in the chair and coughed violently but passed it off as though he were merely clearing his throat. "Like I said, nearly everything. Looks like I'll be King instead." He gave Longinus a devilish smile.

By the time the sun rose on the day of the coronation, all seemed to forget that the King standing before them was not the one they had expected. The people no longer cared that both Xander and Rivers were dead, for all they cared about was the Sun's blessing, and King Randolph had it, for no clouds dared dampen the radiance that illuminated the ex-legate's skin. *Surely*, the prefect told herself, *this King will bring us to true glory*. It would mean much for her and her people.

Rivers died of a weak lung from his travels north. This was the official claim according to the royal palace's autopsy. Their word was final as it was an extension of the Sun's will. It was with a heavy heart that the prefect's uncle accepted the crown. Longinus knew better than that. The blood on her uncle's coat the other night was proof of something more nefarious afoot. She never let her uncle know her suspicion just as she never let anyone know she was not a man.

"I am not worthy," Randolph told the people of Ignistad. He looked down at them from his castle, constructed with the bricks and concrete of the Old Days. Its bleached columns and finely cut archways were meant to pay homage to a white colored house to the East. King Xander claimed it was the castle of the Old Days' kings, and he wanted to recreate it within Ænæria. "The Sun's Chosen was like a brother to me, and he carried a weight on his shoulders that I never envied, but I promise each of you that I will stay true to his legacy."

Randolph never spoke a word about the late Legate Rivers, and no one dared to mention the oddity of the 'coincidence' that led to Rivers's demise. Not in public, anyway. There were whispers though, treasonous things Longinus had heard of when nary a noble was awake to hear it, and she was disguised as her true self out at a back-alley tavern.

There was no celebration after the coronation. Her uncle, the King, instead hosted a meeting for the remaining nine legates. Three had died and a fourth was now the King. *What will they discuss?* the prefect questioned in wonder. Imagination took over the reins of her conscious mind as she swam through the possibilities. She did not need to speculate for long because she was invited to the meeting as well.

Midnight on the longest day of the year. That was the time she was to meet her uncle and the legates at the great hall. It was a blessed day in Ænæria, for it was the day the Sun offered her greatest blessings. King Randolph didn't intended to waste more than a second of the Eternal Mother's grace on this day.

The prefect arrived just two minutes before midnight, for sleep caught her in an unwinnable battle after the tiresome day she had had training for whatever may come. She stared into looking glasses and inspected herself in man's clothing and tight binding. She practiced deepening her voice and standing as tall as she could. She added paints to her face to bring out her cheekbones and appear masculine, just as she had every day of her life since her father died. She fasted during the day and feasted at night. All this to prepare her body and mind, purging all self-doubt in preparation for the meeting. The prefect wanted to be ready for anything the solstice may bring her. And yet, she found herself almost late to what could be the most important moment of her life.

The grand hall was a familiar place to the prefect. She had accompanied her uncle to the room many times during the planning for the northern expedition. Not much had changed since she had last seen it: the gold rimmed chairs of stone and the marble center table still stood beneath the skylight, illuminated by the Sun's jealous sister, the Moon. Unlike before, the prefect noted, all golden statues of Xander had been removed and were now replaced with platinum effigies of her uncle. The prefect gulped and offered a wry smile to herself as she thought about how long Randolph had truly been planning this.

Seated at the center of the table was, of course, King Randolph. To his right was Legate Glendir with Legate Lorenz to his left. He assumed this meant they were now First and Second Legates, respectively. As the prefect walked toward the rectangular marble table, she noted a man with an unfamiliar face, marred by a half-missing nose, sitting to the right of the only empty chair around the table. To its left was a stranger wearing a black hood, covering his face from view. Across his shoulder was an orange-tinted bow that seemed to be made of bodark wood. *Reminds me of Limmetrad's bow,* Longinus thought to herself.

Next to the hooded man was a ghost, or so she thought. Bald from head to chin with an illuminated gloss from the skylight above sat Gatron, the dead legate of Plutonua. He and the stranger were the only two men around the table not to look directly at the prefect as the red double doors slammed behind her.

"Longinus!" the King cried, jumping from his table. "So kind of you to join us! Please, take the empty seat, and we may begin!"

Longinus gritted her teeth by the mention of the cursed name that buried her true identity almost from memory. She walked past the various legates, some thin old men, others barrel-chested and battle-tested and barely older than herself. All were loyal to a fault—except for Randolph, only loyal to himself. Where Gatron's loyalties lay, Longinus did not know. She took her seat between the hooded stranger and the half-nosed man.

"Legates," the King said proudly, "as many of you know, this is my nephew, Longinus. As of tonight, he will be the legate of our youngest province, Bacchuso. Do you accept, my dear nephew?"

Longinus seated herself at the table and bowed to her uncle. "Of course, sir. As you command." *What is he doing? He said he would let me be myself once he became king, and there has never a she-legate before.*

Randolph removed his crown and replaced it with his hat, grinning deviously as he did so. "Very good, my boy." He put his feet up on the table and leaned against his gold-rimmed throne. Longinus could feel the tension in the room at the disrespectful gesture made by their King. *Is it disrespectful though,* she wondered, *if it's done by a man chosen by the Sun?*

"*Ah*, allow me to introduce our newcomers before we get started, Legate Longinus. First off, you know of Legate Gatron. It appears he is among the living after all. His capture and defeat but a mere rumor and mix up. He will continue to be my eyes and ears in Plutonua." Randolph waved toward Gatron, who avoided Longinus's eyes but offered a subtle nod.

"To your right is our new representative from Juptora, Legate Juarez."

Legate Juarez snorted through his half-nose and gave a gruff, "Hello," to Longinus.

"And lastly, I will reveal to all of you who our stranger in the hood is. I apologize for the suspense, but it really is much more fun to have everyone here and to only do the introductions once. This will be our representative to Vestinia and will offer us quite the advantage in our war to come."

The legates shifted in their seats, seemingly just as unaware of plans for war as Longinus. *It makes sense why he told me about the eye and other Vaults,* she realized.

"I think it is long since time that we have a woman with us, for she is made more in the image of the Sun than any one of us. May I introduce all of you to our newest member of Ænæria!"

Longinus's blood boiled, and she did all she could to contain her anger. *Another she-legate? Then he has not forgotten. Uncle wants me to keep up this farce.* She gritted her teeth and clenched her fists in fury.

The hooded woman stood from her seat and removed her hood, revealing her tough face and should length hair of fire. All but one of the legates clapped with a profound applause and gusto. Gatron slowly put his hands together and attempted to hide the fear in his eyes as the woman glared at him with an intense and daunting smile that screamed *I know your secret*.

"Everyone," Randolph hollered, in an attempt to quiet his legates. It was clear the King was quite proud of himself, giddy with excitement as he could barely keep still in his chair with his legs propped up under the moonlight. "Meet Arynn of Vänalleato!"

SEVEN OF THE ÆNÆRIAN PROVINCES WITH THE PENTERIC ALLIANCE TO THE SOUTH, AS CHARTED BY MASTER SIEGFRIED OF VÄNALLEATO

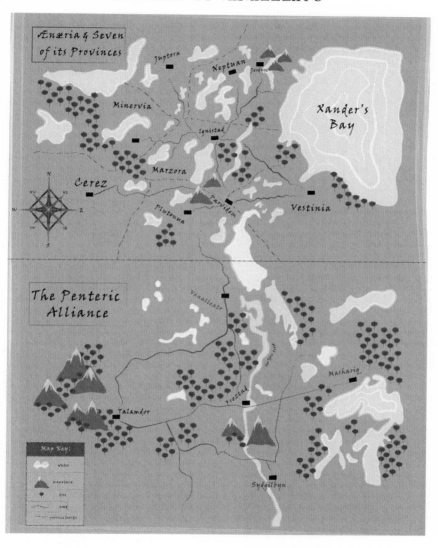

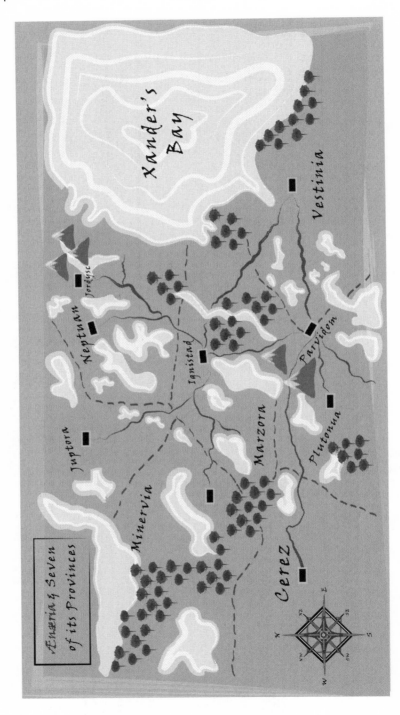

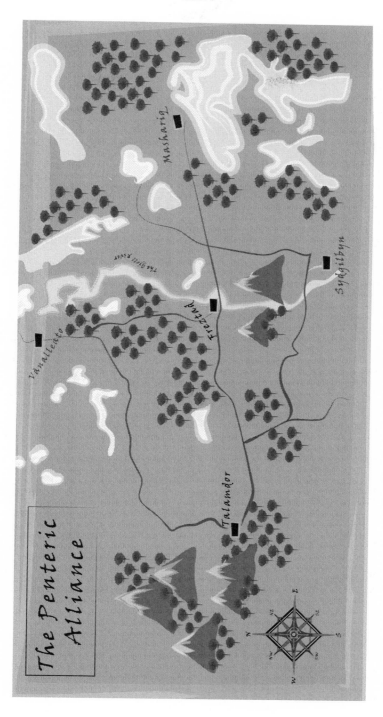

AFTERWORD

I look fondly on the night I sat in my college dorm with my friend and roommate, Alex, discussing my desire to write a novel. My imagination has always been an important aspect of my life, and for the longest time I had wanted to use to it for more than just daydreaming. It was a school night when Alex and I talked about what a good story needed, and if I had enough creativity to come up with a story that would not only entertain, but enlighten and touch you, the reader. I told him, as I am telling you now, that I wanted to write a book that reflected the hardships in my life, specifically the illness and death of my mother. This novel was written as a creative and therapeutic outlet to cope with the dying of my mother and the many changes I went through at the time. I also wanted the world I was creating to reflect my own rather cynical worldview with an added hint of idealism. A post-apocalyptic setting seemed to be the best way to do this. With this foundation, Alex and I discussed various plots, characters, and themes that the novel could utilize. We discussed the idea of a villain and how a story is only as strong as its antagonist. I also credit Alex with coming up with the idea of characters racing against time to find a vault filled with seeds. I therefore could not have come up with the same story without his input. With those ideas in mind, I started writing an outline and coming up with characters and subplots to work with. Then, as I started to actually write, the story seemed to come to life and write itself. It is a very different story than what Alex and I had originally discussed, and I'm excited for him to finally read it and see how it turned out.

Of course, I'm excited to see how all of you, the readers, will react to it, too.

There are a lot of themes and motifs in this novel. Some were quite deliberate: death, morality, equality, and environmentalism. There were also some that seemed to inadvertently seep from my non-conscious mind onto the pages, only to be later brought to my attention by the novel's initial reviewers. These included topics such as friendship, young leadership, and tolerance. I believe these worked their way into the novel because they are among my own values, and I was able to write about them in a more natural manner.

The setting is perhaps the most important aspect of the book. It is a world ravaged by war and the cataclysm of climate change. Yes, climate change. It is a very real threat that we cannot afford to ignore. Perhaps everyone alive today will avoid the majority of its consequences, but climate change is a threat beyond those who are living now. It's a threat to our children and grandchildren; to the Bens and Roses of the future. The thematic elements of environmentalism are scattered throughout the story and demonstrate my strong opinion on the subject.

The subject of climate change also strongly represents the topic of death, the novel's ultimate theme. Death, as I see it, is the only certainty in life. Our perspective on death is often influenced by religion and societal norms, and we therefore often fool ourselves into believing we do not need to explore our feelings about the subject. A goal of this story—and the series that I hope it will become—is to challenge your perception of death. Is it the end? Does it hurt? How do you want to die? Is it wrong to be responsible for one's death? What does it *really* mean to be alive? I found myself asking these questions as my mother moved between hospitals, a nursing home, and hospice. I asked myself these questions when she died, and I was still writing the first draft. I am asking myself these questions while writing these words. I hope you will also ask yourself these questions because Death is the one certainty waiting for us. It is only a question of when.

Stay tuned for Book 2, which I plan to publish in late 2019 or early 2020. The current working title is *The Scorched Earth*, though it may change, just as this book was originally titled *The Vault Guardian* before I changed that to the series title.

See my blog, at https://tvgcosmicraces.blogspot.com/, for updates and more information about themes, characters, and further works.

ACKNOWLEDGMENTS

I offer my greatest thanks to those who helped me along the way with the creative development of this novel. They gave me invaluable insight that led to the development of this story and its characters.

Alex, for your creative ideas and help in developing something that you knew was important to me.

Priya, for being the first person to read my novel as it was being written, back when it was a mere skeleton of what it has become. You helped me get on my feet as a first-time writer and pointed out details that I would have never noticed on my own.

Clarissa, for helping me come up with ideas and being a wonderful girlfriend with whom I could share this experience. You were supportive and inspirational throughout the entire writing process, and you never doubted me for a second.

Dad, for being the first person to read through the novel after the first draft was finished. Your grammatical feedback was exceptionally useful, and I appreciate your expertise on the subject. Also, thanks for being a pretty cool father.

Elena, for your commitment to bringing my characters to life, sharing this with your dad, and for putting up with my constant pestering. I hope to work with you on my future works.

Sam, for your dedication to my novel and editing while working in rural Cambodia. I look forward to seeing you change the world.

Rachael, for sending my draft to Sam and taking an interest in something outside your normal genre.

Uncle Joe, for being my godfather and taking this journey with me.

Brian, for being a supportive roommate during these edits and taking an interest in my story.

Zack, for getting back into reading just for me, editing like your life depended on it, and for meeting with me to discuss your thoughts and feelings on the story.

Rosaria, for being my grandmother, one of my biggest role models, and for supporting me throughout my life.

Mom, for helping me become the person I am now. I hope you are watching me from the Great Dream with the other Ascendants. I wish you would have gotten a chance to read this, because I made it for you.

GLOSSARY

Ænæria—A theocratic kingdom founded by King Xander 15 years prior to the events of *The King's Gambit*. It is made up of 13 provinces that were once independent tribes making up the Northern Realm.

Alejandra—A codename for the leader of the Miners Guild. Her real name is known only to her family. She is the mother of Mandi, daughter of Risa, wife to Heath, and niece of Takashi Kabedge.

Alphonse Limmetrad—Benedict Limmetrad's father and Lydia Limmetrad's brother. He is the former Chief of Freztad before disappearing to pursue the mysteries of the Vault.

Apollin—Province of Ænæria east of Neptuan and across the sea from Bacchuso.

Arma, Silas, Dyl, and Ming—Slavers working from the Plutonua province of Ænæria.

Arynn—Daughter of Siegfried, the cartographer of Vänalleato. She is 17 years old and an aspiring navigator. She is easily recognized by her bright red hair and blue eyes.

Ascendants—The spirits of the dead living within the Great Dream according to the beliefs of Vänalleatian natives. Called Ancestors by Ænærians.

Bacchuso—A disputed territory between the Ænærians and its natives. It is a large island that lies across the sea from the Apollin Province.

Benedict Limmetrad— The son of Alphonse Limmetrad. He is 16 years old for the majority of *The King's Gambit*. He works as a farmer in Freztad and is an aspiring Sentinel. He and Rose are the only children in the village to have survived the plague.

Blood Bugs—Vernacular for mosquitos. They are often blamed for the plague that occurred on the Gjoll River 10 years before the events of *The King's Gambit*.

Hunter Flies—Vernacular for dragonflies. They are raised for the purpose of keeping the blood bug population under control.

Cerez—The agricultural province of Ænæria, west of Plutonua. It is the only province with fertile farmland, though it pales in comparison to Freztad. Its primary produce is the poppy flower, which is used for its analgesic properites.

Darius—At the age of 15 he deserted the Rhion of Holy Ænærian Army in hopes of becoming a member of the Miners Guild.

Deus ex Machina—Latin translation for "God from the Machine," as well as the title of Chapter 21.

Diania—Ænærian Province north of Neptuan.

Elders—Priests of Vänalleato who preach the words and beliefs of the Grand Elder.

Enochians—The mysterious creators of the Vaults.

Eternal Mother—The worshipped deity of Ænæria. Synonymous with the Eternal Sun.

Faaip de Oiad—Enochian translation for "Voice of God," as well as the title of the prologue, an account given by Mimir to a woman named Sam. This account is given after the events of *The King's Gambit*.

Felix—A young boy from Vänalleato with a rare combination of black skin, blonde hair, and blue eyes. He is the adoptive son of the blacksmith Wulkan.

Freztad—Farm and trade village next to the Gjoll River. At the center of the Penteric Alliance, Freztad serves as its capital.

Gal and Skalle—Brothers from a group of people known as Orks from the eastern land known as Ney. They are hairless and have skull tattoos over their faces.

Gjoll River—River that flows north past Freztad and into a large lake by Vänalleato. According to Vänalleatian belief, it is a holy river with a strong connection to the Great Dream. The cremated remains of their deceased are released into the river. Many Freztadians believe the Gjoll is the reason their farm flourishes.

Grand Elder—Leader of Vänalleato. He is believed to be the reincarnation of the founder of Vänalleato and their belief in the Great Dream.

Great Dream—The afterlife according to the belief of the Vänalleatians. All souls enter the Great Dream where they are free and can aid in the affairs of the living.

Heath—Military strategist of the Miners Guild. He is the wife of Alejandra and father of Mandi.

Ignistad—Capital city of Ænæria at the center of the Marzora Province.

Jarl Geon—The current leader of the settlement of Sydgilbyn as well as the commander of their army.

Jean—Alphonse's wife and Benedict's mother.

Jordysc—A settlement north of Ignistad. It is the base of the Miners Guild.

King Xander—He is also known as the Eternal Mother's Chosen. After leaving Freztad, he united 13 of the kingdoms within the Northern Realm and founded Ænæria.

Legate Fenwin—Legate of the Vestinia Province. Fenwin is King Xander's third-in-command. He is the only known proficient user of sun-swords, solar powered swords that are prototypical replicas of the legendary Voidsweeper.

Legate Gatron—Legate of the Plutonua Province. He is the legate responsible for training Darius as a Rhion.

Legate Randolph—Legate of the Minervia Province. Randolph is King Xander's fourth-in-command. Despite being so high-spirited, Randolph is a military man who fights without mercy. His nephew is Longinus.

Legate Rivers—Legate of the Neptuan Province. He is King Xander's second-in-command. He has a mild demeanor but is believed to be highly intelligent.

Longinus—Prefect of the Minervia Province. He is 19 years old and was raised by Randolph, his uncle, after his father died and dishonored their family.

Lydia Limmetrad—Official Chief of Freztad, though she has not acted as such in the last 3 years before the events of *The King's Gambit* due to her melancholia and losing the use of her legs. She was exposed to the plague 10 years before the events of *The King's Gambit* and slowly experienced an ascending paralysis. She is the mother of Rose Limmetrad and sister to Alphonse.

Mandi—An intelligence agent of the Miners Guild. She is 18 years old and has a large burn on the left side of her face. Health and Alejandra are her parents, and Risa is her grandmother.

Marcus and Jesse—Husband and wife, respectively, living in Svaldway. They are among the founders of the Miners Guild.

Marzora—Capital Province of Ænæria. There is no legate in Marzora as King Xander oversees it directly.

Mashariq—Western settlement of the Penteric Alliance. Its leader is given the title of 'Sheik' or 'Sheika.' It is currently led by Sheika Thalia. They are most renowned for their fishing and skill as boat builders.

Mathias the Exile—He was of the first generation to be born and raised after the end of the Old Days. He united a tribe of people to find Freztad and is the first Limmetrad.

Mercura—The smallest Ænærian province.

Mimir—The first guardian of the Grand Vault. His sole purpose is to preserve its integrity.

Miners Guild—An underground organization scattered throughout Ænæria dedicated to overthrowing King Xander's regime.

Minervia—Ænærian province east of Marzora. It is overseen by Legate Randolph.

Neith and Yeong—Two Sentinels (female and male, respectively) who, along with Zechariah, accompany Rose to Ænæria.

Neptuan—Fishing and naval province north of Marzora. It is overseen by Legate Rivers.

Ney—Land far east of the Penteric Alliance. Its natives call themselves Orks.

Northern Realm—Ænæria and the other lands surrounding it. It was once known as the Northern Kingdoms before King Xander's rule.

Old Days—Denotes the time before the cataclysmic events that led to the fall of Earth's civilizations. Nearly all technology and traditions have died since then, along with the vast majority of humanity.

Orks of Ney—Inhabitants of Ney. They have had very little interaction with outsiders.

Parvidom—Crossroads town between Plutonua and Vestinia. It is the largest trading hub in Ænæria and crucial to their economic stability.

Pawel—A young boy whose family avoided the Ænæria census and is trying to escape to the Penteric Alliance.

Penteric Alliance—The pact between five settlements south of the Northern Realm. It is also used to refer to the land between the settlements' borders. It is made up of Freztad its capital, found at the center of the Alliance's borders, Sydgilbyn in the South, Vänalleato in the North, Talamdor in the West, and Mashariq in the East.

Plague—A great sickness that overcame many settlements near large bodies of water about 10 years before the events of *The King's Gambit*. Many believe blood bugs to be the culprit of the plague because anyone who was bitten in that time period came down with a long and debilitating sickness. Every child bitten in Freztad died, except for Benedict.

Plutonua—Ænærian province bordering Vänalleato's territory. It is overseen by Legate Gatron. Both Darius and Trinity are originally from here.

Prefect—A high ranking military officer in an Ænærian province, second only to the legate. They have the authority to give orders to their subordinate Rhion.

Rakshi—Commander of the Freztadian Sentinels. She is close friends with the twins Kristos and Zechariah as well as Ben and Rose. She is 23 years old and a prodigy swordswoman and archer.

Rhion—Title of an Ænærian soldier.

Risa—One of the founding members of the Miners Guild. She is the sister of Takashi Kabedge, mother to Alejandra, and grandmother to Mandi.

Rohan and Zoya—Father and mother to Rakshi. They are both originally from Vänalleato but moved to Freztad shortly after Rakshi was born.

Roryk—A Rhion of Plutonua working undercover to aid the Miners Guild.

Rose Limmetrad—Daughter of Lydia Limmetrad and Julius. She is 15 years old and the acting Chief of Freztad. She is an exceptionally skilled archer. Her bright green eyes are her defining feature.

Sam—A woman who listens to Mimir's tale in the first chapter.

Sentinel—The title of a Freztadian guard. They are responsible for keeping the village safe as well as patrolling the roads within its borders.

Sera—Arynn's best friend who disappeared two years prior to the events of *The King's Gambit*. It is believed that she was one of the first to be kidnapped by slavers near Vänalleato. Her disappearance led to the Elders' decision to not allow women to leave the town alone.

Sheika Thalia—The leader of Mashariq, the eastern settlement of the Penteric Alliance.

Siegfried—Master cartographer of Vänalleato. He has travelled all over the Penteric Alliance and nearly all of Ænæria. He is the father of Arynn. His defining features are his bald head and red beard.

Sierra—A large white wolf who follows Ben on his journey. She was named by Arynn.

Sleipnir—A moody and difficult gelding who typically only cooperates for his owner, Rose. After the attack on Freztad he and many other animals ran away from the village.

Sol Invictus—The motto of Ænæria. It means 'Invincible Sun.' It is used to inspire strength among Ænærians.

Sols—Round and metal coins used as currency in Ænæria. There are copper, silver, and gold coins.

Sun-Chariot—Solar powered trucks used by high ranking Ænærians or for special missions. They are believed to be from one of the Vaults, though no one seems to how it was opened.

Sung—Solar powered guns used by high ranking Ænærians or for special missions. They are believed to be from one of the Vaults, though no one seems to know how it was opened.

Sydgilbyn—A desert settlement south of Freztad. They are known for their military expertise and large population.

Takashi Kabedge—One of the oldest residents of Freztad. He is a mentor and parent figure to Ben just as he was to Julius. He owns the farm in Freztad and a food shop where he is a chef. He is Vic's husband and Risa's brother.

Thane Morgiana—Leader of Talamdor, the western settlement of the Penteric Alliance.

The Argr—A fearsome fighter of Ignistad's gladiatorial arena. The term is also known by some to be a term of emasculation.

Tree of Mathias—A large linden tree (often called lime tree, as well) at the center of Freztad. Only the western facing half of the Tree still has leaves and flowers. On rare occasions it will grow seeds as well. The eastern facing half is dead and has never bloomed since its discovery. The Limmetrad name is derived from the tree.

Trinity—A former slave from Plutonua who learned the art of healing. She is 16 years old, and her master freed her two years earlier than required when he was dying. Between that time and the events of *The King's Gambit* she moved to Ignistad and had a relationship with Darius.

Valhaven—The oldest building in Freztad and the ancestral home of the Limmetrad family. It is used to hold meetings for the villagers and leaders of the Penteric Alliance.

Vänalleato—A settlement atop a very small mountain overlooking the mouth of the Gjoll River. Its leader is the Grand Elder and its people have a deeply spiritual culture. The town is most well-known for its farming of blood bugs.

Vaults—Secure and mysterious buildings left over from the Old Days. It is believed that the only way to enter the Vaults is through special blood. They are believed to hold secrets from the past and perhaps even the sungs and sun-chariots used by Ænærians. There are two known Vaults, the Great Vault near the North Pole and the Broken Vault far to the East, which was opened when Alphonse found it.

Venaz—Ænærian province far northwest of Ignistad.

Vestinia—Ænæria province east of Plutonua and south of Marzora. It is overseen by Legate Fenwin.

Vic—Takashi Kabedge's husband. He helped raise both Benedict and Julius when they were young. Before becoming gravely ill, he was a teacher in Freztad and farmer alongside Takashi Kabedge.

Voidsweeper—A legendary blade that has been lost and found over again for generations. It has immense power somewhat similar to that of a sung.

Vulcestus—The eastern most Ænærian province, most renowned for its engineering.

Warden Chen—Warden of the Vestinia prison, north of Parvidom.

Wastelander—Bandits who live outside of organized civilization. They wander the land without laws and often pillage small towns or outposts for food and supplies.

Wulkan—Blacksmith of Vänalleato and adoptive father of Felix. He is easily recognized by his blonde hair, red beard, and very large build.

Zechariah and Kristos—Twin Sentinels of Freztad. They are best friends with Rakshi and quite close with Benedict. They are both about 26 years old. Zechariah is one of the most skilled Sentinels and departed with Rose during the events of *The King's Gambit*.

Zevi—Meat butcher of Freztad and betrothed to Rakshi.

PRONUNCIATION GUIDE

Ænæria—ah-NAIR-ee-ah
Alejandra—Alay-HON-drah
Alphonse—AL-fonz
Argr—ARR-ger
Bacchuso—ba-KU-so
Cerez—SEER-ez
Darius—DAIR-ee-us
Deus ex Machina—DAY-oos EKS MOK-in-ah
Enochian—Eh-NOKEE-in
Faaip De Oiad—FAH-eep DAY oh-EYE-id
Freztad—frez-TAD
Gal—GOLL
Gatron—GAT-tron
Geon—GEE-yon
Gjoll—gee-YOLL
Ignistad—ig-ni-STOD
Jarl—YARL
Jordysc—YOOR-disk
Legate—Leg-IT
Limmetrad—lim-eh-TROD

Longinus—LAWN-jin-is
Mandi—MON-dee
Marzora—mar-ZORA
Mashariq—mosh-a-REEK
Mercura—mer-KYOORA
Minerveria—min-ERV-ee-ah
Morgiana—MOORG-ee-ona
Neith—NAYTH
Neptuan—nep-TOO-on
Ney—NAY
Parvidom—PARV-i-dom
Pawel—POWL
Rakshi—ROK-shee
Rhion—REE-on
Siegfried—sig-FREED
Skalle—SKAYL
Sleipnir—SLAYP-neer
Sol—SOLE
Sydgilbyn—SIJ-ill-bin
Talamdor—Tal-am-DOOR
Thalia—TAL-ee-ah
Vänalleato—von-ALL-ee-ot-toe
Venaz—VEE-naz
Vulcestus—VOL-kes-tus
Yeong—YUNG
Zevi—ZEV-ee

Made in the USA
Middletown, DE
08 March 2019